IN SEARCH OF A KILLER

"I thought I explained all this," Olivia said. "I've been in to the police department before. No one took me seriously. Just like you."

"Try me," Bentz suggested. "Just tell me what you saw."

'Well ... where to begin? I'd have these nightmares, more fragmented than this last one, but intense. It wasn't a vision of someone being violently murdered like last night ... but rather short images, every other day or so, of a victim being left to starve to death. She ... she was trapped somewhere like a crypt of some kind and she was screaming and crying. And I felt him. His presence."

"The killer?"

"Yes. Whoever abducted her and left her to die would come and visit her, shine a flashlight into her terrified eyes, then leave. So I only got glimpses of where she was being held, only quick images of the surroundings. Anything else?" she asked.

"Yeah, a couple of things. I'll want a list of everyone you know. Family, friends, anyone you work with or see at school."

"You think my friends are involved."

"That's the problem. I don't know who is, but if I take what you're telling me at face value, then somehow you're connected with the killer ... right? There's something between the two of you ... I mean, I assume that's the way it works."

She nodded. "Sometimes ..." She let her voice fade away and didn't go on.

"Sometimes what?"

"It sounds so crazy, but sometimes I get this feeling ... it's like crystals of ice over the back of my neck, and I feel that he's close ... closer than I ever imagined ..."

Books by Lisa Jackson

TREASURES

INTIMACIES

WISHES

WHISPERS

TWICE KISSED

UNSPOKEN

IF SHE ONLY KNEW

HOT BLOODED

COLD BLOODED

Published by Zebra Books

COLD BLOODED

Lisa Jackson

ZEBRA BOOKS
KENSINGTON PUBLISHING CORP.

ZEBRA BOOKS are published by

Kensington Publishing Corp.
850 Third Avenue
New York, NY 10022

ISBN: 0-7394-2575-7

To Robin Rue, agent extraordinaire—thanks for all!

Acknowledgments

First and foremost I would like to thank the City of New Orleans Police Department for their help and courtesy, even though I bent the rules a tad to accommodate this story.

I would also like to thank the following individuals who offered their support, knowledge and expertise, without whom this book would not have been written. Thanks to Nancy Berland, Nancy Bush, Matthew Crose, Michael Crose, Alexis Harrington, Mary Clare Kersten, Carol Maloy, K.C. McNeeley, Arla Melum, Ken Melum, Ari Okano, Betty and Jack Pederson, Sally Peters, Robin Rue, Jon Salem, John Scognamiglio, Larry and Linda Sparks, Laura Stanulis, Mark and Celia Stinson, and Jane Thornton. If I've missed anyone, my apologies.

Prologue

He saw her.

Half-running, head bent, fingers clutched at the hood of her coat, she hurried through the darkness to the small church.

From his hiding spot beneath the magnolia tree, The Chosen One waited. His blood began to sing through his veins as he crouched in the darkness, every muscle tense, nerves strung tight as piano wire.

How easy it would be to catch her In three swift strides he could be upon her and drag her away. While her father waited inside. That particular thought appealed to him, was warm seduction.

But it wasn't her time, he reminded himself. There were others.

She paused beneath the overhang near the front doors, tossing off her hood and shaking her hair free. Long and wavy, the strands gleamed a tempting red brown in the lamplight. The Chosen One swallowed and felt the first stirring between his legs.

He wanted her.

So badly he ached.

Just looking at her, his senses were heightened. He heard his heart beating, felt his blood pulse through his veins, smelled the heavy odor of the Mississippi River winding dark and slow through the town where traffic whined on slick streets and sin was waged at every corner.

As she disappeared through the doors, he edged deeper into the dense foliage of the grounds to his hiding spot near the flawed stained-glass window. A tiny panel of glass had been removed and replaced by a small clear pane, giving a perfect view into the nave. Crouching, The Chosen One peered through this portal and he watched as she walked down the aisle, genuflected, then slid into the pew to take her seat next to her father. The bastard cop.

They exchanged a few words before she planted herself next to him.

Once seated, she fidgeted in the pew. Looked bored. As if she'd rather be anywhere than at evening mass with her father. She flipped her long hair this way and that, glanced at the others as they entered, slumped onto her lower back to bite at one fingernail as dozens of candles burned.

The Chosen One let his gaze move to the cop.

The enemy.

He was a solid man, over six feet. His jaw was square, his eyes deep-set and world-weary, showing his forty-plus years. Rick Bentz was a detective whose tarnished reputation had been polished to a recent sheen, his past sins forgotten if not forgiven. In his black suit and starched shirt, he appeared more uncomfortable than his daughter, definitely out of place in the house of God.

As well he should be.

Tugging on his tie, Bentz leaned closer to the girl and whispered into her ear. Immediately she stopped biting at her nails and straightened in the pew. She folded her arms over her abdomen defiantly and inadvertently raised her breasts, making them plump a bit at the neckline of her dress. White supple flesh against turquoise silk.

The Chosen One imagined what was hidden beneath that smooth fabric . . . rosebud nipples, virgin skin, and lower, a dark nest of curls the same reddish brown as that luxurious tangle of copper that tumbled to her shoulders.

He thought of her as the princess.

Her father's pride and joy.

Athlete, scholar, and . . . a little naughty. Rebellious. It was there, in her eyes. He'd seen it before. Heard it in her deep, sexy laughter.

She glanced toward the window with her wide green eyes. The Chosen One froze in his hiding spot.

Her mouth pulled into a tiny, defiant pout.

His cock responded. Just a little twinge.

He imagined what those lips might do with the right sort of prodding . . . Closed his eyes, felt the cool caress of the rain running down his neck as his fingers strayed to his crotch.

His erection stiffened to full mast. Hard. Throbbing. Anticipating.

Soon, Princess, he thought. *Soon. But I must take care of the others first. Then it will be your turn.*

Be patient.

Beep! Beep! Beep!

His eyes flew open at the sound of his watch's timer. He clicked off the alarm and bit back a swear word. That was careless. Unlike him. Angry with himself, The Chosen One took one last glimpse of the church's interior and found the princess still staring at the window. As if she knew he was there.

Quickly he ducked from beneath the tree and jogged through the curtain of rain. He'd stayed much too long. Furious with himself, he picked up his pace, long legs sprinting easily across the wet lawn to the corner, where he turned down a narrow alley, ran three blocks, then doubled back to a parking space in front of an abandoned, boarded-over building that had once been a garage.

He was sweating, not from exertion but anxiety as he climbed into the older car with its tinted windows. He stripped off his running clothes and gloves, then folded them neatly into a leather duffel.

Soon it would be time.

Soon Rick Bentz would feel the pain of losing that which he held most dear.

But first Bentz needed to know what was at risk; he had to feel real fear—a dark, gnawing dread that would eat at him when he realized that everything he did, everywhere he turned, every place he'd once held sacred, would no longer be safe.

A smile crept across The Chosen One's jaw as he withdrew a towel from his bag. Quickly he swiped the rough terry cloth over his face and neck. Then he took the time to check the rearview mirror. Blue eyes stared back at him. Hungry eyes. "Bedroom eyes," he'd been told by more than one woman who was foolish enough to think he could be seduced.

But . . . beneath his gaze he caught the merest glimmer of a shadow, something wrong, out of sync in the reflection. As if someone were watching him. He snapped his head around, stared through the foggy rear window to see if the mirror's reflection had caught someone peering into the car. He squinted through the raindrops and fog of condensation.

Nothing moved outside.

There was no one around on this deserted street. And yet he felt . . . a connection somewhere. This wasn't the first time; he'd sensed a presence on several occasions. Each time the feeling became a little more certain, a tad more intense. Sweat rolled down his temples. His heart hammered wildly.

Paranoia . . . that's what it is. Stay cool. Keep focused.

There was no one in this desolate part of town, no one who could possibly see through the smoky glass windows of the sedan on this gloomy night.

He had to calm down. Be patient. Everything was coming together.

Rick Bentz's worst nightmare had already begun.

He just didn't know it yet.

Chapter One

"You need a woman," Reuben Montoya observed as he pulled the police cruiser into the lot of Bentz's apartment.

"Good. Maybe I could borrow one of yours." Bentz reached for the handle of the door. What he didn't need was any advice from a young cop with more balls than brains as evidenced by the earring winking in Montoya's ear and the neatly trimmed goatee covering his chin. The younger detective was smart as hell, but still a little wet behind the ears. And he didn't know when to keep his nose in his own business.

"Hey, I'm a one-woman man these days," Montoya insisted and Bentz snorted.

"Right."

"I mean it." Montoya slammed the cruiser's gearshift lever into park, then reached into his jacket pocket for a pack of cigarettes.

"If you say so."

"I could set you up." Montoya was a young cop, not quite thirty, with smooth bronze skin, a killer smile, and

enough ambition to propel him out of his poor Hispanic
roots and through college on an athletic scholarship. Not
only had he kicked the living hell out of a soccer ball, but
he'd made the dean's list every semester and then, upon
graduation, with his future as bright as the damned sun, he
decided to become a cop.

Go figure.

Montoya shook out a filter tip, lit up, and blew a cloud
of smoke. "I know this nice older lady, a friend of my
mother's—"

"Can it." Bentz shot him a look meant to shut him up.
"Forget it. I'm okay."

Montoya didn't back off. "You're definitely *not* okay.
You live alone, never go out, and work your tail off for a
department that doesn't appreciate you. That's your life."

"I'll bring it up when I'm up for my next raise," he said
and climbed out of the passenger seat. It was a cool night;
the wind rolling off the river had a winter edge to it.

"All I'm sayin' is that you need a life, man. Your kid's
gone off to school and you should have some fun."

"I have plenty."

"My ass."

" 'Night, Montoya." He slammed the door of the Crown
Vic shut, then made his way into the building. A woman.
Yeah, that would solve his problems. He grabbed the evening
paper and his mail on the ground level, then climbed up the
stairs to his second-floor unit. What did Montoya know?

Shit. That's what the kid knew: shit.

Bentz had learned long ago that women only added to
his problems; and he'd learned from the master.

Jennifer.

Beautiful.

Intelligent.

Sexy as hell.

His wife.

The one woman he'd given his heart to; the only woman
he'd allowed to break it and break it she had. On more than

one occasion. With the same damned man. He unlocked the door and snapped on the lights.

Hurt me once, shame on you.

Hurt me twice, shame on me.

Tossing his keys onto the desk, he shed his jacket and yanked off his tie. God, he could use a beer and a smoke. But not a woman. Trouble was, he'd sworn off all three. No messages on the answering machine. Montoya was right. His social life was nil. He worked out by pounding the hell out of a boxing bag that hung in the second bedroom, didn't even belong to a bowling league or golf club. He'd given up sailing and hunting years ago, along with high-stakes poker and Jim Beam.

Rolling up his sleeves, he walked to the refrigerator and stared at the dismal contents. Even the freezer, where he usually kept a couple of those frozen man-sized microwave meals, was empty. He grabbed a can of nonalcoholic beer and popped the top, then clicked on the TV. A sportscaster started rattling off the day's scores while highlights flashed in rapid-fire images across the screen.

He settled into his recliner and told himself that Montoya was way off base. He didn't need a social life. He had his work and he still had Kristi, even if she was off at school in Baton Rouge. He glanced at the telephone and thought about calling her, but he'd phoned last Sunday and had sensed she was irritated; hated him intruding on her new-found freedom at college, acted as if he was checking up on her.

He turned his attention back to the tube, where highlights of Monday night's Saints game was being replayed. He'd grab a sandwich at the local po'boy shop two blocks over then open up his briefcase and catch up on some paperwork. He had a couple of reports to write and he wanted to pull his notes together; then there were a few open cases that were going stale; he'd need to look them over again, see if there was anything he missed the first, second, third, and fourth times through.

He had plenty to do.

Montoya was wrong. Bentz didn't need a woman.
He was pretty sure no one did.

Olivia didn't like the lawyer. Never had. Never would. She couldn't imagine how her grandmother could have trusted anyone so obviously crooked. Ramsey John Dodd, who liked to be called RJ, was as oily as Grannie Gin's fried chicken and twice as plump. "'. . . so the estate's all wrapped up, the taxes and fees paid, all the heirs having gotten their disbursements. If you want to sell the house, now's the time.'' From the other side of his oversized desk in this hole-in-the-wall he called an office, Ramsey John tented his pudgy hands together and patted his fingertips. Behind him, trapped between the blinds and the only window in the airless office, a fly that should have died days ago buzzed in frustration, banging against the glass.

"I'm still not sure about moving."

"Well, when and if you decide, I could put you in touch with a good real estate man."

I'll just bet you could.

"Wally's a real go-getter."

"I'll let you know," she said, standing abruptly to end the conversation and help disguise the fact that she was lying through her teeth. She wouldn't give any associate of RJ Dodd the time of day much less any business.

He shrugged the shoulders of his too-tight suit as if it were no matter, but Olivia sensed his disappointment. No doubt he would have gotten a kickback for any referral that panned out.

"Thanks for all your help."

"My pleasure."

She shook his sweaty palm and dropped it.

Her grandmother could usually smell a con man six miles away. How in the world had she ended up with this snake? *Because his services come cheap,* was the obvious answer. Aside from that, RJ was a nephew of one of Grannie's friends.

"Just one thing that troubles me," RJ said as he forced himself from his squeaky chair.

"What's that?"

"How come you ended up with the house and contents, and your mama, she only got the insurance money?"

"You're the lawyer. You tell me."

"Virginia would never say."

Olivia offered him a weak smile. He was fishing and she didn't understand why. "I guess Grannie just liked me better."

His fleshy jaw tightened. "That could be, I suppose. I didn't know her very well, just enough to figure out that she was an odd woman, you know. Some people around these parts claim she was a voodoo priestess. That she read fortunes in tarot cards and tea leaves and the like, you know. ESP."

"Well, you can't always believe what you hear, can you?" she said, trying to change the subject. It touched a little too close to home.

"They say you inherited it."

"Is that what you want to know, Mr. Dodd? If I'm psychic?"

"It's RJ," he reminded her, grinning and showing off the hint of a gold molar. "No reason to get your back up. I was just makin' conversation."

"Why don't you ask my mother about all this?"

"Bernadette claims she didn't inherit the gift if that's what you want to call it, but that you did."

"Oh, I see . . . it skips a generation. Of course." Olivia smiled at him as if to say only an idiot would believe such prattle. There was no reason to confirm or deny the rumors. She knew only too well how true they were. It just wasn't any of Ramsey Dodd's business. She hoped it would never be.

"Listen," he suggested, stepping more agilely around the desk than a man his size should have been capable of. "A word of advice. Free." He seemed to drop his usual pomposity. "I know your grannie thought a lot of you. I also know that she was . . . an unusual woman, that because of her visions, she was considered odd. Some people trusted her with their lives. My aunt was one of 'em. But others, they thought she was into the dark arts or crazy or both. It didn't make her life any easier, so if I was you, I'd keep my mouth closed about any of that vision shit.''

"I'll remember that."

"Do that . . . It would have behooved your grandmother."

"Is there anything else?" she asked.

"Nope. That's it. You take care."

"I will. Thanks again for all your help." She stuffed the manila folder he'd given her into her backpack.

"It's been a pleasure workin' with you. Now, if you change your mind about sellin' the place, just give me a jingle and I'll have Wally call ya . . ."

She didn't wait for him to escort her to the door, but showed herself out through the paneled reception area where a single secretary was poised at a desk situated on a shabby carpet that stretched between three offices, two of which looked vacant as the name plates upon the doors had been unscrewed, leaving telltale holes in the thin veneer. Grannie sure could pick 'em.

Outside, she crossed a parking lot where the potholes had been patched and climbed into her truck. So RJ knew about her trips to the police department. Great. It was probably all over town, would probably get back to her boss at the Third Eye and even to the University, where she was taking graduate classes.

Wonderful. She rammed the old Ford Ranger into gear and roared out of the lot. She didn't want to think about the visions she'd had, the glimmers of evil that she sometimes felt rather than saw. Disjointed, kaleidoscopic shards of horrid events that cut through her brain, made her skin rise in goose bumps, and troubled her so much that she'd actually visited the local police.

Where she was considered a nutcase and had been practically laughed out of the building.

Heat climbed her neck at the thought. She flipped on the

radio and took a corner a little too fast. The Ranger's tires screeched in protest.

Sometimes being Virginia Dubois's granddaughter was more pain than it was worth.

"Forgive me, Father, for I have sinned," the naked woman whispered, unable to speak loudly, unable to scream because of the tight collar at her neck. On her knees, chained to the pedestal sink, she obviously didn't begin to recognize the magnitude of her sins or the reason that she was being punished, that he was actually saving her.

"Tell me," The Chosen One whispered. "What sins?"

"For . . . for . . ." Her terrified eyes bulged and blinked as she tried to think, but she wasn't penitent. Just scared. Saying what she hoped would convince him to set her free. Tears streamed down her cheeks. "For all my sins," she said desperately, trying to please him, not knowing it was impossible; that her destiny was preordained.

She was quivering with fear and shivering in the cold, but that would soon change. A bit of smoke was already beginning to waft into the tiny bathroom through the vents. Flames would soon follow. There wasn't much time. "Please," she rasped. "Let me go, for the love of God!"

"What would you know about God's love?" he demanded, then, tamping down his anger, he placed a gloved hand upon her head, as if to calm her, and from somewhere outside, through the cracked window he heard a car backfire on the wintry streets. He had to finish this. Now. Before the fire attracted attention. "You're a sinner, Cecilia, and as such you will have to pay for your sins."

"You've got the wrong woman! I'm not . . . her . . . I'm not Cecilia. Please. Let me go. I won't say a word, I promise, no one will ever know this happened, I swear." She clutched at the hem of his alb. Desperate. And dirty. She was a whore. Like the others. He turned his attention to the radio sitting on the windowsill and swiftly turned the knob. The sound of familiar music wafted through the speakers, fading to the sound of a woman's sultry voice.

"This is Dr. Sam, with one last thought on this date when John F. Kennedy, one of our finest presidents, was killed . . . Take care of yourself, New Orleans. Good night and God bless. No matter what your troubles are today, there's always tomorrow . . . Sweet dreams . . ."

He turned the dial, switching stations, and heard the static and chirps of announcers' voices until he found what he wanted: pipe organ music. Full. As if echoing in a cathedral.

Now it could be done.

As the whore watched, he withdrew his sword from behind the shower curtain.

"Oh, God. No!" She was frantic now, pulling at the chain as the collar tightened even further.

"It's too late." His voice was measured and calm, but inside he was shaking, trembling, not with fear but anticipation. Adrenalin, his favorite drug, sang through his veins. From the corner of his eye he noticed flames beginning to lick through the screen of the vent. The time had come.

"No, please, don't . . . oh, God . . ." She was clawing at her tether now, vainly trying to hide behind the pedestal as the collar tightened, her wrists and ankles bleeding and raw from her bonds. "You've got the wrong woman!"

His pulse throbbed, pounded in his brain. For a second he felt a tingle against the back of his neck, like the breath of Satan. He glanced at the mirror, searching the shimmering surface, looking beneath the reflection of his own image, his face hidden in a tight black mask, but feeling as if someone were watching through the glass. Witnessing his act.

But that was impossible.

Sweat slid into his eyes as he lifted his sword so high his arm ached. Smoke burned in his lungs. Blood lust ran through his veins as he grabbed a fistful of hair in his free hand. He stared down at her perfect neck surrounded by the choke collar. He was hard between his legs, his erection nearly painful. Oh, how he would love to thrust into her body, to taste of her before absolving her of her sins. But that was not his mission. Denying himself of such wicked pleasure was his own act of martyrdom.

"For your sins, Cecilia," he said, biting out the words as ripples of pleasure passed through him, "and in the name of the Father, the Son, and the Holy Spirit, I commit your soul to God."

Chapter Two

"No!"

Olivia's eyes flew open.

Her own scream echoed through her small bedroom. The dog gave up a sharp "Woof!"

"Oh, God, no." Her heart was a drum, her body drenched in sweat, the vivid dream lingering as clearly as if she'd just witnessed a murder. Again. Oh, God, it was happening again.

The vision was so damned real. Her nostrils still stung from the smell of smoke, her ears rang with that eerie pipe organ music, her mouth was dry as cotton, her throat raw from her scream. A blinding headache started at the base of her skull and moved upward.

She glanced at the clock. Three-fifteen. Her hands shook as she pushed the hair from her face.

At the foot of the old bed, her grandmother's mutt lifted his head and was staring at her. Yawning, he emitted another warning bark.

"Come here, you," she said, patting the pillow as Hairy

S stretched. He was all scraggly bits of fur, mottled gray and brown with splotches of white, heavy eyebrows that hinted of some schnauzer hidden back in his bloodlines. He whined, then belly-swamped up to the pillows next to her. Absently, she pulled him close, needing something to cling to. She ruffled his coarse coat and wished she could tell him it would be all right. But it wouldn't. She knew better. She buried her face in his fur and tried to calm down. Maybe it was a mistake . . . maybe it was just a dream . . . maybe . . . no way. She knew what the images meant.

"Crap."

She scooted up to a sitting position. *Calm down.* But she was still shaking, the headache beginning to pound. Hairy S wriggled out of her arms.

"Damn you, Grannie Gin," she muttered as the sounds of the night floated in through the open window, the rustle of the wind moving through the trees underscored by the hum of traffic, eighteen-wheelers on the distant freeway.

Dropping her head into her hands, she massaged her temples. *Why me? Why?* The visions had started at a young age, before she could really remember, but they had been less defined then, and rare. In the off-and-on-again times when her mother had lived with them, the times between husbands.

Bernadette had never wanted to believe that her daughter had inherited her grandmother's psychic gift.

"Coincidence," Bernadette had told her child often enough, or, "You're making this up. It's just a cheap attempt to get attention! Now, knock it off, Livvie, and quit listening to Grandma. She's touched in the head, you know, and if you aren't careful . . . You hear me?" she'd said sharply, shaking her daughter as if to drive out the monsters in her brain. "If you aren't careful, you'll be touched too, not by some ridiculous gift of sight as Grannie claims, but by the devil. Satan never sleeps. Do you hear me? Never."

Once Bernadette had pointed a long red-tipped nail at the end of her eldest daughter's nose. They had been in the kitchen of this very house where the smells of bacon grease, wood smoke, and cheap perfume had adhered to pine cabinets yellowed with age. A fan had sat near the ancient toaster, rotating on the corner of the countertop and blowing hot air around the tiny, sparse room.

As Olivia recalled, Bernadette had just gotten off the day shift down at Charlene's restaurant at the truck stop near the Interstate. She was standing on the cracked linoleum floor in bare feet, a white blouse, and the ever-present black skirt of a waitress. One strap of her bra was visible and a tiny gold cross hung from a chain around her neck and lay nestled in that deep cleft between her breasts. "Listen, child," she'd said seriously, her expression intense. "I'm not kidding. All this mumbo jumbo and hints about voodoo are just bullshit, you hear me? Bull*shit*. Your grandma has delusions of being some damned voodoo priestess or some such nonsense, but she's not. Just because way back when there was some octoroon blood mixed in with the rest, doesn't make her a . . . a . . . damned fortune teller, now, does it? She's not a psychic and neither are you. Okay?"

Bernadette had straightened, adjusted her short black skirt, and sighed. " 'Course it doesn't," she'd added, more, it seemed, to convince herself than Olivia. "Now, go outside, will ya, ride your bike or skateboard or whatever." She picked up an open pack of Virginia Slims on the counter, shook out a cigarette, and lit it quickly. With smoke seeping out of her nostrils, she stood on her tiptoes and reached into an upper cabinet, where she pulled out a fifth of whiskey.

"Mama's got herself a whopper of a headache," she'd explained as she found a short glass, cracked ice cubes from a plastic tray, and poured herself a healthy drink, which she'd explained was her reward for a hard day's labor while enduring the leers, winks, and occasional pinches at the truck stop. Only after taking a sip and leaning her hips against the counter did she look at her daughter again. "You're an odd one, Livvie," she'd said with a sigh. "I love ya to death, you know I do, but you're different." With the cigarette planted firmly between her lips, she'd reached forward and grabbed Olivia's chin, moving her head left, then right. Narrowed eyes studied Olivia's profile through the smoke.

"You're pretty enough," Bernadette finally allowed, straightening and flicking ashes into the sink, "and if you use your head and don't go spouting off all this crazy talk, you'll land yourself a good man, maybe even a rich man. So don't go scarin' 'em off with all this weird talk, y'hear me? No decent man'll have you if ya do." She'd rolled the drink in her hands and watched the ice cubes clink together. "Believe me, I know." A sad smile had curved her lips, which showed only a hint of lipstick applied much earlier in the day. "Someday, honey, you're gonna git yerself outta this dump"—she fluttered her fingers to take in all of Grannie Gin's cabin—"and into a fancy house, just like Scarlett Damned O'Hara." She managed a wider grin, showing off straight, impossibly white teeth. "And when you do, you're gonna take care of your mama, y'hear?"

Now, thinking back, Olivia sighed. *Oh, Mama, if you only knew.* Olivia would have done anything to make the demons in her mind be still. But lately, those dreams she'd repressed had come back with a vengeance.

Ever since she'd returned to Louisiana.

She had to do something about the visions. She had to do something about tonight.

The woman's dead, Olivia. There's nothing you can do for her and no one's going to believe you. You know that. You've tried to contact the authorities before. You've tried to convince your family, your friends, even your damned fiancé. No one believed you then. No one will now.

Besides, it was a dream. That's all. Just a dream.

Slowly she edged off the bed, dragging her grandmother's quilt with her, then unlocked the French doors to the verandah. The dog trotted after her as Olivia stepped into the cool winter of early morning, the floorboards smooth beneath her bare feet. The bayou was quiet, mist rising slowly, huge cypress trees guarding the sluggish waters that lapped near the back of the house. She leaned a hand against the rail, worn smooth by the touch of human hands over the past

hundred years. Some creature of the darkness scuttled
through the brush, rustling dry leaves and snapping thin
branches on its way into the swamp. Goose bumps sprouted
on Olivia's arms. As she gazed across the still, dark waters,
she tried to shake the dream from her mind, but it remained
steadfast, clinging with razor-sharp talons, digging deep into
her brain, refusing to be dismissed.

It was more than a nightmare.

Olivia knew it with horrid certainty.

It wasn't the first time she'd "witnessed" someone's
death. They had come and gone over the years, but whenever
she was here, in this part of bayou country, the visions had
preyed upon her. It was one of the reasons she'd stayed
away so long.

Yet, here she was. Once again in Louisiana. And the
nightmares had already begun, back with a blinding, soul-
scraping fury that scared her to death. "It's your fault," she
muttered as if Grannie Gin, bless her voodoo-lovin' soul,
could hear her.

Olivia's fingers gripped the railing. As clearly as if she'd
been in that minuscule bathroom, Olivia saw the murder
again. Smoke rose as the masked priest lifted his sword and
swung downward, not once, but three times. . . .

Olivia squeezed her eyes shut, but the vision wouldn't go
away. *A priest.* A man of God!

She had to do something.

Now.

Somewhere tonight a woman had been murdered. Violently.

By rote Olivia sketched a quick sign of the cross over
her chest. She rubbed her arms and pulled the quilt more
snugly around her as a soft November breeze sighed through
the trees overhead and the dank smell of the swamp filled
her nostrils. She couldn't pretend this hadn't happened even
though no matter what, no one would believe her.

Turning quickly, she hurried inside, Grannie's quilt billowing after her. Hairy S was right on her heels, toenails
clicking across the hardwood floor as she made her way to

the desk. Flipping on a small lamp, she scrounged through the dusty cubbyholes, discarding pens, note cards, thimbles and rubber bands until she found the scrap of paper she'd been looking for, a tattered piece of newspaper. It was an article that had been in the *Times-Picayune* after the latest rash of murders in the Crescent City had occurred. According to the report, a detective by the name of Rick Bentz had been instrumental in solving the bizarre killings. He'd been the man who had discovered the link in the crimes and how they were related to Dr. Sam, Samantha Leeds, host of the talk-radio program *Midnight Confessions*.

The same radio show Olivia had heard tonight in the vision.

She shuddered as she scanned the article she'd torn from the paper months ago.

Bentz and his partner Ruben Montoya, were given credit for breaking the "Rosary Killer" case where several prostitutes had been killed by "Father John," a man who had stalked the city of New Orleans a few months back. *Father John*. The killer who was obsessed with Dr. Sam and her radio show, a sadist who would demand his victims don red wigs so that they would look like Dr. Sam, a murderer who scripted the dialogue for his victims, insisting they repent for their crimes . . . just as she'd seen the priest in her vision demand his victim's pleas for mercy and forgiveness.

Her blood turned to ice.

First a man calling himself Father John and now a priest.

She had to talk to Detective Bentz. ASAP. No one else at the police station had even listened to her—just written her off as a lunatic. But then, she was used to the ridicule. Maybe Rick Bentz would be different. Maybe he'd listen to her.

He had to.

She dropped the blanket and reached for her jeans and a sweatshirt she'd tossed over the bedpost and grabbed a bottle of ibuprofen from the night table. She downed four tablets dry and hoped they'd take the edge off her headache. She had to think clearly, to explain . . .

Slinging the strap of her purse over her shoulder, she slid into a pair of moccasins and flew down the stairs. Hairy S scrambled after her. But as she dashed past the bookcase in the alcove near the front door, she felt a draft—a whisper across her skin, something evil.

She stopped short. Glanced out the window. The dog growled, the hairs on the back of his neck standing up. Again, through the open window, she heard the rustle of dry leaves, a gust of wind through brittle branches. Was it her imagination or was someone outside . . . lurking in the darkness?

Fear pulsed through her blood. She moved close to the window, peered through the mist and darkness, but saw no one. The night was suddenly still, the rush of wind having died.

She slammed the window shut, locked it, and snapped the blinds closed. This was no time to get spooked. But at the bookcase she felt it again, that icy sensation.

You're overreacting. Stop it, Livvie!

Her breath was shallow, the hairs lifting on the back of her arms, as if there were someone in the room with her. She caught her reflection in the mirror mounted next to the bookcase and shivered. Her hair was wild and uncombed, her face pale beneath a few freckles, her lips bloodless. She looked as scared as she was.

But she had to go. . . . She dug into her purse and grabbed her key ring, held the longest and sharpest key in her fingers as if it were some kind of weapon, then headed for the front door. Hairy S followed after her, his tail between his legs.

"You have to stay here," she insisted, but as she opened the door, the scrappy little mutt streaked through, tearing through the fallen leaves to her beat-up truck. Olivia locked the door behind her, checked over her shoulder, and jogged to the driveway, where the dog was whining and jumping against the cab of her pickup. "Fine, get in." She opened the driver's side and Hairy S hurtled inside. He took his favorite spot on the passenger's side of the bench seat, propping his tiny feet on the dash, his tongue lolling as he panted. "This isn't a joyride," Olivia said as she backed into a turnout, the beams of her headlights splashing over the face of her little cabin. She saw no strangers lurking in the shadows, no dark figure hiding behind the wicker furniture on the porch. Maybe her vivid imagination had run wild again.

It had to be.

Still her heart pumped wildly.

She shoved her old Ford Ranger into gear. With a rumble, the pickup shot forward, turning up gravel in its wake. The lane was long and wound through stands of cypress and palmettos, across a small bridge and onto the main road.

New Orleans was a good twenty-minute drive. She pushed the speed limit. But she didn't want to bother with any other police officer, no other detective. No. She wanted Bentz. It was too early for him to be on duty. But she'd wait. As long as it took.

As the road turned south, she noticed a glimmer of light that grew into a faint glow on the horizon, an orange haze that was visible through the thick stands of cypress and live oak.

Her insides twisted.

The fire.

Dear God.

She knew before the firemen or the police that somewhere in that hellish inferno was the body of a woman; the woman she'd seen in her vision.

Chapter Three

"Uh-oh." Reuben Montoya's voice held the knell of doom.

Bentz looked up from his stack of paperwork as Montoya, carrying two paper cups of coffee, slipped through the open door of his office.

He handed Bentz one of the cups, then leaned a hip against the file cabinet of Rick Bentz's office. In his trademark black leather jacket and black jeans, he let his gaze wander back through the half-open door, past the maze of cubicles and desks in the outer office, to the stairway.

"What?" Rick asked from behind the desk and a mountain of paperwork that never seemed to diminish. Crime was big business in New Orleans.

"Trouble."

"There's always trouble."

"No, you don't understand, the resident nutcase is here again."

"Again?" Bentz repeated, looking out the door to see the object of Montoya's interest, a petite woman with wild gold-colored curls, smooth white skin, and attitude written all over her. In faded jeans and a New Orleans Saints sweatshirt that had seen better days, she was charging straight toward Bentz's office.

"She's been calling Brinkman, claims she's a psychic and that she sees murders before they take place," Montoya explained.

"And Brinkman says?"

"What he always says. 'Bullshit.' He doesn't believe in any of that crap."

At that moment, she barreled into the room. Her cheeks were flushed, her pointed chin set in what Bentz took as angry determination. Her eyes, the color of fine malt whiskey, bored straight through him.

"Detective Bentz?" she asked without so much as a glance in Montoya's direction.

"Yeah. I'm Bentz."

"Good. I need to talk to you."

By this time Bentz was half standing. He flipped a hand at Montoya. "And this is Detective Reuben Montoya, my partner."

"Reuben *D.* Montoya. I go by Diego." Montoya added.

Bentz lifted a brow. *Diego?* Since when? Oh . . . Since a beautiful female entered the room. Montoya might have referred to this woman as a nutcase but he was interested in her—of course he was—it was the younger man's MO whenever a good-looking woman was nearby. Regardless, apparently, of her mental condition. And in spite of his talk the other night of being a one-woman man. Montoya's male radar was always on alert.

She barely gave Montoya a second glance as Bentz offered his hand. "I read about you in the *Times,*" she said.

Great. Another citizen who thought he was a damned hero. To her credit, her gaze leveled straight at Bentz and she didn't give Montoya's flirtation a passing glance. Her grip was surprisingly strong as she gave his palm a hand shake then released her fingers. "You can't believe everything you read."

"Trust me, I don't."

He waved her into a chair. "So what's on your mind?"

"A murder."

At least she didn't beat around the bush. He pulled a legal pad from beneath a pile of half-finished reports. "Whose?"

"A woman." She fell into a chair and he noticed the smudges of exhaustion beneath her eyes, the little lines pinching the corners of her mouth. A faint scent of jasmine entered with her. "I don't know. He called her Cecilia but she said that wasn't her name and . . . and she never told him what her name was."

"Told who?"

"The killer," she said, staring at him as if he were as dense as granite.

"Wait a minute. Let's start over," he said. "You witnessed a woman being killed, right? You were there?" he asked.

She hesitated before answering. "No."

"No?"

"But I saw it."

Wonderful. Just what he needed to start the day right. Bentz clicked his pen. "Where did the murder take place, Miss—?"

"Benchet. I'm Olivia Benchet, and I don't know where it happened . . . but I saw someone, a woman about twenty-five, I'd guess, being killed." Olivia's face paled and she swallowed hard. "She . . . she had shoulder-length blond hair, blue eyes, a few freckles, and . . . and kind of a heart-shaped face. She was thin, but not skinny . . . in . . . good shape as if she worked out or . . . oh, God." Olivia closed her eyes, took in a deep, shuddering breath, then slowly let it out. A second later her lids opened and she seemed calmer, in control. Again the scent of jasmine teased his nostrils.

"Wait a minute. We'd better back up. You *heard* him say her name and you *saw* him kill a woman, but you weren't there?" Shit. Montoya had called this one, and the Cheshire cat smile beginning to stretch across his chin indicated he knew it.

"That's right."

"Was it on film?"

"No," she said, then rushed on, "I think I should explain something."

That would be a good start. She leaned forward in her chair, and then, as if trying to grasp something, anything, she opened and closed her hands. *Here it comes,* Bentz thought. *The part where it all falls apart but she tries to convince us that this outrageous story is true.* She was, no doubt as Montoya had explained, a bonafide nutcase.

"I'm able see some things right before or as they're happening. In my mind. Even though I'm not there. I know it sounds bizarre, even crazy, but it's true."

"You're a psychic." *Or a psychotic.*

"I don't know if you'd call me that. I think of myself as having a little bit of ESP."

"A little bit?"

"It comes and goes. Last night, while I was sleeping, this was very real. I mean, I was *there.*"

Hell, this just got better and better. She'd been asleep. Great. "So you were dreaming."

"It was more than that."

"And all of your dreams, do they come true?"

"No. Of course not!" She threw her hands into the air. "I already told you I know this sounds nuts, but just hear me out, okay? And please, don't make any judgment calls. I'm telling you these 'dreams,' if you want to call them that, are different. I can't explain it. They're beyond real. Beyond surreal."

I'll bet. Bentz rubbed the back of his neck as he studied her. She was so earnest. She wasn't lying. Whatever it was she was peddling here, she believed every word of it.

"I woke up and I could still smell the smoke, feel the heat, hear her cries for help. I mean, *I was there.* Not physically, but ..."

"Spiritually?" he offered.

Montoya suggested, "Mentally. Or telepathically."

"However you want to explain it," she said, starting to sound irritated.

"I can't."

"I know. Neither can I," she admitted.

Because it's inexplicable.

"I know . . . I mean, I understand that you're used to working with facts. Cold, hard evidence. I don't blame you, but surely you've worked with psychics or people who have a different level of sensitivity, or psychic prowess. I've read about police departments using psychics to help solve particularly difficult cases."

"That's when they run out of that hard evidence," he said to her, "when they actually have a dead body or missing person and have exhausted all other conventional avenues."

"There's nothing conventional about this."

"Amen," Montoya said and she tossed a sharp look over her shoulder.

"My grandmother, she had the same gift, but not my mother." Her lips twisted into a wry, self-deprecating smile. "Lucky me," she said. Her smooth forehead was suddenly lined, her eyebrows pulled together, and she leaned back in her chair as if exhausted.

"It's genetic?"

"I don't know how it works, okay? That's just what happened in my family. And it's not always at night, in dreams. Sometimes it can happen in the middle of the day, driving down the Interstate."

"Could be dangerous."

"That's right, it is. And it's . . . a royal pain telling people about it and trying to make them understand. To believe."

"It's a big leap for most of us mere mortals," Bentz agreed.

Behind her Montoya tried to keep his expression bland, but there was a glimmer in his dark eyes as he took a sip of coffee. He didn't say it, but *I told you so* was written all over him.

"I already admitted that I know it sounds crazy," she said, as if she, too, felt the skepticism in the small room.

She seemed so small and out of place in the station where, though it was barely eight in the morning, the place was a beehive of activity. The door to Bentz's office was ajar and through the opening he caught glimpses of officers and civilians, heard snatches of conversation and muffled laughter, watched as more than one suspect was dragged to a desk for a statement. But this woman didn't belong here. Whatever she was, it wasn't a cop, a criminal, or, he suspected, a valid witness.

Slumping down in the chair, she rubbed her shoulders as if she were cold to her bones though the room was stuffy, hot enough that he'd cracked the window open. The sounds of the city waking up wafted inside—pedestrians walking and talking, the tires from passing cars whirring, engines rumbling, and pigeons cooing and flapping their wings from an upper ledge. She ran long fingers along her jaw. "I shouldn't have come here," she said as if to herself. "I knew you wouldn't believe me . . . but I had to try."

"Detective Montoya, maybe you could scour up some coffee for Ms. Benchet?"

"I'm fine—" she protested, but Montoya was already out the door.

Olivia leaned forward, as if now that they were alone she could confide in him. "You have to believe me, Detective Bentz. A woman was murdered early this morning. Brutally. I saw it."

"But you weren't there."

"No, no, in my mind's eye."

"While you were sleeping," he pointed out.

"It wasn't a dream!" she said emphatically, not so much angry as desperate. "I know the difference." Montoya, carrying a paper coffee cup, slipped into the room again. "The priest tortured her and—"

"Priest?" Montoya repeated as he handed her the cup. Some of his cocksure bravado slipped. "A priest was the killer?"

"Yes. He was dressed in robes. Vestments."

Bentz scowled as he understood why she'd singled him

out. He set the pen on his notepad and leaned back in his chair. "Let me guess. You read about Montoya and me solving the other case this past summer, so you thought that we'd be able to help out. Because we're kind of experts on the whole Catholic-homicide thing and you've seen a priest." He tried to keep the sarcasm out of his voice.

"I hoped so," she admitted, and she looked so guileless he had the unexpected urge to believe her. But he knew better. "Oh, I get it," she said, and those amber eyes sparked as the light dawned. "You actually think I read about the serial killer last summer, and because I didn't have anything better to do, I just bopped down here with a wild story about a priest to try and stir things up, right? To gain some attention, my 'fifteen minutes or seconds of fame'?"

He didn't reply.

"Oh, give me a break. Who would do that? Come on!"

"Ms. Benchet—"

"Don't patronize me, okay, and it's Olivia. Let's get that straight, right now. I realize my story sounds hideous, and believe me it was, but I witnessed the murder, as surely as if I was in that tiny bathroom."

"A bathroom?" Montoya interjected again.

"That's where it happened. Where a priest, a man who was supposed to have dedicated his life to God, killed a woman he had chained to a sink."

Montoya arched a brow. "So, Ms. Benchet—Olivia— you'd recognize the killer?"

"No." She shook her head and bit down hard on her lip. "He was wearing a mask—like a black ski mask that covered his entire head."

"Now we've got a priest in a mask," Bentz repeated.

"*Yes!*" Her eyes flashed angrily.

"And this murder that you witnessed though you weren't there, happened in a bathroom?"

"I told you the woman was chained to the sink and—" She shuddered. "God, it was awful. The flames were coming in through the vent and he didn't seem to care; it was like he expected the fire somehow, but that wasn't enough."

"Not enough?" Bentz asked, dreading what was to follow.

"No. He had a sword," she whispered, visibly shaking and squeezing her eyes shut as if to close off the memory. "He swung down three times at her bowed head."

"Jesus!" Montoya muttered.

Tears formed in Olivia Benchet's eyes and she blinked several times. Either she was one hell of an actress, or she really believed her own lies. "It—it was horrible. Horrible."

Bentz glanced at Montoya as he found a box of tissues and handed it to Olivia. She pulled out a couple and looked embarrassed as she wiped her eyes. "I'm sorry."

"Don't even think about it," he said. He wasn't sure what was going on, but one way or another, Olivia Benchet was at the end of her decidedly frayed rope. He decided to go by the book and take her statement formally. Just in case. Crackpot or not, she was scared to death. "Let's start over. I'll tape this if that's all right with you."

"Please . . . fine . . . whatever." She waved her fingers as if she didn't care what he did, then sipped her coffee as Bentz found his recorder, put in a fresh tape, and pressed the record button. "November twenty-second, this is an interview with Olivia Benchet. Detective Rick Bentz and Detective Reuben Montoya are with the witness." Angling the microphone so that she could speak into it easily, he said, "Now, Ms. Benchet, please spell your name for me and give me your address. . . ."

As the tape whirred and he took notes, Olivia cradled a cup of coffee and spoke in soft, calmer tones. She told him she lived out of the city, in bayou country, gave him her address and phone number along with the name of the shop where she worked—the Third Eye, just off Jackson Square. Before moving to Louisiana a few months back to care for her ailing grandmother, she'd lived in Tucson.

With Bentz's prodding she repeated much of what she'd already said, and as Montoya watched, Bentz scribbled notes, listening as she explained her "vision" only hours earlier, that she was certain she'd "seen" a priest who had chained a naked woman to a sink in a smoky room and that the woman had repeatedly begged for mercy.

Olivia's voice was a low whisper, nearly a drone, almost as if she was in some kind of trance, detached from Bentz's small office with its piles of files, overflowing wastebasket, and dying Boston fern littering the floor with dried, curled fronds.

". . . after he was certain that the radio was playing the right song, some kind of hymn, then he used the sword," she said, describing again that he'd swung three times. "I sensed he was in a hurry, probably because of the fire or a fear of being caught, but after he was finished, while the flames were beginning to come up from the vent, he took the time to dig into his pocket. He pulled a chain or a necklace of some kind and hung it over the shower head. The radio was playing some weird music and the smoke was so thick I could barely see, but I think he stripped off his robes and left them there."

"So he was naked?" Montoya interjected. He was leaning against the door frame, his arms folded over his chest, his forgotten cup of coffee in one hand. "You could see identifying marks. Like tattoos or birthmarks or moles . . ."

"He wasn't naked. He was wearing something like a wet suit or one of those tight biking suits, all black."

"And a ski mask that covered his entire head."

"And gloves?" Montoya asked.

"Yes." A muscle worked in her jaw and she glanced through the open window. "I think . . . I mean I got this eerie feeling . . . that somehow he knew, or he sensed, that I was watching him."

Chapter Four

A nutcase. Pure and simple. He hated to think it of her because she seemed so convinced of what she'd seen, but Bentz decided Montoya was right. Intriguing as she was, Olivia Benchet was certifiable. Pretty—with her wild light brown hair and full lips—but certifiable. Sitting across from him, alternately seeming small and vulnerable, then angry and tough, always animated, she was desperate for him to buy into her story.

So far he wasn't.

"This priest-slash-killer. How did he know you were watching him? Did he see you?" Reuben asked.

"I don't know. I can't explain it, but I swear he looked at me."

Montoya persisted. "How could he see you? You weren't there, right? You were at your grandmother's house . . . this was kind of like a foggy dream."

"There was smoke but I could see through it. I felt like I was staring through glass or clear plastic, a window, maybe . . ." Letting out a discouraged sigh, she set her unfinished cup of coffee on the desk, then pushed her unruly hair from her eyes. "I realize you don't want to believe me, that it would be easier if I just disappeared, but I know this happened." She leveled her gaze at Bentz. "I'd bet my life on it."

Bentz glanced down at the legal pad in front of him. He heard the sounds of phones ringing, conversations buzzing, keyboards clicking from the outer office and felt like he was wasting his time, but decided to hear her out. "Okay. So go on. You said the priest took off his clothes. What happened then? Where did he go?"

"He left. Went out the door of the room."

"Didn't you follow him?"

"I don't think I could have. It doesn't work like that."

"What does it work like?"

"I wish I knew. I usually just get glimpses. Pieces that I have trouble putting together. This was much more complete, but . . . but then . . . I woke up."

Convenient, Bentz thought, but didn't comment, and when he did speak, tried to keep the skepticism from his voice. "Do you remember anything else? For example, was there anything distinguishing that would help us locate the house or apartment where this happened?"

"The building was on fire," she snapped. "I'd think that would narrow the search down a little."

He didn't rise to the bait. "You're sure it was in New Orleans?"

"The radio was playing. I recognized one of the programs. So it was in the vicinity, I think, and . . . I can't explain it, but it *felt* like he was in the city or nearby . . . oh, God." She sighed and shook her head. "You still don't believe me, do you?"

"I'm just sorting through what you're saying, trying to get to the facts." Whether she intended to or not, she was bothering him, getting under his skin. So sure of what she'd seen one minute yet admitting that she knew she sounded like a loon the next. One second on the verge of tears, the next mad as hell. He had a dozen questions, but didn't want to overwhelm her. And if she was lying, he relied on the old adage: Give her enough rope and she'd hang herself.

"So," Bentz said gently, "all you know is that someone was murdered, nearly beheaded, by a priest you can't identify, in a building you can't describe, but you somehow think it happened here. In New Orleans."

She looked at her hands. "Yes. I—I can't tell you where specifically. But I do know it happened this morning."

"Because that's when you were dreaming."

Her cheeks flushed. "No . . . I assume the visions occur simultaneously with the act, but I'm not certain about it. However, as I mentioned earlier, *Detective,* there was a radio in that damned bathroom and the host of the late-night program, *Midnight Confessions,* Dr. Sam, was talking about it being a significant day in history, the day President Kennedy was assassinated. That's today, the twenty-second."

"Sure is," Montoya said.

"So is that significant?"

"I don't know!"

"Look," she said, pointing a finger straight at him, those gold eyes snapping fire, "I've been in before. I've talked to Detective Brinkman and he just blows me off every time, but when I read about you two, I thought maybe you'd be different. That you might help me. That somehow you could find a way to prevent what happened last night from happening again."

"*If* something happened."

"It did, Detective. I swear on my grandmother's grave." Her face was flushed with color, conviction setting her jaw.

"Except that maybe you just had a bad dream."

"No way in hell. I know the difference."

"Is there anything else you can tell us?" he asked, and she let out a long, protracted sigh.

"No. Not that I can think of. Not now."

Time to end this. He managed a smile he didn't feel. "Look, Ms. Benchet—Olivia—there's not much I can do. I can't very well start a murder investigation without a body, or at least a report of a missing woman matching your girl's description. You haven't given me much to go with here other than you had a pretty bad nightmare.''

"Pretty bad?" she repeated. "Pretty bad? I don't make it a habit to run to the police station every time I have a nightmare. The least you can do is check it out. Start with the fire.''

From his position near the file cabinet, Montoya scratched at his goatee. ''There was a fire. An old house, not far from City Park, off of Esplanade, I think.''

Bentz glared at his partner. "How do you know this already?''

Montoya flashed his practiced grin. "Ear to the ground, eye on the sky, nose to the grindstone.''

Head up the ass, Bentz thought. Sometimes Montoya's practiced cool bugged the hell out of him. "Anyone inside?''

"Don't know. When I heard about it, they were still hosin' down the place.''

Bentz swung his gaze back to Olivia. "Okay. We'll check it out.''

"Good.'' Her gaze centered on his, but her shoulders relaxed a bit, as if she were relieved. "Look, I know you'd like to write me off as a crazy person, but don't, okay? Please.''

He clicked off the recorder and stood, signifying the interview was over. "Thanks for coming in. As I said, we'll look into it and let you know if we find anything.''

"That's all I can ask.'' Reaching into her purse, she withdrew her wallet, unfolded it, and pulled out a business card that read:

Olivia Benchet
Owner
The Crystal Prism
Collectibles, New Age, Spirituals

The phone number and Tucson, Arizona, address had been scratched out and a local number inserted. She slid the card across his desk, past the bifold picture frames where two photographs of his daughter, Kristi, smiled up at him.

"She's pretty," Olivia observed, glancing at the pictures. "Yours?"

"Yeah." He picked up the card. "Look, I'm gonna tell you straight out, Ms. Benchet. All you've brought me is something that looks a helluva lot like a wild goose chase, but if I hear anything, if there's any reports of a missing woman who matches your description, if . . . any bodies are found in a fire . . . I'll be in contact with you."

She nodded, hesitated, and seemed to be struggling with something more. Montoya observed it too, because in his peripheral vision Bentz noticed his partner straighten slightly and say, "You've got something else on your mind?"

Glancing from Montoya to Bentz, she said, "No doubt you'll talk to Detective Brinkman about me. Check me out and I don't blame you, I would, too. So here's the deal; I'm sure the murderer's struck before. I—I didn't have the kind of clear vision I had last night—the visions were much more fragmented. Pieces of glass rather than a whole window. But I sensed, and I can't explain why, that this man—this priest—has not only killed before, but that he's on some kind of mission. A vendetta. He won't quit until he is stopped. There have already been several victims—two, maybe three . . . or more. I'm not as clear as to what happened to them, but they died. Cruelly." She bit at her lower lip, her eyes narrowing thoughtfully. "Something's very wrong in this city. Evil. Last night I saw the whole thing and it was hideous. This mission of his, it's not finished yet. In fact, it's probably just started."

Bingo. Bonafide lunatic. Bentz had heard enough, but Olivia Benchet glanced at the photos of his daughter again. In the first picture Kristi wasn't quite six, grinning widely enough to show that she was missing a front tooth as she entered kindergarten. The other taken just last year was of a pretty, composed seventeen-year-old. She smiled softly, but there was just the hint of defiance in her hazel eyes, a bit of a challenge in the tilt of her chin—the promise of rebellion yet to come.

"You're a father, Detective Bentz, and some monster is out there killing women in this city. How would you feel if the killer zeroed in on her?" She motioned to the double-fold pictures. "That girl he killed last night is someone's daughter, possibly someone's sister or mother." Those whiskey-gold eyes beseeched him again. "I hope you'll call me when you find out I'm telling you the truth because there's a chance that I can help."

He rounded the desk and pushed the door open further, signifying she should leave. "We'll get back to you if anything comes up."

"I asked you not to be condescending," she reminded him, her lips pinching at the corners. "I can't read your mind, thank God, but I'm pretty good at seeing what's in your eyes." She swung out the door.

"Ouch," Montoya said as she walked out. More than one officer turned a head to watch her swing by in her tight hip-hugging jeans and sweatshirt. Her back was ramrod stiff, her chin held high. Bentz never took his eyes off her, but she didn't so much as glance over her shoulder and he hated the fact that he still smelled a tinge of her perfume.

Montoya let out a long, low whistle. "What a piece of . . . work."

"Yep." Bentz fingered the card she'd left him and watched as she disappeared down the stairs. He gave himself a swift mental kick. He wasn't a horny kid anymore. Not like Montoya. Sure, she was an attractive woman, but big deal. They were a dime a dozen. And not all of them were prancing around with a significant amount of screws loose. He tapped the edge of her business card against the calluses of his other palm.

"Just another beautiful looney tune," Montoya said thoughtfully. "We've got our share down here."

"Amen to that," Bentz said. "But she's been in Tucson for a while."

"Hey, they're not hurtin' in the weirdc department, either. Isn't that where they see all the damned UFOs?"

"Roswell, New Mexico."

"Close enough." Montoya zipped up his leather jacket, then flipped the collar to cover the back of his neck. "Too much desert sun if you ask me."

"I didn't."

Montoya ignored the comment, downed the dregs of his coffee, and crushed the cup in his fist "Their brains get baked. You've seen those cow skulls. The sun does that. Strips the bones bare of any flesh or gray matter."

"Even if they're alive?"

"It starts slow." Montoya flashed his killer smile again as he tossed his empty cup into the trash.

"What time was that fire?" Bentz asked, wishing he could just dismiss Olivia Benchet.

"Early this morning. Three or four."

That jelled with Olivia's story. *Midnight Confessions,* Dr. Sam's popular talk show, had been expanded on some nights of the week. She now signed off at three on Friday mornings.

"A priest," Montoya muttered under his breath. "I don't think so."

Neither did Bentz. Even though he had his own bone to pick with the Catholic Church and one priest in particular. The guy was a bastard, but as low as he would stoop in or out of his fancy vestments, the good father wouldn't commit murder. Bentz was convinced of it.

The phone jangled and he moved back to the desk, grabbing the receiver. "Bentz."

"Yeah, Rick. It's Stan Pagliano."

The hairs on the back of Bentz's neck rose. He played cards with Stan every six months or so. Stan was a single dad, too, with a daughter Kristi's age. And he was with the New Orleans Fire Department. "What's up?" He rounded his desk, stretching the cord tight.

"I've been workin' half the night. We had ourselves a bad one not far from Bayou St. John. Small house. By the time the first call came in, it was too late."

"Someone inside?"

"Yeah. What's left of her . . . Well, we think it's a woman. Hard to tell. Not much left. The ME and the crime scene team are here, but I thought you might want to poke around. The deal is this, Rick, this isn't someone who fell asleep in bed while smokin' a damned cigarette. Looks like arson and there was a woman trapped inside; she was chained to the sink, man. Her hands and feet were *chained* there. She had something around her neck, too, and the body's burned bad, but it's—it's—her head." He let out a breath and Bentz knew what was coming. "It was nearly severed. Sick stuff."

Bentz's skin crawled. He glanced at the door, wishing he could call Olivia Benchet back into the room.

"There are some other things, too. The crime scene team will get it all, but it might not hurt for you to take a look before everything's bagged and tagged."

"I'm on my way," Bentz said. His gut clenched tight as Stan rattled off the address. He hung up and was reaching for his jacket when his eyes met Montoya's. "There was someone killed in the fire over by Esplanade. Probably a woman. Burned beyond recognition, her hands and feet chained to the sink, her head nearly severed."

"Holy shit," Montoya muttered, sucking in his breath.

Bentz stuffed his Glock into his shoulder holster. "Precisely."

Chapter Five

Kristi Bentz dragged her body from the Olympic-sized pool. Two miles. The longest she'd swum in six months and it felt good. She grabbed her towel from the hook over the benches against the wall and breathed deeply. Her nose was filled with chlorine, her ears plugged though she heard the echo of voices of the few other swimmers out this early. Ms. Carter, a masculine-looking swim coach wearing sweats and a whistle, was patrolling the area, padding in plastic slip-ons along the concrete siding, picking up kick boards and a pair of goggles that had been left.

Mist covered the windows, but through the foggy glass, Kristi noticed that students were hurrying to their classes, cutting across the quad by the athletic facility. She glanced at the clock.

Shit. It was seven forty-five. If she didn't hustle, she'd be late to her first class. Dripping, she reached for a towel and noticed something out of place in her peripheral vision, something dark through the windows. She turned, got a glimpse of a figure through the foggy glass—a man about six feet tall, peering inside. So why didn't he just walk through the door?

And what did she care? So what if the guy was looking? He was probably some guy getting his jollies out of watching girls in swimsuits. A lame nerd who didn't have the guts to ask a girl out.

Pathetic pervert.

She wrapped the towel around her, hurried into the locker room and took a quick, hot shower. The voyeur pushed out of her mind, she changed into jeans and a sweater. Quickly she snapped her hair back in a ponytail, slapped on some lipstick and mascara, then hauling her backpack, jogged across campus. Most of the kids who were awake at this hour had already disappeared into the lecture halls. Only a few were hurrying along the concrete paths crisscrossing the lawns between the ancient brick buildings. She glanced past the library to Adam's Hall where she had English with Dr. Northrup back to back with Psychology with Dr. Sutter, both of whom were odd ducks in her estimation. They were so . . . intense. Northrup thought Shakespeare was a God, for Christ's sake, and Sutter gave out tons of homework. Tons! If only she'd registered early and gotten into classes by some of the easier professors, but, as usual, she'd signed up late and ended up with Northrup, Sutter, and Dr. Franz, another gem of a professor. Talk about a nutcase!

She jogged down a path to her favorite class. Philosophy of Religion. But it wasn't the subject matter that interested her, or the curmudgeon of a professor—Dr. Zaroster. God, he was as ancient as the books he taught from, but his T.A. Brian Thomas, a grad student. Now *he* was a reason to get up early and never miss a class. If Dr. Sutter or Dr. Franz had T.A.s like Brian, maybe she wouldn't oversleep or skip class.

Kristi smiled at the thought of Brian. He'd showed her special attention during a couple of discussion groups and she'd been flattered. Tall, with thick hair and a body to die for, he'd flashed a shy smile in her direction more often than not. She'd caught him watching her upon occasion during the lectures, then quickly look away when she glanced in his direction. As if he didn't want her to see him.

Well, it hadn't worked. She hurried into the lecture hall and walked down the steps to take a seat in the front of the auditorium. Zaroster was just opening his book. The cranky professor shot Kristi an irritated glance.

Big deal. So she was a minute or two late. She'd wanted to make an entrance. So Brian would notice . . . only . . . he wasn't in the cavernous room. Kristi pulled out her notebook and paper. Others were already writing furiously; a couple even had palm pilots and were furiously entering data. Zaroster's high-pitched voice started filling the cavernous room as he flipped through the pages of some musty old tome.

She hazarded a glance around the room and then she saw him. At the back of the lecture hall, in the top row, handing out some kind of quiz. She must've missed that part by coming in late.

Oh well . . . she'd wing it. How tough could a quiz on the Buddha be?

She looked over her shoulder and caught Brian looking at her. She smiled, and to her surprise, he smiled back.

Oh, God. Her heart did a major flip. She felt the color rush up her face and she glanced down for just a second. Caught her breath. He was so much older than she was— probably closer to thirty than twenty.

So what? Who cared?

And what about Jay?

She felt a moment's guilt. Jay was her boyfriend. Or had been. But since she'd left New Orleans and started college, their relationship had turned rocky. She glanced at the ring on her finger. A promise ring. The kind you get before you get engaged. It seemed foolish now. Adolescent.

She worked it off her finger as old man Zaroster droned on, then slipped the simple silver band into her pocket. Then she hazarded one last glance over her shoulder. Brian was only two rows above her, still handing out the tests. His eyes didn't meet hers again, but she wasn't worried.

Sooner or later he'd ask her out. She'd bet on it.

The air smelled bad.

Smoky and damp, filled with the scent of wet ashes and charred wood.

Bentz glowered at the crime scene where a burned-out shell of a house smoldered in the morning light. Roped off by yellow tape, saturated by the firemen's hoses, a few blackened timbers remained standing around the smokestack of a crumbling chimney. In the yard, half a dozen crepe myrtles and live oak trees had been singed, matching the seared siding and roofs of neighboring houses.

Rubbing the back of his neck, he stared at the soggy, smelly mess. The crime scene staff were already working, carefully sifting through the rubble, a photographer and vidiographer scanning the site, preserving a visual image of the remains. Uniformed officers were keeping out the curious, and department vehicles, some with lights flashing, were parked across the street, closing access. One news crew was still filming; another was already packing up a van to leave.

Good. The press was always a nuisance.

The deceased had already been examined, photographed, and taken away in a bag. Bentz had taken a look and nearly lost the contents of his stomach. He'd witnessed a lot in nearly twenty years of being a cop, but what had happened to this woman was up there with the worst he'd seen.

One fire truck remained. Several police cars and a police van were parked at odd angles around the perimeter of the site. Some of the neighbors were still hanging around, asking questions, or talking among themselves as a wintry sun peeked through a bank of thick gray clouds layering over the city. Bentz had talked to a couple of the officers and the ME and was still trying to piece together how in the hell Olivia Benchet had called this one.

Right on the money.

As if she'd been here. Bentz found a pack of gum in his pocket and removed a stick of spearmint from its wrapper. What the hell was with that woman? If she hadn't been here, in the room or looking through a window, how could she have known what had happened in the house?

Stan Pagliano walked up. His face was smudged with soot and dirt, the lines webbing across his forehead appearing deeper than usual. "Man, this was a nasty one," he was saying, "but then they all are."

"What happened?" Bentz had heard the story from one of the cops on the scene, but wanted Stan's assessment.

"From what I understand, a neighbor got up to go to the bathroom, looked out the window, and saw the flames. By the time he called it in, it was too late to save the house. The first truck got here within three minutes, but by then the whole house was fully involved. We were lucky to save the surrounding property." He motioned to the single-story homes, most of them identical shotgun doubles with decorative supports, hip roofs, a door on each side, and narrow windows in between. "Near as we can tell, the fire started in a closet in the back, one that housed an old furnace . . . and for some reason the fire moved from the firebox through one of the vents, almost as if it followed a trail of something slow burning to the bathroom . . . strange." His dark eyes met Bentz's. "But then there was the victim—chained, for Christ's sake. *Chained.* What kind of sick bastard would do something like that?" He reached beneath his sooty yellow slicker and found a crumpled pack of cigarettes. He shook one out and offered a filter tip to Bentz, but much as he craved a smoke, he shook his head.

"Oh, yeah, you quit, right?" Stan flicked his lighter to the end of his Winston and inhaled deeply. "You know, Bethie always tried to get me to quit, for years. All that shit they hear about secondhand smoke in school, then just last summer she dropped her purse and guess what fell out? A half-pack of Marlboro lights." He said this through a cloud of smoke. "Go figure."

"They start to grow up and realize that we've been lyin'

to 'em half the time," Bentz said, watching as Montoya talked to several people clustered around the street. The neighbors.

"Ten to one the victim was young. Not much older than Beth Ann or Kristi, unless I miss my guess," Stan said, and Olivia Benchet's words burned through Bentz's mind: *You're a father, Detective Bentz . . . How would you feel if the killer zeroed in on your daughter?*

"Hey, Stan, over here. Give a hand, would ya?" another fireman called from the remaining truck.

"Right there." He took a long drag, then nodded to Bentz. "Talk to ya later," Stan said. "And Rick—"

"Yeah?"

"Nail this shit head, would ya?"

"You got it." Bentz watched Stan jog toward the truck.

Montoya had finished with the neighbors. Skirting the crime scene, he wended his way through the parked vehicles, then leapt over a puddle on the street. "What's the ME have to say?" he asked.

"He'll send us a report, but from what he observed, it looks like our 'witness,' if that's what you want to call her, definitely knew what was going on."

"Makes ya wonder, doesn't it?" Montoya observed.

"I think we'd better check her out, front, back, sideways, and inside out." He stuffed his fists into the pockets of his slacks. "There's more to her story." Frowning, considering Olivia Benchet and how downright determined and innocent she appeared, he wondered what he'd dig up. Probably nothing he'd like. "I'll talk to her again, and you, check out her background. The grandmother, mother, boyfriend, if she's married, how many times, where she went to school, all that stuff."

"You got it." Montoya gave a quick nod.

"So what did you find out? Any of the neighbors see anything?"

Montoya snorted. "Not much. No one remembers anything suspicious, or if they did, they're keepin' it to themselves. Aside from the guy takin' a leak in the pink house, there''—he gestured to a shotgun house next to the one that had burned—''none of the neighbors so much as looked out their windows until they heard the sirens. *Then* they smelled smoke and noticed that the neighborhood was glowing like a damned nuclear explosion.'' He shook his head, disgusted. ''The neighbor who noticed the fire, Elvin Gerard, he saw the flames, woke up his wife, Lois, and called nine-one-one. End of story. Except that he claims the house was a rental duplex, but it had been empty for a month or so. Both sides of the unit vacant.''

''But someone was there tonight.''

''Yeah.'' Montoya flipped open a little notebook. ''According to Gerard, the house had been owned by an elderly couple, the Jalinskys. First he died, then the wife within the year. Their kids inherited it and rented it out through a local management firm, Benchmark Realty. No one's been there, except someone from Benchmark showing it to potential renters and a janitorial company that cleaned up the mess from the previous tenants.''

The firemen were beginning to retrieve the hoses, the neighbors were disbursing, and even the last television crew was packing it in. A police officer was taking down the barricades on the street and waving cars with rubbernecking drivers through.

''I'll check with Benchmark, get a list of who's been asking about the place,'' Bentz said. ''Anything else?''

''Yeah. Maybe. The only break we've got is one of the neighbors pulled out his video camera and caught the fire on film just as the fire department arrived.''

''You get the tape?'' Bentz was interested.

''Yep. The guy was only too happy to oblige.'' Montoya reached into his jacket pocket and withdrew a cassette. ''I think we'll have to suffer through the Hendersons' trip to Disney World, but after that we can take a look at the fire.''

''Maybe we'll get lucky and see something on the tape,'' Bentz said, not believing it for a moment. The killer would have been long gone by the time the groggy neighbor had focused on the inferno, unless the murderer had gotten his rocks off by sticking around to view the havoc wrought by his work. It happened upon occasion and then the police got lucky. But it was a long shot. Right now, the most serious link they had to the crime so far was Olivia Benchet. Bentz's eyes narrowed on the soggy mass that had once been a house and thought about Olivia Benchet's bizarre story—a naked chained victim, a priest with a radio and a sword, and the anniversary of JFK's assassination.

"I'll check with missing persons, see if we can figure out who the victim is, then talk to Ms. Benchet again."

"You're not buying the ESP-voodoo thing." Montoya swallowed a smirk.

"Not yet." They started walking to their Crown Victoria. "We've got to figure out what makes her tick. You talk to Brinkman. Pull out anything he's got on her, no matter how insignificant. He must have notes or a file or something. And see if she talked to anyone else, here in the city or in the surrounding parishes. She acts like there are other murders, so check around and I'll contact the FBI. They can put it through their computer."

"They'll want another task force, if this is linked."

"Fine."

"I didn't think you liked working with the Feds." They dodged a few remaining firemen and thick hoses.

"Nah. That's not it. Long as they don't get in my way."

They reached the cruiser and Bentz slid into the passenger side. He wasn't going to leave any stone unturned when it came to the psychic—just what the hell was her angle?

"So, maybe we should check out the local priests," Montoya suggested as he climbed behind the steering wheel.

"Maybe. And while we're at it, maybe we can find one with a rap sheet for arson and murder," Bentz joked.

Montoya snorted a laugh as he started the car. "The nutcase's vision was right on the money, wasn't it?"

"Either that or she was involved."

"Ya think?"

Bentz shook his head as he conjured up the desperation in Olivia's eyes, the genuine fear in her expression, the way her teeth sank into her lower lip and worried it when she was telling her story. "I don't know what to think."

Montoya backed up and jockeyed the Crown Vic between the other rigs. "If she was involved, why come to us? Nah, that doesn't wash."

Bentz didn't think so either, but weirder things had happened. He wasn't leaving anything to chance. "We'll see."

"Yeah, I'll check with DMV, Vital statistics, the SSA."

"Once I get the preliminary information on her and the ME's report, I'm going to have another chat with her."

"Man, she really nailed this one. I mean *nailed* it. Ten to one we find a burned-out radio and some necklace on the shower head, just like she said." Montoya's dark eyes held his for a second. "Somethin's up with that woman."

"It sure is, *Diego.*"

"Hey, that's what I go by these days," Montoya shot back as he turned off the side street.

"Why?"

"My heritage." He patted the video sticking out of his jacket pocket.

"My ass." Bentz stared out the window. "Diego," he snorted.

"It just sounds good, don't ya think?"

"Whatever." Bentz didn't care. Chewing his tasteless gum, Bentz glanced at the video cassette and wondered what it would show. Probably nothing. Unless the tape caught the image of a fleeing suspect, or someone in the crowd of curious onlookers at the scene whom none of the neighbors recognized, and who might be the killer watching the aftermath of his destruction. Or possibly one of the neighbors himself. Either way, Olivia Benchet was the best lead they had.

Chapter Six

The phone was jangling as Olivia opened the front door. Dropping her bag on the kitchen table, she swept up the receiver while Hairy S streaked into the living room. "Hello?" she said, cradling the receiver between her shoulder and ear as she unwrapped the cover to the bird's cage. Green feathers ruffled as Chia, the parrot, gave off a sharp whistle.

"Livvie?" Sarah's usually upbeat voice was soft. Sober. That could mean only one thing. Trouble with her husband. Again. Leo Restin had a problem with fidelity. A major problem. Monogamy wasn't in the man's vocabulary. He just couldn't seem to keep his hands off other women. He'd even had the nerve to come on to Olivia, his wife's business partner, a few months back. Leo's unwanted attention was one of the reasons that had propelled her from Tucson. She'd told him to back off, threatened to confide in Sarah, but he just pressed on. Insufferable jerk.

"What's up?" Olivia asked with a wink at Chia.

"It's Leo."

Big surprise.

"He's disappeared again."

That usually meant he was with a woman. Olivia wrapped the cord of the phone around her hand and stared out the window to the mists rising off the bayou.

"He just doesn't give up, does he?" She didn't respond. "You know what you should do, Sarah."

Sarah sighed. "I don't believe in divorce, Olivia. I know it's crazy, but I still love him."

"He's using you."

"I just have to wait until Leo grows up."

That could well be forever. "He's thirty-five," Olivia pointed out. "How long do you think it'll take?"

"I don't know, but I really love him," she said. Her voice wobbled a bit. "I know, I sound pathetic, like one of those loser women who puts up with everything because she loves the jerk. But I really do care about him and . . . and you don't know what he's like when there's no one else around. He can be so sweet."

"That's why so many women fall for him."

Sarah sucked in her breath.

"Sorry—I couldn't help it," Olivia said quickly. "I hate to see you keep getting hurt. If you keep letting him, he'll keep doing it."

"I know, I know, but *nobody* in my family gets divorced. I'd be the first one in my direct lineage."

"Did all the others put up with this kind of garbage?"

"I guess. I don't know. I grew up believing that everyone got married and lived happily ever after. Oh, they might fight and yell and even break up for a while, but in the end, it all worked out."

"Fairy tales."

"Divorce isn't easy."

"It shouldn't be. Getting married should be harder."

Sarah chuckled. "Yeah, maybe. So how's it going there?"

"Not great," Olivia said, but didn't explain about her vision. Sarah, despite her flirting with New Age religion, had solid roots in Catholicism. Another lapsed believer, but one, Olivia sensed, ready to return to the fold. Wasn't she one herself? "It's not going to be as easy as I thought to sell this place." She glanced around her grandmother's cabin with its gleaming wood walls and floors shining with over a hundred years' worth of patina. Tall windows with narrow panes offered a spectacular view of the bayou. The insulation was practically nil, the plumbing and electricity added decades after the original construction and now were outdated and probably dangerous. "I have a lot of work to do before I put it on the market and then I'm not sure I want to. It's been in my family forever."

"So you haven't decided if you're going to stay in New Orleans?"

"I know I'll stick it out until I finish my master's. Then, who knows?"

"Still working for that little store in the square?"

"Part-time. Around school." She leaned a hip against the counter and thought of the eclectic clientele of the Third Eye. Located in a cubbyhole across from Jackson Square, the store boasted an inventory of everything from dried alligator heads to religious artifacts. New Age to voodoo with a smattering of Christianity in between. "How's business in Tucson?"

"Great," Sarah said as if she meant it. "I met with a new artist who's going to display her things in the back nook. Consignment, and I've got a couple new lines of crystal pendants that are selling like crazy. But I miss you. It's not the same."

"Didn't you hire someone?"

"Oh, yeah. I hired a *girl*, not a partner. A girl with tattoos on her arms and not just rings in her nose and eyebrows, and wherever else she can find a tiny fold of skin, but safety pins! Can you imagine? She looks like she should be working for a tailor, not a New Age shop."

Olivia laughed. For the first time that morning. "Careful, Sarah, your parochial school roots are beginning to show."

"Forbid the thought."

"Next thing I know, you'll be wearing a plaid skirt, blazer, and knee socks to work."

"Very funny."

"I thought so." Olivia glanced at her grandmother's tattered cane rocker at rest near a pot overflowing with the shiny leaves of an ever-growing jade plant.

"Oh, I've got a beep, I'd better go. . . . ."

"Talk to you later," Olivia said, knowing that Sarah was eager to get off the phone and check the other line. Sarah, the eternal optimist, probably thought the caller would be a recalcitrant Leo, tired of the new woman and ready to crawl back on his hands and knees, to beg forgiveness from his loving saint of a wife.

Hairy S gave off a bark and twirled in tight little circles at the back door. "Wanna go out?" Olivia asked as she swung the door open and the dog scurried outside. Storm clouds gathered on the horizon and the air was sticky with the threat of rain. The dog ran the length of the porch to disappear into a thatch of tall grass and cypress, sniffing the ground searching for squirrels or possum or whatever marsh bird he could scare up.

Olivia's stomach rumbled. It was ten in the morning and she'd been up for seven hours, existing only on coffee and adrenalin. She opened the refrigerator and scowled at the lack of groceries—two eggs, a chunk of cheese, a half-loaf of bread, and a bottle of catsup. "Omelette time," she remarked, as she heard Hairy S pad inside. "How about you?" She opened the pantry, where a half-full bag of dog chow was tucked beneath three shelves of canned peaches, apricots, and pears that her grandmother had preserved. At the thought of the old woman, Olivia felt a pang of sadness. It was just damned hard to lose someone who loved you so unconditionally.

After measuring a cup of dry food into Hairy S's dish, she added parrot seed to Chia's cage and stroked the parrot's smooth green feathers. "Isn't she beautiful?" Grannie had asked when she'd first brought the bird home. "They're messy as all get-out, I know it, but Wanda owed me some money and offered me Chia. I couldn't resist.'' Grannie's eyes had twinkled and Chia had been a member of the family ever since.

"Grannie was right, you know. You are beautiful,'' Olivia told the bird, who stretched her brilliant wings and picked up some of the seeds in her dish.

Olivia turned on the radio and stuffed two slices of bread into the toaster. As the dog made short work of his breakfast, she fired up the stove and whisked the eggs together. Patsy Cline sang about love lost. *Great. Just what I need to hear. What an upper,* she thought as the eggs began to bubble and she grated the wedge of cheese. The final notes of the song began to fade, and "Ramblin' Rob,'' the deejay, cut in to give some story about the old country classic recorded shortly before the star's death. His deep, baritone voice slid easily out of the speakers and he spoke as if he knew all of his listeners personally. Which Olivia liked.

In the few short months she'd been back in Louisiana, Olivia had come to recognize some of the local newscasters and deejays. The radio station she listened to more often than not was WSLJ, the same station where Samantha Leeds aka "Dr. Sam'' dispensed her nightly advice to her callers, the same station she'd "heard'' last night during the vision.

The damned vision.

She felt that same icy presence rush through her soul each time she thought about that horrifying murder. *So don't. Don't think about it.* But even as she was mentally reprimanding herself, a jagged memory of the victim begging for forgiveness skittered through Olivia's brain. Distracted, she slid her knuckles along the side of the grater. "Ouch. Damn.'' Blood oozed up from her skin and quickly she sucked on her fingers, then turned on the faucet and let cold water run over her hand. "I'm an idiot,'' she muttered at Hairy S. "Truly an idiot.''

The truth of the matter was Olivia was troubled because she couldn't put the nightmare behind her. She'd hoped talking to the police would help. But Bentz's blatant doubts had stopped her cold. She'd thought, from reading the article in the paper, that he might be different, more receptive, but he'd been nearly as bad as Brinkman. "Jerk," she muttered.

Maybe Bentz's doubts are well founded. Maybe it was all just a dream, a really horrible, bad dream.

"Yeah, and maybe I'm the Queen of England," she growled as she wrapped a paper towel around her fingers and managed to sprinkle a handful of mozzarella onto the eggs.

The toast popped.

Olivia slid the slices onto a plate and was reaching for the tub of margarine when she heard the newscast. ". . . a three-alarm fire last night took the life of one woman who has yet to be identified. The blaze broke out near three this morning near Bayou St. John . . ."

Olivia sank against the counter and listened to the short bit of information. The press had only the basics. A fire. A woman dead. Suspected arson. Nothing about homicide. Nothing about a murderer escaping into the night.

But Rick Bentz knew.

And he'd be calling.

She didn't have to be a psychic to know that much.

Chapter Seven

The real estate management firm wasn't much help. Bentz stopped by after grabbing his own car at the station only to learn that Oscar Cantrell, the owner of Benchmark Realty, was out. But the secretary, Marlene, a spacey brunette in red plastic-rimmed glasses, assured Bentz that the house where the fire had taken place had been vacant since September when some students at Tulane University had skipped out on several months' rent.

"It's always a crap shoot when you rent to college kids," Marlene confided, and added that the five boys who had rented both sides of the building had turned out to be partiers. They'd done some damage to the house which the cleaning and security deposits hadn't covered. Now the owners, a brother and sister who lived in separate states, were thinking about selling.

Marlene had talked a little breathlessly, all the while chewing gum and gesturing wildly with her hands. "We handle everything as the owners are out of state. Wes, that's the brother, he lives in Montgomery, and Mandy—she's married and her last name is Sieverson now—she's in Houston. They can't get along to save their souls.'' She popped her gum. ''Mandy, she wanted to upgrade the place—it was really two units, you know, but Wes didn't want to put a dime into it.'' Dark, heavily penciled eyebrows rose above the thin red rims, as if she were about to impart the wisdom of the ages. ''His mother wasn't even cold in her grave when he called up and asked about selling the place. He was pretty adamant, let me tell you, but Mandy wouldn't go along with it. She's married, as I said, and she wants to keep the house for an investment—you know, fix it up. But with Wes, now that's a different story. He went ballistic when those last tenants skipped out, let me tell you. Had himself one tremendous hissy fit and wanted the boss to make up the difference.'' She rolled her eyes and clucked her tongue. ''Oh, yeah, like that was gonna happen.''

''I'd like a list of anyone who's been interested in the house since it's been vacated as well as anyone you hired who did the work to repair the place.''

''No problem,'' Marlene assured him as her fingers flew over the keyboard of her computer. ''It'll be just a sec. We keep a log on each property—kinda like a diary, you know.'' An ancient printer chugged out a few pages in counterpoint to her rapid gum chewing, and within minutes, the secretary, far more efficient than she'd first seemed, handed him the printout.

She answered a few more questions, but aside from being a purveyor of all kinds of gossip, when push came to shove, Marlene wasn't a helluva lot of help. Bentz made a note to check out the owners and their recent travel schedules, just to make sure they hadn't blown into town and had decided to torch the place for the insurance money.

Except that an insurance fraud didn't begin to explain why some woman had been tortured and killed in the house. Stan Pagliano's words played over and over in his mind. ''Her hands and feet were chained . . . but it's her head . . . it was nearly severed.''

Later, Stan had asked him what kind of sick bastard would commit such a horrendous crime.

Bentz didn't know.

But there was someone who might.

Olivia Benchet. The lady had called this one, right on the money.

"I'm tellin' ya, she's a nutcase pure and simple," Brinkman said when Bentz caught up with him in the hallway near one of the interrogation rooms. "I talked to her twice and each time she came in with these cockamamie, bullshit stories about murders she'd seen, visions about someone being killed. But she couldn't give me anything concrete. No body. No murder scene. No damned smokin' gun. Nothin'. If ya ask me, and seein' as you tracked me down, then yeah, you did, she doesn't have all her wheels on the pavement . . . and she might just be ridin' a unicycle."

Bentz wasn't in the mood for bad jokes. As they walked to the stairs, weaving their way past a group of uniformed cops, he said, "I just want to see the reports. This time there was a body and a murder scene, and if not a gun, a sword, for cryin' out loud."

"I heard about that one. Over off Esplanade, right?"

"That's the one."

"Christ. And she called it?" Brinkman shook his head. He was bald, a horseshoe of black hair surrounding a freckled bald spot, the lights over the staircase gleaming on his pate. They climbed the stairs, their shoes ringing on the steps as a couple other cops descended. "Brutal."

"So why do you think she's come in with bullshit before and then came through this time?"

"Dumb-ass luck? Hell if I know." Brinkman walked through the doors to a reception area surrounded by offices. "But I have to admit, I was curious about her. She seemed so certain she was right. So I did some checkin', called around. Turns out she comes from a long line of crazies. Her grandma claimed she was a voodoo priestess or some such shit just because she was an octoroon, and her mother's been married four or five times, and then there's the father, who's spent most of his life in the State Pen in Mississippi—"

"Hang on. What's that all about?" Bentz asked as they reached the doors on the second floor.

"You didn't know? Old Reggie Benchet iced a man," Brinkman said, shoving his glasses up to the bridge of his nose, a smile creeping across his lips as he realized he'd imparted new information. "It's all in my report. Reginald Benchet got out earlier this year."

"And?"

"Far as I know, he's kept his nose clean." Brinkman smiled. "A real model citizen. Found God, or somethin'. I'll send the info to you and then you can decide how much of Olivia Benchet's story you believe. If she knew what was happenin' when the girl was offed, I'd bet she was in on it . . . nah, she doesn't seem like the murderin' type. Oh, I got it." Brinkman snapped his thick fingers. "She saw it. In a dream."

"That's what she says."

"And you buy that? If so, I got some land in Florida—"

"Forget it, Brinkman. Just send me your notes," Bentz said, irritated. He didn't buy the vision theory either, but he couldn't believe that the woman was in on the murder in any way, shape, or form. "Maybe we should give her the benefit of the doubt."

"Oh, Christ, now you're soundin' like one of them damned bleedin' hearts." He shook his head and snorted. "Just when I was beginning to think you might be a decent cop after all."

"Just get me the report," Bentz snapped.

"Forgive me, Father, for I have sinned." The Chosen One knelt at the altar and saw his own distorted visage in the shiny surface of the chalice. Candles burned and flickered, and through the walls of his drafty sanctuary he smelled the river. Musty. Damp. The current moved restlessly and would not be deterred. They had a lot in common, he and the Mississippi. They both held secrets beneath their surfaces, secrets that would never be revealed.

"I am prideful, Father, and I . . ." He swallowed hard, knew he had to admit his horrid sin. "I . . . I've lusted after those women, and though I feel your power, Father, my . . . my flesh is weak. So weak. I pray for your strength and your forgiveness . . ."

He closed his eyes, listened, and through his straining ears he heard the voice of God meting out his penance.

After whispering a nearly inaudible "Amen," and deftly making the sign of the cross, he stood and slowly walked to the closet where his albs hung . . . one less today. His favorite. Left to burn. Because of the whore.

Her picture was there as well. He took it from the closet and carefully taped it on the calendar he kept on the wall, carefully covering the space for the date, November twenty-second, the Feast Day of Saint Cecilia. Ah . . . she'd been so trusting . . . until it had been too late. He didn't think of that now. Couldn't. He had penance. He strode back to the closet.

With gentle fingers, he slid the vestments aside and turning the combination lock, opened his most private of places, the spot where he kept all that was valuable and worldly to him. He added a long lock of golden hair to his other treasures, other bits of hair and fingernails, then sifted through the medals and chains until his fingers encountered the weapon. Ah.

A tiny, featherlight whip with sharp stones embedded in the ribbon-like lashes, sparkling gems that cut with razor-sharp slits, nice, neat little cuts that barely scraped the surface, not enough to cause much bleeding, just enough to create sufficient pain to remind him that he, like all mortals, was born in original sin.

The Chosen One slipped out of his clothes and, naked, knelt at the altar once again, bowing his head, murmuring a prayer of atonement.

Not for the killing. Now he understood. That had been necessary. As always. God's will. Even the violence, had it not been preordained? Had he not followed the Holy Father's commands to rid the earth of the vile sinners on the day God had selected?

Yes, but he'd felt lust, that vibrant raw hunger that even now stole through his bloodstream. Hot. Dark. Wanting.

He could not be weak. He drew in a deep breath. Readied himself. Held his weapon high, then cracked his wrist.

Slap!

The leather fingers bit into his shoulder and he stiffened.

Pain, glorious pain, swept through him. His blood rushed through his veins. Heat centered in his groin.

He drew back the whip and snapped his wrist again.

Slap!

The sharp little stones stung. Like the bite of a hundred wasps. He sucked in his breath. Felt the ooze of a bit of blood. Enough to wash him of his sins.

Again. He flicked his hand. Hard.

Slap!

His erection began to throb. Painfully. Deliciously.

He thought of the woman. The way her pale curls fell upon her smooth white neck. Cecilia. Whore. Daughter of Satan. She was so fine . . . her body perfect . . . that smooth neck beckoning . . . for his blade, or his mouth? He imagined mounting her as she knelt, her body quivering, her lips begging forgiveness, his teeth catching hold of her nape as he thrust inside her. Hot. Moist. Slick. Even now he envisioned her heavy breasts hanging downward, rosy nipples nearly scraping the floor. How he would have liked to have stroked them, pinched those nipples, heard her cry out as he plunged deeper inside her.

Sinner! Defiler! You are weak with your want of her!

He cracked the whip harshly.

Slap!

Pain tore through his flesh. He sucked his breath through his teeth.

Again! The leather fingers sizzled in the air.

Slap!

His body jerked.

Yes! The whore deserved to die.

He drew back. Braced himself. Cocked his wrist.

Slap!

Tears ran from his eyes as he felt the holy light bathe him. He would fight his lust, his weakness, and he would kill again to rid the earth of Satan's whores.

It was God's will.

Chapter Eight

Olivia heard the crunch of tires on the drive and glanced out the window facing the lane just as Rick Bentz stretched out of his cruiser. Even beneath the moss-bearded oaks, he appeared the big man that he was, muscular, nearly stocky, with deep-set eyes and an I've-seen-it-all expression. He was wearing a jacket that fit loosely around his waist but stretched over his shoulders, casual slacks, and a white shirt. And a shoulder holster. She caught a glimpse of smooth leather and the butt of a gun.

Some women might find him handsome, she thought grudgingly. He had a certain appeal with his square jaw and thick brown hair. His face was lined and craggy enough to be interesting, the bit of gray at his temples not unattractive. But besides the gun, it was the glint in his flinty eyes and the set of his jaw—all hard-edged determination—that reminded her he was a cop.

And off-limits.

Not that she was looking. But she'd noticed he didn't

wear a wedding ring and she'd read somewhere that he was divorced, and that his ex-wife had died.

She'd sworn off men after the last near-miss at the altar. Besides, Bentz wasn't her type.

She opened the door before he knocked, and Hairy S rounded the corner from the kitchen to start barking like crazy. "Stop it!" Olivia commanded, and the dog, for once, actually shut up. Olivia met Bentz's eyes. "You found her, didn't you?"

"We found someone."

Oh, God. Deep inside she'd harbored the tiniest shred of hope that she'd been wrong. That, as this detective had thought, she'd just experienced a really bad nightmare. But of course, even that iota of hope had been misguided. "It's the woman I told you about. The one in the fire."

"I'd like to talk to you about her."

About time. "Come in." She pushed the door open further and the dog bolted through.

"Thanks." Hands in the pockets of his slacks, he walked into her house, his gaze skimming over the bookcase, potted plants, lumpy couch, and scattered chairs. "We'll have to backtrack some, go over some of the things you said earlier."

"No problem. I've got most of the afternoon, then I've got to meet my professor around four."

"That late on a Friday?" He seemed even bigger in the kitchen, taking up space in this little cabin with its low ceilings and yellowed pine walls. Pushing six-two or -three, he ducked around a hurricane lantern that hung from the ceiling, a fixture Grannie Gin had refused to replace just in case the electricity was ever cut off. From her cage, Chia shrieked as she moved from one end of her perch to the other, warily eyeing the intruder.

"Hush, Chia!" she ordered. "Another of my grandmother's orphans. Chia doesn't like to go unnoticed. Has to have her say."

"Typical female."

"What?" Olivia's eyes narrowed.

"It was a joke," he explained.

"A poor one."

"Right. So, you have to meet with your professor later."

"Yes. Dr. Leeds at Tulane."

She felt it then, as surely as if she'd turned on the air-conditioning, the atmosphere in the room got suddenly colder. It was as if Bentz's sense of humor evaporated.

Something glinted in his steely eyes.

"You know him?" she asked.

"We've met." From his pocket he withdrew the same small recorder he'd used earlier. "This shouldn't take too long." He set the recorder on the kitchen table, where a Thanksgiving cactus was trying to bloom. Speaking into the small microphone, he said that he was continuing the interview, gave the date and time, and after spelling Olivia's name, indicated that he was in her house with her. But he didn't sit down at the table, instead stood resting his hips on the counter.

"You said you moved back to Louisiana recently. When was that? Last summer?"

"Yes. I came in late July when my grandmother got sick." She pointed to one of the framed photographs she'd hung on the wall near the back porch.

"This is a picture of us. A long time ago." In the shot, Grannie, gray hair braided in a single plait, was swinging a bare-footed Olivia off the ground. Olivia was dressed in ragged shorts and a T-shirt, had been around five at the time, and her head was thrown back in pure delight. Sunlight streamed through the trees and dappled the dry grass. In the background a hedge was in full bloom, showing off pink blooms, and the only dark spot in the photo was the hint of a shadow creeping from the bottom of the frame.

Bentz noted it as well. "Who took the picture?"

The muscles in the back of Olivia's neck tightened. "My father. One of the few times he deigned to show up."

"He didn't raise you?" Bentz asked.

She took in a deep breath. "My father? He wasn't exactly the Ward Cleaver type of model dad. He didn't hang around much. For the most part, Grannie Gin raised me." She didn't like talking about her family. "Dysfunctional" didn't begin to describe it. "Oh . . . I'm sorry . . . could I get you some coffee . . . or, God, I don't think I have anything else."

"Only if you want it."

"Desperately," she admitted. "This is . . . nerve-racking."

To her surprise, he actually smiled, showing off just a hint of white teeth. "I know. Sure. Coffee would be great."

She knew he was just trying to calm her, but that was fine. She needed to be calm. Standing on her tiptoes, Olivia stretched to reach onto the top shelf of one of the few cupboards, the one where she kept the "good" dishes she never used. Bentz came to the rescue and retrieved two porcelain coffee cups.

"Thanks." She set the cups on the counter and checked the glass pot of hours-old coffee still warming in the coffee-maker. "Okay . . . you asked about my family, which isn't my favorite subject. My grandfather was killed in the war. My grandma never remarried. She spent most of her time taking care of everyone else."

"Who's everyone else?"

"Basically me. My mother when she was around. My sister, Chandra, until she died. She was only two. Wading pool accident," Olivia said, using the same phraseology she always did when anyone asked about her family. Accident. So simple. But it hadn't been. Maybe death never was.

"Where's your mother now?"

"Good question." She poured the coffee. "Actually, I think she's in Houston with her husband, Jeb Martin, who, for the record, is a real SOB."

"You don't like him."

Lifting a shoulder, she said, "He's as good as any of them, I suppose, but no, I don't like him, and I really don't see what all this has to do with what happened this morning."

"Maybe nothing. But it's not every day someone charges into my office claiming to witness a murder the way you did."

She didn't argue. At least he was listening. She handed him a cup. "I've got milk, no sugar."

"Black's fine."

"I inherited this house and haven't decided how long I'm staying."

As the tape recorded, Bentz walked to the window and stared at the bayou, sunlight filtering through the trees, murky water stretching away from the cabin and small yard. "What about your father?"

She closed her eyes. May as well get it over with. "I haven't heard from him in years. He . . . he's in jail—prison in Mississippi, I think. The last time I saw him, I was in grade school." She expected more questions about her father, but thankfully he let the subject drop.

"So what about Tucson?"

"What about it?"

"Why'd you leave?"

"I thought I explained that. My grandmother was sick, and I'd already applied for grad school. I got accepted at Tulane, and I decided it was fate, or destiny, so I moved back. My partner bought out my interest in the shop."

The dog whined at the door to the porch and Olivia cracked it open to let him in. Hairy S shot through, a streak of scraggly fur. "My grandmother's," Olivia explained before Bentz asked. "I inherited him. Hairy S . . . named after Grannie Gin's favorite president, only spelled a little differently."

"Not much of a watchdog."

"*Au contraire,* Detective. This guy's tough as they come, aren't you?" she asked, scratching the dog's ear.

"I usually advise a rottweiler or pit bull."

"Thanks, but I'll keep Hairy."

"And the bird."

"Definitely the bird."

He glanced around the little house. "You're a long way from the neighbors and you have pretty damned scary night-mares. Aren't you afraid? You reported that you sensed the

killer caught a glimpse of you somehow. It's so isolated out
here. Aren't you nervous that he might come after you?''

"I don't think he knows who I am."

''Yet.''

She remembered the feeling that someone had been watching her through the windows, the cold sensation that had
run through her blood. ''I try not to live my life in fear.
I've got the dog, my grandmother's shotgun, and I keep the
place locked. I'm careful,'' she said. ''You have to remember. I grew up here. It's home.''

"A security system wouldn't hurt."

''Maybe you're right,'' she agreed. ''I'll think about it.''

"Think hard." Bentz scooted out one of the cane-backed
chairs at the small table. ''Okay, let's talk about last night,''
he suggested, retrieving a small pad from his jacket pocket.
''Can anyone confirm that you were here?''

''Here, at the house . . . no . . . I was alone . . . hey, wait
a minute,'' she said, disbelieving. ''Now . . . what are you
saying? Do I need an alibi?''

''Do you?''

''No. I'm the one who brought this to you, remember? I
just told you I live alone. With my dog.''

''I'm just establishing what happened. You went to bed
as usual and . . .''

''And I was asleep for about three hours, I guess.'' She
glared at him as she took a chair on the opposite side of the
table. ''Look, I don't know how to explain it, okay? I used
to get these . . . dreams or visions as a little kid . . . things
that were happening . . . but it wasn't all the time and it was
. . . different, I suppose.'' She glanced out the French doors
and frowned. How many times had she tried to explain what
she saw? How many times had she been disbelieved or
laughed at or called a freak? Rick Bentz, detective or not,
was just the same as all the others she'd tried and failed to
convince.

Gray eyes assessed her.

''I came to the station to try and help you. I assume you're
here for the same reason, that after you found that woman,

you actually *want* my help. I can't tell you any more than I already did.''

"What about the killer? Tell me about him.''

"I've thought about that,'' she said, trying to tamp down her anger. The nerve of the man, even to suggest . . . She took a deep breath and told herself to just get through this. "As I said, he was dressed like a priest and kept demanding that the girl confess her sins. But I'm not sure he really was a priest, I mean, there's no way I could know if he actually took vows.''

"You didn't see his face because of the mask, but you heard his voice.''

"Yes. Over the organ music that was playing from the radio.''

"Would you recognize his voice if you heard it again?''

"I don't know,'' Olivia admitted, thinking hard. "He whispered.''

Furrows deepened in Bentz's brow. "How tall was he? Could you tell when he stripped off the vestments? What size of man?''

"He was fit . . . athletic-looking. Probably around six feet, but that's just a guess. It didn't seem that he had much body fat, but he wasn't rail-thin either. He didn't look like a long-distance runner. Maybe it was the outfit, but I thought . . . I had the impression that he was built like a skier or maybe a swimmer because he had wide shoulders but a narrow waist and hips.''

"You said you thought he looked at you.''

"Yes. He looked up and stared hard.''

"But you weren't there,'' Bentz clarified, finally picking up his cup and taking a swallow.

"No—it was as if he sensed me.''

"So you have some what? Telepathic link to him?''

She shook her head. "I wish I knew or understood it . . . but when it happens, I get a headache and afterward I'm exhausted.''

"How many times has this happened before?''

"Several," she admitted. "But never this clear. Never so vivid." She sipped her coffee, but didn't taste a drop.

"What color were his eyes?"

"I didn't see a color," she said with a sigh. "The room was smoky and he was squinting . . ."

Bentz looked annoyed. "So even though you had some kind of view of him, you don't remember anything that could distinguish the priest in a crowd."

"No." She gritted her teeth. Bit back the sharp retort that formed on her tongue because Detective Bentz was going through the motions but he still didn't believe her. "You think I'm making this up."

A muscle worked in his jaw. "It's all pretty farfetched."

"Then how could I know this much?"

He leaned forward, and for the first time she noticed the striations of color in his gray eyes, the brackets deepening at the corners of his mouth. "That's the question, isn't it? How do you know this much?"

"I already told you, Detective, but obviously you don't trust me. You seem to think I was somehow involved in this macabre murder and then I was stupid enough to run to the police station so that I could be ridiculed and then found out!"

"That's pretty farfetched, too."

"Then why'd you come all the way out here?"

"I'd like to get to the truth."

"Believe me, not any more than I would," she shot back, angry. What a fool she'd been to think he might actually believe her. That he'd see the evidence and trust her.

A muscle throbbed in Bentz's temple. "Is there anything else you want to tell me?"

"Is there anything else you'd like to ask me?"

"That should do it, but I might have more questions later."

"Of course." She couldn't keep the sarcasm from her voice even though she told herself not to bait the man.

He clicked off his recorder and slid it into his pocket. "If you think of anything else—"

"Trust me, you'll be the first to know."

He flipped his notebook closed.

"You know, Bentz, I was hoping that you would believe me."

"Whether I believe you or not isn't the issue," he said as he kicked back his chair. "What dces matter is if you can give me information so that I can catch this sick bastard. Before he strikes again. Maybe you should time your visions a little better. Like *before* something happens. Rather than afterward. Now, *that* would help."

Chapter Nine

"Okay, let's fire this baby up," Montoya said as he slipped a cassette into the small television/VCR that sat on the end of one filing cabinet in Bentz's office. As usual, he was wearing his trademark leather jacket and smelling of smoke. "This is a copy of the Hendersons' video of the fire. I had it converted from the camera disk onto video tape and a CD so that we can play it on the computer. The original's in Evidence."

Bentz climbed out of his chair and rounded the desk as Montoya pushed the appropriate buttons and images of the fire flashed onto the screen. The tape was shaky and blurry in spots as the cameraman panned the street. Neighbors and gawkers had gathered. Bits of conversation and gasps punctuated the sounds of street traffic, as clusters of people stood gaping at the house. With a crash of breaking glass, a window exploded. "Jesus!" the cameraman yelled as flames licked skyward from the roof. "Monica, for God's sake! Keep the kids back . . . I said . . . no, get them in the house. Now! They can watch the tape later. Move it." Some younger voices complained and a baby cried, but the cameraman kept his lens trained on the conflagration. Black smoke billowed upward as sirens screamed. The camera moved to catch a fire truck with its lights flashing as it roared up the street. It was followed by another truck, a rescue van, and police cars. Rescue teams spilled from the vehicles. "Get back," policemen yelled as firefighters trained hoses onto the building. "Can you get inside . . . Here . . ." Stan Pagliano's voice yelled from a distance. Bentz watched the firefighters push through the door to battle flames and check for survivors.

His jaw tightened when he thought of the woman trapped inside . . . chained to the damned sink. Firemen rushed and barked orders, cruisers with their lights flashing parked at the perimeter of the roped-off area while the crowd of onlookers grew. *Here we go,* Bentz thought as he stared at the indistinct images.

"Okay, those two . . ." Montoya said, pointing to an elderly man and woman. "They're the Gerards. They called in the fire. Live next door and that one"—he indicated a bald man in his early thirties—"lives on the next street . . ." There was a family huddled beneath one of the trees, and a tiny frail-looking woman with her dog. There were other images as well, mostly indistinct as the cameraman focused his lens on the burning house.

"Not much here," Montoya said, sipping coffee from a paper cup as he stared at the screen.

"Wait." The camera panned the crowd again to show a group of teenagers, three boys and a girl staring at the flames, then knots of the curious huddled together in the shadows. "Rewind it," Bentz growled as he caught an image just outside the light of one of the street lamps, too far in the shadows to be illuminated by the hellish reflection of the fire. Montoya pushed the rewind button, then hit Play again. The images moved on the screen. "Stop. There."

Montoya froze the picture. The frame was fuzzy, but there was a lone person, barely in the shot, too blurred to tell if it was a man or woman. "What about that guy?" Bentz pointed to the screen where the shadowy figure lurked beneath a tree.

"What about him?"

"He's the only one in the crowd who's not with someone else. He's alone. Standing off by himself."

Narrowing his eyes at the small screen, Montoya said, "There could be others with him who were just out of the shot, though." He pointed to the screen. "See there to his left. Someone could be just out of the frame, someone Henderson didn't catch on the video."

"Maybe. Maybe not."

"And there could be more people on the other side of the street that Henderson didn't catch on film."

"But we've got this guy. Mark that frame. Have it enlarged and refocused if possible to try and get a sharper image." Bentz squinted, staring hard at the murky figure. Could this be their guy? Could they have gotten that lucky? He didn't believe it; couldn't trust luck, but right now, it was all they had. "While you're at it, have every frame that shows any of the bystanders blown up, too. Our guy will try to blend in, not look out of place."

"I'll get paper and digital copies." Montoya hit the play button again and they watched the rest of the tape in silence. There wasn't much more. Carl Henderson had trained his viewfinder on the blaze and the subsequent shots were of firemen with hoses trained on the house and huge geysers of water arcing over the roof, attempting to douse the flames.

When it was over, Montoya punched the tape from the player and pocketed the cassette. "I'll get the pictures to you ASAP. Did you talk to our star witness again? The nutcase?"

"Olivia Benchet? Yeah." Though Bentz agreed that Olivia was certifiable, it rankled him to hear Montoya voice his thoughts.

"So what's her story?"

"She's back in Louisiana because her grandmother died a few months back. Olivia moved here to be with the old lady when she got sick. The grandma kicked off and Olivia stayed on. She's working on her master's at Tulane."

"What does she study? Voodoo? Isn't that what the grandma was into?"

"Close enough. Psychology." Bentz had already done his research on her, checked with the University, gotten a copy of her transcript and schedule of classes from a somewhat reluctant registrar.

"Psychology? Another one? I thought we were finished with shrinks after closing the Rosary Killer case."

"Mental illness seems to be going around these days."

"So what's wrong with Prozac? Forget talkin' to some shrink. Just take a pill. It's a helluva lot easier." Montoya adjusted the collar of his jacket. A diamond stud glittered in his earlobe. Damned dandy, that's what he was. "If you ask me, they all got into the profession cuz there's somethin' not working in their own brains. They go visit a psychologist, find out they like lyin' on leather sofas and talkin' about themselves, and before you know it, we got ourselves a glut of head doctors hangin' out shingles or giving out advice on the damned radio. Jesus, just think of it. A shrink who thinks she has"—he stopped to make air quotes with the fingers of both hands—" 'visions.' That's heavy. Worse yet, she had a grandma who was a voodoo priestess—isn't that what she said? That's what we need right now. Next thing ya know there'll be a murder, some kind of sacrifice with a bunch of dead chickens."

"Don't even go there, okay?" Bentz said, irritated.

"Yeah, well, just you wait."

"Get this. One of her professors is Dr. Jeremy Leeds."

"No shit?" For once Montoya was struck dumb. "It's a small world."

"Sometimes too small."

"You got anything on her?"

"Some. Preliminary stuff. I've done some checking and I have Brinkman's notes." Bentz took his chair again and flipped through the reports he'd gathered so far. "The student info at Tulane checks out. Looks like she's never been married, but came close. She left a guy at the altar and split to Tucson about six years ago. The guy, Ted Brown, was pissed, chased her down, then married someone on the rebound. That lasted less than a year.

"Ms. Benchet hasn't been in trouble with the law except for a couple of speeding violations and some kind of animal rights sit-in in Phoenix a few years back." He glanced up at Montoya. "I've already called the Tucson authorities. Figured they might know something, but either she didn't have these visions in the desert or she never bothered telling the police."

"So she goes West and they stop."

"Or she keeps 'em to herself."

"Not her MO," Montoya said, leaning a hip against the desk. "What else?"

"She worked odd jobs to put herself through college, anything from waitressing to an insurance company claims clerk. Does art on the side. She sold her New Age gift-slash-art business in Tucson to her partner. When she came back here, it was a natural that she landed a job at this touristy-crap New Age shop called the Third Eye on Jackson Square."

"So she claims to hate these visions that she inherited from her grannie, but she keeps hanging out with the New Age and spiritual stuff." Montoya grimaced. "It doesn't wash. And neither does her not bein' married or at least shackin' up with some guy. A good-lookin' woman like her? What's up with that?"

"Don't know."

"You didn't ask?"

"Nope," Bentz said. "I didn't have the info on the first trip down the altar until I looked through some of Brinkman's notes."

Montoya lifted a brow. "I thought her eligibility state might be the first thing you asked her. I saw the way you looked at her today. Couldn't take your eyes off her and I don't blame you, she's one fine-lookin' lady. And that ass—"

"I was looking at her because she came in here peddling some pretty off-the-wall stuff that just happened to be right on," Bentz cut in.

"If you say so, man," Montoya said, his grin spreading wide in a way that irritated the hell out of Bentz.

"Get over yourself, Diego. She's a nutcase." But deep down, the younger cop was right. They both knew it. There was a lot about Olivia Benchet that just didn't fit together. She was an enigma. An interesting puzzle. He'd left her house but he hadn't been able to push her out of his mind. All day long as he tracked down clues to the murder near Bayou St. John as well as dealt with the other cases demanding his attention, the anger that sparked in her gold eyes and the desperation that etched her features had stayed with him. When he'd returned here, he'd read through everything Brinkman had tossed his way and done some more checking himself.

She was a crackpot, all his instincts told him so, and yet she believed her own lies or illusions or whatever the hell they were.

And though he didn't know quite why, he wanted to believe her as well. Maybe it was because they had nothing else to go on. He didn't see her as being involved in the murder and arson, so what did that leave? That she was telling the damned truth.

He found an opened pack of Juicy Fruit and unwrapped a stick, doubled it over, and jammed it into his mouth. It wasn't the same as a smoke, but it would have to do. For now. "There's something else in Brinkman's report. I'm not sure it has any relevance. Olivia's old man has done time at the Mississippi State Pen. Assault. Murder Two. A business partner who supposedly cheated him."

Montoya gave a long, low whistle. "And he's out now?"

"Yeah, just last January after serving twenty-two years. Time off for good behavior."

"Jesus H. Christ. Not exactly *Ozzie and Harriet.* You ask her about it?"

"Not yet. Thought I'd do some research first. She alluded to the fact that she hadn't seen her old man in a long time."

"Yeah, because he was in stir," Montoya commented. "Man. Where is he now?"

"In Lafayette. Working at a car wash and checkin' in with his parole officer like clockwork."

"A model citizen."

"You got it. But we'll check him out. Put him at the top of the 'persons of interest' list. Find out if he's got an alibi."

Montoya reached for his cigarettes, thought better of it, and stuffed the pack back into his pocket. "This keeps gettin' weirder and weirder. But yeah, let's have a talk with her old man. Now, what about Olivia; did she tell you any more about her visions?" Montoya prodded. "This isn't the first time, right? She said that when she came in here. So what about the others?"

"According to her, none of them were as clear as this one. We didn't go into the other cases today, but you can look over what Brinkman has. Something about a woman in a cave with hieroglyphics. Here." He fished out Brinkman's notes and tossed them to Montoya.

The phone jangled and Bentz grabbed the receiver before the second ring. "Bentz."

"Hey, Dad."

Kristi's voice always made him smile. "Hey, kiddo— what's up?" He held up an index finger, signifying to Montoya that he'd be a minute. Montoya gave him an exaggerated wink, as if he were talking to some "hot babe," but got the message and, taking Brinkman's report with him, slipped through the partially opened door.

"I just wanted to check in," Kristi was saying. "I've got an hour before my next class and I thought I should call and give you the rundown. My last class before Thanksgiving will be over Tuesday at four, so you can pick me up anytime after that."

Bentz flipped through his calendar, surprised that the month was getting away from him. "I could be there by six, maybe sooner if I turned on my lights and siren."

"Oh, that would be a great idea," she mocked. "You really don't have to drive up and get me, you know. I can find a ride."

"I want to, honey. It's not a problem. Baton Rouge isn't that far. Besides I'd like another look at the campus I'm paying for."

"But if you're busy . . ." Her voice trailed off.

He glanced at the pile of paperwork on his desk, the bulletin board on the wall behind him with shots of the victims of homicides yet to be solved. "I'll be there," he said automatically before picking up on the fact that she might be giving him a hint. Rather than an out. Leaning forward, he glanced at the pictures of her as a child and, now, as a woman. "You still want me to come get you. Right?"

"Well, yeah, of course, but it'll be kinda crazy up here with everyone leaving for Thanksgiving and all. And I've got some stuff I've got to do at the house that might hold me up. I figured coming up here might not be your thing."

"Or *your* thing," he said, recognizing a touch of resentment in her voice. He'd insisted she rush and pledge a sorority house. He wanted to know that she'd have a built-in support system at All Saints College, that she wouldn't be pressuring him to let her lease an apartment at the age of eighteen. He wanted her to grow up, he was trying to let go, but he wanted her to be safe. From the corner of his eye he caught a glimpse of the latest grisly crime scene with a mutilated woman. He knew as well as anyone how dangerous the world could be. That's why he'd spent an arm and a leg on tae kwon do and firearm lessons.

"Yeah . . .well, I just thought I'd check in."

"I'll see you next week." He offered her an olive branch. "If it works better for you to ride down with friends, just let me know."

"Okay, but . . ." She sighed loudly and he imagined she was shoving a tangle of red-brown hair from her eyes. ". . . here's the thing. There's this girl Mindy and she got all excited. Her mom's single, and oh, guess what? She

just happens to be a cop and she's coming to pick up
Mindy. They're going out to dinner before driving back
to Shreveport. So, of course, Mindy thinks it would be
waaaay coooool if you two hooked up.''

"But you don't think so?"

"Mindy's a dweeb. And her mom's a detective. God, can
you imagine? The two of you?"

Bentz laughed. "Don't worry, I'll come up and it'll be
just you and me. Tell Mindy that I have to get back right
away or that I'm already involved with someone . . . or
something.''

"You? Involved? You mean like with a woman? In a
relationship?''

"Yeah.''

"But . . . . you're not.''

"How do you know?''

There was silence on the line, then a little nervous laughter. "Oh, yeah? Right. And when would you have time for
a relationship? Give me a break, Dad, you are like *married*
to your job.'' She chuckled and the sound reminded him of
her mother's laugh—deep-throated, kind of naughty.

Jennifer Nichols's laugh had caught his attention when
he was little more than a kid himself, barely out of high
school, and it had never let go. He'd thought she was beautiful with her long, dark hair, mischievous eyes and sassy
tongue. They'd been attracted to each other immediately,
their affair torridly passionate. She'd had a temper, but he
was a man who could handle her moods and when he'd
proposed barely five months after meeting her, she'd
accepted. She'd expressed a few doubts about marrying a
cop and imagined she could convince him to go to law
school; he'd thought he could tame her reckless spirit.
They'd both been wrong. He'd sensed it at the wedding,
seeing her walk down the cathedral aisle in her lacy white
dress barely nine months from the day he'd first seen her.
Her veil hadn't been able to hide the imperious lift of her
chin and as awed as he'd been by her, he'd sensed theirs
wouldn't be an easy path. But he hadn't cared. He'd loved

her too damned much. Even through the bad times. Even when she'd betrayed him. . . .

"What woman would want to get 'involved' with a homicide dick?" Kristi demanded.

"You don't think your old man has a social life?"

"I *know* he doesn't."

"Then maybe I *should* meet your friend's mother."

"Yeah," she tossed back at him. "That would be good, Dad, real good." She snorted. "Save me," she muttered, then caught her breath. "Damn it all."

"What?"

"I forgot my stupid term paper! It's back in my room on the other side of campus. Shit. I gotta go, Dad." The line went dead and Bentz didn't hang up for a second. He glanced at her graduation picture smiling at him from the desk frame. She'd grown up fast. Faster than most. Kristi had seen far too much in her eighteen years, been robbed of some of her innocence at a tender age. And it was his fault. His and Jennifer's.

What kid wouldn't have a chip on her shoulder after going through what Kristi did? Not only had she buried a mother and watched her old man pull himself out of a bottle, she had to deal with the fact that both her parents had lied to her from the get-go.

Not exactly *Ozzie and Harriet,* Montoya had remarked. Didn't he know that there was no such thing?

Chapter Ten

Melinda Jaskiel, his immediate superior and the reason he had this job with the department, breezed in. Melinda was usually all business. He'd never seen her in anything but a suit. With her hair cropped short, rimless glasses, and a no-nonsense attitude, she was professional to the letter. Middle-aged, divorced, and physically fit, she handled the men she oversaw with an iron fist hidden within a kid glove.

"Tell me about the murder off Esplanade." She folded her arms over her chest and leaned a shoulder against the door frame. "I read the preliminary report on this one and heard a rumor that you have an 'eye' witness who wasn't there."

"That's about the size of it."

"So—what do you think? Does this woman really have visions? ESP?"

"She seems to have firsthand knowledge of what came down. I think it was more than a lucky guess."

One side of Melinda's lips pulled upward. "Always the master of understatement, aren't you, Bentz?"

"You know it's my personal mission to serve, protect, and filter out the crap."

"And you're doing a fine job of it," Jaskiel assured him.

"I don't put much stock in psychic mumbo jumbo. ESP usually means Easy Sucker Punch or Exceptional Shit Pile."

"Maybe you should try to keep an open mind, okay? There are cases on record where psychics did actually help the police."

"Yeah, I know," he admitted grudgingly. He'd had a partner in L.A. who worked with a psychic. The woman had helped him with a couple of cases but hadn't been able to predict that a kid would point a toy pistol at him one night and Bentz, thinking the twelve-year-old intended to shoot, had taken him out. Nope, the damned psychic hadn't said a peep before the tragedy. Bentz had ended up on probation, then promptly decided Jack Daniels was his best friend. His job in the City of Angels ended. He'd been lucky Melinda Jaskiel had seen something in a broken-down cop and hired him when every other department in the country had decided he wasn't worth the trouble. "You know what they say is the problem with having an open mind?"

"That your brains will fall out? I've heard that one, Rick."

Bentz smiled. "I was going to say people might accuse you of being a pansy ass and not having an opinion."

"I doubt if that'll be your problem." She shook her head. "And since when do you care what people think?"

His grin widened and he winked. "Not people, Jaskiel. Just you."

"Save that for someone who'll believe it. So how're you handling this?"

He gave her the rundown, everything from the vision, to the videotape, to the information from Benchmark Realty and Brinkman's reports on Olivia's previous visits to the Department. "Olivia Benchet knows more than she should. It makes me wonder why"—he held up a hand—"except that, of course, she's a psychic and just happens to 'see' murders."

Melinda sent him a withering smile. "So does the lady have an alibi?"

"Just her dog and he's not talkin'."

"Seriously."

"She was home in bed. Asleep. The vision woke her up."

Melinda thought a second. Couldn't seem to put her mind around it. "I assume you're checking her out."

"Done deal."

"Okay, so keep me posted on the case. When you see the evidence report and the ME's report, let me know." She started out the door, but thought better of it. "And, Bentz, don't pull any of that rogue-cop crap on me, okay? We need to play this by the book."

"Wouldn't *dream* of it."

"My ass."

"And it's a nice one," Bentz said.

"Careful. There is such a thing as sexual harassment these days."

"You love it and you know it," he said. "Besides you're the boss."

"Keep that in mind. Now, let's give the witness in this case, Ms. Benchet, some credibility. Okay? It's odd and she could be jerking our collective chains, but just maybe she does have some kind of visions. Look into it." Jaskiel patted the door frame, then left.

"You got it," Bentz muttered under his breath. So he was supposed to believe whatever Olivia Benchet peddled his way? He was supposed to buy that she had some psychic experience. How? Was she connected to the killer? The victim? The house where it happened? Why did she "see" this particular murder? Why not others? Did she confess to the priest? Or maybe he confessed to her. What the hell was the connection? Bentz stretched out of his chair and scratched his chin. Keep an open mind. Shit. He didn't know if he could. Believe that a woman actually "saw" a murder miles away?

That would be a trick.

* * *

So Bentz doesn't believe you. So what?
Not exactly a surprise, is it?

Olivia's grip tightened on the steering wheel of her truck as she wound her way into the Garden District on her way to the University. She'd hoped that Detective Bentz would trust her, that he would sense she was desperate, but of course, he was just like all the others. *Men,* she thought disgustedly as she stopped, waiting to turn into the University while the streetcar clacked past. No, that wasn't fair. She'd run into her share of women skeptics as well. Starting with her mother.

It was late afternoon, shadows lengthening over the nearby colleges of Tulane and Loyola. She parked in a designated spot, then jogged to the psychology department. Images of Detective Bentz chased after her, but she was determined to push his handsome, craggy face, and all thoughts of the murder aside. At least for the moment. She made her way up a flight of stairs to the office of Dr. Jeremy Leeds, her professor and, she thought, noting the irony, the ex-husband of Dr. Sam, the radio psychologist at WSLJ. Olivia didn't much like the guy; he seemed pretty stuck on himself, but as he was her assigned counselor, she had to put up with him for a year or so.

No one was seated at the secretary's desk, so she wended her way through a labyrinthine hallway and knocked on the door to Leeds's private office. No answer. She tried again, her knuckles, where she'd scraped them earlier on the cheese grater, aching a little. "Dr. Leeds?" she said just as she heard footsteps rounding a corner.

"Olivia! Sorry I'm late." His smile was wide. Apologetic. In his mid-forties, with strong features, a long, straight nose and a neatly trimmed beard, he shoved open the door and held it for her. His shoes were polished to a gloss, his casual jacket looking as if it had cost a small fortune. Natty was the word that came to mind whenever she thought of Dr. Leeds. Well, 'natty' and 'fake'; there was just something about him that didn't ring true. Nothing she could put her finger on, but something. "I had to run down the hall to catch a colleague, Dr. Sutter, before he left for the day. He's only here part time and it's the weekend, you know, so I was fortunate to grab him." Leeds was patting down his pockets for his keys and rattling on, as if he were nervous. "Dr. Sutter and I are offering a two-day seminar in the spring you might be interested in. You've heard of him? Ah!" Leeds found his key ring as Olivia lifted a shoulder. All she knew about Sutter was by reputation, that he was a difficult taskmaster. Leeds inserted his key into the lock. "Anyway, he and I started talking, and well, I guess I'm playing the part of the absentminded professor."

She didn't think so. Jeremy Leeds was sharp as a straight-edged razor. There was something too smooth about him. Cold. She felt it now, just being near him.

"Come on in."

She took a chair near a small window and flipped open her folder of notes, all of which she'd taken before last night. Before, she was certain, her life had changed forever. Dr. Leeds slid into his chair on the other side of the desk— as tidy as Detective Bentz's had been cluttered. A calendar sat on one corner, a humidor of cigars on the other. The room was small and compact, with a smattering of degrees and artwork hung on the walls. "So, what have you got there?" he asked, indicating her work. "A premise for your thesis?" He slid a pair of wire-rimmed glasses up his nose.

"Just the germ of an idea."

"Oh?" He was interested. His eyebrows lifted. "Did you want me to go over it?"

"Actually I just wanted to run some thoughts by you. It's not on paper yet."

"Of course." He leaned back in his chair, tented his fingers, and waited.

"I'd like to do my thesis on aberrant psychology as it applies to religion."

"Really?" His smile faded.

"I'm thinking of the psychology of prayer and penitence as it applies to Judeo-Christian theology."

"That's quite a mouthful. Don't you think it would be better suited if your area of expertise was theology or philosophy?"

"I think I could make it work. And it's what interests me," she added, not inclined to explain any further. "You offer undergrad classes on aberrant psychology and criminal psychology and I thought I'd sit in, if that was okay."

"Yes, yes, that's not a problem." He nodded, turning the idea over in his mind. "Tell you what. Go ahead and run with this, but bring me a written proposal, an outline of your thesis, and we'll go from there. How does that sound?"

Just peachy, she thought, but said, "Great. I'll call and we'll set up an appointment."

"Good, good." He stood—ever the gentleman—and she left feeling that at least one small detail of her life was back in place. She'd been struggling with a concept for her thesis. If nothing else, the murder last night had sharpened her focus.

She hurried downstairs and outside, where the shadows had turned to dead-on night. Though it wasn't quite five, darkness had blanketed the city and street lamps were glowing, giving the grounds an eerie feel. Olivia had always thought the massive limestone facade of Gibson Hall looked as if it belonged to part of a medieval castle, and now, in the darkness with the first few drops of rain beginning to fall, it seemed more imposing than ever.

Crossing the thick grass, she headed for the parking lot, found her truck, and slid behind the wheel. She wasn't alone. Other students hurried by, but somehow tonight, after the events early this morning, she felt isolated. Detached. She plunged the key into the ignition and pulled out of the parking space. Knowing she was probably making a huge mistake, she drove deeper into the city. For a macabre reason she didn't understand, she felt compelled to drive by the scene of the crime.

Just like the killers are supposed to do.

* * *

Traffic was messy. It had begun to rain in earnest and huge drops fell from the sky, pelting the streets and running down the windshield so fast that the wipers could barely slap them away. Taillights glowed red, seeming to smear through the glass as she wound her way to the other side of Canal Street and through the French Quarter, where umbrella-wielding pedestrians filled the sidewalks and sometimes spilled into the streets. She turned on the radio. WSLJ was playing jazz and it grated on her nerves. Maybe it was just from being overly tired and wrung out, but she couldn't stand the thought of vocal interpretations and riffs. She found a country station and cranked up the volume.

Better to listen to pining and heartache.

Yeah, right. She clicked off the radio.

On the east side of City Park she squinted at the street signs until she found one she recognized, then rolled down the narrow street until she came to the charred, burned-out building. Not much was left, she thought as she pulled close to the curb and climbed out of her little truck.

Crime scene tape roped off part of the yard and all of the debris and ash. Her shoes were no match for the water rushing through the street, and the jacket she kept in the cab had no hood. Nonetheless, she threw it over her shoulders and waded across the street to stare at the soggy, blackened rubble. Rain peppered her face and ran through her hair as she remembered the vivid scene from her vision. The victim—that horrified blond woman—had died horribly here, somewhere in the burned shell of a house. At the hands of a priest.

Shivering, she whispered, "Who *are* you, you bastard?" She'd thought if she came here, actually stepped onto the soil where the horrid event took place, she might get a glimmer, a flash of him, might *feel* him again and gain some clue to his identity. Traffic crawled behind her but the rain muffled much of the city's noise as it poured from the sky and dripped off the surrounding trees.

She closed her eyes. Listened to her own heartbeat. Felt something. A prickle that brought a slight chill, as if the killer had passed her on the street. "Come on, come on," she said, her eyes still closed as she turned her face skyward, felt the harsh wash of rain and strained to see something, to hear something, to smell—

"See anything?"

She nearly jumped out of her skin. Fists clenched, she whirled.

In the sheeting rain, Detective Bentz was standing less than a foot away from her.

"Oh, God, you scared me," she said, her heart pounding in her ears, adrenalin rushing through her bloodstream. "But . . . no . . . I don't see anything but rubble."

He nodded. Wearing a baseball cap with the symbol for the New Orleans Police Department emblazoned upon it and a water-repellant jacket, he asked, "What were you doing? Just now."

She felt foolish. Embarrassment washed up the back of her neck. "It was just an exercise. I thought maybe if I actually came to the scene of the crime, I might get more of a sense of him."

"The killer?"

"Yeah." She glanced at the Jeep double-parked on the street. "Did you follow me here?"

"Nah. Headin' home. Thought I'd swing by. Maybe see somethin' or get a glimmer—a hunch—of what went on now that it's quiet here. Kinda like you were doin'." He gave her a quick once-over. "You're getting wet."

She smiled. "Now I know why you're a detective. It's your keen sense of observation." Raindrops caught in her eyelashes and dripped from her nose. "There's just no gettin' anything past you, is there?"

"I like to think not," he said but gave her the barest of smiles, one that seemed genuine and she'd begun to realize was rare. "How about I buy you a cup of coffee . . . or dinner, before you get completely soaked?"

"What . . . like in a date?" she blurted out before thinking.

Of course not, Livvie. Don't be a goose! Cripes! A date? What kind of romantic ninny are you? She swiped at the rain running down her cheeks. "Or as in you want to pump me for more information because you've finally figured out that I'm the best resource you've got?"

"Whatever you want to call it. I know a place where you can get great Cajun shrimp and those spicy curli-cue fries," he said, twirling a finger. "It's a hole-in-the-wall, but has great food."

She couldn't believe he was serious. "I really didn't figure you for a curly fry kind of guy."

"And you claim you have ESP. Only goes to show ya."

"Bentz, are you trying to flirt with me?"

His smile fell away. "Just trying to get you out of the downpour so that you would talk to me." He was all business again. Kind of gruff. As if she'd inadvertently tromped all over his male ego. Funny, he didn't seem to be the kind of man who had an ego problem . . . but then he didn't seem like the kind who would go for the damned curly fries, either.

"Okay. Where to?"

"I'll drive." He ushered her to the Jeep and she told herself that she was making another incomprehensible mistake.

"I could follow you."

"There's not much parking around there."

"Fine, whatever."

He opened the door to his Jeep and she slid into the passenger seat. It looked pretty much like every other four by four on the road, no police-issue shotgun at ready, no wire mesh or glass separating the front seat from the back, no handcuffs dangling from the glove compartment. But there was a slicker in the back with the police department logo, and of course, he was armed with a handgun.

He drove through the rain-washed city streets with the expertise of someone who maneuvers cars through tight spots all the time. They cruised across Esplanade and into the Quarter to St. Peter, where he forced the Jeep into what appeared an impossibly small space. "It's not The Ritz."

"Good. Cuz I'm not dressed for it."

They ducked under a dripping awning and into a narrow restaurant that smelled of grease and spices. Behind a long counter cooks sweated over boiling pots of shrimp and sizzling baskets of french fries. Bentz led her to a table near the back, past a bar where bottles of beer were packed in metal tubs of ice. He held one of the café chairs for her where, from her vantage point, she could see a glass door that opened to a rear courtyard at the back of the restaurant.

Bentz settled into a café chair on the opposite side of a red-checked tablecloth, and as the waiter appeared said, "We'll have a double."

"A double?" Olivia repeated.

"I always eat the same thing. You'll like it."

"I don't get to choose?"

Bentz grinned. "Next time you pick."

As if there was going to be a next time. "Okay."

"You want somethin' to drink? Beer?"

"Sure. A lite."

"And my usual," he said to the waiter, who even with his shaved head, didn't look old enough to serve anything remotely alcoholic but returned within seconds with two opened bottles. Bentz's boasted zero percent alcohol.

"Still on duty?" she asked.

"Always. Cheers." He tapped the long neck of his bottle against hers, then took a long swallow.

"So what is it you want to know, Detective?" she asked over the clink of flatware and buzz of conversation. "You're not assigned to tail me or anything like that, are you?"

"Not exactly."

He took a long swallow from his bottle and in the soft lighting from a kerosene lantern with a red shade, he looked less formidable than he had earlier; more approachable. He was good-looking in a rough-hewn way and he had a decent smile beneath those dark eyes.

"I was told to keep an 'open mind,' that's how it was

phrased, about you. So when I ran into you at the crime scene, I thought I'd try to do just that. Listen to what you have to say.''

''And figure out what makes me tick?''

Again the flash of that enigmatic smile. ''Somehow I don't think that's possible.''

From somewhere behind her there was a crash of glass and metal hitting the hard brick floor.

''Oops,'' Bentz said, raising his thick eyebrows. She looked over her shoulder and saw a tray of broken glass, cutlery strewn helter-skelter, foaming beer running in rivulets through the cracks in the floor, and dozens of prawns, shrimp, and crawfish sliding under tables and between customers' feet.

''Watch out, they're escaping,'' Olivia whispered and Bentz laughed.

A stricken waitress from whose fingers the tray had obviously tumbled was gasping in horror as the bartender, a big black man, tossed her a towel and a busboy hurried to a closet to retrieve a mop and bucket. ''Smooth move,'' Bentz muttered, amused.

''The girl is traumatized.''

''She'll get over it. I did the same thing once. My first job. In high school. I not only dropped a tray of drinks, I splashed them over six patrons at the country club. Every one of those ladies was dressed in silk, I think. Anyway, that was my first and last day there. God, I'd forgotten about that.'' He took a swig from his bottle.

Olivia didn't want to think of Bentz as a butter-fingered teenager, or anything other than the detective he was. ''From bus boy to cop in two easy moves?''

''Not quite.'' His lips pinched a little. ''I've had my share of missteps along the way.''

He didn't elaborate and Olivia couldn't help but wonder if the reason he was drinking nonalcoholic beer had to do with one of those missteps. The waiter brought a double order of shrimp—served in buckets—along with two massive baskets of fries. The shrimp were blazing red, the fries, as promised, were spiraled and covered with some kind of hot salty spice. Bentz dumped his shrimp onto his paper-covered tray, cracked off the shrimp's head, peeled off the shell and legs, then tossed the waste into his bucket as he plopped the meat into his mouth.

Olivia followed suit, her fingers smearing with the liquid from the shrimp and staining from the spices and grease from the fries.

As Bentz promised, the food was fabulous. Maybe there was more to this man than first met the eye. Maybe the gruff detective hid a more refined soul—*oh yeah, right, tearing a crustacean apart with bare hands hardly suggests any sense of sophistication. Face it, Livvie, he's a bruiser. All brash, suspicious, male cop. Remember that. He still thinks you were somehow involved with that murder. He just hasn't figured out how. He believes in what he can see, touch, hear, and smell . . . Don't trust him for a second!*

"So, tell me about this 'gift' you've got," he suggested as he finished his first near-beer and the waiter set two more bottles onto the table. "When did it kick in? Right from the beginning? I mean were you born with it, or did something, some incident, start the ball rolling?" He cracked the back off a shrimp.

"You mean like was I dropped on my head as an infant? Or did I faint in high school and wake up suddenly able to see events that weren't happening to me?" she asked.

"If that's what happened."

"It's not," she snapped, her temper rising. "It's just what most people expect to hear."

"Hey, whoa," he said, lifting a hand. "I didn't mean to push any hot buttons." He seemed sincere and she felt a little foolish for jumping off the deep end.

"Sorry . . . conditioned reflex. It's hard to explain, but yes, I had this as a kid. Right from the get-go. Grannie Gin told me it was a gift and my mother told me it was all in my head, that I should keep quiet about it. I think she grew up embarrassed by her own mother's gift. People would come over and Grannie, even though she was a vastly reli-

gious woman, would read tarot cards and tea leaves and all
that stuff. Bernadette, that's my mother, thought it was weird,
which, I guess, it was. It always just seemed a part of my
grandmother and I understood it, just not why it happened
to me, too.''

''You don't like it, but you work with all that New Age
and voodoo stuff.''

''I know. It's like I hate my gift but I have this weird,
almost macabre fascination about it.''

''Brinkman mentioned you'd come in and talked to him
about other murders.''

''So you talked with him.''

''Had to. That a problem?''

''No. Not at all.'' She'd picked up a shrimp but dropped
it back into her bucket. ''I thought I explained all this. I've
been in to the police department before. No one, especially
Detective Brinkman, took me seriously. Just like you.''

''Try me,'' he suggested and, when she hesitated, peeled
another shrimp. ''Tell me your side of it. Firsthand.''

''It's in Brinkman's reports, I'm sure.''

''But I want your perspective.'' He leaned back in his
chair, wiped his mouth, and stared at her. ''No recorders.
No notes. Just tell me what you saw.''

She hesitated.

''Come on, Olivia. You started this,'' he said, and she
noticed how his hair fell over his eyes and how tiny crow's
feet fanned from his eyes, as if he squinted a lot. A thoughtful
man.

''You're right. I did. Okay . . . Well . . . Where to begin?
Let's start with last summer, that was the most recent. I
remember it because it happened around the time my grandmother died. I was flying back and forth from Tucson in
those weeks and each time I got to Louisiana I'd have these
nightmares, more fragmented than this last one, but intense.''
She studied his reaction. There was none. He ate, listened,
sipped from his bottle, and didn't reach for a notepad or
pen. Maybe he thought she was making it up. Maybe he
was actually starting to believe her.

"Go on," he urged. "What was the dream about?"

"It was different in that it recurred. Very faint when I was in Tucson but extremely vivid when I was back here. It wasn't a vision of someone being violently murdered like last night . . . but rather short images, every other day or so, of a victim being left to starve to death. She . . . she was trapped somewhere like a crypt of some kind and she was screaming and crying. There were symbols on the walls, pictures of blurry images and writing . . . some kind of inscription that I couldn't make out. She was getting weaker every day, I could sense it. And I felt him. His presence." Olivia held Bentz's stare. He'd quit eating, was just watching her intently, as if looking for a crack in her story, a lie.

"The killer?"

"Yes. Whoever abducted her and left her to die would come and visit her, shine a flashlight into her terrified eyes, then leave. So I only got glimpses of where she was being held, only quick images of the surroundings. He . . . he left a vial there . . . I think, probably to taunt her. It could have been water, or maybe something she could take to end her life quickly, but it was just out of reach. She, too, was chained." Inside, Olivia shivered. "Last night the woman died violently, but this one was just the opposite, at least in the beginning . . . In some ways it seemed worse . . . a horrid waiting game where the victim was left in the dark to starve to death or die of thirst."

"Which she did."

"Yes . . . but . . . and this image is vague, but I think there was more. It was around the end of July or first of August. I know because Grannie was getting really sick. I flew to Tucson, closed up my apartment, and drove back here all in the span of five days. In that time things shifted. I had images of something more hideous."

"What?"

She drew in a deep breath. "I think the girl was eventually . . . beheaded."

Bentz's lips flattened. "Like the one last night."

"Yes," she whispered. "Like the one last night."

Bentz didn't know what to think. Was the woman completely off her rocker? Seriously mental? Or was there something to all this voodoo/psychic mumbo jumbo. She looked so damned normal as she sat across the table from him, her damp hair curling tighter as it dried, her fingers greasy from the food, her eyebrows knitted, her lips pulled into a tight little knot. But it was her eyes that got to him, her steady gaze that defied him to believe her, the haunted shadows just beneath the surface. "Could you draw the symbols for me?" he asked.

"Not from memory, no, but I wrote them down. Any night that I had that particular nightmare, I scribbled down what I remembered. They're at home. I could drop them by Monday, on my way to work."

"How about I get them from you tomorrow?"

"It's a long drive."

He offered her a smile and motioned for the waiter, indicating he wanted the check. "I'm a bachelor. The only thing I was going to do was watch football and do laundry."

"Fine," she said. "Whatever." She picked up a prawn and he watched as she peeled it and plopped it into her mouth. "Anything else?" she asked, licking the butter from her lips and it almost seemed like a come-on. Ridiculous. But there was something about her, something a little bit naughty, that fascinated him. *Just like Jennifer.*

"Yeah, a couple of things. I'll want a list of everyone you know. Family, friends, anyone you work with or see at school."

"You think my friends are involved."

"That's the problem. I don't know who is, but if I take what you're telling me at face value, then somehow you're connected with the killer ... right? There's something between the two of you ... I mean, I assume that's the way it works. It's not a lightning bolt from heaven, and you don't see random murders being committed. You think what you view is the work of one man."

She nodded. "Sometimes ..." She let her voice fade away and didn't go on. The sounds of the restaurant seemed more intense. Waitresses calling out orders, conversation, the faint sound of Dixieland playing from concealed speakers, the rattle of trays of dishes.

"Sometimes what?"

"It sounds so crazy, but sometimes I get this feeling . . . it's like crystals of ice drizzled over the back of my neck, and I feel that he's close . . . that somehow I've trod in his footsteps . . ." She must've read the doubt in his eyes, because she reached for her beer and took a long swallow. "I told you it sounded whacked out."

"But it could help. Think about it. Who would be the connection? How the hell does this telepathy or whatever it is work?"

"All I know is that it's more intense since I came to New Orleans and the murders are happening here, so it has to be someone close by."

"Agreed," he said, and though it took a lot to scare Bentz, he felt a frisson of dread; whoever the killer was, there was an element of the intangible at work and that made him all the more dangerous.

Bentz paid the check and gave her a ride to her car parked near the charred ruins. The rain had stopped, but the crime scene was gloomy and dark. "You said you stopped by here in the hopes that you could sense what had happened, right?"

She nodded as she climbed out of his Jeep. Bentz pocketed his keys and leaned a hip against the fender.

"So . . . are you getting anything?"

"It's not quite the same as a radar signal," she said, but walked closer to the tape, staring at what had been a cozy little duplex. "No . . . nothing." She shook her head and frowned. "But if I 'get anything,' I'll let you know. Thanks for dinner."

"My pleasure," he said automatically and she looked up at him sharply, silently accusing him of the lie.

"It was business for you, Detective Bentz, and I have a feeling that it always is with you." She climbed into her truck, fired the engine, and tore off down the narrow streets, the taillights of her pickup winking bright red in the night.

Bentz eased behind the wheel of his Jeep and switched on the ignition. He could follow her. Make sure she was going home. He thought he might just do that. Why not? Jaskiel had authorized it, and even though he was off duty, he could spare a few hours.

He wheeled away from the curb. What bothered him about the tail wasn't that he was following her, but that he was more than curious. More than interested because of the case. She was sexy as hell. And an oddball. A kook. A whacko.

But she knew more than anyone else about the killing. Like it or not, he had to believe her.

Chapter Eleven

The phone rang. Once, twice, three times. Jangling through Kristi's groggy brain. From beneath the covers of the bed in her dorm room she groaned; she didn't want to wake up. She glanced at the clock. Ten-thirty. On a Saturday. What kind of idiot would be calling now. *Dad*, she thought, burrowing under the covers and letting the answering machine pick up. "Hi, this is Kristi. You know what to do," her recorded voice intoned.

After a beep, she heard a moment's hesitation, then a deep voice. "Hi, I hope I've got Kristi Bentz. This is Brian Thomas. You might not remember me, but I'm T.A. for Dr. Zaroster and—"

Kristi shot out of bed. Grabbed the phone. "Hi," she said breathlessly. "I know who you are." God, who on campus didn't? *Don't get your hopes up, he's probably calling to tell you that you flunked the quiz on the Buddha yesterday.*

"So you were screening your calls."

"No, um, I was . . . well, if you want to know the truth, I wasn't up yet, but I am now."

"Out late?" he asked and she kicked herself.

"Of course, but I was studying in the library." She giggled and fell back on the bed. They both knew it was a lie, but she didn't want to admit that she'd been to a frat party and had drunk more than she should have. As it was, her head ached and her mouth was cotton-dry. "What's up?" Around the headache she tried to sound cheery.

"I was wondering if you'd like to go out."

Her mouth fell open. She sat bolt upright. He wanted a date? A *date?* Her heart was about to leap out of her chest, but she told herself to sound cool. If that was possible. She'd told herself he'd call, but she hadn't expected it so soon. Her silly heart began to pound wildly.

"Look, I really shouldn't because you're a student in Zaroster's class, but I figure what could it hurt?"

Exactly!

"But if this makes you uncomfortable, you know, because I'm the T.A.—"

"No! I mean that's not it. I'd love to go out with you."

"Good." He sounded relieved.

"So where? When?"

"Tonight. Around seven. Dinner and a late movie. Whatever you want. If you're not busy."

She couldn't believe her good luck. A date with Brian Thomas! She'd had a major crush on him since the beginning of the term. "That would be great."

"I'll pick you up . . . You're at Cramer Hall, right?"

"How did you know—?"

"We at the Theology Department are all-knowing," he said, joking. "It comes with the whole God-like territory."

"Right," she mocked.

"Actually I have authority. I looked it up in your records. You're a DG."

"Yeah, I pledged Delta Gamma," she admitted, but he knew more than he should and it bugged her. Maybe she should have been flattered by him nosing around in her records, but she wasn't. "I, um, thought all that stuff was pretty secure."

"It is, but some of us, the privileged, know the codes."

"Oh, yeah?" He wasn't even a professor. It didn't seem right somehow. "You're one of the privileged?" Man, he sounded kinda stuck on himself. And she thought he was shy. It occurred to her that it might not even be Brian on the other end of the phone, but some creep who'd figured out that she had a crush on him. Brian had always seemed cooler than this.

So who would it be and why would he have access to your student records?

"I'll see you at seven." He was so sure of himself.

"Okay—"

He clicked off and she fell back onto the bed with a huge smile on her face. She couldn't believe that he'd actually called. He'd seemed so reserved in class. Serious. And yet on the phone . . .

She glanced over to the bulletin board tacked onto the wall above her desk. In one corner was a picture of Jay and her, just last year, at their high school senior prom. She was wearing a long black dress, he was dressed in a tuxedo. He was bending her backward, one of her legs was kicked out and a long-stemmed rose was clutched between her teeth as they mugged for the camera. She'd sworn that night that she loved him. And she did. Or she had . . . but he'd stayed in New Orleans where he planned to eventually take over his father's roofing business. For now, he was on the crew, tarring roofs, nailing asphalt shingles, starting at the bottom. He wanted her to quit college and marry him, but she'd begged off, knew she was too young for that kind of commitment.

Since then, their relationship wasn't what it had been.

She'd considered breaking up with him, just hadn't gotten around to it, wasn't sure it was the right move.

But this morning's phone call changed everything.

She threw off the bedclothes and noticed that her roommate Lucretia was already gone, the top bunk evacuated. As usual. Lucretia was a bookworm of the highest order, always freaked out about this test or that. The hours she wasn't in the library studying, she was here, cracking the books. She never went out. *Never.* It was like she was in jail or something.

Stretching, Kristi considered working out in the pool before she had to do her duties at the sorority house, then she really did have to hit the books; she had a paper due in Sutter's class, and she didn't dare turn it in late—that guy was way too intense; sometimes she caught him staring at her as if she were a puzzle, a psychological enigma. It was almost as bad as Dr. Northrup. Now that guy was just plain weird. He watched her, too. As if he expected to catch her cheating or something. It made her skin crawl. She groaned because there was probably going to be a quiz in Northrup's class today. But after that . . . She glanced at the clock again and grinned. Nine hours from now she'd be in heaven.

True to his word, Bentz showed up around two in the afternoon. Olivia was trying to sweep up bird feathers and seed, when she heard Hairy S suddenly going berserk and yapping his fool head off. Leaving the broom and dustpan propped against the back door, she walked through the kitchen and peered through the windows. Bentz's Jeep rolled down the lane. Leaves scattered in the afternoon sunlight and clouds shifted above the trees. The dog wouldn't let up for a second.

"Hush!" she ordered, but Hairy S jumped at the front door and barked wildly as Bentz cut the engine and unfolded himself from the rig. Olivia barely recognized him. Gone were the slacks, crisp white shirt, tie and jacket. Instead he wore beat-up jeans, a sweater and athletic shoes. His hair ruffled in the wind and he looked more like a dad going to his kid's soccer game than a world-weary cop.

As Bentz climbed the two steps to the front porch, Olivia scooped up a yapping and snarling Hairy S, then opened the door.

"Doesn't he ever calm down?" Bentz asked.

"Not until he gets to know you." Hairy's eyes were

trained on Bentz and he was wiggling like crazy, yapping and growling as if he were about to tear the detective limb from limb.

"And how long does that take?"

"Longer than a couple of days. Same with Chia, so I wouldn't be putting your nose too close to her cage." Hairy S was still barking. "Knock it off!" she ordered, and the dog, chastised a bit, satisfied himself with a growl of disapproval. Olivia put him on the floor and he started sniffing the hem of Bentz's jeans. "He's all bark and no bite."

"But not the bird."

Olivia smiled. "You can test her if you want."

"I think I'll take your word for it."

"That's probably a wise choice. So, is your laundry all done?" she asked, unable not to needle him.

"Yep." He flashed a smile—one of those rare, genuine ones that lit up his eyes. "I even managed to unload the dishwasher, too. But damn, I just didn't have time for the vacuum."

"Very funny."

"I thought so."

She couldn't help but return his grin. "I'm surprised you didn't bag out, that you didn't find something better to do."

"I think I just ran through my list of options."

"What about fishing or hunting or golfing . . . You said you were going to watch football—"

"I listened to the game on the way over. LSU needs help."

"Don't they always?"

"Uh-uh-uh. You're talkin' to a die-hard fan here."

"I'll remember that. Come on in." They walked to the kitchen and she felt a little more at ease with him in her house. Maybe it was because he was dressed-down, or because the visit wasn't official, or maybe she was just getting used to him. It was hard to imagine that less than forty-eight hours ago, he was just a name on a piece of newsprint. Now he was this . . . presence in her life.

Oh, get over yourself. He's a cop. Doing his job. End of subject.

"So—the inscription?" he asked, leaning a jean-clad hip against the counter.

"Oh, right. Up in my room. Just a sec." She sprinted up the stairs to her bedroom. Hairy S, ever faithful, galloped ahead. In the drawer of her night table she withdrew two sheets of paper, one with a list she'd compiled last night of everyone she knew who lived within fifty miles and the other she'd taken from her computer's printer the last night of the dreams when she awoke to find Grannie Gin had died. On another page, she'd written the strange markings that she'd seen in the vision. Now, her good mood evaporated as she glanced down at the meaningless symbols and letters and she felt that same chill she always did upon reliving the vision.

"Don't even go there," she told herself as she hastened out of the room and down the stairs with an excited mutt leading the way.

"Loyal, isn't he?" Bentz observed.

"Very." *Unlike the men I've known.* "Here's the symbols and a list of my friends and family." She handed him the sheets and he was instantly absorbed, scrutinizing the hieroglyphics as he dropped into a chair at the table.

"So this is what was written in the crypt when you had the dreams?" he asked.

"What I could remember when I woke up, yes." She walked to a spot behind him where she could look over his shoulder, and as she stared at the symbols and letters, she shivered, remembering all too clearly the victim's plight. "Go over it again, would you?"

"Sure. What I can remember. But those dreams, if you want to call them that, weren't as vivid, at least not at first." Yet she recalled them clearly. With the same bone-chilling intensity as the last. "It was basically the same dream over and over, with just slightly different variations." She rubbed her arms and glanced through the window. Winter sunlight pierced through the filigree of naked branches, to spangle the dark water, but the day seemed suddenly frigid and lifeless, filled with shadows that shifted and distorted, always changing. How many times had she thought of the terrified woman trapped in a living tomb? How many nights had the image become a nightmare that she saw over and over again? "The most awful dream was when I think he actually killed her. It was the same night my grandmother died. August eleventh.

"I reported this all to Detective Brinkman for all the good it did." Her eyes held his for an instant, then she glanced away. "Same old story. No body, no missing persons, no witnesses . . . just me. The lunatic."

"Is that what you are?" he asked.

A small smile lifted one side of her mouth. This time when her gaze found his, she wouldn't let it falter. "What do you think?"

When he didn't answer, her smile twisted into a self-deprecating smirk. "Let me guess. That I'm not playing with a full deck? I'm a bottle short of a six-pack? That the gates are closed, the lights flashing, but a train ain't coming? I've heard 'em all. You have to believe, Detective Bentz, I'm *not* one of those idiots who tries to make a scene with the police just to get some attention. And you know it. Because that girl in the house the other night was murdered just the way I told you she would be. And there was at least another one. Maybe more. Someone was left in the dark with those"—she pointed to the paper spread in front of him—"those damned markings!"

"Okay, okay. Let's start over. Calm down, okay. I'm sorry. I'm here, aren't I? Listening to you. Trying to make some sense of it."

Her blood was still boiling, but she nodded, tried to rein in her temper.

"Okay . . . so what do you make of these?" he asked, picking up the sheet and indicating her sketches. "I saw this in Brinkman's report, but they didn't mean anything to me. Chicken scratches. What do you think?"

She leaned over his shoulder and silently cursed herself

for catching a waft of his aftershave. Pointing a finger at the symbols, she said, "I'm not sure what they mean. Remember, I caught only glimpses of these things as a light—probably the beam of a flashlight—swept the room." She stared at the images she'd memorized. "I think the first one is an anchor and those"—she moved her finger to indicate a group of pointed lines—"those three are probably arrows—one with an arc over it, like it's supposed to be a bow or something or on fire. At least that was the impression I got." She touched the next image. "This is some kind of flower, I think, but the rest ... I don't know. This"— she indicated a group of letters with her fingertip—"is the inscription, but I only caught quick looks at the letters and I tried to write them down in the order they were scratched onto the walls of the tomb but they were just flashes, glimpses, all that I could remember."

She read the strange message she'd tried to decipher a hundred times before: *LUM . . . NA . . . PA . . . E . . . CU . . . FI*

"Lum-na-pa-e-cu-fi," he pronounced.

"Some of the letters are missing," she said, "and I've tried a million times to fill in the blanks. Luminary, luminous . . . Napa—like Napa Valley in California . . . I don't know. It could be a foreign language or part of an acronym or . . . anything. Maybe even gibberish. Maybe it was written on the wall before the woman was held captive, maybe it has nothing to do with her. I don't know." She gazed over his shoulder at the partial words and they made no more sense to her than they did the first time she'd seen them. Squinting, she leaned forward for a closer look, her breasts brushing the back of his sweater until she felt the muscles of his back tense. Realizing just how close she'd gotten, she quickly stepped back, breaking contact.

Embarrassed, she pulled out a chair and dropped into it. She motioned toward the sheet of computer paper. "It's like one of those word-jumble puzzles in the Sunday paper. Except you can't go to page fifty-one and find the answer."

His eyes narrowed a fraction. Not a hint of a smile. All

business again. "Mind if I take this? It's clearer than Brinkman's copy."

"Go ahead."

"Any other visions?" He was staring at her as if trying to sort out the lies from the truth, the smooth sanity from any shards of craziness.

"Off and on."

"All different?"

"Yes. Nothing as clear."

"Done by the same guy?"

"I . . . I don't know . . . But it seems that way as I obviously don't visualize every murder committed, not even some that happen in my town, but I see some, Detective Bentz, and they're so clear they literally make my skin crawl."

Nodding, he flipped to the second page and scanned it quickly. "Names, addresses, and phone numbers." He glanced up. "I'm impressed."

"I'm determined to catch this bastard." She leaned back in the chair. "So . . . are you going to keep following me? Like last night." She'd seen his Jeep in her rearview mirror as she'd driven home last night.

"Maybe I just wanted to see that you got home safely."

"And maybe that's a cop-out. Literally."

His jaw slid to one side. "Okay, I'll level with you."

"That would be a plus."

"I did want to see where you went and there's something else. I'm starting to believe you and I'm starting to get worried. I wasn't kidding about an alarm system and a Rottweiler."

"So now you're going to be my own private bodyguard?" she asked, tilting her head and trying to figure him out.

"I think my boss might have some issues with that although you're pretty damned valuable—with this gift and all."

"And all, Detective Bentz?"

He folded the paper and slid it into the pocket of his jeans. "You can drop the 'detective,' " he said.

"And call you what?"

"I go by Rick but most people refer to me as Bentz."

She realized this was an olive branch of some kind and figured she could use all that was offered. "Okay, Bentz, only if you call me Livvie or Olivia. I answer to both."

"It's a deal."

"So you finally believe me?" she asked and he slanted her half a smile.

Something flickered in his gaze. "Let's just say I'm keeping an open mind."

"And it's killing you."

His grin stretched wider. "It's not what I'm known for." He pushed himself to his feet. "Thanks for your help," he said as they walked through the house and onto the front porch. Hairy S streaked off, whining, hot on the trail of some invisible creature. "I'll let you know if we find anyone trapped in a crypt somewhere."

"I hope to God you don't," she said, "but I know someone will. Someday."

"Maybe by then we will have caught the guy." He hesitated and for a second she wondered if he was going to shake her hand, give her a hug, or kiss her. Instead he just inclined his head. "I'll let you know."

Olivia watched as he strode to his Jeep and got in. He backed the four-by-four into the turnaround by her truck, then waved and drove off, his rig bouncing down the rutted lane and out of sight behind the thick stands of cypress and oak. Leaning a shoulder against the door frame, she wondered how long he'd last, if indeed he would keep that open mind, then told herself it didn't matter.

The visions came to her.

She was the one who had to figure out where they came from. Otherwise she'd never convince anyone to take her seriously. She wrapped her arms around her middle and wondered why it was so damned important that Rick Bentz trust her. After all, he was just another cop who'd seen it all. So what if she saw something deeper than the crusty, no-nonsense exterior he put forth? What did it matter that

she noticed how wide his shoulders were and the way his
jeans hugged his hips? Who cared that there was a deeper,
more complicated side to the man than first met the eye?
She couldn't afford to find him attractive. Getting involved
with him would be a major mistake.

Major.

Nor could she sit around and wait for Rick Bentz or
anyone else from the police department to take her seriously.
She'd have to find some more proof or a link or something.
Before the killer, whoever the bastard was, struck again.

She decided to start with St. Luke's.

Chapter Twelve

Olivia pulled on the parking brake and looked through her windshield at the church. It was larger than she'd expected, a whitewashed building with arched stained-glass windows, a single spire, and a bell tower separated from the rest of the church as it rose toward the gray cloud-covered sky. She'd chosen St. Luke's because of its proximity to the French Quarter. A few blocks off Esplanade, the two-hundred-year-old bastion of Catholic faith was the closest church to the crime scene. It seemed the logical place to start when one was looking for a murdering priest.

"A fool's mission," she told herself as she got out of her pickup and cinched the belt of her coat more tightly around her middle. She hoped that somewhere in St. Luke's offices, or the vestibule, there might be information, pamphlets about the church, its priests and staff and hopefully something about the other churches in the city.

It was Saturday. No one was hanging around in the vestibule. She tested the main doors and they opened easily.

Inside, the building was vast but inviting. The ceiling was two full stories above the tiled floor and decorated with painted inlays framed in gold. The nave was lit by dim lights and dozens of candles, their flames flickering against the rough masonry walls. Most of the dark pews were empty, only a few devout individuals inside.

Olivia paused to stare at the altar and felt something. A need. An ache to believe. She'd never been particularly religious, but had tagged along to mass at her grandmother's prodding. "When your troubles are too much," Grannie had said, clutching Olivia's hand, "it's time to talk to God. To visit His house."

Yet she was here not to pray, but to pry.

She made a quick sign of the cross and began her search, looking for the church office or a rack containing information about when the services would be held. If she didn't find what she wanted here, then she'd visit St. Louis Cathedral by Jackson Square. It was the oldest and most famous in the city, and it was half a block from the store where she worked. If all else failed, there was the Internet.

Father McClaren watched the woman hurry into the vestibule and felt a forbidden emotion he quickly tamped down. She was windblown, her curly hair unruly and damp, her face flushed, her perfect lips turned into a pout. She crossed herself as if anxious or troubled and she seemed out of place with the regulars, the parishioners who made their daily pilgrimage to the church. Even in the half-light he noticed that her eyes were a unique gold color, that her teeth worried a pouty lower lip. She seemed as if she were searching for something. Or someone.

Another lost soul who stopped long enough to sign the guest register he and Father O'Hara had placed near the front doors.

"Can I help you?" he asked, approaching.

"I think I'd like to speak to a priest." She was slightly

breathless and he noticed a few sparse freckles across the bridge of her nose.

"You *think?*"

"Yes. No. I mean I'm sure I want to." She seemed a little rattled, but he was used to that.

"I'm a priest," he said, and she looked at him as if he had claimed he was from outer space or that she thought he was trying to pick her up in a bar. "Really. Father James McClaren."

Obviously she wasn't one of the flock.

"Oh." Her eyebrows knit, and she still hesitated, almost as if what he'd told her was somehow a bit frightening. Strange. "I didn't think you were allowed to wear jeans in church," she clarified, still eyeing him with what? Suspicion?

"It's probably not a great idea," he admitted, indicating the faded Levi's, "but I was just cutting through on my way to the cloister. I didn't think anyone would catch me and I'm pretty sure God won't mind."

She lifted an eyebrow. Obviously he wasn't what she'd expected. But then he never was.

"Are you here for reconciliation?" he asked, motioning to the confessionals positioned near the altar. "Father O'Hara is officially on duty and I'll round him up for you."

"No," she said suddenly. "I'm not here to confess anything, I just need to talk . . . to someone." She stared steadily at him with those whiskey-colored eyes surrounded by thick dark lashes and mounted over cheekbones that didn't quit. She was, all in all, a gorgeous woman.

Women were the bane of his existence. Especially beautiful ones.

"Could I talk with you?" she asked, seeming to overcome her reticence a bit. "I mean, when you've got a minute."

"How about now?" He wanted to think that it was his sense of purpose, his calling, his pact with God and Church that made him accept her offer, though at the back of his mind he knew there was another reason, not quite as honorable, at play. "I'm not in that much of a hurry." He touched her lightly on the arm and pointed her in the direction of the courtyard. "We can talk now if you'll put up with me playing handyman. There's a clog in one of the downspouts in the cloister and the regular guy is laid up with the flu. Just give me a minute."

Olivia decided to trust him even though she felt a little nervous. Hadn't she just witnessed a physically fit priest killing that poor woman?

You can't distrust every athletic-looking minister you run into. What would be the chances that this priest was the ogre of your vision?

Besides, she just wanted to talk to someone about her gift and the burden that came with it. She had no intention of telling the priest about the murders or that she'd seen another man of the cloth killing an innocent woman, but she wanted to touch the Church in some way, to speak to a man of God, to make a connection.

Father James guided her past the last row of pews and through a door to the cloister, where the covered porch surrounded a square of marble and a center fountain and marble sculpture of the Virgin and baby Jesus. Cold wind swept across the open area and dark clouds hovered above the city.

"This'll just take a minute," he said as he unlocked a door and retrieved a broom, pair of gloves, bucket, and ladder from the closet. As she watched, holding her hair from her eyes, he positioned the ladder near a corner of the roof where a downspout spilled into a gutter. Donning the gloves, he climbed onto the ladder and pulled soggy leaves and debris from the gutter. "Messy business," he said, and shoved the handle of the broom into the downspout. "But then God's work is never done." He looked down at her and smiled. It was a great smile. White teeth against late-afternoon beard-shadow in a square jaw that could have been taken from the Marlboro man. The guy was way too handsome to be a priest.

She had a twinge of *déjà vu,* as if she'd met him somewhere before. A silly idea. This guy, she would have remembered.

He finished with the gutter and she tried not to notice how the fabric of his jeans tightened over his butt as he climbed down and folded the ladder. What was wrong with her? Her libido, so long dormant, was suddenly all too alive. For all the wrong men.

"If you're too cold, we can go inside, but I like it here. Outside, but sheltered. Something closer to God about it." He snapped the ladder closed and placed it, bucket, and gloves into the closet.

"If the priest business ever slows down, you can always get a job as a maintenance guy," she observed as he locked the door.

He laughed and rammed a stiff set of fingers through his near-black hair, pushing it off his forehead. "Not exactly a higher calling. So, tell me what's on your mind?"

"You won't believe it."

"Try me." Again the smile. "I've heard it all."

"Okay," she said as they walked the perimeter of the courtyard, under the overhang. The smell of the Mississippi wafted over the two-hundred-year-old walls of the church. "My name is Olivia," she said. "Benchet. I moved here a few months ago to be with my grandmother before she died. I inherited her house and something else. It's a gift, they say, kind of like ESP."

"Kind of?"

"I see things, Father. Sometimes ugly things." She stuffed her hands into her pockets and wondered how much she should confide. Dry leaves danced across the stone floor of the cloister. "Sometimes things that make me doubt my faith." She slanted him a glance, but he was looking straight ahead, his brows knit, his nose a little red from the cold.

"We all have doubts now and again," he said. "Even priests."

"Do priests sin?" she asked.

"What do you think?" he asked and his lips tightened a fraction. "Unfortunately we are human."

She wondered. The man she saw in her visions wasn't human at all. He was hideous. A beast. The embodiment of evil. All dressed up in fine vestments. The clouds opened up and poured rain from the sky and the thick drops tumbled down the sloping roof to gurgle in the eaves.

"So you believe that I have this 'sight'?"

"God works in mysterious ways."

"Come on, that's not an answer."

"No, I guess it's not. Kind of an overused cliché." He stopped at the door to the chapel. "How about this? I think there are gifts God bestows upon all of us. Some we can see, or touch, or prove, if you will. Others are intangible, but gifts nonetheless. We're lucky if we recognize what we've got."

"What if I consider my particular gift a curse?"

"Then you should try to look at it another way. Turn it around. God wants us to use whatever gifts he bestows upon us to benefit mankind and to glorify Him. I bet if you look hard enough you can find something positive in your sight."

"That'll be tough."

"I'm sure you can do it," he said with an encouraging smile that touched his eyes.

If you only knew. She was tempted to confide in him, to tell him what she'd seen, but thought better of it. "I'll give it a shot," she promised, wondering if she was lying to a man of God. "So, are you and Father O'Hara the only priests here, at Saint Luke's?"

"For the moment. Sometimes we have visiting priests who conduct the service. And for the record, it's Monsignor O'Hara. Sometimes he's a little fussy about that."

"Oh. I'll try to remember. So do you know other priests in New Orleans, the ones who work in different parishes?"

"Of course." He smiled as if amused. "Why?"

"Just curious," she said, and that really wasn't a lie. As much as she wanted to trust this man of God, she knew that if she confided the horrid truth to him, she was bound to alienate him. Right now, she just needed a friend in the

Church. Someone she could talk to. "Thanks for your time." She offered her hand.

He wrapped chilled fingers around her palm. "Come back anytime you have questions, Olivia. And . . . you might want to attend mass once in a while. Talking with me is fine, but maybe you need to speak to the Father directly."

"I can do that from home, can't I?"

"Of course, but God's house is a welcome home." He smiled and she felt better. "Here." He reached into his pocket and withdrew his wallet. From inside he pulled out a business card. "You're welcome to come, to call me anytime and the door to St. Luke's is always open." He pressed the card into her outstretched hand. "I'll look for you."

Don't hold your breath, she thought, turning the card over.

"Don't tell me . . . you didn't know priests carried business cards. Or use e-mail, right? Well, not all do. I find it just makes things easier. And making business cards with a computer is a snap."

She laughed, feeling more at ease, then tucked the card into her purse. "Thanks."

"Don't thank me. There's a higher power at work here." Father James held the door for her and watched her cross the parking lot to a red truck. She was an interesting woman. Troubled. Beautiful. And she'd lied to him. Well, if not lied at least hedged: he saw it in her eyes. He wondered why, but he tried not to judge. Never. For there was no man who should judge another.

He'd learned long ago that judgment should be left to God.

Didn't he know himself what it was to sin?

What it was to feel the pull of evil?

How hard it was not to transgress?

He'd have to be careful, he thought, remembering how easily sin had come knocking on his door, and how quickly, eagerly, he'd opened it. He'd promised God as well as himself that he'd never unlock it again.

He hoped he hadn't lied.

The Internet was a bust. Olivia clicked off her laptop and rubbed the kinks from the back of her neck. Seated on her grandmother's old couch in the living room, she picked up her now-cold cup of tea, and frowned. Well, what had she expected? That all the priests in the state of Louisiana would have their pictures and personal bios on a website? *WWW.WeAreSouthernPriests.com?* And even if she had found photos and personal tidbits on the web, what would that prove? She couldn't pick the guy out of the crowd anyway. And maybe he wasn't even a priest. Maybe he'd just donned an alb that he usually saved for Mardi Gras. One that he let burn in the fire.

That made more sense.

"Give it up," she told herself, and carried her cup into the kitchen to deposit it in the sink. It was late afternoon, the sun sinking fast, darkness shading the bayou. The rain had let up, but the clouds still rolled across the sky, making the day dreary and glum. Hairy S was curled on a rag rug near the back door. He looked up and thumped his tail on the floor before yawning broadly and resting his chin on his paws again. Chia whistled softly, then tossed water from her dish over her head.

Olivia glanced at the caned-back chair where Rick Bentz had sat only hours before. The big man with the world-weary expression until he smiled, and then, look out. He transformed into a handsome, if determined male with intelligent eyes and a cutting sense of humor. She liked that. He could take it as well as dish it out. An interesting man, but off-limits. He was a cop; his interest in her was purely professional and he thought she was a crackpot. She could read it in his eyes.

Then there was Father James McClaren. Hollywood handsome with intense blue eyes and just enough gray at his temples to make him interesting. Talk about off-limits! He was a priest, devoted to God and a life of celibacy. What a waste, she thought, remembering him climbing the ladder and the way her gaze had strayed to his buttocks and thighs . . .

"You've been alone too long, Benchet," she groused at herself, disbelieving. Lately her libido seemed to be making up for lost time. She, who after the last broken engagement had sworn off men for good. And now she was thinking ludicrous, sexy thoughts about two men she could never even date, much less have a future with. "Bentz is right, you're a maniac," she muttered.

Hairy S jumped to his feet and growled.

"What?"

He began barking crazily and scrambled to the front door, making enough racket to raise the dead in the surrounding three parishes.

"Cut it out!" Olivia ordered and followed him to the front door, half expecting to hear the peal of chimes. She smiled inwardly. It had to be Bentz. Back with some clue or question.

But as she looked out the window, she saw no one. Hairy was still barking, jumping up to the window, acting as if there was someone on the other side of the door.

The hairs on the back of Olivia's arms rose. She moved, angling herself so she could look down the length of the front porch through the window. But she saw nothing. Not even a shadow. She thought about her grandmother's shotgun tucked into the closet under the stairs. "Just in case," Grannie had said. "You just never know about people anymore. I'm ashamed to say it, but I don't trust 'em like I used to."

Me neither, Olivia thought now. Remembering Bentz's warning, she went to the closet, pulled out the gun, and finding a box of shells on the shelf over the coats, loaded the darned thing, throwing the bolt. Then, telling herself that she would call the security people first thing Monday morning, she walked to the front door and cracked it open. Outside there wasn't a sound. Not a sigh of wind, not a croak of a bullfrog, not the hum of insects. The world was still. As if everything had come to a halt. She stepped onto the porch and Hairy S, sticking closer to her, began to growl, low and deep, as if he were afraid.

"It's all right," she said to the dog, but even to her own ears the words sounded false. Hopeful. Founded on nothing.

He whimpered.

"Come here." Picking up the dog from the worn porch boards with her free hand, Olivia stared into the twilight. Shadows seemed to shift or was it a trick of the fading light? The air was cool and still, the clouds overhead barely visible but motionless. She curled her fingers into the scruff of fur at Hairy S's neck and he whined, shivering. "Let's go inside," she whispered and backed into the house, locking the door firmly behind her, wondering if she'd ever have the nerve to actually fire the gun.

She wasn't one to be scared. Living alone wasn't usually a problem, but tonight she wished she had someone with her. Someone big, strong, and unafraid. Rick Bentz's face flashed through her mind. He was big. Strong. Determined. And he wore a sidearm. Then there was James McClaren. He had God on his side. Definitely better than a weapon.

"Fool," she muttered, shaking her head at the turn of her thoughts. Was she so desperate for a man, she wondered as she tucked the shotgun into the closet. Never. She wasn't going to buy into that relying-on-the-stronger-sex theory. She had only to look at the men in her own life—her father, the con, or her fiancé, the cheat. There had been other boy-friends, all short-lived, all of whom had some major flaw that she hadn't been able to see herself living with or compro-mising over. Not that all of the men she had dated had declared their undying love for her—well, other than Ted. But she just plain wasn't interested.

But now?

What's with thinking about the cop and the priest? *You, Olivia, need some serious counseling. Serious.* She glanced at herself in the mirror mounted over the bookcase near the front door. She felt it again.

That stark coldness. Like black ice, deceptively benign, it lured, created a false sense of security. She saw beyond her own reflection and into the darkness . . . heard the sounds of the night, felt a pulse . . . an ache . . . a blood lust that ran through her veins . . .

"Oh, God," she whispered, shivering as she recognized the scent of the hunt, the black adrenalin rush at the thought of the kill. Her heart pumped wildly. Her pulse pounded in her ears.

"No . . . no . . ." Her knees went weak and she leaned against the table, felt the worn edges of her grandmother's Bible with the tips of her fingers. But her eyes stared deep into the glass and saw only the stygian night.

Through the monster's eyes.

He was hunting again.

Chapter Thirteen

"Bastard," Kristi hissed, looking at the clock in her dorm room. Seven thirty-five and no sign of Brian. She'd dressed in black hip-hugging jeans and a red sweater that showed off just a hint of her abdomen if she reached her hand over her head, and had spent nearly an hour with her makeup and hair, which was about fifty minutes more than she usually allowed. And he was standing her up.

Glowering at the telephone, she willed it to ring. "Come on, come on."

Lucretia walked into the room carrying a Coke and a white sack from the local fast-food Mexican spot, located just a block off-campus. Black corkscrew curls bounced around her face. "You're still here?" she asked, sloughing off a jacket that was already dripping onto the carpet. "I thought you had a hot date."

"So did I."

"No show?"

"Not yet."

"Maybe you should call him and see what's up. Does he

have a cell phone?'' She opened the bag, peered in, and withdrew some kind of taco wrapped in brightly colored paper.

''I don't know. I don't have his number,'' Kristi said, frowning. She'd checked caller ID, but Brian's last call had come in as an anonymous call, which made the service that her paranoid cop of a dad insist she have absolutely worthless.

''Maybe he got sick,'' Lucretia suggested as she unwrapped a soft taco and took a bite.

And maybe he just set you up. He probably could tell that you had a crush on him and he was just playing with you— a silly little freshman interested in a thirty-year-old grad student on his way to his doctorate. Face it, Kristi, he's not going to show. ''Then he could have called.''

''Well, it's not *that* late. Maybe he just got detained. Traffic or . . . I don't know . . .'' Lucretia drank from her Coke and sat on her desk chair.

''He still could have phoned,'' Kristi said, burned.

''Well, then he's a jerk. And you should probably stick with Jay anyway. At least he loves you.''

That much Kristi knew. ''Jay's good, but he's kinda boring.''

''But he's true-blue.''

Which you're not, Lucretia didn't add, but Kristi read it in her eyes. Lucretia had dated only one boy in her life and she stuck to him like glue. They went to different colleges, rarely saw each other, spent hundreds of dollars on phone cards, but stuck it out. Lucretia spent every weekend that she wasn't with her boyfriend in this cracker box of a room, studying night and day.

Which, in Kristi's opinion was *zero* fun. Probably less than zero.

''Oh, by the way. Someone else called.'' She searched her desk and found a tiny scrap of paper. ''A guy named Willie Davis.''

Kristi groaned. ''He's the kid I told you about. The guy who always sits behind me in Psych and I can feel him staring at me.'' She took the piece of paper from Lucretia's hand and wadded it in her fist. "He's harmless, but I'm not interested. He's a nerd, but he likes me. The only thing good about him is that Dr. Sutter seems to have a thing against him. He's always calling on Willie in class and that takes the pressure off me.'' She tossed Willie's name and number into the trash. "If he calls again, tell him that I'm out, or that I dropped out or to drop dead or any of the above.''

"I'm sick of lying for you.'' Lucretia shook her head. "You deal with him.''

"I will,'' Kristi snapped, irritated with Lucretia and especially with Brian. The jerk. Why the hell didn't he show up? Irritated, she grabbed her jacket. "I'm going out.''

"Without Brian?'' Lucretia's eyes rounded as she took another bite from her taco.

"Yeah, without him.''

"But you shouldn't go out alone, Kristi. The sorority's rules are—''

"Meant to be broken. I'm leaving. Alone.''

"But . . . But what should I tell him if he calls?''

To go screw himself. "That I'm out,'' she said as she took off, pushing her arms down the sleeves of her jacket and hurrying down the hall to the stairwell. She heard a phone ringing as she reached the door to the stairs, but she wasn't about to turn around and run down the hall and see if it was for her. If he called, fine. He could live with the fact that she wasn't about to sit around for any boy.

Not even if he was the sexiest guy on campus.

He watched from the shadows. Saw her shoot out of the glass doors of Cramer Hall and across the street toward the quad. She was perfect, with her long, athletic legs and tight, swimmer's body. Her hair streamed behind her as she jogged, glinting with just a hint of red in the blue haze of the security lamps. And she was alone. Just as he'd hoped.

Kristi Bentz was soon to become St. Lucy.

If he could wait that long.

A fine mist shrouded the grounds, rising up from the grass and bushes, creating a dense, shifting curtain, and clouds blocked any moonlight.

He wanted her. Tonight. December thirteenth seemed much too far away.

Silently following the same path she'd taken, keeping a safe distance behind her hurried steps, he thought of ways to take her . . . to keep her until the perfect time . . . to prolong the thrill. He could stalk her, capture her, and hold her for just the right moment. The day of her salvation was preordained. December thirteenth, still over three weeks away. Could he wait that long? Would the sacrifice of another satisfy him, for there was one before her. But this one . . . she was the one he wanted. The fact that she was Bentz's daughter, the princess, only added to the intensity of his need.

He slid through the shadows.

She would be a match for him. Unlike the others, the cop's daughter had spirit and fire. He imagined what he would do to her. Surely God would forgive him one transgression, surely he would be absolved for touching her . . . feeling her soft, supple flesh and hard muscles . . . He'd watched her in the pool, cutting through the water, turning, and later, in those perfect moments when she'd climbed out of the water and snapped the bottom of her swimming suit over her tight buttocks, he'd glimpsed the curve of her rump, eyed the length of her leg, observed her shaking the water from her hair.

His cock stiffened, rising and wanting. Was she a virgin? Or was she tainted? Another whore? Would he be the first, were he to break his vows and mount her?

The thought of shackling her, of keeping her, of touching her and teasing her, made him groan. *This is not part of the plan. She's not the one. Not yet.* But he couldn't resist. She was a siren, a Jezebel, and he was weak . . . so weak.

She dashed along an alley separating the fraternity and

sorority houses, then crossed a street and didn't stop for another block. He kept after her and watched as she rounded a corner to follow the seduction of neon lights sizzling in the window of a popular spot where college kids tended bar and rarely checked the patrons' IDs.

One sign was the name of a popular beer written in pulsing blue script; the other was a pink martini glass complete with olive, tipped invitingly. Beckoning.

She walked brazenly into the bar though she was underage and her father was a cop. Yes, she was bold.

"Tsk, tsk, tsk," he whispered, his pulse pounding, his erection stiff. "Naughty, naughty."

She never so much as looked over her shoulder.

He followed her in.

Bentz ignored the open pizza box. He'd eaten three slices while watching ESPN and downing a beer—or what he now referred to as a beer. But his mind was still on Olivia Benchet and the case surrounding the Jane Doe in the fire.

He'd contacted the Lafayette Police. They were supposed to be questioning Reggie Benchet. When they rounded him up, they'd call. So far nothing.

Bentz had given up trying to figure out the meaning of the symbols that Olivia Benchet had scribbled on the paper, and he'd faxed them to a cryptographer who worked for the department. He'd taken a copy of the list of her friends and family and given it to a civilian staffer, but he was going through it himself anyway, acquainting himself with the people with whom she was close.

Resting a heel on his coffee table, he glanced at the screen, then back to the papers spread on the couch beside him. He knew psychics who had worked with the LAPD. But they worked from being at the scene, or working with items of clothing or the habitats of suspects. Never had he dealt with someone who'd actually seen through the eyes of the killer.

Or through a mirror or reflective surface, a macabre takeoff on the magic mirror in *Snow White*. Damned weird.

It didn't make sense. Yet he believed her. There just wasn't any logical explanation. His television was on low as he was catching the latest basketball scores, but he concentrated on the list. Her family was odd and he was double-checking the whereabouts of her father. An ex-con on parole after serving time for murder was a pretty big red flag. Then there was the ex-boyfriend, Ted Brown, now divorced, working for the railroad and living across the river in Gretna. He'd had a few brushes with the law. Officers had been called out to his apartment three times for domestic squabbles. Twice with his wife and once with a girlfriend. Supposedly he'd been brandishing a knife, but the charges had been dropped each time.

"Nice guy," Bentz observed, wondering how Olivia could have come close to marrying the jerk. Ted Brown warranted being checked out. Spurned ex-lovers tended to be hostile and nasty.

Bentz wondered if Olivia still talked to Brown. Saw him? Was close to him? Was it enough of a connection if he was the killer? That was what bothered Bentz: the damned connection. What was it that linked Olivia Benchet with the killer? Who the hell was he? *How* did she see him, and did it work two ways? Why didn't she see his face every waking moment, why just the killings? Was the killer in tune with her? Did he know her name? She was a threat to him. If he knew who she was, she was potentially in serious danger. Serious.

He clicked his pen nervously. Didn't like the train of his thoughts. He saw the mother's name. Bernadette Dubois Benchet Martin. He circled her name because it wasn't complete. According to Brinkman, Bernadette had been married "five times" so there were a few husbands missing. He'd have to check that. And what about the kid who'd drowned? The sister, Chandra?

Bentz had added three deceased people to Olivia's list. Chandra and her grandparents Virginia and Montcliff

Dubois. There were another set of grandparents he hadn't
tracked down, uncles, aunts, and cousins that he intended
to call. Any blood relative, though why he thought there
might be a genetic connection to the killer, he wasn't sure.
It just made some kind of sense to him.

What about half-brothers? Half-sisters? If Bernadette had
been married so often, surely Olivia had a couple of half-
siblings tucked away. And Reggie could have spread his
seed around. He could have any number of offspring.

Shit. The list could go on forever, and Bentz wanted to
nail this guy by his balls before he hurt anyone else. Before
he figured out that Olivia Benchet was witnessing what he
was doing.

Thoughtfully, as the sports anchor switched from basketball to football stats and the Saints' chance at the Super
Bowl, Bentz drew a question mark by the name of Chandra,
Olivia's only sibling. Something wasn't right there. Call it
a hunch or intuition; he sensed there was more to the story.

As there was with the burned house where the victim was
found. The department had started sifting through people
who had inquired about the duplex, but so far nothing had
clicked.

They needed a break and soon.

His pager beeped. Bentz looked down at the readout and
recognized Olivia Benchet's number. He tensed. She
wouldn't call unless it was important. Unless it was trouble.
In one motion, he hit the mute button on the TV and grabbed
the cordless phone and punched in her number.

She picked up before the second ring. "Hello?"

"It's Bentz."

"He's hunting again," she said and her voice was shaking.

"What?" Bentz was on his feet, reaching for his jacket,
sidearm, and keys.

"I . . . I felt him again. And he's hunting. Right now."

"Where?"

"I don't know," she admitted, her voice tight. "I just
caught glimpses. But he's out there tonight and he's following some girl. I couldn't see her face. It was too damned

dark, but . . . oh, God, he wants her. He's conflicted about taking her tonight or waiting. I don't know what that means, but I'm afraid he's going to kill her tonight. Unless we can stop him.''

Chapter Fourteen

"Make sure your doors are locked tight. I'll be right over. As soon as I'm on my way, I'll call back on the cell." Bentz was already out the door as he hung up. Before he reached the first floor of the apartment building, he'd strapped on his shoulder holster and jammed his arms through the sleeves of his jacket.

Shouldering open the door, he dashed to his parking space and was on the street within five minutes. He placed a quick call to Montoya, left a message, then tore up the streets to the freeway. Once heading out of town, he dialed Olivia. "It's me," he said as he blended into the thin stream of Saturday night traffic. "Now, start from the beginning. Tell me what you saw."

"I was here alone and . . . I just looked into the mirror, and it sounds crazy, I know, but I was suddenly not seeing my reflection, but something beneath it. It was like I was looking through another set of eyes. *His* eyes." She sounded calmer than when she'd first called him, but she was still frightened. He listened to what happened, told her to hang tight, and floored it.

Her house was usually more than half an hour away. He made it there in twenty minutes, his Jeep bouncing down her lane as his tires flung mud from the rutted lane. Leaves danced across his windshield and across the swath of his headlights. His chest was tight, his mind racing. A few days ago, he wouldn't have given the woman the time of day and now he was driving like a maniac, worried sick for her safety, assuming what she was seeing was the truth.

Through the trees he saw her cottage, warm patches of light glowing through the windows. As the Jeep slid to a stop, she flipped on the porch light, flung open the door, and the dog shot out to bark, run in circles, and lift his leg while she stood on the porch. Bentz's pulse, already pounding, skyrocketed. God, she was beautiful with those long legs and wild hair and worried eyes. He unfolded himself from the car, jogged to the porch, and as he clambered up the two short steps, she flung herself into his arms.

"Thanks for coming," she said, smelling of jasmine, and he held her for a minute, longer than he should have.

"Are you all right?"

"Yes . . . I think so . . . come in."

He let his arms drop and noticed that she flushed a bright shade of scarlet, as if she was embarrassed by her emotional display. She whistled to the dog, who sped into the house and made a beeline for the kitchen. Olivia locked the door, then motioned toward a short bookcase with a worn, leather-bound Bible sitting on the top shelf. Mounted on the wall over the bookcase was a mirror with a beveled edge and dark frame. "This is where I saw it," she said, looking into the glass and swallowing. Bentz, standing behind her, saw nothing more than their reflection, him standing over half a foot taller than she.

"And now?"

"Nothing. Just you and me." Her eyebrows drew together. "But it was dark," she said, and reached to the wall to switch off the overhead light. Instantly the tiny hallway darkened. Again they gazed into the mirror, and Bentz heard her swift intake of breath, watched as she stared into the mirror. She tensed, and he touched her lightly on the shoulder, hoping to offer her strength and support. "There's nothing . . ." she said at last, relaxing. "Nothing." She shook her head and sighed. "I should have known, this isn't something that I can call up, it just happens." She shoved her hair from her eyes and caught his gaze in the darkened glass. "I'm sorry. You came all the way out here for nothing."

"Maybe not. Let's go over it again. Maybe if you talk it through, show me exactly what happened, we'll learn something." He offered her a bit of a smile and she turned, her arm brushing his chest, the scent of her perfume tantalizing.

"If you think so."

"I don't know what to think."

"Neither do I," she admitted. "I guess we may as well give it a shot." She started up the stairs and Hairy S sped up ahead of her. "I was up here."

The old steps creaked as he climbed. All the while he tried not to watch her round little rump as she ascended or the way the denim stretched tight over her buttocks. He forced his eyes to the upper floor, which consisted of a short hallway, small bath, and two bedrooms tucked under the eaves. He caught a glimpse of the larger room that faced the rear of the house. A four-poster sat in the middle of one wall and French doors led to a verandah. The rest of the furniture consisted of a bureau and desk. Olivia led him to the other bedroom. It was smaller and cozy, filled with a twin bed, a small sofa, a bureau, and a desk where a laptop computer was set up. Textbooks filled a floor-to-ceiling bookcase. "I was here. Doing some research," she explained, "and nothing seemed out of the ordinary, then I went downstairs . . ." Again he followed her, this time watching her sun-streaked hair bounce as she made her way to the first floor, ". . . and as I passed by here . . ." She looked into the mirror again, her fingers reaching forward as she touched the cover of a Bible resting on the top of the short bookcase. ". . . I felt something." She shivered as if experiencing a chill. This time he didn't touch her, but let her gaze into the glass, to recreate what she'd felt, to try and reconnect with the monster who was stalking the streets of New Orleans.

He didn't know when he'd started believing her, but against his deep-rooted skepticism she'd found a way to convince him that somehow, some way, she had a connection to the killer.

It was his job to figure out how.

"I don't feel him," she whispered. "He's gone." Shaking her head and sighing, she turned to face Bentz. "But I did. Tonight. I felt him tonight."

"I know." He looked into her eyes and something deep inside him shifted. A wall he'd worked so hard to erect began to crumble. She was so earnest here in the half-light that filtered into the hallway from the living room. Her gold eyes were clouded with worry, the skin over those high cheekbones stretched taut with concern.

"You believe me?"

"I believe you saw something, yes. I don't know what it was or what it means or how it happens, but in some way, Olivia, I think you're linked to the murderer."

"Dear God," she whispered. "How?"

"That's what we've got to figure out." He wanted to comfort her. To wrap his arms around her and hold her tight. To press a kiss upon her crown and even brush one across her lips. But he didn't. Despite his conflicting emotions, he restrained himself. He was too involved as it was.

To his surprise, she took the initiative and, standing on her tiptoes, pressed a featherlight kiss against his cheek. "Thanks for coming," she said hoarsely then, as if embarrassed all over again, cleared her throat. "Have a seat," she said, gesturing to the living room. "And I'll buy you a beer."

Hairy S hurried down the steps. Bentz settled for some kind of flavored coffee and sat on one corner of the couch while Olivia curled up in the other corner. The dog hopped onto the cushion between them and circled three times before plopping down. Bentz asked dozens of questions. She answered, but he learned nothing. "You have no idea who he is or the identity of the woman he was chasing?"

"No . . . I only saw her back, but she was jogging and I got the impression she was young. He followed her through some alleys that I didn't recognize, past huge, well-kept mansions and across a busy street toward a business district. Again, I didn't recognize anything," she admitted, concentrating. "The woman hurried into a bar and I caught a glimpse of neon lights—a pink martini glass."

That was something. But not much. "There are hundreds of bars around here."

"I'm not even sure it was New Orleans."

"Then where?"

"I don't know." They sipped coffee and he asked her question after question, trying to make her think about the vision, about her family, about her "gift." He got nowhere. His cell phone blasted and he picked it up.

"Got your message," Montoya said. "What up?"

Bentz explained and Montoya swore under his breath. "So it looks like we're gonna have another one."

"Let's hope not. She didn't witness a murder this time. Just a hunt."

"That's enough," Montoya muttered. "Has she ever seen a hunt before?"

"No. I asked her that."

"So now she's getting more peeks. Maybe that's a good thing. Maybe she'll pick up on something before he strikes again." Montoya was finally buying her story as well. But then he had to. It was all they had to go on.

Bentz hung up, asked a few more questions, and assuring himself that she had calmed down and that the house was secure, decided he had to leave. "Call me anytime," he said as he walked to the door.

One side of her mouth lifted. "I will."

"And really, get an alarm system." He reached for the doorknob, then hesitated. "I'd feel a lot better about it."

"Are you worried about me, Detective?" she asked, amused.

"Yeah, I am."

"Because I'm the only witness you've got?" She was teasing him, flirting with him.

"Yeah, that's it," he said, and watched as she raised a dubious brow. "That and the fact that I'd hate to see anything happen to that cute ass of yours."

She laughed. "What about the rest of me?"

"Goes without saying."

"You're a real charmer, aren't you, Bentz?"

"I try my best." He opened the door, hesitated again, and then, knowing he was making one of the worst mistakes of his life, muttered, "Oh, hell," and grabbed her again. She let out a gasp as he bent down, kissed her hard, and lifted her off her feet. She was breathless as he set her down. "Don't mess with me, Benchet," he said with a wink. "And lock the damned door behind me."

Olivia was left with her head spinning. She watched him climb into his Jeep, then closed the door and threw the dead bolt. Sagging against the aging panels, she wondered why she'd baited him, why she'd flirted with him.

Because you're lonely and scared, and Rick Bentz is sexy as hell. She heard the sound of his Jeep's engine roar to life then fade as he drove off. The house seemed suddenly emptier. No longer cozy.

You can't be falling for him, she told herself. *No way. No how. It's just that you're terrified and he's a big man, a strong man, someone you can lean on.*

That had to be it. And yet when she touched her lips with her fingertips, she relived that breath-stopping kiss and realized with a sense of doom that she was lying to herself.

If she didn't watch it, she'd imagine herself in love with Detective Rick Bentz and that would only spell disaster.

* * *

Kristi was midway through her second beer and pissed as hell. She'd found some friends in the bar and pretended that she wasn't mad, but she was, and when she saw Brian wending his way through the tables to their booth, she turned and made a point of staring out the window.

"Don't look now," Marianne whispered from the other side of the booth as she took a drag on her cigarette, "but I think someone's here to eat some crow."

"Good. I hope he chokes on the feathers."

"Give the guy a break. Hear what he has to say," Jennie said, grabbing a handful of pretzels.

"Kristi?" Brian's voice was deep. She felt his fingertips on her shoulder and jerked away. "We need to talk."

Still steamed, she angled her face toward him and sipped her beer. "About?"

"Why I was late."

"You weren't late. You didn't show."

"I did. Just about five minutes after you left, according to your roommate. I figured I might find you here."

"How?"

"It's the local hangout." He was leaning over slightly. His face was wet. He smelled of musky aftershave and rainwater. "My car broke down."

"You could've called."

"The battery ran down on my cell. It died when I called roadside assistance for someone to come jump me."

"There are pay phones."

"I didn't think I'd be that late." He glanced past her to her two friends, who were swallowing smiles and staring at him unabashedly. "Come on . . . let me take you to dinner."

"I think I'd better stay here."

He gave her the ghost of a smile. "You're really going to make me suffer for this, aren't you?"

"You deserve it."

"Just give me a chance to make it up to you."

"I don't think so."

Marianne stubbed out her cigarette. "Give the guy a break, Kristi."

Kristi's eyes narrowed on her friend.

"Tell ya what," Brian said, "I'll take you on at pool or darts. Your choice. If I win, we go to dinner."

"And if I win?" Kristi asked.

"Then you choose the punishment."

"That might be dangerous," she teased, warming up. He was just so hot. "I have a pretty wild imagination. You could be humiliated."

Something sparked in his sexy eyes. "Then maybe I should lose on purpose," he said and she laughed.

"Okay, you're on." She drained her beer and felt a little lightheaded as she got to her feet.

"Watch out," Marianne warned. "Kristi's really good."

"So am I," Brian assured her as she made her way to the dart board and grabbed a handful of darts.

She had the weird sensation that someone was watching her, someone besides her girlfriends. She glanced around the bar and saw no one really staring at her. Oh, there were a couple of guys playing pool who glanced up and winked at her and she was afraid the bartender was studying her as if he suddenly questioned her fake ID, but no one sinister. Still, she couldn't shake the eerie sensation. "But there is one thing."

"Yeah?"

Brian clamped steel-tough fingers around her wrist. She hadn't realized until then how much bigger he was than she. "One rule."

"So now there are rules? Great. Okay, what is it?"

"If I lose, and I don't intend to, you can't ask me to change your grade in Zaroster's class. I like you, but I'm not going to screw up my life over this, okay? You're on your own in philosophy."

"Oh, darn, and I thought this was my big chance to score an A."

"I mean it."

"Fine, but anything else goes?" she asked and his fingers loosened a bit, the tips rubbing against the inside of her wrist.

"That's right," he said, that wicked light in his eyes flaring again. "Anything at all."

Chapter Fifteen

Bentz spent Sunday morning working on the case. He'd checked with the department, and though there had been a gang-related knifing on the waterfront, and a hit-and-run out by the airport, no one had reported another murder that would suggest Olivia Benchet's private killer was on the loose again.

But then she hadn't witnessed a murder, only someone stalking a woman.

He'd also run down some leads, called people who had viewed the house on Bayou St. John where the murder had been committed and checked the people visible on Carl Henderson's video against the list of witnesses who'd viewed the fire. Three people on the video, a young couple and the guy in the shadows, hadn't been identified. Everyone else was accounted for.

The Lafayette Police had talked to Reggie Benchet and were faxing a report, but so far, there was no indication he'd been in New Orleans during the time of the last killing—they were still checking his alibi.

Bentz had created a list of sign companies specializing in neon lighting and another of bars in the area. Maybe someone would remember a pink martini glass, though Olivia's recent vision had nothing to do with any murder.

So far.

Then there were the churches and the priests who officiated. He had lists of those as well.

Tired of the paperwork and trails leading nowhere, he took a break and worked out in the back bedroom. Stripped to his boxer shorts, he pounded the hell out of a punching bag. It worked his muscles, relieved stress, and had peeled off about fifteen pounds in the past six months. He was getting so goddamned healthy he could barely stand himself.

No booze.

No cigarettes.

No women.

Unless he counted Olivia Benchet, whom he'd known only a few days and had kissed once. It was a helluva kiss. But it wasn't exactly a relationship.

Sweat began to run down his back. He was living the life of a bloody priest. Montoya had accused him of having no social life and the truth of the matter was the young buck was right. "Hell," Bentz growled and pummeled the bag until his muscles screamed and he was soaked. Breathing hard, he leaned against the bag and let it rock slowly as he caught his breath. He glanced around Kristi's room. Aside from the punching bag, it was just as she'd left it with its double bed, aqua-colored spread, and matching curtains. It smelled dusty and unused and he decided he'd go the distance and vacuum and dust, maybe even have a bouquet of flowers on the bedside table waiting for her. He looked at the spot and frowned when he noticed the photograph of Jennifer, still at the side of Kristi's bed.

Taken years before, faded slightly, the shot was a picture of the two of them. Kristi had been around seven at the time and the picture had been taken by one of Jennifer's friends as mother and daughter had climbed off a roller coaster. Their faces were flushed, their hair wild, their eyes alight with the thrill of the ride. Funny, he didn't feel the old anger anymore, just a deep sadness with a bit of an edge. Their marriage had been doomed, of course, from the onset. Jennifer had been miserable married to a cop, who had been overly ambitious and spent long hours away from her. He'd sensed something had been wrong from the get-go, but had thought things would smooth out. He hadn't read the warning signs, until she, tearfully and eight month's pregnant, couldn't keep up the charade and explained that the baby wasn't his.

God in heaven, he'd never known such pain. And when he found out who the son of a bitch was who'd impregnated his wife . . . . no wonder he'd begun to drink. Oh, sure, he'd claimed Kristi, had determined from the moment he'd set eyes on the baby in the hospital that he would raise her as his own, but the seeds of distrust had been planted deep. The marriage had disintegrated to a hollow shell of what it should have been. Bentz had spent long hours at work or at a bar near the precinct in L.A. He'd told himself he was doing the right thing, but now he wasn't so sure. He'd never forgotten his wife's betrayal, never really forgiven her. Not even after her death. Now, however, he could put that rage into perspective, tuck it away. It didn't matter much anymore. Jennifer was dead and Kristi, left without a mother, felt all the more abandoned, all the more rebellious toward him.

But maybe that rebellion would mellow now that they weren't living under the same roof. If they both didn't let their tempers and sharp tongues get the better of them. He walked out of her room, closed the door and headed for the shower. Yeah, he thought, he'd definitely spring for the flowers.

In the meantime he had work to do.

Business was slow at the Third-Eye on the Sunday before Thanksgiving. Olivia waited on a few customers, restocked shelves and dusted some of the artifacts before stringing gold tinsel along the shelves and cupboards housing the stock. Glassy-eyed alligator heads stared at her, candles, virgin wicks unburned stood at attention and mirrors reflected her image as she climbed onto a small step stool, draping the glittery tinsel. New Age prisms sparkled, books collected dust, and voodoo dolls hung suspended from the ceiling along with Christmas ornaments. Religious artifacts were tucked into drawers or cubbyholes of the antique desks, tables, armoires, and sewing machines that served as display cases. "Eclectic" didn't begin to cover the merchandise offered for sale.

At four o'clock Tawilda, back from a cigarette and coffee break, urged Olivia to "take a load off for a few minutes." Tawilda was a reed-thin African-American woman. She wore vibrantly colored saris and slipped matching beads onto the tiny braids clustered in her long hair. With a model's high cheekbones, and a series of bracelets running up one arm, Tawilda was as exotic as some of the merchandise. "I can handle things for a few minutes. Go get yourself some fresh air, girl," she insisted as she swept through a curtain of beads hanging in the doorway to the back rooms. A minute later she returned without her coat and purse. The beads danced again. "Go on. Git. I can handle things here."

Olivia needed a break.

"I'll be back in fifteen."

Tawilda waved an elegant hand. "Knock yerself out. Make it twenty or twenty-five. Ain't nobody shoppin' here today. It's not like I'm gonna be swamped or nothin'."

"If you say so." Olivia grabbed her jacket and purse and headed outside. Across the street was Jackson Square. A spiked wrought-iron fence surrounded the manicured grounds where paths converged at a statue of Andrew Jackson. Olivia wasn't interested in the park. Instead she tightened the cinch of her jacket and walked swiftly to St. Louis Cathedral. Only a few pedestrians were out and a stiff breeze rolling off the Mississippi was colder than usual. Pigeons scattered and a lone trombone player, his case lying open, played something bluesy on the street corner.

The cathedral with its three imposing spires knifing sharply into the darkness was not only a grand, imposing structure but the oldest active cathedral in America, a building that had been rebuilt twice and was, Olivia felt, the center of Catholicism in the Crescent City.

She walked inside, where tall arches and stained glass surrounded the nave. She gazed at the altar and blended in with a handful of tourists who milled just inside the door. A sprinkling of the pious or troubled knelt in the foremost pews, their heads bent as they faced the altar. A tall man in an overcoat brushed past her and their eyes connected for a second.

"Leo?" Olivia called as he hurried by. Was Sarah Restin's missing husband here, in New Orleans? No way. She took a step to follow him, but he was out a side door in a flash.

"Livvie?" she heard faintly.

Olivia froze at the sound of her mother's voice. But that was impossible. Bernadette was in Houston.

A light touch on her sleeve and she nearly catapulted out of her skin. She glanced back to see the woman who had borne her, paler than she remembered, wearing a cape that reached her ankles and spike-heeled boots. Bernadette's hair was tucked beneath a wide-brimmed hat and sunglasses covered her eyes.

Olivia was stunned. She hadn't seen nor heard from her mother since Grannie Gin's funeral.

"What are you doing here?"

"Looking for you," Bernadette replied, slightly out of breath. "I stopped in at the shop and that black girl said you'd just left. I ran to catch up and I was lucky enough to see you walk through the front doors, so I hurried to catch you."

"But why . . . ?"

"Come on, let me buy you a cup of coffee or something."

"Mom, I have to go back to work."

"The other girl said she'd watch the store. Really, Livvie, it's important." It had to be. Otherwise she wouldn't be here. Bernadette inclined her head toward the front doors and Olivia walked into the square with her mother, a woman she barely knew, didn't understand, and wasn't sure she liked. As far as love went, well, that mother-daughter thing was a little nebulous. She felt the chill of the winter wind and it settled deep in her soul. As much as Olivia had wanted and tried for her mother's approval as a child, disavowed it as a teenager, ached for it as a twenty-year-old, she now realized and accepted that Bernadette Dubois Benchet and whatever other names she'd tagged on, didn't have the capacity to give nor, probably, receive unconditional love. It was a concept Bernadette just didn't understand.

They found a café that served coffee and alcohol around the clock. A jazz man was seated in the corner, playing a guitar and harmonica simultaneously, his notes soulful. From the heart. Bernadette took off her hat and hung it, along with her jacket, over the top of the post separating the booths, then slid onto the bench opposite her daughter. In the flickering light from the hurricane lantern on the table, her long dark hair took on a burnished, coppery color. The sunglasses remained.

"How are you, Livvie?"

"Okay, I guess."

"School going well?"

"As well as can be expected. How about you?"

Her mother's smile was faint. "I suppose. I, uh, I know how close you were to your grandmother and I wonder how you've been doing since she's been gone."

"I miss her."

"I know." Bernadette nodded. "Believe it or not, I do, too. She was . . . a character. All that silliness with the tarot cards and mind reading or whatever it was."

A waiter appeared and they ordered café au lait and beignets. "I don't have much time."

Bernadette nodded, rolled her lips over her teeth as if now, when she finally had Olivia's attention, she wasn't quite sure if she should confide in her "What were you doing in the cathedral?"

"Looking around."

"I don't remember you as being particularly religious."

"Maybe I've had a change of heart," Olivia said as the waiter carried a wide tray to their booth. She didn't elaborate as they were served. Only when the waiter had deposited their coffee and a basket of beignets covered in powdered sugar on the table did she ask, "What's on your mind, Bernadette?"

Olivia's mother took in a deep breath. Her fingernails tapped on the tabletop. "I heard from your father." Her voice was a whisper, and tiny lines dared pinch the corners of her mouth.

The sperm donor. Great. Olivia stiffened at the very thought of the man who had sired her. "Oh, yeah? What did he want?" She picked up her cup, took an experimental sip as the jazzman concluded his set, and several people clapped. "Let me guess. Money."

"Well, that, too. There's always that." Bernadette picked up a pastry and tore it in two. "But this time there's more. He wants to see you."

Olivia nearly choked on a swallow. "Give me a break."

"It's true. He called last week sometime."

"I thought he was still locked up," Olivia said bitterly. That her father was a felon and that she hadn't been told still bothered her. She'd found out from a "friend." Connie Earnhardt had only been too happy to let it slip when they were in high school. Grannie Gin and Bernadette had thought it best to let Olivia think Reggie Benchet was in the Armed Forces somewhere on the far corners of the earth instead of in the Mississippi State Penitentiary. Incarcerated for armed robbery, assault with a deadly weapon, and murder.

"He's been out since the first of the year. He called me a few months ago. Jeb found out and there was hell to pay." Her glossy lips turned down at the corners, and in the soft light Olivia noticed that her mother wore more makeup than usual, a thicker coating of base and powder, probably in deference to her age. As beautiful as she was, Bernadette couldn't stop the footsteps of Father Time from marching across her skin and leaving footprints of wrinkles and age spots upon her face.

Picking at her beignet, Bernadette said, "Reggie disappeared again for a while, but now he's back. He's called three times in the last two weeks and he insists he wants to see you. You're all he has left now."

"Forget it." Olivia shook her head, pushed her coffee aside. "He dumped you, me, and Chandra, killed someone, and ended up in prison, for God's sake. He made a mess of his life. I'm not interested. Believe it or not, I've got my own life. There are things I've got to do."

"So that's why you were at St. Louis Cathedral?"

Olivia couldn't confide in her mother. She had as a child and Bernadette's reaction had only made things worse. "Everyone needs a little faith sometimes," she hedged and glanced at her watch. "I really have to go."

"Well, okay . . . but I think you should know that I gave Reggie your number."

"You did *what?*"

"He has the right to know," Bernadette said stubbornly, raising her chin a bit. "He is your father."

"You just wanted him off your back."

Bernadette stiffened, and though Olivia couldn't read the expression in her eyes because of the sunglasses, she expected anger was flaring in those green orbs. "He did his time and paid his debt to society. He has the right—"

"What about mine, Bernadette? What about *my* rights?" she demanded. Then she shut up. This was a no-win argument. Reining in her fury, she changed the subject. "So what's with the dark glasses, Mom? It's twilight, and if you haven't noticed, this restaurant isn't exactly well lit. Why are you wearing shades?"

The corners of her mouth pinching, Bernadette ignored the questions. As if they hadn't been asked. Finally she sighed. "I guess I should have expected this reaction from you. I'd thought, no, hoped that maybe you'd grown up, Livvie. I guess I was wrong."

Way to go, Mom, Olivia thought. She remembered the

way her mother had always argued, forever on the attack. To Bernadette's way of thinking, a best defense was a strong offense. "I don't know why I wasted my time. Well, I told you about Reggie's request. Now it's up to you."

"You have to admit he hasn't been exactly a stellar dad."

"Fine. We both know that. I passed along the message. That's all I needed to do." She stood abruptly and fished in her purse for her wallet.

"I'll get this," Olivia said, but Bernadette was having none of that today. She found a twenty-dollar bill and dropped it onto the table. "There's one other thing, Olivia," she said icily. "You may as well know, I'm leaving Jeb."

She shouldn't have been surprised, as her mother not only had horrid taste in men, but felt compelled to marry them, then divorce when the blush of love subsided. Olivia suspected that Bernadette thought that if she had the right partner she could find a fairy tale romance complete with happy ending, but so far all her princes had turned out to be frogs. Or worse. Ogres. "That's probably a good idea."

"I . . . I hope so." Bernadette was standing now but some of her fire seemed to have been doused.

"Is there a reason?"

"We . . . we don't get along." Her lower lip quivered in a distinctly un-Bernadette-like fashion. "And it's gotten worse. He found out that I lied about how much my inheritance was."

"Why did you keep it from him?" Olivia asked, not wanting to know the answer.

"So I could have something. Something of my own." Bernadette swallowed hard, then tucked her hair into her hat again. As she did, the candlelight shifted and Olivia thought she saw a blemish under the thick layer of powder on Bernadette's cheek. A bluish smudge.

"Mom?" Olivia asked, dread mounting.

Bernadette's head snapped up sharply at the familiarity. It had been years since Olivia had referred to her by anything other than her given name. "What?"

"What's going on?" Olivia stood and focused hard on

the discoloration beneath Bernadette's makeup. A bruise. As if Bernadette had banged her head against something.

Or been hit.

"Take off your glasses."

"No. Not now."

Olivia did it for her. Though Bernadette backed away, Olivia snagged the frames and pulled them from her mother's face. "Oh, God, he hit you," she said angrily. Bernadette's eyes were swollen, the whites reddish, black circles beneath them.

"I'll be all right."

"Are you crazy?" Olivia exploded. " You'll *never* be all right. That son of a bitch should be in jail. It was Jeb who did this, right? That's why you're leaving him."

"I have to go now," Bernadette said. "And you're late for work."

"Screw work!"

Her mother started to walk away, but Olivia grabbed her elbow. From the nearby tables and booths, patrons stared at them, conversation died.

"This is assault, Bernadette. You have to go to the police. You have to report him, make him stop. I know a cop who—"

"I'm not going to the police, Livvie."

"But that bastard—"

"*Shh!* This is my problem. I'll handle it," Bernadette said, slipping the shaded lenses onto the bridge of her broken nose again. "You just worry about your father, okay? Don't cause a scene!" Yanking her sleeve away from Olivia's fingers, she hurried, head down, through the glass door.

"Is everything all right?" a nervous little man with a pencil-thin mustache asked from a nearby table. He was blinking rapidly.

"Fine. It's fine," Olivia said, though she didn't believe a word of it. Nothing was right tonight. Nothing at all.

Chapter Sixteen

The library was nearly empty, only a few students hunched over books on Sunday night. Just the die-hards. Or those without someplace better to go, Olivia thought as she shut the reference book and stretched her spine. She'd closed up the shop at six then driven to the campus, where she'd spent the last three hours studying and trying to forget her visit from her mother, attempting to convince herself that whatever problems Bernadette was having with her current husband, she couldn't help.

Or could she?

Had her mother come not to tell her about Reggie, but to try and mend what seemed impossibly tattered mother-daughter fences? *You didn't even give her a chance*, her mind nagged, guilt storming through her soul. *Catholic upbringing.* Compliments of Grannie Gin. Bernadette certainly didn't have much to do with it.

Pausing at the desk to check out two books on the psychology of sociopaths, she remembered the last time she'd seen her mother. At Grannie Gin's funeral.

It had been a muggy day, the kind when hot air seemed to adhere to her skin. Bernadette had been distant, but that wasn't unusual as she'd sat through the mass. She'd listened to the service, dropped a rose on Grannie's casket, shown up at the house where the few members of the family, distant cousins for the most part, and some friends had gathered, but she'd kept mostly to herself, chain-smoking on the back porch and sipping from a never-finished drink of Jack Daniels. She'd seemed lost in thought, and the few times Olivia had approached her, she'd been subdued, tears slowly tracking from beneath her black veil.

Now, Olivia realized, she'd never taken off her hat or the lacy veil for fear that a bruise might show through.

Again Olivia felt a pang of guilt as she walked, keys clutched in one hand, outside to her truck. The night was cool, winter threatening to grasp hold of the Crescent City. There were only a few students crisscrossing the campus, knots of kids in two- or threesomes hurrying along the walkways. Olivia was the only person walking alone, she realized, and for the first time in her life, it bothered her. Not just because of the cool, dark night and the recent dreams, but because she was unconnected, flying solo when most of the world was coupled up.

Which was ridiculous. She had only to look at her mother, or her friend Sarah, or remember Ted, the man she nearly married, to realize how much better off she was alone. The only two men she'd found remotely interesting in the past couple of years were a world-weary cop and a priest, both, she guessed, who carried a ton of baggage with them. What was wrong with her?

It must be the holidays. Everyone gets a little nuts during the holidays. Isn't that when the most suicides occur?

She turned the collar of her jacket up and heard the sounds of a stereo playing from one open dorm window and laughter from another.

So what if you're alone? And why do you always pick men who are unavailable? Off-limits? Because you don't want to get involved, not really. You know, Livvie, you might just be a candidate for a psychological study ... or the subject of one of those trashy afternoon talk shows. "Women who love men who can't love them because they're already married to their careers."

"Idiot," she muttered as the path cut through a copse of trees. It was darker here and she was alone. All of the other students had disappeared into the buildings on campus. *So what?* She hurried along the path.

Click, click, click.

A noise came from behind her.

Her heart squeezed. *It's nothing. Just your overactive imagination.*

She glanced over her shoulder to the darkened shrubbery flanking the buildings. No one.

Stop it, she told herself. *No reason to be jumpy.*

But she heard the noise again and her heart began to thud. She started to run.

"Hey! Watch out! On your right," a gruff voice yelled.

She leapt to the left, out of the thicket to the parking lot.

From the darkness a bicyclist blew past her in a flash of silver spokes and glossy helmet reflecting in the blue light from the security lamps. *Click, click, click,* the cyclist shifted gears and was swallowed by the night.

So that was it! A sound she'd heard hundreds of times.

You're losing it, Benchet, she thought, relieved as she spied her pickup, the only vehicle in the lot right where she'd parked it. She jogged across the pockmarked asphalt, unlocked the truck, and slid behind the steering wheel. *Get a grip!* She fired the engine and gunned it, toppling the sack of groceries she'd picked up earlier. "Great."

A few minutes later she was on the freeway heading out of the city. She turned on the radio and heard Trish LaBelle's voice giving out advice over the airwaves. Trish had been with WNAB before joining the staff at WSLJ. Her program was in the early evening, about over now, Olivia thought, then there was Gator Brown's light jazz, which led into Dr. Sam's popular late-night advice program. Trish's format was different. She pretaped questions from viewers, then interspersed the questions and answers with music that seemed to fit the mood.

Olivia listened for a few minutes, but as she stared through the windshield, she thought of Bernadette's message that Reggie Benchet wanted to see her.

Why would her father want to connect now, after all these years of no contact? Why? She drove in silence, by rote, maneuvering her Ranger off the freeway. Rain began to fall, the drops flashing in the glare of her headlights. She barely remembered her father; didn't want to start a relationship now. Lost in thought, she drove down the winding country road and stopped only to pick up the mail at the end of the lane. What would she say if Reggie Benchet called her? What was there to say? As she drove on, her truck's headlights flashed against the stark trunks of the giant cypress and oaks surrounding the cabin, and as the truck crossed the small bridge to her grandmother's cottage, she caught her first glimpse of the little house she'd called home all of her growing-up years. A home devoid of a father, and often as not a mother.

But she'd had Grannie. And God, how she missed that little scrap of a woman.

She parked, picked up the strewn groceries, and tossed them into the paper bag with her mail. As she walked to the front door, she could hear Hairy S barking his fool head off. Tonight she didn't care that he was acting like an idiot as she unlocked the door and made her way inside.

She was still caught up in the events of the past couple of days. Rapid-fire thoughts burst through her mind. Images of the blackened shell of a house where the girl was killed, of a priest with a long sword, of Father James stretching upward on the ladder, of her mother's bruised face. And then there was the kiss she'd shared with Bentz in this very house, a long, passionate kiss that had touched her heart as well as curled her toes.

Dear God, she was a hopeless romantic. He was a cop, for crying out loud, a homicide dick who looked at her as some kind of freak.

She set the mail on the dining room table, then greeted Hairy S properly, petting him and scratching him behind his ears as he twirled in frantic little circles at her feet. "Need to go out?" she asked as she hung up her coat. The dog yipped. She opened the French doors off the small kitchen. Barking madly, he raced outside, across the porch and into the shadows, hot on the trail of a squirrel or possum or heaven-only-knew-what-other swamp critter. "Avoid the gators, would you?" she called after him, then winked at Chia. "He's an idiot, isn't he?"

The parrot squawked and hopped from one perch to the next in her tall cage. Her eyes dilated and retracted above the bright band of red and gold over her beak.

"We women, we're a whole lot smarter," Olivia said as Chia made a cooing sound, ruffled her feathers, and showed off her black tongue. "A whole lot."

Yeah, right. Then why the confusion over the men in your life?

Rather than listen to the nag in her head, Olivia played her telephone messages. The first was from the contractor she'd contacted about the alarm, promising to be out and give her a bid in an installation the Monday after Thanksgiving. The second was Sarah again.

"Olivia. When you have a minute, would you give me a call? I, um, I still haven't heard from Leo and I know it's only been a couple of days since I talked to you . . . He's probably okay, but damn it, I found a woman's earring in my bed . . . can you believe that, in *my* bed? Crap. What a jerk! You're right about him . . . I know it, I know it, I know it." Olivia's heart sank. She heard the pain in Sarah's voice. The humiliation. "Well, um, just call me when you get a chance, okay?"

After Sarah's call, there was a long hesitation on the phone, as if whoever had called didn't know what to say, but then he eventually hung up. It was odd, she thought and replayed it again . . . was there music in the background . . . a song she recognized? Yeah . . . something from her past, a Springsteen song . . . then she recognized it. *Tunnel of Love.* Ted's favorite.

"Damn," she said, her skin crawling. Could her ex-fiancé have really tracked her down? She thought of him, how angry he'd been with her, how he'd followed her to Tucson only to finally give up. After she'd threatened him with a restraining order.

She ignored the call and went on to the next, a message from Dr. Leeds's secretary asking for a date when she could meet with him again. The last call was from Detective Bentz asking her to call him at the station in the morning. His message was all business, but she smiled at the sound of his voice and pushed aside the eerie feeling that the earlier unspoken message had left. "Silly girl," she told herself and called the station only to be told that he was gone. She considered trying to locate him at home or his cell, then thought better of it. She glanced at the clock. It was too late to catch anyone at the University, so decided to phone the psychology department in the morning, and rang up Sarah in Tucson, only to hear Sarah's answering machine pick up. Olivia left a message, hung up the cordless phone, and in the porch light, saw the dog jumping crazily at the back door. "I'm coming," she said, reaching for the door handle and letting him inside. "Hungry?"

Hairy S danced at his dish. She poured some fresh kiblets into his bowl, then unpacked her groceries and threw a frozen dinner into the microwave.

"Turkey à l' orange," she said to the dog. "Only six grams of fat." Hairy, nose buried deep in his dish, made no indication he'd heard a word. What a day, she thought, as the microwave dinged and she gingerly took off the plastic wrap as orange-smelling steam wafted up. A can of diet cola and her meal was complete. She glanced at the photo of herself and Grannie Gin, the one she'd pointed out to Bentz. She'd been so carefree then, hadn't really needed a father. She hadn't yet been to school, hadn't suffered the embarrassment of not knowing him, hadn't borne the indignity of learning, compliments of Connie Earnhardt, that he was in prison in Mississippi.

Olivia had only vague images of the sperm donor and those, she was certain, were due to the few old snapshots she'd seen of a man in a sailor's uniform, a handsome, athletic man who had swept Bernadette Dubois off her seventeen-year-old feet. It had been a whirlwind romance and the details were sketchy. Virginia Dubois hadn't approved and Olivia, barely in high school, had caught snatches of conversation she wasn't supposed to hear. While lingering at the foot of the stairs, her ears straining, her fingers curled over the railing, she'd listened over the thudding of her heart.

"He left you, don't you remember that?" Grannie Gin had demanded while frying bacon. The hickory-smoked scent wafted through the dining room as the strips sizzled noisily in the pan. "And you were pregnant."

"He didn't know . . ." Bernadette had protested, sobbing. "I didn't tell him."

"And that was a good thing. The truth came out early enough. I said it then and I'll say it now, Reginald Benchet is no-count and never will be." Grannie Gin had sighed heavily. "You've got one child left, Bernadette," Grannie had said and added a handful of onions into the hot grease. Though Olivia couldn't see what was happening, she smelled the onions, had witnessed the ritual dozens of times. The slices hit the pan with a grease-splattering hiss. "You'd best tend to Livvie. Forget Reggie. He was bad from the day he was born. Branded by the devil, I tell ya. I knew his mother and his grandmother. Both loose women with the morals of alley cats and his daddy . . . pure evil."

"You don't know anything of the sort," Bernadette had argued, then blew her nose.

"I do. I've seen what that man can do."

"How . . . oh, for the love of God, don't tell me you had one of your visions about him." There was a break in the conversation when all Olivia had heard was the sputter of the grease cooking and a woodpecker tapping on some part of the house. She'd bit her lower lip and watched the lace curtains in the dining room flutter with a breeze. "That's it, isn't it?" Bernadette had accused. "You think you've seen something when really you've just dreamt it up. That's crazy talk and we both know it. And it's bad for Livvie. You're filling her head with all this nonsense and now she's started mumbling about seein' things . . . like she saw her sister die *before* Chandra drowned. That's your fault, you know."

"The child might have the gift."

"The gift, the gift, forget the damned gift. It doesn't exist and I'm sick to death of hearing about it. And let's face it. Livvie claimed she'd seen Chandra die because she killed her."

"Hush! That's nonsense."

"It is not. They were fighting, weren't they? Livvie was older. Bigger. She pushed Chandra back in the wading pool and . . . and . . . my baby drowned. Right out there," she'd said, her voice elevating an octave. Olivia, tears filling her eyes, had known her mother was pointing a long, accusing finger past the back porch to the yard. Even a few years later, the scene was as fresh as it had been on the day when the "accident" had happened and she could still see Chandra's face beneath the water. Grass and dead yellow jackets and crickets had floated on the surface and Chandra's wide blue eyes stared upward past the scum. She'd fallen into the pool, hitting her head and Olivia hadn't been able to save her.

"Enough!" Grannie said harshly. "It was an accident. You remember that."

"And you blame me. Because I was asleep. God, Mama, don't you think I know that you've blamed me? I see it every time I look into your eyes."

"You weren't just asleep. You were passed out. Olivia tried to wake you . . . Oh, well . . . what's the use? It's over and done. Just don't blame Livvie, whatever you do. And if she claims she has the sight, then I believe her."

"She just says it to please you. It's crazy talk and I don't

want her to hear any more about it, do you hear me?''
Bernadette insisted. ''Do you know how awful it was growing up being called the daughter of the crazy woman? Do
you? The kid whose mother could tell the future for a lousy
two bucks? People think you're a lunatic, and I don't want
my daughter exposed to it. You quit fillin' her head with
all these foolish notions, y'hear.''

''Then you start actin' like a mother. Take care of her.
Quit runnin' around with every man who looks your way.''

''I'm not gonna listen to any more of this.''

''And keep your pants up and your legs crossed.''

''Mama!''

There was a pause. Olivia's fingers had ached from clutching the banister so hard. ''Just protect Olivia,'' Grannie had
said as the scrape of her cooking fork sounded against the
cast-iron pan. ''Keep her away from Reggie. Don't let him
come 'round here.''

''He won't. We're divorced.''

''And you're engaged to another man; you'd best not
forget it.'' Olivia imagined her grandmother pointing the
blackened tines of her bone-handled fork at her daughter.
''I'll do what I think is best for Livvie. Until you prove that
you're a decent mother.''

Silently swiping at her tears with the back of her hand,
Olivia had crept up the stairs and buried herself deep in the
covers of her bed.

She'd never seen her father after that. Nor much of Bernadette after she'd remarried.

So why the visit today, she wondered now.

After cleaning the few dishes, she whistled to Hairy S
and headed up the stairs to the second bedroom, the one
she'd slept in growing up. The single bed with its saggy
mattress was still in place, tucked under the sloped ceiling,
and the fold-out couch her mother used when she stayed
was on the opposite side of the room. A bureau with a round
mirror stood between the hallway door and the closet and
a desk was pushed beneath the single window near a bookcase. It was the desk she'd used growing up, and with the

addition of a file cabinet, it now was home to her laptop computer and printer.

She sat at the computer and intended to study; she had two classes in the morning, the last until after Thanksgiving, but as she pulled one of her textbooks from the small bookcase, she felt a chill, deep in the marrow of her bones, the same horrid coldness she'd experienced the night the girl had died. And the other night.

Oh, God, was he doing it again? So soon? She swallowed back her fear and glanced out the window to the dark night. A tiny sliver of moon, visible through the leafless branches of the trees, hung low in the sky. Maybe she was mistaken . . . she didn't actually "see" anything, no, this was just a feeling, a dark sensation that crawled across her skin. Movement. That was it. She felt him. He was moving.

And hunting again.

The darkness closed in on him and like a creature of the night, his senses became sharper. Keener. The Chosen One heard his own heartbeat, smelled the scents of perfume and stale smoke lingering in the damp air, felt the sharp pang of blood lust coursing through his veins.

Find her. Take her . . . it's time.

Running on silent footsteps he loped across the wet grass of the campus and heard the strains of jazz emanating from an open window in one of the dorms. Knots of students tarried together and the sweet smell of marijuana settled in the dark alleys. He rounded a corner to a more secluded part of the campus, a back alley that was sometimes used by students rushing into the city.

He felt inside his pocket, assured himself that his weapon was at his fingertips and a smile slid over his mouth. A stun gun. Silent. Quick. But not deadly. So perfect for abduction. He knew she should be coming this way. Had overheard her conversation in class.

But the killing couldn't be here . . . no . . . He needed privacy, time to create the ritual. His mouth went dry at the thought and his crotch tightened, a hard-on swelling even as he ran. Just the thought of it . . . watching her beg for mercy, pleading with him when he knew that her fate was sealed.

He saw her in the distance.

Alone.

Head bent against the rain and wind.

His fingers surrounded his little weapon as he crept through the shadows, waiting for the perfect moment. He licked his lips and reminded himself to be patient. He couldn't make a mistake. Not tonight.

Not ever.

After all, he had a pact with God.

She looked up as he approached. Smiled in recognition. Started to speak as he pulled the gun from his pocket and shot. She gasped. Her purse dropped to the ground. He grabbed it and caught her before she fell. Her hood slid off and her black hair framed her ghost-white face. "What—?" she whispered hoarsely. "No–" She could barely catch her breath.

He grinned as he swept her easily into his arms and carried her to his older car. "Be quiet, Catherine," he whispered, "or I'll have to punish you again."

"No—I'm not—"

He set her down and gave her another long, hard jolt. She cried out, but he picked her up again. "I mean it. Behave." She was whimpering now. Scared. Would probably piss all over his trunk.

He opened the latch and the lid sprang open. She was fighting him with what little strength she had and it only served to make him harder. He thought that just this once he could allow himself the pleasure of her, but knew that God would disapprove.

He had to remember his mission.

"Don't," she cried and he zapped her one final time, lusting after her as her body convulsed, showing off her white neck. She would make the perfect sacrifice. He slammed down the lid of the trunk.

God would be pleased.

"Hey, man, don't you ever go home?" Montoya asked, slipping his arms through the sleeves of his black leather jacket as he passed by Bentz's office. "It's Sunday night."

"Don't you?" Rick leaned back in his desk chair and it creaked in protest. He had the window cracked open. The sounds of the city, horns blaring, voices filtering skyward and a mournful tune from a saxophone slipped inside.

Montoya flashed his knock-'em-dead smile and strolled into the room. He set a hip on the corner of Rick's desk. "Not unless I have to. I'm a player."

"You'd like to think so."

"Hey, I *know* it."

Cocky son of a bitch. Make that young, cocky son of a bitch. He'd learn. Montoya was a good cop, but he was still green enough to think that he could change the world, that what he did mattered, that justice would always be served. He was clever enough, downright smart. The problem was Montoya still had more balls than brains. "If you say so. I thought you had a steady these days."

"I do," Montoya said with a grin. "But that doesn't mean I can't look, does it?" He glanced at his watch. "Why don't you call it a night? I'll buy you a beer. Even the alcohol free shit, though I don't know why you bother."

"And make you keep the ladies waiting?" Bentz arched a knowing eyebrow. "I'll take a rain check."

Montoya clucked his tongue as he headed for the stairs. "You're missin' out," he called over his shoulder as he disappeared.

"So be it." Rick glanced at the computer screen glowing on his desk. He had several cases he was working on, one where a battered woman had grabbed her husband's hunting rifle and opened up on him rather than subject herself to another beating and another arson case where one of the owners died in the blaze. Then there was the knifing, a fight between gang members that left one dead, the other barely hanging on.

But Bentz had put those cases out of his mind for the moment. Because as he'd skimmed the evidence report on the Jane Doe in the fire one more time, something had clicked. A sharp little spark in his brain. He remembered what it was that had been nagging at him.

The saint's medals.

This wasn't the first homicide scene where a chain with a medal had been left. There had been two others that he remembered, perhaps more that he didn't yet know about. He typed in a case file on his keyboard and within seconds crime scene photos of the recent victim flickered on the monitor. His jaw tightened as he stared at the nude body of a woman not much older than his own daughter. The victim had been found in her apartment in the Garden District. Her date of death July twenty-second. Her name had been Catherine Adams, if you went by the DMV or Social Security Administration, but she'd also been known as Cassie Alexa or Princess Alexandra. It all depended if you knew her as a pretty, part-time student at Tulane, or a sexy exotic dancer down on Bourbon Street, or as a hooker. No matter what the name, she'd been murdered. Strangled. And posed. Lying facedown on an area rug, her arms stretched outward, her head placed near a wall that was decorated with a picture of Christ, her toes pointed to an opposing wall where a portrait of Martin Luther King hung. Her head had been shaved, a skein of her own hair wound through her fingers, her mocha-colored naked body reeking of patchouli.

At the top of his list of suspects was Marc Duvall, her boyfriend/pimp who'd been known to knock her around and blacken her eyes upon occasion. He'd skipped town and probably the country. Just disappeared into thin air. Or was dead himself.

The other case was even more sketchy. Another Jane Doe. Her body burned beyond recognition and left at the statue

of Joan of Arc in the Quarter. So far no one had been able
to identify the charred remains found on the last day of May.
He flipped the images on the screen, and as hardened as he
was, the sight of the blackened, disfigured body laid at the
feet of the magnificent statue of St. Joan astride her horse
bothered him.

He wouldn't have thought that the two were connected
except for one single piece of evidence linking them: the
small chain with a saint's medal dangling from it. Left at
the scene.

Three dead women.

All killed differently.

But all left with a saint's medal near their bodies.

A coincidence?

Bentz didn't think so. He hadn't linked the two murders
this summer. They hadn't matched the signature of the
Rosary Killer and there wasn't much that connected them
. . . He hadn't thought about the medals because he'd thought
they were personal items; they didn't match. But he'd blown
it. The link had been there all the time. And now there was
a third. Much as it sickened him, he was certain a serial
killer was stalking the streets of New Orleans again.

The press would eat it up, but the public had to be warned
and the FBI notified, its computer records searched for other
murders, not just localized in the New Orleans area, that
were similar.

He knew the question that would be on everyone's mind.

Was the Rosary Killer resurrected?

Or was the city being stalked by a whole new sicko? One
connected in some strange way to Olivia Benchet?

Chapter Seventeen

The evidence report and Medical Examiner's report were waiting on Bentz's desk Monday morning. Sipping from a cup of coffee hot enough to scald his lips, he sifted through the pages as carefully as the crime scene team had combed the scene. What he read didn't surprise him. Basically, after he sorted through the medical terms, he concluded that the victim had died because someone had tried to hack her head off. The ME had decided, because of the way the bone had been cut, that there had been more than one blow to the back of the neck with some kind of long-bladed knife, machete, or sword.

Just like Olivia Benchet had maintained. Which, he supposed, squinting, shouldn't surprise him.

What kind of monster was on the loose? He'd seen violence in his days with the LAPD, even more so here just this past summer. The Rosary Killer had his own special brand of cruelty and he certainly had ties to the Catholic Church . . . but he was dead. Bentz had taken care of that himself.

Or so he'd thought.

The body had never been recovered from the swamp where he'd been shot. Maybe the bastard had resurrected himself somehow.

"Son of a bitch." The thought of "Father John," as he'd called himself, resurrecting himself wasn't pretty. But what was happening here wasn't "Father John's" MO. This was different.

And what about Olivia's far-fetched story of a woman entombed, then beheaded? Another nightmare? He didn't think so. He'd even copied the page of notes Olivia had given him and along with people within the department had, against rules, shown the weird notations to a friend of his who'd once worked for the CIA and who loved codes, puzzles, cryptograms, crossword puzzles, any word game imaginable. Bud Dell was as likely as anyone to crack it although guys in the force were working on it as well.

So far, Bud and the others had come up with nothing.

The phone rang. He answered on the second ring. "Detective Bentz."

"It's Olivia," she said and he couldn't help but smile. "You called last night."

"Yeah. Just checkin' on you. Everything okay?" Leaning back in his chair, he stretched the phone cord taut. "No more visions?"

"Not last night."

"Good."

"I was afraid you'd found another victim."

"No," he said and conjured up Olivia's face.

"Good. So you were just checking up on me?"

"You've been pretty spooked lately. And yeah, I just wanted to see that you were all right."

"Oh . . ." She hesitated. "Thanks."

"You call if there's anything, *any*thing that makes you feel uncomfortable, okay?"

"I will," she promised, still obviously taken aback by his concern, then recovering, managed a quick "Take care," and rang off. Bentz looked at the receiver in his hand. What the hell was going on with him? He'd called her yesterday because he'd felt compelled to talk to her, to make certain she was all right. He didn't like her living alone in the middle of the damned bayou with only that silly excuse of a dog for protection. She was seeing some very weird shit and he was afraid that somehow, some way her life might be in danger.

Maybe Kristi was right. Maybe he was just another paranoid cop, but he couldn't shake the feeling that Olivia, because of her connection with the killer, was in the crosshairs of peril.

And what the devil was that connection, he wondered for the dozenth time as the phones rang in the outer office. Cops, suspects, and witnesses talked while keyboards clicked as information was entered into computers. How did Olivia know the killer—she had to know him, didn't she? He scratched his chin thoughtfully. She'd sworn another person was being hunted, but hadn't seen another killing. But there were clues—the damned martini glass sign in the bar still nagged at him. How did it all piece together?

Maybe it didn't. Maybe his sudden faith in her visions wasn't founded. Oh, hell, what did he know? This case was getting to him. The phone call to Olivia Bentz was proof enough of that. It had been above and beyond the call of duty and certainly out of the normal set of rules he'd established for himself.

Hell, he was getting personally involved with her and that was sure to be a mistake.

He read through the evidence report again and stopped midway down the page where a chain was listed, a small chain, not the large one used to tether the victim, but a tiny linkage with a medal swinging from it. The saint's medal. The lab had worked on it and determined that it was of St. Cecilia. It had been left at the scene, charred and swinging from the showerhead, just as Olivia had said it had been. Cecilia. As in the woman's name, according to Olivia Benchet.

He double-checked. Sure enough, the saint's medal found

on the victim near the statue was of St. Joan of Arc, that made sense, but the one found with Cathy Adams in the Garden District was of St. Mary Magdalene. Different. What was that all about? He also noted something he'd missed before: that each woman seemed to have one spot on their heads shaved. He hadn't made the connection as Cathy Adam's entire head had been shaved, but now, in reexamining the ME's report, it seemed odd that both women had lost nearly a square inch of their hair before their bodies had been burned. Either the murderer had done it himself, taking a trophy, or they both belonged to some weird cult, which was unlikely.

Something niggled at the back of Bentz's mind, something important, though he couldn't quite retrieve it. It had to do with the rosary killings . . . what the devil was it?

The phone rang and he lost the thought, caught up in a conversation with an assistant D.A. about a knifing down by Canal, not far from the casino. What had happened to Cecilia would have to wait.

Kristi dropped her backpack onto the floor. She'd already gone to her early-morning swim—earlier than usual—and she needed the next half-hour to get ready to see Brian again in Zaroster's class, then she had to study. She had a test in Psych tomorrow, and a paper due in English, no doubt a quiz in bonehead math and a paper due in Philosophy all before she left for Thanksgiving.

And . . . more importantly . . . she was supposed to meet Brian again. He'd been very adamant that they spend Sunday studying as he wanted to see her tonight before she left for home.

She couldn't believe how they'd clicked the other night— well, after she'd gotten over being pissed and beaten him royally at darts. She wondered if he'd let her win and she should've insisted he be her slave or something for the payoff. Instead she'd settled for an expensive dinner and told him that he still owed her . . . At that point he'd suggested "double or nothing" and she'd leapt at the chance to best him. That was the problem with her—the athlete within loved to compete. Besides . . . double or nothing with no rules, that sounded pretty interesting . . . even dangerous.

He was different from any of the boys she'd dated. Lots more mature, deep, even pensive. They'd spent most of Saturday night together, talking, drinking, and making out. She'd found out that he'd grown up somewhere around Chicago, had gotten his undergraduate degree at Notre Dame, and had come to All Saints for graduate work. He was a complex man, not a simple boy whose only aspiration was to get married, have some kids, preferably boys who could play football, and someday own his father's roofing business.

She'd outgrown Jay; that much was obvious.

But she doubted she'd ever outgrow Brian. He was so . . . mature . . . so . . . experienced. She tingled at the thought of how he'd kissed, like it would be the last one he'd ever experience.

Kristi smiled at the thought as she pulled off her T-shirt and caught a glimpse of her torso, clad only in a black bra, in her mirror. *Not too bad,* she thought, swinging around for a full view.

She'd like to have bigger boobs, of course, but then she wasn't into plastic surgery or hormones, so for now, she'd content herself that she had a tiny waist and a flat abdomen. Though her shoulders were wider than most girls', probably from years of swimming, and she weighed a few pounds more than the average in her sorority house, she looked pretty damned good. All muscle. No fat. Athletic. Besides, she thought, the whole waif-like anorexic look was overrated and the way some of the girls attained it through cigarettes, uppers, and cocaine wasn't for her. Not that she didn't like a drink or two and had been known to smoke weed once and again, but she just didn't want to get into that whole drug scene. She'd experimented enough in high school and given her dad a good bunch of his gray hair while trying ecstasy and hallucinogenic mushrooms.

Well, what could you expect, when you're a teenager and you find out that your dad's not really your dad and your mom . . . *Don't even go there. It's over and done. Rick's a good guy. A real good guy and you know it now. He is your dad. He's always been there for you. Always. Even though he knew you weren't really his kid.* Frowning at the path of her thoughts, she concentrated on her image in the glass and liked what she saw. She tossed her head, letting a sweep of red-brown hair fall over one side of her face as she'd seen models do in the shampoo commercials on TV.

Again she smiled. Her hair was long, layered and a thick burnished mahogany. She'd sprung for highlights this fall so the strands gleamed red in the sunlight and Brian loved it. He'd buried his face in it several times when they were making out Saturday night and he'd told her how beautiful it was. She'd let him take off her top and his fingers had caressed her breasts in a way that made her hot when she thought of it. Feather-light touches that created all sorts of conflicting emotions . . . She *wanted* to do it with him, but she hadn't. Knew better.

Good old Catholic upbringing, she thought. Though her father had been lax about taking her to church, when her mother had been alive, Kristi had been enrolled in parochial schools and never missed mass or Catechism or youth instruction. And yet Jennifer herself hadn't adhered to the sacrament of marriage, now, had she?

At least not according to Rick Bentz, who had decided, when she'd graduated from high school that she needed to know the truth. So he'd laid it out to her, explained why the marriage had gone sour, that her mother had been involved with the man who had sired her. Not just once. Oh, no. Jennifer had slept with the guy way back when Kristi had been conceived, broken off the affair, then started up again, nearly fifteen years later, just prior to her death.

Kristi hadn't wanted to believe that Rick Bentz wasn't her father. But once she'd seen the evidence herself, in the form of a letter Jennifer had written two days before driving off the road and into a tree, she'd been convinced. The letter had been addressed to Kristi, but Bentz had decided his daughter should be spared the truth until she graduated from high school, so he'd hidden it away for over four years.

Bastard, she thought, angry all over again.

Swiping tears from her eyes, she remembered every word on the single yellowed piece of paper. The lines that burned in her mind still brought tears to her eyes.

I'm so sorry, honey. Believe me when I tell you that I love you more than life itself. But I've been involved with the man who is really your father again and I'm afraid it's going to ruin my marriage and break Rick's heart. . . .

"Thanks, Mom. Thanks a lot." Kristi sniffed loudly. Wouldn't break down. She was convinced Jennifer had committed suicide. She'd loaded herself up on pills and driven off the road two days after her husband had caught her in bed with another man. In Kristi's estimation Jennifer had taken the coward's way out by writing the damned letter and getting behind the wheel.

Ever since she'd found out the truth at the beginning of last summer, Kristi had been mad as hell at her mother, at the man who had raised her and at the goddamned son of a bitch who couldn't keep his hands off of Jennifer, the man who had spawned her. Pathetic, that's what it was. Pathetic.

Kristi didn't want to think about it right now. Well, really, not ever. She'd taken enough psychology already this term to recognize that she was in denial big time, but she didn't care. She'd rather concentrate on Saturday night and Brian. After a bad start, the date had been wonderful, she thought.

Yanking a sweater over her head she wished she wasn't going home to New Orleans for Thanksgiving. Not that she wouldn't have an okay time with her dad, but their relationship had been rocky for years and now she had someone new. A real boyfriend. An older man.

Wouldn't her overprotective father flip when he found out? She pulled her hair through the neck hole of the sweater and couldn't help but grin. She still liked jerking the old man's chain.

So what would happen if when he came to pick her up,

she'd have him meet Brian and then blithely announce she'd invited Brian for Thanksgiving? He didn't seem to have anywhere to go; at least she thought he didn't. But then she didn't know much about him other than he taught at the college and was working on his doctorate.

So dinner tonight with Brian, and later . . . who knew? A naughty smile caressed her lips. She couldn't wait!

"Check this out," Montoya said as he swaggered into Bentz's office just before ten. His Cheshire cat smile was stretched wide, his earring winked in the fluorescent lights suspended overhead, and his black leather jacket gleamed as if it were brand new.

"What?" Bentz was on his second cup of coffee waiting for a callback from the Covington Police. A secretary for an insurance company was missing. Her boyfriend, Dustin Townsend, had called earlier; no one had seen Stephanie Jane Keller since Friday afternoon when he'd driven her into town. According the Townsend, Stephanie was five foot six inches, about a hundred and twenty pounds, and played tennis regularly. Blue eyes, blond hair. He'd sounded upset on the telephone, frantic with worry, and reluctantly given Bentz the name of Stephanie's dentist. The department had formally asked for the dental records, which had been faxed and were now being matched. Townsend himself was on his way, agreeing to bring pictures of Stephanie with him.

"I've got some interesting information on Ms. Benchet," Montoya announced, swinging a leg over the corner of Bentz's desk. The muscles in the back of Rick's neck tightened. "Well, really on her old lady. Bernadette Dubois . . . She's been married five times and that doesn't count a misstep or two with engagements that didn't pan out. Not too shabby for a woman who's barely in her fifties. There was Olivia's father, Reggie Benchet."

"The felon."

"Ex-con."

"Still a felon in my book," Bentz said.

"Yep. Assault. Resisting arrest. Murder two. A few other things. A helluva guy. Anyway, Bernadette had the good sense to divorce him after a couple of kids. But he's just the first. She has a string of husbands. She left every one of them. And she's working on her most recent. According to court records, she's already filed papers against the current Mr. Bernadette, a guy by the name of Jeb Martin. He works for an oil company in Houston. They got married about four years ago and apparently wedded bliss didn't last long. Martin's got a nasty temper when he drinks—been arrested several times."

"Sounds like a pattern." Bentz knew his partner was leading up to something.

"Well, number one and number five are alike and the third husband, Bill Yates, the trucker, I think he was a rebound thing. Only lasted eighteen months. Number four was Scott Lafever, a musician who didn't live through his last OD. But here's the kicker. Guess who was the second husband?"

"The one right after Reggie Benchet?"

Montoya nodded, then dropped the bomb. "Our good friend, Oscar Cantrell."

"The owner of Benchmark Realty?" Bentz asked.

"One and the same." Montoya, obviously pleased with himself, stroked his goatee. "I don't know about you, but I think there might be a connection there, seeing as Oscar's management company rented the house where one of our Jane Does was killed."

"Maybe we should have a talk with him."

"I tried. Already called his house—no answer, just a machine—then I rang up Benchmark a few minutes ago and talked to Cantrell's secretary, I think you met her."

"Marlene Something-or-Other."

"Anderson."

"Right. The talker," Bentz said, remembering the chatty brunette with the wild glasses.

"That's the one. She claims he's still away on business

and will be out until after the holiday weekend. Oscar Cantrell isn't due back into town until next Monday.''

"She can't get hold of him?'' Bentz asked, disbelieving. "Doesn't the guy have a cell phone?''

"You'd think. I tried to sweet talk her and, when that didn't work, strong arm her a little, but she wasn't having anything to do with it. Got snippy.''

"Snippy? With you?'' Bentz grinned. That he would like to have seen. Most women melted like butter in the hot sun when Reuben Diego Montoya turned on the charm. Maybe there was more to gossiping Marlene Anderson than met the eye.

"Hard to believe, but it happens,'' Montoya grumbled.

"So the connection is that one of Olivia Benchet's short-term stepfathers owns the house where the murder took place?''

"Got anything better?''

Bentz's stomach burned fire. He reached into the top drawer of his desk, found a bottle of Tums, and shook out the last two tablets. He plopped them into his mouth and chewed. "Don't know. I'm waiting for a possible ID on the Jane Doe.'' He gave Montoya a quick rundown on Stephanie Jane Keller. ". . . the boyfriend should be here soon. With pictures.''

"In case we have to reconstruct?''

Bentz nodded, but he had something different in mind. A test. For Olivia. He'd get snapshots of a dozen women in the department, add in Stephanie's photo, and see if Olivia could pick her out of the photographic "lineup.'' Though he was beginning to buy into her claims of ESP, the pragmatic, real-cop side of him was still having trouble accepting it.

"You think the boyfriend could be involved?'' Montoya asked.

"Always a possibility. If the Jane Doe does turn out to be Stephanie Keller, then we'll check out the boyfriend, her family, other friends and acquaintances and see if other than being killed by the same murderer, she has any connection to Cathy Adams.''

''And Olivia Benchet.''

''I'll check that out, too.''

''Thought you might.'' Montoya's dark eyes narrowed. ''You know, Bentz, if you weren't such a hard-ass, I'd think you might have a thing for our resident kook.''

''I swore off women long ago.''

''Oh, right.'' Montoya nodded. ''Because of your ex-wife. Man, that lady must've done a number on you. What was it? Did you catch her doing the wild thing with someone else?''

Bentz didn't reply.

''That's it, isn't it? Who was it?''

''It's ancient history. What happened occurred a long time ago,'' Bentz said, unwilling to dredge up all the muck again. It had been over eighteen years and when he stopped to think about it, how Jennifer had admitted that the child she was carrying wasn't his, how it had hurt like hell, he figured she'd only told him because he might find out if the baby needed blood work. There had been problems with the pregnancy and Jennifer, always one to overplay everything, had thought the baby might need surgery and her blood would be typed and it might not match Rick's. So she'd told him the truth and vowed she'd broken off the affair, that she loved Rick, that she wanted to make the marriage work, that the man who had sired the baby didn't want the child, couldn't support it, and the affair was over almost before it had begun. Bentz had been blindsided and nearly poured himself into a bottle, but he'd stuck around and never once regretted claiming Kristi as his own. ''Look,'' he said to Montoya. ''What happened to me doesn't matter anymore.''

Montoya snorted. ''Then why haven't you hooked up with another woman?''

''Maybe I've been too busy.''

''With what? Work? Christ, Bentz, we all need a social life.''

''Do we?'' He leaned back in his chair until it creaked.

"Yeah, and don't give me any garbage about you bein' too old. I know better."

"You don't know Jack shit."

Montoya clucked his tongue. "You need to get out more, Bentz. You really do."

"You get out enough for both of us."

"Not anymore. *Nooooo,*" he said with a wink. "I told you. I'm a one-woman man these days."

"Oh, right."

"It's true. I've met a fine woman. A *fiiiiinnnnne* woman."

"You meet one every week."

"This one's different."

"Until next week."

Montoya scoffed, but didn't continue the argument. "Okay, so now that you think we've got a serial killer in our fair city, what about the media?"

"Jaskiel's working with the public information officer. There should be a press release and conference later today."

"You gonna be there?"

"Not unless I'm asked. Jaskiel will take care of it. She'll make sure the public gets the right information." They didn't have to discuss the fact that, though the public would be warned about the killer and some of the information would be released, the police department would keep back important pieces that only they and the killer would know in order to catch the right culprit and flush out any mental cases who might claim to be the killer just for some sort of attention. Leaning forward, Bentz tapped his pencil on the desk. "So what's new with the video of the fire?"

"The lab's still working on it. I've seen pictures. So far nothing. But the guy who took the film, he wants to make sure he has the rights to it. You know, if it becomes valuable to the case."

"And what? *The Enquirer* wants a copy?"

"I think that's his major concern, yeah. There's been talk on the street about a serial killer and Henderson is all of a sudden thinking he might have something as valuable as the Zapruder film of the Kennedy assassination."

"Great. Didn't he sign a release?"

"Sure, but now he's hired himself an attorney. After the press release, I'm sure he's gonna make a lot more noise."

"Let him," Bentz grumbled just as the phone shrilled. Bentz picked up before the second ring. "Bentz."

A secretary informed him that Dustin Townsend wanted to see him. "Send him up," Bentz said and within five minutes a distraught man appeared in his doorway. Townsend was somewhere around thirty. Prematurely balding, he carried the start of a beer belly. His eyes were bloodshot and he appeared nervous. "Can you tell me anything?" he asked after quick introductions were disposed of.

"Not until we've done some tests and comparisons. They're checking the dental records now."

"Oh, God, it can't be Stephanie," he said, his face ashen, his chin not quite steady. "I mean, I saw her Friday afternoon. No . . . there's got to be some other explanation."

"I hope so," Bentz said and didn't glance at Montoya. How many times had they heard the same fears expressed by disbelieving family members? Unfortunately every victim had family and friends, lovers, parents or children, someone who cared. "Is that the picture of Stephanie?" he asked, indicating a small sack clutched in Townsend's fingers.

"Oh . . . yeah. I, um, I brought a few." He offered Bentz the bag. Complete with a full set of fingerprints. Should they need them.

"Thanks. Why don't you show me what's inside?"

Townsend was more than willing to fan out three pictures of a gorgeous, vibrant-looking girl. One where she was standing in hip-hugging jeans and a tank top; another where she was dressed in shorts and a sleeveless top, her hair scraped back in a knot on her head, her face speckled with sweat, a tennis racket held loosely over her shoulder; and a third that was a glamour-type head shot with Stephanie looking over her shoulder, her eyes slumberous and sexy.

"She's pretty."

Townsend nodded and sat on the chair in Bentz's office, his hands clasped between his knees, his voice low as he answered enough questions to convince Bentz that he was either innocent or a damned good liar. He left half an hour later and Montoya shook his head and reached into his pocket for his pack of cigarettes. "I don't think he's our guy."

"Me, neither. But check his alibi. He said he dropped her off at a car dealership where she was having some work done on her Taurus, then she was going to her night class at Loyola and she planned to spend the weekend with friends. The friends said she didn't show up and they eventually tracked down Townsend. He called the police in Covington yesterday and that's where we are. Her car's in the shop, just as he said. The owner remembers her. That's all we know. I'm getting a list of the other people enrolled in the class from the University and I've already got a call in to her professor to try and figure out who last saw her alive. It shouldn't take too long to have the dental records prove whether or not she's our Jane Doe."

"And if she is?"

"Then we'll take a harder look at the boyfriend." Bentz reached for his jacket as Montoya slid a filter tip from the pack. "I'm going to check at Loyola. If the Jane Doe is Stephanie Keller, then two of our victims attended college and the universities butt up to each other."

"He's picking off coeds."

"So he could go to school at one of the universities himself," Bentz said. "Or works there."

"Loyola—Catholic?"

"Yep. It merged with the Jesuit College of the Immaculate Conception over a hundred years ago. It's supposed to be the largest Catholic University in the South."

"And Tulane."

Bentz shook his head. "Originally a medical school, now lots of business."

"How do you know these things?" Montoya seemed amazed. He was usually one step ahead of the game, at least when it came to what was happening within the department, but Bentz invariably dug deeper on the crime scene stuff.

"I checked. The minute I heard that another victim might

have been a student, I did a little research. It's all here.'' He flipped a copy of a text on New Orleans across his paper-strewn desk.

''Maybe. In the meantime I'll see what I can dig up on Oscar Cantrell and Bernadette Dubois.''

''Let me guess,'' Montoya said as he started for the door. ''Another interview with the visionary.'' His dark eyes gleamed.

''I figured I'd show her pictures of this girl and some others—see if she can pick Stephanie out as the victim she claims to have seen. I'll make copies on my way out. You got a better idea?''

Montoya's grin grew. ''Nope. I think it's a damned good plan.'' He crammed the cigarette into the side of his mouth. ''Damned good.''

Chapter Eighteen

The bell over the shop door tinkled. Olivia was stocking shelves in the back room. She shoved a box of aromatic candles onto a stack, then swept through the beaded doorway to find Bentz making his way along a narrow aisle filled with baskets of incense, bath beads, and candles.

"Early Christmas shopping?" she asked.

He glanced at a five-inch crystal pyramid. Next to it was a tiny Japanese sand garden. On the next table was a tiny waterfall. "I think I'll pass."

"I can get you a deal on slightly used tarot cards," she teased, unable to stop from baiting him as his shoulder brushed against a silver star that was part of a wind chime set. The chimes pealed softly over the background of sitar music piped in from the speakers mounted on the highest shelves.

"Another time."

"I take it this isn't a social call," she said, reading the serious expression in the lines of his face. Suddenly she understood. "You caught the guy," she guessed, crossing her fingers and hoping against hope.

"Nothing like that, but we did get a possible ID on the body."

"Who?"

"I can't say. Not until we know for certain and the family's been notified."

"Then why are you here?" she asked and stupidly, for a split second, she wondered if he'd come to see her, and her heartbeat increased. She remembered the kiss they'd shared in her house and she wondered if it had affected him as much as it had her.

He reached into his pocket and withdrew a manila envelope. Within were color copies of snapshots of half a dozen women, all between twenty-five and thirty-five, some smiling, some not, all seemingly fit and all attractive. He handed the pictures to Olivia.

"Are all of these women missing?" she asked, horrified. *Oh, God, please say that the monster hasn't killed them.*

"No. I just wondered if any of them looked like someone you've 'seen' in your visions."

"What?" she asked, then understood. "Oh, I get it. You're testing me, right?" She was disappointed. "Always the skeptic, aren't you?"

"Gotta be."

"I suppose." She flipped through the pictures, studying each face and stopping when she came to a tawny-skinned woman with a wide smile in a bikini. "I . . . I feel like I've seen her before," she said, confused. "But she's not the one . . . oh, God." Her heart nearly stopped as she gazed at one of the snapshots of a girl holding a tennis racquet. Cold recognition swept over her. "This one," she whispered, dropping the rest of the snapshots as if they burned her fingers. "This is the woman he called Cecilia. I'm sure of it." In her mind's eye, she again saw the brutal images of the woman kneeling, begging, desperately clutching the priest's robe. Olivia's knees turned to water and the contents of her stomach curdled. She took in a deep breath and sagged heavily against the counter.

Bentz was quick. He grabbed the crook of her arm. "Steady," he said as the door opened and Tawilda, lugging a shopping bag, stepped inside.

"Hey! Livvie, are you okay?" she asked, bustling down the aisle, the bracelets circling her wrist jangling. "Who the hell are you?" Dark eyes flashed at Bentz.

"It's okay. He's—"

Bentz flashed his badge. "Rick Bentz. New Orleans Police."

"Police? What happened? Did we get robbed or somethin'?" Tawilda asked.

"Ms. Benchet is helping us with a case."

"What case?" Tawilda's eyes were round. Then they narrowed on Olivia. "You didn't tell me anything about a case. What's goin' on?"

"She's not at liberty to discuss it now," Bentz said. "In fact, it would really help out if you could tend to the store while I speak with Ms. Benchet for a few minutes alone." He glanced at Olivia. "I'll buy you a cup of coffee."

Olivia pulled her arm out of Bentz's grasp.

"Is she bein' arrested? Don't you have to read her rights to her or somethin'?"

"She's not being arrested," Bentz said.

"It's all right, Tawilda." Olivia forced a smile. "But if you wouldn't mind, I think I need to talk to him."

"I do mind. I *mind* that you didn't tell me about this," Tawilda snapped. "I knew something was up with you, girl. You've been acting strange for the last couple of days and I thought it might have somethin' to do with your mama comin' to town, but it's more than that, isn't it?" She gave Bentz the once-over with her dark eyes. "Oh, go on." With a shooing motion of her long fingers, she gestured for Bentz and Olivia to go out the door. "I'll handle things here, it's about time for you to be off anyway. Now, you do whatever it is you have to, just don't you be holdin' out on me, y'hear?''

"Wouldn't dream of it, '' Olivia drawled. "I owe you one.''

"You owe me a million, but who's countin'?''

"You are. Every single one.''

"Well, maybe.'' Tawilda rolled her eyes. "And I intend to collect.''

"You will,'' Olivia insisted, then said to Bentz, "Give me a minute to get my things.'' She ducked through the beaded archway and into the back rooms to the office, where she located her purse stuffed inside a closet. In one motion, she tugged her jacket from a brass hook and stuffed her arms down the sleeves. Finger-combing her hair, she made her way past boxes of inventory yet to be catalogued and stocked, then rattled the beads as she returned to the front of the store.

Bentz was waiting at a display of dried alligator heads sporting Santa caps. "The perfect gift for that hard-to-buy-for someone,'' Olivia quipped as he held the door open for her. Along with a blast of cold air, two middle-aged women bustled into the shop.

"I'll remember that on Christmas Eve when I go shopping. Aunt Edna's a bitch to buy for. I'd been thinking along the lines of chocolates or a new pair of slippers but I bet what she'd really like is the gator head with the red hat.''

"Wouldn't anyone?'' Olivia stuffed her hands into the pockets of her jacket. The smell of the river was thick, the wind blowing across its muddy depths cold and raw. "So were you trying to lay a trap for me?'' Olivia asked as they walked toward Decatur Street. The sidewalks were crowded with pedestrians bustling in and out of the shops and restaurants facing the streets. Cars, trucks, and carriages drawn by mules filled the streets. On one corner a street mime was standing motionless. In front of him an upturned hat, sprinkled with a few dollars and coins, was an open invitation for donations.

"I just wanted to see if we were on the right track."

"That girl, the one with the tennis racquet, is the one."

"And the other one? How do you know her?"

"I don't. Not really," she said, thinking hard. Tiny pictures of the woman, cracked shards, cut through her brain. "The image I got of her wasn't as intense, but I feel like I've seen her before. And yes, in my dreams. Last summer, when I was here taking care of Grannie, I think. I had several nightmares. About her. It was in bits and pieces, but . . . I'm sure she's the woman. Someone was shaving her head . . . and positioning her . . . and choking her."

Bentz guided her into a café that boasted strong coffee and even stronger drinks. They took a table near the window where the street was visible through the glass and a candle was flickering in a small hurricane lantern. "Was the same guy you saw the other night, the priest, was he choking her?"

"I don't know," she admitted. "As I said, I only saw bits and pieces."

"And the guy in the cave with the woman who was left to starve?"

"I already told you, I'm not sure." She shook her head as a waitress took their orders for coffee then moved to the next table. "It must be. But I don't remember a priest . . . just . . . there was something the same about it . . . besides the terrified woman, there was. . . a necklace or chain. Like the one I saw the other night, the one the priest left over the showerhead." She shuddered at the intense memory, the scent of fear and smoke. She glanced at Bentz across the table, his features shadowed in the dark room, warm candlelight playing upon his skin. His eyes were a dark gray. Intense. Suspicious and yet . . . there was another emotion in their steely depths. She hadn't remembered the connection of the chain at the time, but now it seemed important. "You have to believe me, Bentz. I'm not making this up. I couldn't."

"I know." He nodded as the coffee was deposited.

"Anything else?" the waitress, a gum-chewing girl of about eighteen, asked. Bentz looked at Olivia.

"You want something?"

"No . . . this is fine." She wrapped her fingers around the cup and the waitress, popping the gum, sauntered off. "So. Did I pass?" she asked as Bentz leaned back in the booth. "The pictures. Did I pick out the right ones?"

He nodded over the clink of spoons swirling in cups and soft conversation. "Right on the money."

"So now you're wondering, *What's her connection? It can't be that she actually has ESP or whatever you want to call it, so she must have some other way of knowing what happened at the murder scene.* Right?"

"It's crossed my mind," he admitted and her temper snapped.

She shot to her feet, banging the table and sloshing coffee from her cup. "Well, when you figure it out, would you let me know? It would help me out, too. I wouldn't feel like I was going out of my mind."

"You're not," he said. "Please. Sit down." He motioned toward the other side of the booth and reluctantly she took a seat again. "There's something else I want to talk to you about."

"What?" she asked and sensed she wasn't going to like the subject matter. She dabbed at the spilled coffee with a napkin.

"Your mother."

"What about her?"

"She was married to Oscar Cantrell."

Husband number three. "She was married to a lot of people," Olivia said, then immediately regretted her flippant tone. "Okay, right, she was married to Cantrell for a while."

"You ever meet him?"

"At the wedding, but that was it. My mother and I aren't particularly close. I thought I told you all this." She dropped the wet napkin onto the table.

"Bear with me," he said and she got the impression he was leading up to something; something she wouldn't like. "It turns out that the house where the last Jane Doe was killed the other night is owned by some people who live out of state. They rent it through a management company, Benchmark Realty."

She waited but he didn't elaborate. "So?"

"Benchmark Realty is owned by Oscar Cantrell."

"What?" she whispered, disbelieving. "Do you think he's involved?"

"We're checking," Bentz said, not elaborating.

"As I said, I met Oscar at the wedding. He was short, maybe five-six or -seven, and he wasn't built like the man I saw."

"He could've lost weight."

This sounded all wrong. She remembered Oscar. A teddy bear of a man with a big nose, red cheeks, and a quick, wide smile—the salesman's salesman. A far cry from the intense, reined-in anger she felt in the murderer. "Why would Oscar use a place that could be so easily traced to him? That would be stupid." She was certain Oscar Cantrell wasn't the suspect. "Doesn't he have an alibi?" She looked at Bentz, who was sipping his coffee and studying her over the rim.

"We're checking that out."

"My mother wasn't married to him but about two years, I think. Maybe two and a half on the outside, so if you think that there's a connection to me through Oscar, you're barking up the wrong tree. As I said, I only met him once."

"You ever meet any of his family? A brother? Father?"

"No. During the time that Bernadette was married to Oscar, I lived with my grandmother."

"Did they have any children?"

"No! I don't have any half-siblings. I only had my sister and she died years ago."

He nodded, as if he understood, but Olivia saw the shad-

ows in his gaze. "What is it?" she asked. "You don't
believe me?"

"Just trying to piece this all together."

"Don't you trust anyone?" she demanded. "What is it
with you, Bentz? Are you so jaded from your job that you
can't believe anyone or is it more than that? Did something
happen to you personally?"

His lips twitched. "Why don't you tell me? You're the
psychic."

That did it. He'd been hard-nosed from the minute he'd
stepped into the shop. Suspicious all over again. "I'm outta
here." She snagged her purse from beneath the table.

"Wait a minute," he said as several heads swiveled from
the nearby booths.

"Forget it. I'm sick to death of being second-guessed. I
know this doesn't make a lot of sense to you, okay? It
doesn't make any sense to me, either. But there it is. I
thought . . . I mean . . . don't you believe me? Didn't you
say that . . . Oh, hell, it doesn't matter!" She huffed off and
wondered why she bothered trying to explain anything to
the bull-headed cop. She heard him slapping bills onto the
table and felt his arm on her as she reached the front door.

"Olivia—"

"Can it, Bentz. Whatever it is you want to say, just can
it. I'm not interested. I've done my part, my good citizen
bit, and I've suffered enough of your disbelief and suspicion
and your insults. Enough already."

"You can't blame me for being skeptical."

She spun on him, bumping into his chest. "I can and I
will. Take me at face value or leave me the hell alone."
She was overreacting, but she didn't care. Who the hell was
he to second-guess her? To mock her? She expected more
from him and, damn him, he kept letting her down. One
minute he seemed to trust her, to open up to her, to even
go so far as kiss her, for God's sake, then the next thing
she knew they were back to this, the hard-nosed cop with
all the questions.

She darted across the street, dashing through traffic, hearing a horn blast as she jaywalked. She half-expected Bentz to pursue her and slap a ticket on her, but she made it back to the shop without being accosted and didn't bother looking over her shoulder to see if he was still standing on the other side of the street staring after her.

It didn't matter.

Because the feelings she had for him, the desperation she felt to make him believe her, not just to solve the crime, unfortunately, but for personal reasons she had no right to feel, were ludicrous. She was being a fool. Of the highest order. A fool of a woman over a man.

That, she told herself, was going to stop. Pronto.

The Chosen One was restless. Edgy. Irritated as he paced in his chapel. He'd read the accounts of the fire in Bayou St. John. No mention of the sacrifice. Just a victim who'd died in the blaze. As if she'd accidentally succumbed to the flames.

Ahh . . . Cecilia. What a beauty she was.

The police were withholding evidence, of course, but they were morons. Cretins. He'd watched them arrive, a pathetic group and they hadn't yet connected his "crimes." That's what the imbeciles would call them—crimes. Like he was a common criminal. They had no idea of his mission, that what he was doing was God's work. And he was far from finished.

No amount of prayer could calm him. He reached into his closet to his private cache and fingered the pieces of fingernails and toenails, the tiny trophies he'd taken and he relived each encounter. Closing his eyes, aware that his cock was stiffening, he saw himself in the mirrors he'd set upon his altar, the way he'd been able to see his victims' fear and his own mastery in the reflective glass, the way they'd begged. He'd ached for each of them, suffered the torment of wanting to claim their blasphemous, heathen bodies. The

Jezebels had been so outwardly innocent, so inwardly evil. There were so many of them.

One more important than the rest. The cop's daughter. That one was personal. Smiling, he thought of her . . . soon . . . soon.

Deep in the recess he found the braid, the one he'd so carefully woven, strands of different colored hair winking in the light from his candles . . . brown, black, blond . . . but no red. A flaw. One he would have to correct. He rolled the plait between his fingers, imagined each terrified face of the whores, remembered cutting a lock of hair first, while they still believed they would live, while they were sending up prayers of repentance for crimes they didn't believe they'd committed, then tucking the trophy under his neoprene suit, close to his body. Foolish cunts. Daughters of Satan. Whores each and every one.

Slowly he parted his bath robe, letting it fall open. His cock was hard. Throbbing. Standing at attention. He dragged the braid across himself, feeling the light caress, as soft and teasing as a harlot's lips. He stiffened, sensing the driving need to release. His blood pounded through his veins, thundered in his ears, ached in his groin. Oh . . . for just the touch of one mouth upon him . . . one evil kiss . . . He felt the need to touch himself, to let go, but he didn't. No. He would not give in to the base desire to relieve himself.

Instead he imagined the whores' faces. Beautiful. Seductive. Wicked. Tear-stained in fear, begging him to let them service him, bargaining for their wretched lives. He smiled. Sweat ran down his back and face. They were his in death. Did they not know he'd saved them? Martyred them?

But he needed another . . . a soul to save . . . another Jezebel to add to his harem of the dead. . . one more lock to add to his braid . . . tonight.

He had the place. It was ready, a crude altar, but a place of sacrifice nonetheless. Hidden. Dark. The weapon waiting.

The time had been preordained. He looked at the calendar. November twenty-fifth, the feast day of St. Catherine of Alexandria, patron saint of maidens . . . of philosophers . . .

of preachers ... of students ... how fitting ... oh, yes, it would be perfect.

It had to happen tonight.

Before the stroke of midnight.

God was waiting.

Chapter Nineteen

Olivia had trouble shaking off her confrontation with Bentz. What was it about the man that made her so crazy? What did she care what he thought? She locked up the shop and was going to pick up her things when the phone rang. The recorder would pick it up, of course, but being as it was near the holidays and all, she plucked the receiver off the phone and said, "The Third Eye. This is Olivia. How can I help you?"

There was silence, but she knew that someone was on the other end.

"Is someone there?" she asked, glancing through the paned windows to the darkened street. The shop itself was shadowed, only the security lights giving any illumination. "Hello?"

"Olivia?" A man's gravelly voice.

"Yes." Hadn't she already identified herself? "Can I help you?"

"I hope so." A second's hesitation as if he were gathering his thoughts. "This is your father."

Her heart plummeted. She didn't say a word. Couldn't.

"You probably don't remember me. I've been away a long time, but I was hopin' that you and I, we could get together."

She leaned against the wall. Frantically her eyes darted around the shop to the darkened displays, as if she expected Reginald Benchet to pop out from behind a Mardi Gras mask or the rack of books on witchcraft. "I . . . I don't think that would be a good idea."

"How do you know?"

"Look, let's just leave things the way they are," she said, sweat prickling her scalp.

"Well, that's the problem, Livvie," he said and the use of her nickname in his thick southern drawl gave her the creeps. "I've been away a long time and I had plenty of time to think. To reassess my life. I didn't call you right away, didn't contact your mother, didn't even come to your grandmother's funeral even though I read her obituary in the paper. I thought I'd give us all some time to get used to the idea that I'm a free man."

I'll never be used to it. "Why would that make any difference?"

"Because I've changed, Livvie. I spent a lot of time alone, and a lot of time reading, reevaluating, even philosophizing. I've let Jesus into my life, into my heart, and I've not only paid my debt to society, but I've repented for my sins and taken Jesus Christ as my personal savior."

"That's good . . ." she said, winding the cord around her fingers and wishing there were some way to break the connection. She didn't need a father now, not the kind of father Reggie Benchet was.

"You bet it is. And I'm going to prove myself."

"How's that?"

"By doing the Lord's work. Spreading His word. I'm a minister now, Livvie, and now that I'm on the outside it's time to visit my daughter. You're the only child I've got left, you know. I've lost the others. When a man spends as much time as I did in prison, he learns what's valuable in life. And it's family, Olivia. Family and God.''

"I don't think I'm ready for this," she said. "In fact, I know I'm not."

"Give it some thought."

Not hardly. "I will," she lied.

"The Lord be with you, Livvie." He hung up before she did. Olivia closed her eyes for a second.

He's your father, her mind nagged, but she wasn't buying it. "He's the sperm donor. Nothing more."

But he's changed. Turned over a new leaf.

Something else she wasn't buying. From what she'd heard about Reggie Benchet, she'd learned that he was a con artist of the highest order, someone who could talk the skin off a rattler. She didn't want anything to do with him.

Yeah, and what if he gets sick and has no money . . . what then? You are flesh and blood. His only kid.

She decided she needed help sorting this all out. After finishing locking up, she reached in her purse, pulled out her wallet, and found the card Father James McClaren had pressed into her hand when she'd found him at St. Louis Cathedral.

"This is a surprise," James said, and he meant it as he looked up from his desk. The secretary had left for the day, as had Father Roy, and now he was faced with Olivia Benchet again, the beautiful woman with the tangled hair and enigmatic eyes. He'd thought about Olivia more than once in the last couple of days. More than he should have. And his thoughts hadn't been pure. Far from it. But that was his personal cross to bear, the demons he had to fight.

"I want to talk to someone," she said, hesitating in the doorway.

"Come in . . . please . . ." He stood and pointed at one of the two side chairs on the other side of the desk. They were wooden, their seats smoothed and polished by fifty

years of backsides of the troubled, the cursed, or the penitent.
"You're here to see me?"

"Yes."

"As a priest?"

She hesitated as she sat and he noticed the curve of her
calf peeking from beneath a slit skirt. Quickly, he looked
away, to the window and the naked branches of the oak tree
that were visible in the blue illumination from nearby street
lamps. A crow was sitting on a lower limb, his head tucked
beneath his wing. "Yes, and, well . . . I haven't been to
mass in years."

"Maybe that's the problem." He offered her a smile and
noticed her lips twitch.

"If so, it's just the tip of the iceberg."

"What's going on with you, Olivia?"

Again there was a moment's hesitation. She worried her
lower lip as if deciding just how much she could confide.
"I think I should start with my family," she said, then found
his eyes again. "That alone could take days."

He lifted his eyebrows. "Why don't you begin and we'll
see where it takes us and how long. I've got all night."

"Even men of God need to sleep," she said.

"What's troubling you, Olivia?"

What isn't? she thought, but said, "I guess I felt compelled
to seek some kind of counseling because of my father. I've
never really known him; he and my mother were divorced
when I was a toddler, and for most of the remaining years
he's been in prison. For murder." Father James didn't so
much as flinch. "But he got out earlier this year, I guess, I
didn't know. My mother told me just recently and now he
wants to meet me. He even called and claimed he's a changed
man, that he's reformed, a minister of some sort, and the
simple truth is I really don't want anything to do with him."

"But . . ." he encouraged.

"But even though I think of him as just a sperm donor,
the truth of the matter is that he is my flesh and blood. I'm
his only living child and my good old Catholic guilt is
rearing its ugly head. He mentioned that I was all he had

left.'' And there was something about the way he'd said it that had bothered her; something was off.

Father James was listening hard, his square jaw balanced on the knuckles of both hands, his blue eyes focused on her. His jaw was dark with beard-shadow and he wore a black shirt and a stiff white cleric's collar. He was just too damned handsome to have given his life to God. There was something about him that reminded her of someone, but she couldn't put her finger on who that could be. Probably some television or B-movie Hollywood hunk who never made much of a name for himself.

He just didn't look the part of a priest. Though he wore cleric's garb and sat in this ancient room with its wide, polished desk, an open Bible in one corner, an arched window offering a view outside the vestibule, Father James McClaren looked as if he belonged on a soccer field or guiding a white-water rafting trip or standing on the bridge of a sailboat.

As if he read her mind, he smiled, showing off straight white teeth. ''I guess I should tell you to search your heart, look into your soul, find the courage to forgive your father for his sins against you.''

''Turn the other cheek and avert my eyes to all he's done?''

''He's paid his debt to society. His punishment has been complete in the eyes of the law, so that leaves what he did to you, which, essentially is abandon you and your mother, the embarrassment to you.''

''Yes.''

''I don't mean to trivialize it. There's nothing trivial about abandonment, especially to a child. I'm sure the ramifications to you and your mother were devastating. And even though you're an adult, it doesn't mean that the pain will just vanish. You can say you don't care, that you're over it, that it was probably for the best, but the scars run deep and are painful. And when the pain is revisited as it is now that your father has contacted you again, it's like the scab over those old wounds is being picked at. It stings. Threatens to bleed again. Burns. Brings back old, wretched memories that we'd hoped and prayed were long forgotten.'' He didn't smile as he looked at her, and Olivia was suddenly aware how dark the room was, that aside from the weak light from the street lamp outside, the only illumination in the room was from a banker's lamp with its dim bulb and green shade.

The corners of the office seemed to shrink, the atmosphere thickening.

Father James said, ''I can't tell you what to do, Olivia. I can only suggest that you pray and talk it over with God. See what He says.'' He spread his hands wide. ''That's probably not the answer you were searching for, but it's the best I've got.''

''Is it?''

''Tell you what. Why don't you go home and think about it? Do some soul-searching, then come back in a couple of days and we'll discuss it again.''

''And in the meantime? If he calls again?''

''Do what your heart tells you.''

''What if my heart tells me to call him every name in the book?'' she asked and he grinned.

''Just make sure it's this book.'' He thumped two fingers on a corner of the Bible resting on his desk.

''Is that what you'd do?''

''It's what I'd *try* to do.'' He sighed through his nose. ''You know, I wear this collar''—he touched the white ring at his neck—''but it doesn't mean I have all the answers. I'm just a man.''

''And here I thought you were touched by God.''

''I guess I'm supposed to say we're all touched by the Father.'' He quirked an eyebrow. ''I suggest you speak with Him. And then listen. He will respond.''

She wasn't so sure, but she didn't argue. After all, she'd come here for Father McClaren's counsel. The least she could do was hear him out. ''Thank you for your time.''

''My pleasure,'' he said and the twinkle in his eye and warm handshake across the desk told her that he meant it. ''Here, let me walk you out.'' He rounded the desk, touched the crook of her arm as he opened the door, then crossed the vestibule to the front doors. Dozens of votive candles were flickering in the dim nave, and a few lights glowed, shining from the exposed beams and reflecting on the stained glass windows. "Perhaps I'll see you at mass this Sunday," he suggested as he shouldered open the door and a cold breeze gusted inside, sending the tiny flames of the candles dancing wildly.

"I'll think about it," she said.

He touched her hand, his fingers brushing the back of her knuckles. "Call me after you talk with God."

She glanced into his eyes . . . blue . . . intense . . . sexy. At odds with his soft-spoken piety. "I will," she promised and he stepped away from her, though she felt his gaze as she bundled her jacket around her and skirted puddles to reach her truck. As she climbed inside and slid behind the steering wheel, she saw him lift a hand and she waved back, then shoved her key in the ignition, pumped the gas, and twisted her wrist. The old engine ground for a second or two and she hesitated, then gave it another try. The tired motor sputtered to life and she wheeled out of the parking lot, the truck bouncing over potholes.

Her heart was pounding way too fast.

Because Father McClaren had touched her. Not her skin. But deeper down. To her soul.

"Don't even think about it," she warned as she looked into the rearview mirror. She couldn't let herself be attracted to a priest. Nor a cop. Two men who were off-limits. Way off-limits. Maybe that was her problem, she thought as she accelerated onto the freeway. Maybe she was only interested in men who weren't safe; men she couldn't possibly be involved with.

So why didn't you confide in Father McClaren about your visions? Why not trust him? Are you afraid he might think of you as another nutcase like Bentz does?

Large drops of rain started to fall, splattering on her windshield. She turned on the wipers and knew she couldn't talk to the priest. Not yet. She'd look like a fruitcake. He already knew about her ex-con of a father, and soon, no doubt, she'd explain about her often-married mother, so right now she wouldn't bring up a grandmother who practiced voodoo along with Catholicism, nor would she mention the fact that she witnessed murders through visions in her mind . . . at least one of which had been committed by a priest.

He'd write her off for good if she mentioned that little fact.

So, for now, she'd hold her tongue.

Chapter Twenty

The names of the saints ran through Bentz's head.
St. Cecilia.
St. Joan of Arc.
St. Mary Magdalene.
Each one different. Each one immortalized on a medal that was purposely left at the scene of the crime.

Why? Bentz wondered as his computer spewed out pages of information on each of the martyred women. What was the significance? Pivoting in his desk chair, he picked up the first page on St. Cecilia, patron saint of musicians, poets, and sinners. He skimmed the account of her life as a Roman girl, then came to the part about her death. His nerves tightened. Cecilia or Cecily was sentenced to death for refusing to repudiate her Christianity. She was supposed to die from suffocation in her bathroom by furnace fumes, and when that didn't work, she was to be beheaded by three blows to the neck, which again failed, and she survived for several days after the attack.

"Jesus," he whispered as he thought of the similarities

to the woman's death in Bayou St. John—the smoky bathroom and then her head nearly severed from her body, in three blows according to the ME as well as Olivia Benchet. The sick bastard who did this was copying the punishment meted out against St. Cecilia—the name Olivia had heard him whisper in her vision.

An eerie sensation swept over Bentz's skin.

He knew that Joan of Arc died from being burned at the stake and the Jane Doe had been horridly burned before her body had been dumped at the statue of Joan in the French Quarter.

But what about Mary Magdalene . . . that part didn't quite fit. He didn't have a record of Mary Magdalene's death, but he did know that she was a sinner—presumably a prostitute—as was Cathy Adams, who was found dead in her Garden District apartment. Cathy's head had been shaved, and the smell of patchouli oil had been present. He read the account of Mary Magdalene's life and how it was recorded in the New Testament by St. Luke that she wiped Christ's feet with her hair and anointed him with ointment.

Bentz felt that eerie sensation again.

Had the killer turned this story of Jesus into something grotesque?

The phone rang. It was the ME in the morgue. "The dental records of the victim from the fire in Bayou St. John match with Stephanie Jane Keller," he said, though Bentz had already convinced himself that the girl who died in the fire was Dustin Townsend's girlfriend.

"You're certain?"

"A hundred percent. She had a lot of dental work done a few years back. I've checked the X-rays and talked to the dentist. She's your girl."

"Thanks." Bentz hung up and tapped his pen on a legal pad situated near the phone. He felt sick inside. He'd seen grizzly deaths—more than he wanted to count—but these killings were so macabre and hideous, gruesomely executed by some kind of weird zealot. A *priest?* No way.

"So think, Bentz. Think." *Stop him before he strikes again.*

What did the three women have in common aside from being murdered in a bizarre fashion?

They all appeared to be under thirty. Two of the three were white, though Cathy Adams was racially mixed. The killer had jumped racial lines, which was odd in and of itself. But not unheard of. He made a note.

Okay, what else?

Until he found out who the Jane Doe left at the statue of Joan of Arc was, he had only Cathy Adams and Stephanie Jane Keller to compare lifestyles and acquaintances and their pasts. They both had boyfriends, though Cathy's hadn't been heard from in months. Marc Duvall, Cathy's pimp/boyfriend, had blown town around the time of the murder and was still a suspect.

Both of the identified victims had lived alone, Cathy in the Garden District of the city, Stephanie in an apartment in Covington, less than a mile from her boyfriend's house. Cathy was a part-time student at Tulane and an exotic dancer. Stephanie was a secretary for an insurance company and took night classes at Loyola.

Which was next door to Tulane University.

A connection? Or a coincidence?

Bentz made it a personal code not to believe in coincidence. He made another note and wondered about the remaining Jane Doe. Another student at one of the universities in the Garden District?

Olivia Benchet's a graduate student at Tulane.

His jaw tightened. He didn't like where this was leading. The thought that Olivia might be in contact with the killer scared him. Big-time.

So what about the priest?

The priest only Olivia saw—and that was in her "vision." Don't go jumping off the deep end here, Bentz. You need more facts to believe that a priest would kill these women.

It didn't make any sense. He scanned his notes again, the ones he'd taken during the interviews with Olivia. He stopped when he came to the sheet of paper with the weird letters and symbols. His eyes narrowed as he thought. Another saint? Or was that stretching it too far . . . grasping at straws? Why would a priest kill women and make them look like martyred saints? That didn't make sense. And why would Olivia be able to see him killing the women? *How?* What was the connection? Bentz was missing something . . . something important.

He ran a hand over his face, heard the hum of computers and buzz of conversation in the outer office, and glanced back on his notes on St. Cecilia once again. The same stuff. Except . . . His gut clenched as he noticed the feast day. November twenty-second. He caught his breath. The day Stephanie Jane Keller was murdered.

The killer had done his work on November twenty-second not because it was the date of the JFK assassination, but because it was the feast day of St. Cecilia.

"Son of a . . ." He flipped through his pages on Joan of Arc. "Feast day . . . May thirtieth." The Jane Doe was found at the foot of the statue of Joan of Arc on May thirty-first. But she could have been killed before midnight, May thirtieth, her feast day. Burned at a damned stake? Where? "Shit." What kind of sick mind were they up against?

And when would he strike again? Jesus, if Bentz remembered correctly, from his days of Catechism, it seemed there was a feast day celebrating some saint's life every time you turned around.

Sweat broke out on his forehead. That meant there wasn't much time.

If you're right, his mind warned. *You could be connecting dots that don't exist.*

Like hell. He knew he was right. The demented bastard was using the holy days for his gruesome work.

Suddenly Bentz wanted a drink. And a smoke.

He opened his desk drawer and scrounged for a piece of tasteless nicotine gum. It wasn't the same; didn't give him the hit a Camel straight did, but it would have to suffice. For now. A drink was out of the question.

Grabbing his jacket, ID, and shoulder holster, he logged out and told a secretary if Montoya showed up he needed to talk to him. Then Bentz hit the rain-drenched streets, paging his partner himself from his cell phone as he unlocked his Jeep. He decided to drive to the one spot in the city that he'd managed to avoid for a long, long while.

Jaw clenched, mind racing with more questions than answers, he cut across town, impatient with the clog of traffic. Ironic that a place he'd shunned was now so damned important that he'd abuse the speed limit to get there. The wipers slapped a torrent of rain from the windshield and the police band crackled, though only if Satan himself was found in New Orleans would Bentz be deterred.

A final turn and he saw the church. A place of faith. His parish, if he had one. Since moving to New Orleans, he'd been here about five times. Always with Kristi. On Christmas, sometimes Easter. Never in between and sometimes he'd skipped a year. It all depended on how he felt about God at the time the holiday rolled around. He parked on the street and stared up at the tall spire of St. Luke's Church. Illuminated by lights on the ground, the steeple rose into the night, seeming to knife into the clouds, unbent by the rain.

It was ironic, he thought, that James had ended up here. What were the chances?

Unless James had requested the transfer.

Wouldn't that beat all? He'd wondered half a dozen times why his half-brother had transferred to the Big Easy.

Bentz pocketed his keys, didn't bother turning up his collar, and made a dash for the front doors. Someone had told him long ago that God was patient. He hoped to hell it was true.

The woman was a problem. A serious problem.

The Chosen One sensed her presence, knew that it was only a matter of time before she led the police closer to him. He knew her name. Olivia Benchet . . . a self-proclaimed psychic. As was her grandmother, a backwoods voodoo priestess. But then The Chosen One knew all about Virginia Dubois.

He'd done his research. It was necessary to understand one's enemies. How else would one prevail?

Standing in the shower's hot spray, he sneered when he thought of the police. Simpletons. Idiots. With all of their sophisticated equipment and computer links, and manpower, they were still running around in circles. He'd listened to the press conference that was meant to warn the constituents of the city about a homicidal maniac; he'd heard that there was a task force in place and that more details would be released when they were available.

Which was a joke. The police didn't care tip their hands and tell too much about what they'd found for fear of a copycat killer, or someone confessing to the crime who had no part of it.

So they were careful.

And stupid.

He held a razor and shaved himself carefully. First one thin blade, then another, and finally a third, so that there was no margin for error. The razors were sharp, honed with precision, and they gently caressed his skin, removed all trace of his hair. He worked his way downward from his hairline, slowly over his face, then his neck and chest and underarms, anywhere there was a hint of body hair. He was careful in that sensitive area surrounding his scrotum and took his time with his legs and feet, watching the dark stubble swirl down the drain in an eddy of lather.

He'd installed a full-length mirror next to the shower, and through the steamy glass doors, he saw his image—bare and clean, white skin red from the hot spray, nary a single hair visible, just rippling muscles beneath taut skin, compliments of a rowing machine, a cross-country ski machine, and weights that he used in his daily regimen. The hair on his head was wet and he considered removing it. He should shave it down to nothingness as one single strand left at a scene would undo him. But a significant change in his appearance would raise suspicion, and in truth, pride and vanity won out over caution. For now, the hair would stay. He combed the wet strands from his face, slicking them to his head. Someday, perhaps . . .

As he stepped out of the shower, he didn't towel off but let the cold air evaporate the moisture on his skin. He'd found his next victim. Oh, there were many to choose from; so many sinners, but this one, the redhead, would do nicely. He'd been watching her for weeks, wondering if she was worthy of the sacrifice, and when he'd spoken to her, he'd known then. If she only knew how he was going to transform her soul. Barefooted, he crossed the smooth wood floor to his closet and reached inside for the medal, a very special medal suspended from a fine chain.

St. Catherine of Alexandria.

He felt his blood begin to heat at the thought of his mission. Tonight . . . before midnight. He imagined her pleading for her life, praying and supplicating, crying and repenting, offering herself to him . . . No matter what she bartered with, no matter how desperately she begged, her blood would flow.

He looped the chain over his wrist and glanced in the mirror again. Tonight would be good. Yes. Another sacrifice.

But then he would have to reassess. Because the grand-daughter of Virginia Dubois, daughter to the slut Bernadette, could ruin things for him.

Unless she became one of the martyred.

He smiled at the thought. She had to die. She was a threat and he had personal reasons to end her life, reasons she couldn't yet fathom. There were others slated to be sacrificed first, of course, but . . . his schedule could be rearranged to allow for this special rite.

Saint Olivia. It had a nice ring to it.

A very nice ring.

Chapter
Twenty-one

"There's someone to see you ... a police officer," Wanda, the church secretary, said as she tapped on the door to the office while simultaneously pushing it open.

Father James McClaren looked over the tops of his reading glasses and read the curiosity in the uplift of Wanda's white eyebrows. Thin and wrinkled with eyes that appeared owlish behind her glasses, she licked her lips nervously.

"His name is ... what?" She turned and James heard a deep voice that he recognized instantly. "Oh yes ... Detective Richard Bentz," she said, looking at Father McClaren again.

James's chest tightened. The soft classical music he'd been listening to seemed to fade. What would bring his half-brother here? Only the direst of circumstances. *Kristi.* James's mouth went dry. "Send him in," he said, turning away from his computer screen. Next week's sermon would have to wait.

As Wanda stepped aside to let Bentz enter, James steeled

himself. Any conversation with Bentz turned into a confrontation.

"Father," Bentz said with a nod and James, standing, forced a smile.

"Thank you, Wanda," James said, slanting a glance at the woman still hovering in the doorway. She got the hint and slipped outside. The door shut with a soft thud. James extended his hand across the desk. He relaxed a little. If something was seriously wrong with Kristi, it would have been evident in the lines on Bentz's face. As it was his half-brother looked worried, but not filled with despair or grief. "Long time, no see. How're ya, Rick?"

Bentz took his hand in a bear-like clasp that was as brief as it was strong. "Okay." He settled into one of the visitor's chairs and James remembered how much, as a boy, he'd looked up to his older brother. How close they'd been. As children, Rick had always been there for him. While growing up, Bentz had shown him how to throw a baseball, shoot a twenty-two and sneak booze from the old man's liquor cabinet. Rick had scoffed at James's piety, and once taken on Freddy Mason when Freddy and some friends had picked a fight with James in the school yard, calling him a sissy and a "Mama's boy." Rick had knocked Freddy flat, then, when the older boys had left with their tails tucked between their collective legs, Rick had turned on his half brother and kicked James's butt from one side of Orange County to the other. He'd told James that Freddy had been right. James *was* a "Mama's boy" and all that candy-assed stuff about God and Church had to be hidden away or he'd get into big trouble. It was time for James to fight his own battles.

The next week James had asked Rick to show him how to box and in the next year, after growing six inches and putting on thirty pounds, James had been able to stand up for himself. They'd been tight way back when and James had always felt awe for his stronger half brother; a kid who'd grown up not knowing his own father, a policeman shot in the line of duty.

Even so, eventually James and Rick had taken far different

paths and eventually James had betrayed his older brother. And he'd been paying for it ever since.

Now, he dropped into his worn desk chair.

"How 'bout you?" Rick asked without so much as a smile, as if he didn't really give a damn. "You okay these days?"

"Can't complain." Drawing in a tight breath James asked a question that had been on his mind for months. "How's Kristi?"

"Fine."

"In school?"

"Yeah." Bentz's eyes dared him to go further.

He took the challenge. "Up at All Saints?"

"That's right."

"She doin' okay?"

"As I said, 'fine'."

"Coming home for Thanksgiving?" James asked, eager for any little tidbit of information about the daughter who had believed he was her uncle until a few months ago.

"Yeah." A muscle worked in the side of Bentz's face as if he, too, were remembering the scene after he'd handed Kristi the condemning letter, then left a message on James's answering machine explaining that he'd finally told her the truth. James had hoped for some kind of bonding, a healing, and he'd been sorely disappointed. Kristi had summarily rejected him, and told him to "Fuck off" when he'd called. The short, furious, one-sided conversation still rang in his ears.

"Don't you ever call me, okay? You're a goddamned hypocrite and I don't want you praying for me, either, just leave me the hell alone!" she'd cried and slammed down the phone. He had prayed for her. Hours. Hoping she would see him. Speak with him, let him explain . . . If she only knew how much he loved her, had loved her mother . . . maybe more than God. When Jennifer had admitted that she was pregnant with his child, he'd offered to quit the priesthood, had been willing to take the heat of his brother's wrath, God's fury, even to accept the specter of being ex-communicated, but she'd refused . . . She couldn't accept the scandal, so they'd covered up the truth for a while. Now, he tapped his desk, feeling shame. Feeling that same familiar guilt.

Rick was still glaring at him. "I didn't come here to talk about her," he said tersely.

James nodded, trying to ignore that particular pang of emptiness whenever he thought about Kristi. "I know. And I guess I'm glad. I was afraid something was wrong with her when you showed up."

"This isn't about her."

"All right, but . . ." He opened his hands and wondered how to ever bridge the gap between them. *Through God*, he'd told himself over and over, but for some reason the Father hadn't seen fit to mend their small family. And that, too, was James's fault. For he'd never forgotten Jennifer and years after Kristi was born, he and the mother of his child had sinned again. He cleared his throat. "I was worried . . . You know, she won't respond to my letters or my e-mail."

"Then leave it be, James," Bentz said, his lips compressed.

"But—"

"I said 'leave it'; if she wants to contact you, she will. Until then you just leave it alone."

"I've prayed and—"

Bentz snorted, the way of nonbelievers but even so, James felt no sense of superiority in his faith. It was prideful, of course, to feel that smugness. And a sin. Even those who desperately needed God's love sometimes rejected James's attempts to lead them to the Father. For those who couldn't find that faith, he felt despair, and, in some cases, unfortunately a sense of superiority. However not today. Not when it came to Kristi. James couldn't rely on his faith for he'd transgressed so badly, wounded his brother so bitterly, that God seemed to have shunned helping him. Rick Bentz had, at one time, been his role model, the older brother James had looked up to and emulated.

But that was before James had met Jennifer. And the weekend that had changed their lives forever.

God help him.

"I'm here on business," Bentz said, getting down to it as he leaned over the desk. "Here's the deal. We've got another sicko loose, a serial killer."

"I saw it on the news."

"Yeah, well, there are certain things I can't talk about, of course, things that we're keeping from the public, so I guess I'm here as a . . . penitent or confessor or whatever it is the Church calls it these days." He made a brushing motion with his hand, as if it was of no consequence. "I just want to make sure that if I talk to you, it'll go no further, right? This is between you, me and God."

"If that's what you want."

"It is." Rick was dead-serious and James recognized the look. He'd seen it in the past. The grim, focused expression had always been a part of Bentz whether he donned it before a boxing match in high school or right before his fist had crashed into James's face and broken his nose. James hadn't seen it coming. But he hadn't known that Jennifer had confessed to Rick that she was carrying his half-brother's child. That one blow had been symbolic of the rift that was to come. James had tried to reconnect with his half brother, to play the role of uncle to his own child, but Rick had only grudgingly allowed it, probably for the sole purpose of hiding the painful truth and to protect Kristi.

"Then, yes. You can trust that this will go no further."

Again the corners of Bentz's mouth tightened, but he didn't comment on trusting his half brother. "The killer has struck three women that we know about, potentially more. The women have a couple of things that link them, but one of the strongest is that I think they were all murdered on a Saint's feast day."

"What?" James didn't think he'd heard correctly.

"It seems they were killed on the feast day purposely. There are clues to back this up."

"Dear God," James whispered, sketching a quick sign

of the cross over himself. "But if that were the case then there could be dozens ... or hundreds of victims." He pointed to the calendar hung over his desk. "Look at today. It's the feast day of St. Catherine of Alexandria, the patron saint of maidens and philosophers and students and preachers."

"Damn." Bentz glared at the calendar, then asked, "How did she die?"

"Horribly. Well, all the martyrs did ... Here ..." He swivelled in his chair and searched the bookcase behind him before he found the heavy book he wanted; one devoted entirely to the saints. What Bentz was speculating was heinous; crimes not only against the victims but the Church itself. To think someone would misconstrue the veneration of those canonized and twist it into murder was unthinkable. Twisted and evil.

As he slid a pair of reading glasses onto his nose, James flipped open the book, scanned the chapters and, thumbing quickly through the pages, found what he was looking for. "Here we go." He pushed the open book across the desk.

The color drained from his half-brother's face. "Tortured by being strapped to a spiked wheel."

"That was the idea, yes."

"Jesus," Bentz whispered, his eyes scanning the page. "Her bonds were miraculously loosened and the spikes flew off to kill the onlookers."

"And when that didn't work she was beheaded."

Bentz nodded slowly, his gaze glued to the text.

"It's said that her blood flowed white. Like milk." James scratched his neck beneath his clerical collar. "And all because she committed the sin of converting people to Christianity." Folding his hands, James leaned over his desk. "If you have a killer who is copying the murders of the saints, you're going to be very busy, I'm afraid. And he won't be satisfied killing only women. Men and children as well will be at risk. There are hundreds of saints ... thousands." Inwardly James shivered. He skewered his half-brother's gaze with his own. "This is unthinkable."

"A lot of unthinkable acts have been performed in the name of God."

"I know."

Bentz flipped through the tome, the lines of his face deepening as he scanned the thin pages. "Do you mind if I take this? I'll return it."

"If it will help. Of course."

"Thanks. Now, I've got something else I hope you can interpret."

"I'll try."

Reaching into his pocket, Bentz withdrew copies of the notes Olivia had taken after her nightmares or "visions" surrounding the woman chained within a crypt. "Does this mean anything to you?" he asked. "Could those notations have anything to do with one of these saints?" He tapped the book with two fingers.

James adjusted his reading glasses. At first the letters and symbols meant nothing. "Is there anything else you can tell me about it?" he asked, studying the symbols.

"Yeah . . . if it's connected with a saint, the feast day would have been in summer, I think. Probably August. Maybe July."

"Philomena," James said as the letters began to connect. He picked up the book again, but he knew before he thumbed through the pages what he would find. "LUMENA, PAXTE, CUMFI. It's Latin, but mixed up. Supposedly these words were found inscribed in red on the tomb of Saint Philomena. When the tiled letters were changed around a little bit, the message read, 'Pax tecum, Filumena,' or 'Peace be with you, Philomena.' "

"What about the symbols?" Bentz asked.

"On the tiles of the tomb." James glanced down at the text. "I suppose they're open to interpretation, but the tomb of this Roman girl was found in 1802. It's thought that aside from the letters, the inscriptions on the tiles were of a lily, a palm, the arrows, anchor and a scourge, see here—" he pointed to the crude drawings. "That's the lily and it means she was a virgin. The palm is symbolic of being a martyr

and the weapons depict the tortures she went through.'' He
pointed to the arrows. ''Even these squiggly lines over the
arrow are supposed to represent fire, but of course, that's
speculation as nothing is recorded about her. She was also
found with a vial of dried blood, presumably hers, within
the tomb.''

''Her own blood? Why?''

James shrugged. ''That's the mystery of Philomena. Not
much is known about her or who she was. Though she's
got a loyal following, the Church has wavered, even sup-
pressing her feast day in the early sixties, I think. She's
gained favor again, at least with some of her supplicants,
those who invoke her name in every sort of need.''

''She performs miracles?'' Bentz asked, obviously skeptical.

''That's right.'' James handed the pages to his half-
brother. ''She was recognized as a saint solely upon her
powerful intercession.''

''You mean she grants prayer requests?''

''Yes.''

''Has she ever granted one for you?'' Bentz asked as he
stood and folded the well-worn piece of paper into his pocket.

''I've yet to ask.'' Again James slid the book across the
desk. ''Anything else I can do for you?''

''Yeah.'' Bentz started for the door. ''Pray.''

''I always do.''

That stopped him cold. He looked over his shoulder and
pinned James in his harsh glare. ''I'm okay, James. I don't
need your prayers except about this case.''

''Old habits die hard.'' James rounded the desk. ''Let me
know if there's anything else I can do.''

''I will.'' Bentz's hand was on the doorknob.

''And would you please tell Kristi that . . . that I wish
her well?''

Every muscle in his half-brother's body tensed. He
rounded. ''What good would that do? She knows the truth,

that you're more than her uncle, okay. She gets it. Let her deal.'' He turned then and torment shadowed the anger that snapped in his eyes. "It's hard enough for a kid to learn that the man who raised her isn't her father. Then add to it that the real father turns out to be an uncle who just happens to also be a priest. That's a helluva lot for a kid to take, don't you think?''

"Yes . . . I know . . . I mean . . .'' The old anguish tore at James's soul. "I've told you I'm sorry. I've talked to God. If I could do everything over . . .''

"What? You wouldn't have gotten it on with my wife? You wouldn't have gotten her pregnant? Kristi wouldn't have been born?'' Bentz raged, then stopped suddenly and the cords in his neck became less visible. "Forget it, James. And next time, let me do the praying. How about that? I'll pray for you, okay? I think you need it a helluva lot more than I do.''

With that he swung out of the door, nearly knocking over Wanda who just happened to be hovering nearby. James let out his breath, made the sign of the cross and sent up another prayer for forgiveness . . . . as he had each and every day for the past eighteen years.

But his half-brother was right. Had he not been seduced by Jennifer, Kristi would never have been born and that, in and of itself, would have been the greatest sin of all. He'd been a seminary student when he'd met his brother's wife. He'd let down his guard one weekend during a time Rick and Jennifer had briefly separated. He could still remember the taste of saltwater on her skin, the feel of hot sand against his back on the beach near Newport . . . Those memories had been with him for years and when she'd offered herself again, years later, when her marriage was on the rocks and she could no longer take being tied to a cop who'd mistakenly shot a kid close to Kristi's age and had begun pouring himself into a bottle . . . James had tried to console her and had ended up making love to her in the marriage bed she shared with his half brother.

Unfortunately Rick had chosen that afternoon to stop by the house.

Within a month Jennifer Nichols Bentz was dead. Had she killed herself? James suspected as much, though her death was ruled an accident. But the antidepressants, the booze, the clear weather conditions didn't explain why her car left the road and slammed into a tree.

James's throat thickened. No wonder his brother hated him. Kristi was right. He was a hypocrite who should have walked away from the priesthood. Instead he'd spent the past eighteen years begging God's forgiveness.

But you couldn't leave her alone, could you? You couldn't resist. And she died. God punished not only you, but your brother and your daughter.

There was a light tap at the door and he looked up, expecting that Bentz had left something and was returning for it. Instead, Monsignor O'Hara swept in. He was a tall, graceful man, soft-spoken, but with a bearing that set him apart from his peers. Wearing a plain alb, he shut the door softly behind him. "Is everything all right?"

What a joke. Nothing was right. "I suppose."

"Mrs. Landry said the police were here."

Of course. Wanda Landry had felt compelled to spread the word. She was a gossip; a pious gossip, but a gossip nonetheless and she seemed to take particular delight in the troubles of others. James suspected that she was involved in the prayer chain primarily to learn of bad news and pass it along. "It was only one policeman who happens to be my half-brother."

"Oh." The monsignor frowned thoughtfully. "I didn't know you had any family around."

"We're not close." *And whose fault is that?*

"Maybe that will change," the monsignor said.

"Perhaps." James didn't elaborate. He figured that his family was his business. Bentz's father had been a policeman killed in the line of duty. His wife had married his partner, who had treated Rick as if he were his own flesh and blood.

However, he'd left the boy with the surname of his biological father—a gift and, perhaps, in retrospect a burden.

"So there's no trouble?" O'Hara asked, a guarded smile stretching across his strong jaw. Though in his fifties, Monsignor O'Hara worked out regularly. There wasn't an ounce of fat on the older man's body. He seemed a sincere, if distant soul though James realized that he knew little of the man with whom he'd been partnered for several years.

"No trouble."

"Good . . . good . . . I'll see you later." As if he really didn't want to hear any bad news, the monsignor lifted a hand and hurried out of the office to leave James alone, sitting at the desk in the green glow of a banker's lamp as the notes from a lonely cello wafted through the empty office. He tried to pray and found no solace in speaking with God. Walking to the window he looked out at the dark, gloomy skies. The wind was beginning to pick up and a branch from the magnolia tree near the front of the building was banging against the church again, as if God were rapping on the walls, reminding him that He was watching. He knew.

James leaned his forehead against the glass and tried to conjure up the monster stalking the streets of the city. A man killing women in the ways some of the saints were martyred. Ugly. Twisted. Who would think of such a thing? And, for God's sake, why?

He suspected there was a lot more his half-brother hadn't told him; he could feel it as he stared into the dark night. And the threat was extreme for Rick to have sought him out.

Or perhaps God was trying to talk to James. There was a chance that God had directed his half-brother to the church, to him, to show James that he was needed. He walked to the bookcase again and found another, well-worn volume on the saints. In this one the pages were so thin they were nearly translucent.

Resting his hips on the edge of the desk, he shuffled through the pages and caught glimpses, images of the portraits of the saints. Painted by the masters, the women who had been canonized appeared virtuous, kind and flawlessly beautiful, the kind of woman any man would want. . . .

Like Olivia Benchet.

Why couldn't he put that woman out of his mind? A dozen times over since their last meeting, James had thought of her, evoking her image and entertaining thoughts decidedly unworthy of his calling.

He looked down at the book again. Olivia was as beautiful as any of the pictures in this ancient tome.

Stop it!

He snapped the book closed but even as he did, he wondered if he would ever see Olivia again. His pulse quickened at the thought of another encounter no matter how brief. She was innocence tangled with sweet, sinful seduction, one of the few women who were able to breach the solid and sanctimonious wall he'd constructed around his heart.

He knew he was good-looking. He'd been told often enough. The jokes that he was wasting his inherent masculinity didn't go unnoticed; some women had speculated that he was gay. Then there were the others, the vulnerable. In his role of advisor and counselor to those in pain or grieving, he'd been given ample opportunity to break his vows of celibacy. Young widows looking for strength and comfort, women who'd been rejected by boyfriends and spouses and were searching for someone to prove they were still attractive, other pushy little flirts who just looked upon him as a challenge, a notch in their garter belts. At each door of temptation, he'd stopped short, steadfastly resisting. Even when the temptation of the flesh had been so strong that he'd spent hours alternately dousing himself with cold water and kneeling on the cold stones of his altar, praying for the strength to resist the invitations thrown his way. In each and every case he'd succeeded.

Except with his brother's wife.

Even now, he closed his eyes and felt shame.

Until a few days ago he'd been prideful enough to think that he could no longer be swayed from his vows of celibacy.

And God had proved once again that he was a weak and frail man.

For that was before he'd looked into the liquid-gold eyes of Olivia Benchet. And now, he feared, he was doomed to sin again.

Chapter Twenty-two

". . . that's right, Saint Philomena. August eleventh," Bentz was saying into the receiver of his cell phone. "See if any coeds from any of the universities were reported missing about that time." God, he hated to think about the connection between the women. College girls. Like Kristi. And she wasn't that far away. It scared the piss out of him.

"I've already started looking," Montoya reported, his voice as clear as if he were sitting in the passenger seat of the Jeep instead of on his own cell phone. "But you really think this is tied into feast days?"

"I'd bet my dad's service revolver on it."

"Damn."

Bentz had spent the last three hours, ever since leaving St. Luke's, running down leads in the Stephanie Keller murder. Now, he was driving into the Quarter. "I talked with the mechanic who saw Stephanie Jane Keller after the boyfriend dropped her off. He was clocked in until nine—they work late—and was home by nine-fifteen to be with the wife and kids. He remembers nothing except that she was in a hurry to get to class. But she never made it, according to her professor. So far, the mechanic was the last one to see her alive."

"Shit."

Bentz's exact thought. "I've called some of her friends. None of 'em think she was going anywhere but to class and that gels as her books and notebook for that class weren't in her car or her apartment. I talked to the team that went through her things. Her friends check out, too, and the last guy she was involved with before Townsend was a guy she worked with, but they broke up because he got transferred to Boston. His alibi checked out, too."

"Great," Montoya muttered, his voice muffled as if he were drawing on a cigarette. "What about her car?"

"I've got people going over it now. Vacuuming, dusting for prints, even looking for blood."

"Maybe we'll learn something."

"I doubt it," Bentz said. "My guess is the guy waited until she was walking the five blocks from the dealership to the university and grabbed her, or maybe even offered her a ride. I think he knows the victims. It would have been someone she trusted. I've got a class list and I'm having everyone called to see if they remember if she made it to class. No one takes roll, y'know."

"Too bad."

"Yeah." Bentz glared into the night.

There were still no more clues on the death of Stephanie Jane Keller and each hour that passed made it less likely the crime would be solved. Where had Stephanie met her attacker? What had happened? How had she been transported to the shotgun house in Bayou St. John? "Keep me posted," Bentz said. "I'm stopping by WSLJ, just to see that no one's getting any crank calls. Then I want to double-check this saints' feast days angle—see if anyone was reported missing from the surrounding colleges on feast days in the summer or early fall."

"You still think the Rosary Killer is back?" Montoya asked.

"I don't know. But I don't like the connection between the murders and the Catholic Church. It's too much like *déjà vu.* I mean, what are the odds? Serial killers are pretty damned rare and this guy's leaving his calling card."

"The signature is different," Montoya reminded him, then swore as a horn blasted through the receiver.

"I know, but I'm saying if it's not the same guy, then there's a chance it's someone he knew."

"What?"

"A mentor or something."

"Hey, whoa—don't you think you're going off the deep end here?"

"Maybe, but it's just a gut feeling that there wouldn't be two serial killers in the same town, connected somehow to the Church, who didn't know each other."

"It's not like they belong to the same country club."

"No? Well, run it by the profiler and the FBI and tell the people who are trying to crack the damned code about St. Philomena."

"You got it. Jesus! That prick cut me off!" There was a muffled sound. Something harsh, then he was back. "Hey, Bentz, guess who I got a call from today?"

Bentz cranked the wheel and crossed two lanes. "I give, who?"

"Marlene, Oscar Cantrell's secretary. Remember her? I guess my little talk earlier today about obstruction of justice got through to her. Anyway, she gave me Cantrell's cell number. I left a message with him. So far he hasn't returned my call."

"Try again."

"Oh, I will," Montoya said. "I'll let you know what the guy says. You know, Bentz, if someone's killing women on saints' feast days, we're screwed. There's another one of those damned feasts every time you turn around."

"Then we just have to stop him," Bentz said as he saw the building housing WSLJ and parked in a loading zone. It was after hours and he really didn't give a shit. He rode up the elevator and was met by a security guard, a reminder that not too long ago this very station had been terrorized by a crazed killer fixated on Dr. Sam.

"Visiting hours are over," the security guard said gruffly, but Bentz flashed his badge.

"I'm looking for Samantha Leeds."

"She's not here," the beefy guard insisted, not budging an inch.

"It's all right, Charlie," a voice behind the guard announced and Bentz looked over the stocky man's shoulder to spy a wasp-thin woman with short black hair and sharp features. "I'm Trish LaBelle, Detective. I recognize you from your picture in the paper." She glanced at the guard. "He's the policeman who cracked the case of the Rosary Killer," then back to Bentz, "Sam's not scheduled to come in until eleven. Is there something I could help you with?" Trish offered a smile. "You know, I'd love to interview you on my program and now that we've got another killer on the loose . . . Oh, that's what this is all about, isn't it?" Her eyes narrowed and Bentz imagined a million wheels turning in her mind. "Wait a minute. You're here to see Samantha—why? Does this have to do with the Rosary Killer?" She snapped her fingers. "His body was never found, was it?" Before he could answer, her mind was racing with lightning-bolt speed. "That's it! You think the Rosary Killer has resurrected himself." Rather than seem horrified at the proposition, she was curious. "Please, Detective, I'd love to interview you."

"Not right now."

"How about in a couple of nights? We'd need to advertise it on my program and Dr. Sam's, of course, and even a couple of spots during Gator's and Ramblin' Rob's programs."

"I don't think so."

"Please, give it some thought."

"Would you tell Samantha that I was here?"

"Deceptive Bentz!" a sultry female voice exclaimed, and he turned to find Samantha Leeds shaking out her umbrella. She straightened, tossing her red hair from her face. A smile curved her lips and she winked at her own joke.

"Very funny," he said, forcing a smile.

"I thought so. But it's good to see you." Her green eyes sparkled. "What's up, Detective? Hoping to get some free on-the-air advice?"

"Maybe later," he said, then cut to the chase. "I need to talk to you, if you've got a minute."

"Always for my favorite cop," she quipped. She led him through the maze-like innards of WSLJ, past rooms of sound equipment and glassed-in studios until they reached a small lunchroom. Dropping her bag onto a round table, she settled into one of the plastic chairs. "So, seriously, before we get down to business, tell me how've you been?"

"Can't complain."

"No?"

"What about you?"

"I guess I can't complain, either. I'm getting married," she said with a wicked grin. "Next month. You'll be getting an invitation."

"I thought you'd sworn off men."

"I had. Then I met Ty. What can I say?"

"My guess is you'll be saying 'I do.' "

She leaned back in her chair. "That's what happens, you know, just when you're ready to give up on the opposite sex, you meet someone. Watch out. It'll happen to you."

He thought about arguing and decided against it. "I'll take your word on it. After all, you're the shrink. How's Ty?"

Her grin widened. "Just finishing his book on the Rosary Killer. He plans to ship it to his agent next week." She sighed. "Then he can get his head into the wedding, but you didn't come here to find out how many bridesmaids I'm having or if the reception should be catered. What's going on?"

Leaning forward, he rested his elbows on the table. "I was wondering if you've gotten any more weird calls."

"You mean weirder than usual," she said with a shake of her head. "People who call up at two or three in the morning aren't your usual nine-to-fivers."

"I mean along the lines of the calls last summer from Father John."

"No." Her expression became instantly sober. "Why? Should I have?"

"I hope not." He outlined what he could about the recent series of murders and noticed that Trish LaBelle was hovering near the doorway, taking in every word. He decided to ignore her as he explained, "The MO and signatures are slightly different from Father John's, but I just have the feeling there's a connection. Serial killers are rare and now we've got a second one within six months of the first. Even overlapping. It's beyond unlikely."

"So you think that someone is copycatting?" she asked, her smooth brow wrinkling.

Trish quit lurking and stepped into the room. "He thinks Father John might not have died in the swamp." She pulled out a chair and took a seat. "Sorry, I'd like to say I just overheard, but I was eavesdropping."

"Nice," Samantha muttered and Bentz remembered there was no love lost between the two women. They'd worked at rival stations with their call-in programs and then, just last summer, Trish had jumped ship and joined WSLJ. Bentz suspected they hadn't warmed up to each other.

Trish ignored Sam's sarcasm. "I have to tell you, Detective, I find all this macabre stuff fascinating."

"You didn't live it," Sam said, but Bentz's eyes had narrowed on the thin, sharp-featured woman.

"Do you?" he asked. "Really find it interesting?"

"Mmmm." She crossed her slim legs and leaned forward to place an elbow on the table and rest her chin on her palm, using her half-turned body to cut Samantha out of the conversation. "The truth is, I'd love to spend some time with you, Detective Bentz, visit the crime scenes, watch you sift through clues, you know, try to catch the bad guy, that sort of thing."

"It can be gruesome. Grown men have been known to lose their lunches at some of the scenes."

"I think I could handle it," she said, her eyebrows

quirking upward, a coy smile tugging at her lips. She was practically begging for an invitation to be a part of the investigation, even flirting a little to get what she wanted. Which wasn't lost on Samantha. Bentz considered the charred, mutilated body of the last victim and was willing to bet two weeks' pay Trish LaBelle would faint dead away if she was ever to see a dead body. "It would be interesting and informative. I'm sure I could work it into my show somehow."

"I don't think so."

"I'd call Eleanor Cavalier. I'm sure she'd approve it."

"Don't bother with the program manager." Time to nip this in the bud. "It's not gonna happen. There are rules about that kind of thing."

Trish was undeterred. "I've read about you, Bentz. You're not exactly one who plays by all the rules."

"He said 'no,' Trish. Take a hint," Sam cut in.

Little lines appeared between Trish's eyebrows. "Look, I want to interview him on my program, okay?"

"Whatever." Sam looked at Bentz.

"I haven't committed," he said as he stood, concluding the short interview. "Phone me if you get any disturbing calls."

"Should she be scared?" Trish asked.

"Everyone should be scared," he said. "I'm not saying that the killer is the same guy, but I'm not sure about that. What I do know is that he's out there, he's dangerous, and unless we catch him, he's not going to stop." Sam grew sober and she rubbed her arms as if reliving the terror she'd survived just this past summer. Even Trish seemed more thoughtful, but she wasn't one to give up easily.

"This is just the reason you should come on to the show," Trish insisted. "To warn the public."

"The department's already made a statement."

Trish wasn't about to be derailed. "I know, but you'd reach more citizens. We could do the interview and parts of it could be replayed during the day, even on Sam's program. WSLJ has a lot of listeners."

"Then they'll hear it on your newscasts."

"Some of them don't hear the news. You'll reach a lot more people this way." She was on a roll now, her hands moving expressively as if she could convince him by the sheer amount of her gestures or coy smiles. "You'd be doing the city a favor, Detective. Just say you'll think about it."

"Okay," he agreed as he stood. "I'll think about it. But don't hold your breath. And Samantha, if you get any calls that make you nervous, let me know."

"If she did that, she'd be out of a job," Trish joked.

Sam ignored her. "You'll be the first to know," she promised. "Thanks for the warning. I'll tell Ty you'll come to the wedding."

"Wouldn't miss it for the world," he said as he left but he knew it was a lie. His experience with marriage had left him the ultimate skeptic. Much as he wished Samantha and Ty Wheeler the best of luck, he just didn't have any faith in the theory of wedded bliss.

Olivia climbed out of the bathtub. The room was steamy and warm as she towel-dried, buffing her skin before she smoothed oil over her body, rubbing deep into her muscles. It had been a long day. Draining. Emotional. She replayed the scenes with her mother, with Bentz, and with Father McClaren through her tired mind and couldn't find a way to stave off a headache that had been pounding the edge of her brain for the past couple of hours. She'd popped four ibuprofen, then soaked over half an hour in the tub, waiting until the hot water had begun to cool slightly, hoping to ease the strain out of her day and keep the migraine at bay.

It wasn't working. As she slid her arms into the sleeves of her robe, she caught her reflection in the mirror. Her hair was piled on her head, wet tendrils framing her face. Mist clouded the glass, distorting her image. Condensation began to run in sharp rivulets, cutting through the fog and giving her a clearer picture of not only her own reflection, but of something darker in the glass, something murky beneath the surface.

"Oh, no," she whispered, her heart nearly stopping.

Not again.

She caught a glimpse of a large wooden wheel, like an oversized wagon wheel with spikes. It turned slowly then disappeared in the mirror's foggy surface. Olivia's stomach clenched. "No . . . no . . ." A woman's tortured face came into view. Olivia jumped back so far she hit the towel bar on the wall behind her. The woman in the vision was screaming, her eyes bulging in fear and pain. Blood matted her dark hair.

Olivia was shaking.

The wheel spun, dancing in and out behind the curtain of condensation on the glass. Olivia's skin prickled. She could barely breathe. Her headache thundered, roaring through her brain. Transfixed in horror, she stared at the mirror.

As some of the condensation evaporated, Olivia caught a better view of a dark place, a cavernous area. She heard tortured screams and water dripping over the creak of ancient gears, then saw the horrendous implement of torture. The woman, stripped naked, was splayed upon the wheel and strapped down. Sharp spikes drove into her body as she struggled and the hideous wheel slowly rotated.

"Don't, please don't!" she shrieked. "Let me go . . . Please . . . Have mercy . . ."

Olivia's headache hammered.

"Help me . . . someone, for the love of God, please, help me . . ." Her voice shook, reverberating in Olivia's brain, pounding with the pain.

"Let her go, you bastard!" Olivia cried.

Then she saw it. Glinting in the damp reflection. A curved sword, its wicked blade catching in some weak, flickering light.

"No! No!" The woman shrieked. "How can you do this to me? I trusted you. Please, please, I'll do anything."

The blade sliced down.

"Stop!!" Olivia snagged a towel from the rack and rubbed frantically at the condensation, swiping away the fog, staring into her own horrified eyes. If she could see more, find out where this was happening . . . but the image had changed, the woman's tortured face fading into the shadows to be replaced by a clearer image, lying just beneath her own reflection. Her heart froze for she was certain she was staring into the face of pure evil. Shrouded in a tight black mask, ice blue eyes found hers and held . . .

Then she heard her name. As clearly as if he'd spoken it. *Olivia.*

"Jesus." She took a step backward again.

Saint Olivia.

"No!" She flung herself at the mirror. "Who are you, you bastard?" she cried, smashing her fist against his masked face. Glass splintered. Shards rained into the sink and onto the floor. Her own image was distorted and fragmented in the remaining pieces still mounted upon the mirror's frame. "You sick, sick son of a bitch." Pain screamed through her hand. "Who the hell are you?" she cried, sobs welling up from deep inside. "Who, damn it?"

Outside the bathroom door Hairy S was barking wildly, clawing at the panels.

Blood dripped and splattered against the glittering slivers in the sink.

Her head raged. The dog howled miserably. Through it all Olivia was left with the tortured image of a woman strapped to a revolving wheel of pain.

"God help us," Olivia whispered, tears running down her face. "God help us all." She stepped back against the wall and somehow opened the door. Sliding down the wall, she let her tears flow freely.

Hairy S whined. She picked him up and buried her face in his unruly fur. What was she going to do? How could she stop this? *How?* "Damn it all to hell." She ran a hand over her face, swiping at the tears, smearing blood over her cheeks and onto the dog.

Something had to be done . . . and soon.

The bastard had killed tonight.

And there would be more.

Saint Olivia. She'd heard her name as surely as if he'd said it. He meant to kill her. She was sure of it. In some hideously painful manner, he was going to murder her.

Unless . . . oh, God . . . unless she found a way to stop him.

Chapter
Twenty-three

Bentz was on the road again and talking on his cell phone. He'd caught up with Norm Stowell. So far the conversation wasn't settling well.

"You've got yourself a problem," the profiler said from somewhere in Arizona. He, too, was on a cell phone and at times the connection sputtered. "Most serial killers start off at a slower pace, they relive the crime for weeks, maybe months before they feel the need to hunt again," Norm told him as Bentz accelerated around a flatbed with only one taillight. "Then as time goes on, the reliving isn't enough of a rush and the killer starts shortening the time between the kills. Escalating. But you've got something different at play here. If you're right about the connection to the saints' feasts days, your killer has a green light. Any female saint's day will do; he'll work it into his plan."

Bentz didn't want to believe it. "But the killings take planning. There are props involved, the scene is staged. And he's got to lure the girls to come with him or convince them to let him in. He takes incredible risks. Take the fire off of

Esplanade. It could have been seen earlier by a neighbor out walking his dog. Bingo, the suspect would have been nabbed. Then there was dumping the Jane Doe at the foot of the statue on a main street in the middle of town, for Christ's sake. That was pretty damned cocky.''

"He's taunting you. 'Look what I can do. See what I can get away with.' He wants you to search for him. He likes the publicity, the feeling of being smarter than you. He could be close to someone on the force. Look for a guy with some kind of security or police background.''

"The witness says he's a priest.''

"Not one of the usual kind,'' Stowell reminded him. "See if you can find any priest with a link to the police. And don't forget that this guy thinks he's on some kind of mission from God. He's empowered. He thinks God is in his corner, so he feels invulnerable, which means there's a better chance that he'll slip up.''

"Let's hope.'' Bentz maneuvered past an eighteen-wheeler that was throwing up road scum. He flipped on his wipers.

"I have a feeling this guy gets to know his victims. That's part of his game, his thrill. Somehow he gets them to trust him. There wasn't any evidence of forced entry with the girl in the Garden District, was there? My guess is that he's charming, they trust him, they allow him to get close, and he starts thinking of them in terms of a saint, or making them a saint. You said the two victims you've identified are part-time students? That's the link. These aren't random women he happens to see. He interacts with them before the kill. Gets them to trust him. All the while he's literally charming their socks off when he's really setting them up. No sign of sexual contact?''

"Not so far.''

There was a long silence when he heard only the wheels of his Jeep turning and the rumble of the other traffic.

"That's odd. Probably has to do with the priest-celibacy thing. Or he's impotent. But usually the kill will get the killer off. I assume you've checked with the local universities.''

Bentz's fingers clutched the steering wheel in a death grip. His stomach burned at the thought of college coeds being hunted and tortured. An image of Kristi shot through his mind and his gut ached even more. "We're trying to find out if the two victims knew each other, took any classes together, ever met. They went to schools that are right next to each other, so the population mixes quite a bit."

"What about the boyfriends?"

"One skipped town months ago, the other has an alibi."

"Air-tight?"

"We're lookin' for a leak. So far he seems on the up and up."

"Double-check him. Especially if he's a white male probably between twenty-five and thirty-five, someone who has a history of violence, maybe trouble in grade school and high school, possibly arrests for cruelty to animals and arson, trouble with women . . . there should be something on him."

"We've got it covered."

"Good. I'll fax you what I've got."

"Thanks." Bentz switched lanes and Stowell rang off. Bentz didn't feel any better than he had when he'd left St. Luke's. It had galled him to face his half-brother again, but he'd known James would see him, would try to help. The sanctimonious bastard. Other than Kristi, Father James McClaren was Bentz's only living relative aside from a few second and third cousins scattered across the country. And James was the one man who had knifed him in the back. More than once.

Within minutes, as he worked the Jeep onto the exit ramp only a few miles from Olivia Benchet's house, the phone rang sharply. "This is Bentz."

"It's Olivia. I need to see you," she said, her voice frantic and breathless. "He's doing it again."

Bentz felt cold as death. He'd expected the call, had even been heading to her house because he'd known the killer would strike on the feast day of Saint Catherine of Alexandria. Or any other saint's day. "I'm already on my way," he said. "I'll be there in ten minutes."

"Thank God."

"Hang in." He clicked off and punched the accelerator. "God damn it!"

The streets were empty in this desolated part of the parish. He blew through one stop sign, then took a sharp corner to the country road that wandered through the bayou. It was dark, the moon shrouded, a damp wind whipping through the stands of oak and cypress that rose like ghosts from the land and water. His Jeep sped across a long, low bridge but it wasn't fast enough. The terror in Olivia's voice spurred him on. He nearly missed the turnoff, but cranked hard on the wheel. The four-by-four shuddered, slowing as he took the corner too fast and cut through the trees of the Benchet tract. Leaves scattered as the Jeep flew across the small bridge near Olivia's cottage.

He stood on the brakes.

The front door of the house flew open.

He sucked in his breath.

Backlit by the lamps of the cabin, she stood in the door-way, a fluffy white robe wrapped around her body, her hair as wild as ever. His heart jolted. He knew then that in a few short days he'd started to fall for this fruitcake of a woman with her bizarre claims of visions and some kind of weird ESP. He experienced the unlikely feeling of coming home. Hell, he'd hadn't had a real home in years.

Bentz was out of the truck in a heartbeat, running. Her stupid dog charged out of the house.

"Hairy!" Olivia raced toward him and seemed oblivious to the mud and wet leaves. "Thank God you're here," she cried, hurtling into his open arms. He caught a glimpse of tear tracks glistening on her cheeks the second before she buried her face in his chest and wrapped her arms around his neck. Instinctively he held her close, smelling the scents of jasmine and lilac over the rush of the wind and the dank smell of the swamp. Her breasts crushed against him. Her hair was damp. No makeup on her face. She clung to him, shaking. He suspected she wore nothing beneath the chenille housecoat, but he didn't let his brain wrap around that image for but a second.

"I saw him. Again. And he was killing a woman . . . on a wheel with horrible nails in it . . . Oh, God, oh, God, oh, God," she cried, her fingers clutching his collar as if she'd never let go. She was breathing with difficulty, fighting sobs, hiccupping with fear. "And then, and then, I think he had a sword . . . he . . ."

"*Shh.*" Bentz held her awkwardly at first, his hands seeming too big to cradle her small body. What was he doing? This was all wrong.

But as she molded to him and the wind sighed through the trees, he loosened up. One hand went to the back of her neck, the other the small of her back. For an instant he wondered what it would be like to make love to her and he remembered kissing her not all that long ago. It seemed only natural to touch his lips to her crown, to feel her soft breath against his bare neck. She turned her face up to stare at him, and it was all he could do not to kiss that sexy, provocative, and definitely frightened mouth. "Come on, let's get you inside."

"I—I'm sorry," she said, as if suddenly realizing what she'd done.

"It's all right. Really." He managed a bit of a smile then whistled to the dog, who found a new interest in the hem of his pants. Bentz draped a steadying arm across her shoulders as they climbed the steps.

"God, I hate that."

"What?"

"Everything." She shot a look up at him as they walked through the open door. "But you know, playing the role of the wimpy, weak female."

"You were scared."

"I was terrified out of my wits. Still am," she said, but the tears had subsided and the hiccups had disappeared.

"I think you'd better tell me about it."

Hairy S, snuffling and snorting, trotted into the house. Bentz closed the door and locked it. He followed Olivia into the kitchen and noticed a thick bandage on her right hand, the drops of blood staining her robe. "What happened?"

"I wish I could say I cut myself shaving," she said, her lips trembling into a smile. The joke fell flat. She blinked hard, still fighting tears. "But I smashed my fist into the bathroom mirror."

"On purpose?" He couldn't believe it.

"Yes. It's stupid but I wanted to strike out, to hit that son of a bitch and I . . ." She stopped and dropped into a chair at the table. The robe gaped open, but she seemed unaware that Bentz could catch more than a glimpse of her breasts. He forced his eyes back to hers. "I guess I should start at the beginning," she was saying as she stared through the windows into the gloomy night.

"That would be good."

"It was about an hour ago, I guess. I was taking a bath. It had been a helluva day . . . Well, you know, you and I had our fight and then my father called—"

"Reggie Benchet phoned you?" he repeated, warning bells going off in his mind. Father or no, the guy was an ex-con. A felon.

"Yeah and . . . well, I had to deal with it. It was weird. I hadn't said one word to him since I was in grade school. It was a short conversation and then I tried to spend some time studying, get my mind off of him. It didn't work, so I was planning to take a bath and crash early, but just as I was stepping out of the tub, I glanced in the mirror and I saw her and that . . . that hideous wheel." Rubbing her arms, she launched into her story of the vision, a chilling reinactment of the death of St. Catherine of Alexandria. Olivia rubbed one temple with her good hand. Her face was drawn and her eyes seemed unfocused, as if she were seeing the vision being replayed in her mind. ". . . and there was nothing I could do," she finally said, again the tears beginning to flow. "I feel so useless."

He placed a hand on her shoulder and she lifted one of hers to touch his fingers. "If it's any consolation, I want you to know that I believe you. I understand about the killings.'' Her fingers tensed as he explained about the pattern that was developing, how the killer was murdering the victims in accordance with the deaths of venerated, martyred saints on the days of their feast. "So we've now got St. Joan of Arc, St. Mary Magdalene, St. Cecilia, all of whose bodies we've recovered."

"You mean there could be more?" She paled.

"I don't know. But you mentioned the woman who was left in a crypt. I think she was playing the role of St. Philomena. Now, we've got a new one, the one tonight."

"Catherine of Alexandria."

He frowned. "We don't know how many others are involved or how long he's been on his killing spree."

"Oh, God," she whispered, swallowing hard. "How many saints are there?"

"Too many." He snorted. "I never thought I'd say that."

She glanced up at him, her eyes troubled, her eyelashes still damp with tears. "What kind of perverted bastard would do this?"

"That's what we have to find out." He tightened his grip on her hand. Attempted to be reassuring. "We'll find him, but I'm going to need your help."

"I'll do anything"

He managed a smile. "I know. Let me make some phone calls." He checked his watch. It was late, after eleven, but he rang up Montoya and the precinct, leaving messages, then walked upstairs to the bathroom. Bits of glass were everywhere—counter, sink, and floor. Blood splattered the basin and tiles. "Looks like a war zone," he joked.

"I was angry," she admitted. "And scared. He was looking at me—straight at me in the mirror—and he could see me, I think, as surely as I could see him." She located a broom and dustpan. Together they cleaned up the mess.

When they were downstairs again, Olivia made tea . . . some kind of ginger-smelling stuff that tasted like flowers. He didn't complain, just sipped it and wished it were a beer. They sat at the small table in her kitchen, the bird making soft noises, the dog settled onto a rag rug as she told her

story, over and over again. Bentz asked a dozen questions.
She didn't always have answers but he was certain she'd
seen another murder. Four days ago he would have scoffed
at the idea, but today he took her word as gospel. It was
after one when he scraped back his chair. "I'd better get
going. Can you think of anything else?"

"Just that his eyes are blue. Icy, intense blue," she said,
suddenly remembering.

"You would recognize him?"

"No, as I said, he was wearing the ski mask again."

"The eye color is something." Of course he could wear
contacts.

"And he knows my name."

"What?"

"I heard him . . . you know, in the vision, he looked
straight at me and it was as if I heard his voice or his
thoughts, but he called me Olivia. Saint Olivia."

"Christ," Bentz swore, then glanced through the windows
to the darkness of the bayou. Gloomy. Isolated. Murky. If
the murderer showed up here, no one would see him. And
he knew who Olivia was. "You know, If you don't mind,
I think I'll stick around here until it gets light."

She hesitated. "Of course . . . I mean that would be fine
. . . but I didn't mean to give you the impression because I
was upset that I'm some kind of frightened helpless female
all alone—"

"You get that security system yet?"

"No—not until after Thanksgiving but—"

"Then I'm staying."

"But—"

"It's not that you're a frightened female, okay? Though
you should be. It's because your life is in danger. I've already
had the department okay a bodyguard."

"I don't live in the city."

"We work with the Sheriff's Department, and besides,
maybe I want to hang out here." He drew in a breath, saw
the questions in her eyes, and decided to come clean. "I
was harsh on you. Not only when you first came into the

station but when we were at the café. I'm sorry. I made a mistake.''

"Yes, you did,'' she said, obviously not giving him an inch on that one. "A major mistake. But I'm over it.'' Was she? She managed a smile. "Apology accepted. And you don't have to stay. Really. I'll be fine here.''

"Well . . .'' He slanted her a smile as a breath of wind rattled a shutter. "Maybe I'd like to stay,'' he said and something sparked in her eyes. Something interested and slightly wicked. Something he didn't want to see.

"That's different. Probably a lie. But different.''

"Go to bed, Olivia. I'll hang out on the couch.''

She shook her head. "I've got a spare bedroom. Come on. It's late.'' She snapped off the lights and started for the stairs. "If you can ignore the junk.''

"Don't worry about a mess,'' he said, double-checking that the doors and windows were locked. "You should see my place.''

"Maybe I'll get the chance someday.''

He didn't respond as he followed her up the stairs and decided this was a mistake. Another one. He was batting a thousand tonight. This house was too cozy and she looked and smelled too damned inviting.

Inside the spare bedroom-cum-office, she tucked away some textbooks and leaned over the bed, plumping the pillows. He tried not to notice the roundness of her rump beneath the robe and ignored the fact that his cock twitched.

"There ya go,'' she said, turning to face him, her face flushed. "Sleep well.'' Standing on her tiptoes, she placed a chaste kiss upon his lips.

That was all it took. He could have resisted an overt come-on; he'd had more than his share of women trying to reach him at a sexual level but this . . . cheekiness . . . her playful smile and the light dancing in her eyes, the challenge he saw on her face, was his undoing. He grabbed her and, as she gasped, kissed her. Hard. His lips covered hers without a question of his intention.

And she responded. As if she'd been waiting for him to

make the first move. She sighed softly, opening her mouth, and his tongue slid easily between those firm lips. The twitch in his pants became a rock-hard erection and all thoughts of keeping her safe, of being vigilant, of catching a twisted killer before he struck again, slipped into the nether reaches of Bentz's mind.

Her fingers slid down his back, rubbing his muscles through his shirt, and all the while he kissed her, he walked her back to her bedroom with its old-fashioned four-poster, only stopping when the back of her calves met the mattress.

He fingered the knot of her robe and the belt loop opened. With one hand he reached inside, scraping the side of her body, tracing the curve of her ribs, waist, and hips. His cock strained. She kissed him as if she would never stop, and a low little moan escaped her throat.

His blood pounded through his brain and he wanted this woman.

Fiercely.

Don't do it, Bentz. Don't!

His mind was a nag.

He ignored it.

With the flat of his hand, he moved to the front of her, to the mound between her legs, her curls bristly beneath the pads of his fingers. Her breathing escalated as his fingers splayed, gently asking. If she pushed him away now, he'd be embarrassed but he could leave.

The air in the room was thick with the unspoken question. Her flesh quivered against the callouses in his palm as he pressed the heel of his hand to her bare skin, gently rubbing.

She moaned again.

Inviting.

Still he hesitated. One hand at the back of her neck, holding her head to his, the other moving in slow, sensual circles against her abdomen. His damned cock ached.

"This could be dangerous," he whispered in the darkness.

"I—I know."

"I don't know how I'll feel in the morning," he admitted, forcing out the words.

"Neither do I."

He kissed her again and she placed her hand on his fly. With a groan, he used his weight to push her onto the mattress and they fell together, kissing, touching, tugging at the clothes that kept them apart.

Her skin felt like silk; she smelled of jasmine and lavender. Her lips tasted of ginger. Her tongue flicked and played with his.

Pushing her robe off her shoulders, he kissed the column of her neck, then lower to the circle of bones at her throat. She bucked. Her fingers scraped off his shirt and tore open his fly. Frantic and wild, her hands caressed him. The room blurred, walls and windows becoming indistinct. His pants and boxers were pushed over his hips and he buried his face in her breasts, kissing, teasing, suckling, while his hands explored all of her.

Oh, God, if they didn't slow down, he'd come before she was ready. He grabbed her hands. "Take it easy, Livvie . . . we've got all night."

Olivia sighed. The want in her pounded through her brain. She couldn't think, could barely breathe as he touched her, kissed her, moved with her. The world swayed and rocked. A part of her knew she was making a horrid mistake, that with the morning light would come embarrassment, or shame, or recriminations. But for tonight, she just wanted to lose herself in this man. Did she love him? Of course not . . . she barely knew him and yet she wanted him so desperately. It had been so long . . . so, so long . . . She was hot, burning inside. Like hot wax, she was melting. His lips pressed urgent kisses to her breasts, his lips playing, his teeth nipping.

Just a tiny hint of pain with the pleasure. Sweat drizzled down her back and her heart was pounding wildly as he kissed her. She clung to him, her fingers raking down the sinewy muscles of his back. She wanted more. So much more . . . all of him.

Tough, hard hands stroked her hips, pushed open her thighs and then, finger by finger, worked their way into the deepest part of her. She was moving against him, wanting more as he touched her intimately. She bucked, crying out. "Oh, oh, God . . ."

"That's it, Livvie," he whispered into her skin. "That's it."

Her fingers dug into his hair and she felt spasm after spasm hit her, propelling her to the edge, taking her higher only to slow just at the brink.

"Ooohh . . . nooo . . . More . . ." she cried and he slid atop her, muscular thighs parting her knees, strong, sturdy body rising above her, barely visible in the darkness, as he pushed, slowly at first, deep into her. She was wet. Hot. Anxious, and as he thrust, she lifted her hips, meeting him. She moved to his rhythm, the room seeming to melt away, the universe centering in the single spot where they were joined, her body throbbing with want.

He was gasping, his skin slick with sweat as he gathered her in his arms, cried out. A second later she spasmed, jerking with the orgasm, calling out his name as he fell upon her. "Rick . . . my God . . . sweet heaven . . ."

She gasped for breath. Her arms held him tight. Tears ran from her eyes. Not from sorrow, or shame, but at the release. For a few seconds they said nothing. The night, thick and warm, wrapped around them as their breathing finally slowed.

"Sooo," he said and she heard the smile in his voice. "Was it good for you?"

"Oh, I suppose it was good enough," she teased and they both laughed.

"Just enough?" He levered up on one elbow to stare down at her in the darkness. "Should we try to improve on that?"

"I was kidding, okay. It was great."

"Nonetheless . . ." A hand moved up her thigh and she giggled.

"You don't have to prove anything to me, Bentz."

"But maybe I have to prove it to myself."

"So now you think you're a triathlete."

"At least biathlete."

"Marathon man?"

"Let's see." His lips found hers again, and this time when they made love, it was slower, the pace calmer, the urgency replaced with expectation. He brought her to the same dizzying heights as before; they weren't frantic, but just as intense and hot . . . inside she melted like butter and lost herself as he joined their bodies, pulling her atop him, moving beneath her, holding her hips firmly as she found the perfect spot. Her breathing was shallow, her blood hot, her skin on fire until at last she exploded only seconds before his own violent release. *"Ooooh,* darlin'," he sighed.

As she gasped for air, he pulled her downward, holding her close.

"Better . . ." she whispered. "Next time—"

"Next time? Oh, hush, woman."

She cuddled into his arms and didn't move. Just felt his lips brush against her forehead as his breathing slowed. She was certain she'd regret this in the morning, but for now, she didn't care.

"We shouldn't . . ." the woman with wild sun-streaked hair and gold eyes said. "We can't." She was walking fast along a path through a sunlit field, a diaphanous dress swirling around her legs and hugging her torso. Her breasts were visible beneath the sheer cloth, her dark nipples inviting. She wore no bra. No panties. Nothing under the sheer, shiny fabric.

James was so hard he ached. "I know . . . but . . . with you it's different."

"You're a priest." She pointed to the collar surrounding his throat. He tried to rip it off. And failed. It was all he was wearing. Just the collar. Otherwise he was naked as the day he was born. The sun felt hot upon his bare skin, and the long, dry grass in the field brushed against his legs.

She started to run away. Grasshoppers flew out of her path. He chased her.

"But I think I'm falling in love with you."

"Love?" She threw back her head and laughed, didn't seem to care that he was naked and hard as he chased her up a small rise. "You love God. Just God."

He caught her at the crest of the hill and dragged her to the ground. Still laughing and breathing hard, she looked up into his eyes. "We shouldn't," she said again, but there was sexy, naughty invitation in her eyes. "It's a sin, you know." Doubts chased through his mind, his vows mocked him as he pushed the flimsy fabric up her legs and smelled her sweet woman-scent.

Somewhere a bell began to ring.

He was stretched out over her, his cock hard and wanting.

The bell pealed again, more urgently. He looked up to see a bell tower . . . sun-baked stucco with a red tile roof . . . pigeons flew around the tall spire where a cross, aflame, pierced the cloudless heavens. But the tower was empty. No bell was swinging from the cross-beams.

"Please . . ." the woman whispered and he looked down to see that her face had changed. She wasn't Olivia any longer. Jennifer Bentz was lying beneath him. Naked. Her body shimmering with perspiration, she was staring up at him, begging him to enter her.

Brrriiiiinnnnggg!

James's eyes flew open.

Sweat drenched his body. The dream began to recede and he breathed hard. Dear Father, what had he been thinking? He was still hard, still ached, and the image of Olivia Benchet, naked beneath the flimsy dress, was imprinted into his brain.

The phone shrieked again.

He fumbled for the receiver. What time was it? He glanced at the clock. Two-fifteen in the morning. What in the world? Someone must've died, or been in an accident. "This is Father McClaren," he mumbled, snapping on the light and realizing he was holding the handset upside down. He flipped the receiver and rubbed his face with his free hand.

"Forgive me, Father, for I have sinned."

The voice was male. A whisper.

"What?" Someone wanted to give confession? Now? Or maybe it was a crank call. Kids. It had happened before. He blinked hard, tried to push the remnants of his vivid dream from his brain.

"Tonight I have taken a life," the raspy voice said again.

"Excuse me?" James said, certain he hadn't heard right and sat bolt upright in bed.

"For God. In the name of the Holy Father. A sinner has been redeemed and now, because of me, has become a saint."

"You're confessing to me?" James asked, the sweat on his body now chilled as he realized the person on the other end of the phone was serious. Dead serious. "You murdered someone?"

"This is my reconciliation. It is between you and me and God," the muffled voice declared and James nearly dropped the phone. A chill, cold as Satan's heart, stole through James's blood.

"Wait a minute—"

"Forgive me, Father, for I have sinned."

Chapter
Twenty-four

Morning light was filtering through the windows.

And the bed was cold.

Empty.

Olivia stared at the ceiling and bit her lip.

What had she done?

Flashes of the night before ran through her brain. Vibrant, erotic images that made her blush as she lay in her bed. She'd slept with Bentz. Made love to him. More than once.

What had she been thinking?

That's the problem, you idiot, you weren't thinking. Not for a minute!

She cringed. What a mistake!

But there was nothing that could be done about it now . . . What was done, was done. She couldn't change last night and didn't know that she would if given the chance. And the experience was definitely worth it. Definitely.

The aroma of hot coffee wafted up the stairs and she heard the muffled bang of a cupboard being shut. So he was still here. That was good.

Right?

Searching, she found her robe, a pool of white chenille, on the floor. Just where she'd tossed it. Good Lord. Shoving her arms through the sleeves, she wrapped the white terry cloth around her naked body and, cinching the belt tight, hurried barefoot down the stairs. She caught her reflection in the mirror near the front door and cringed, then finger-combed her hair as best she could with her good hand as she walked into the kitchen. Coffee brewed in the maker and a copy of a large book lay open on the table. The French doors were flung open, allowing drifts of cold morning air and the smell of smoke to seep into the room.

Bentz, wearing last night's clothes, was staring at the mist rising off the bayou. The fabric of his shirt was stretched taut over his wide shoulders as he leaned over the rail. In one hand a half-smoked cigarette was burning.

"Good morning," she forced out, squaring her shoulders. She was slowly unwrapping the cover to Chia's cage. The bird made a noise and ruffled her brilliant feathers as she stretched her legs. "Good morning to you, too," she added as Chia hopped from one perch to the next.

Bentz turned to face Olivia. His expression said it all.

Her heart dropped.

Regret was evident in the lines around the corners of his mouth and his gray eyes were wary. Suspicious again. "Mornin'." He managed a bit of a smile. "Coffee's on."

"I saw." She folded the cover, felt like a fool, and motioned toward the cigarette. "I didn't know you smoked."

"I don't." He glanced down at his hand, lifted a shoulder, then took a long drag.

She didn't ask the obvious question as she tucked the cover onto a shelf.

"I keep a pack in the Jeep and in the drawer at the station just in case." Smoke drifted from his nostrils.

"In case?"

"In case I really need one." He tossed the butt into the swampy yard, where it sizzled and died.

"For days like today?"

"Yeah. Especially days like today." He looked up at her again. "Besides, I had to go to the Jeep for that." He pointed at the thick volume on the table.

"What is it?" She eyed the book.

"A listing of all the saints."

"I see." The tome was open to a page on Bl. Olivia. "Oh." Her throat constricted. There wasn't much information, just that for her faith and preaching she'd been imprisoned and avoided being burned to death by converting her would-be executioners. Eventually she was beheaded. Olivia shuddered and leaned against the table. In her mind's eye she saw the wicked, curved blade that had been used against the poor woman in her vision. "What a way to start the morning," she said.

"The good news is that her feast day isn't until June tenth."

"Why is she Bl. Olivia, not St. Olivia?"

"I don't know. She's listed as a saint. And there's another. Saint Oliva, no second 'i' in the name." He sorted through the pages until he came to the one in question. Olivia read about St. Oliva. There wasn't much. Just that she was a martyr and executed. Her feast day was March fifth.

"So now I know when he'll try to kill me," she mocked. "Great."

"Not necessarily. I've thought about it. The murderer's MO is to name the victims after the saints, regardless of their given names. So he could change your name to some saint whose feast day is a lot closer." He looked at her with disturbed eyes. "And some of 'em are pretty damned gruesome."

"Did anyone ever tell you that you were a real upper in the morning?" she muttered, refusing to be freaked out. "Please have a cup of coffee or something. I don't need this."

"It's not a joking matter."

"I know. I know." She wrapped her arms around her middle.

"You've got to be careful."

"I am," she said but the look he sent her said otherwise. Chia squawked from her cage and Olivia thought about the night before. About sleeping with a cop. About, if she allowed it, how she could lose her foolish heart to this man. "Okay, you're right," she said, sighing as she leaned against the edge of the table.

"Good." He plowed stiff fingers through his hair. "I called a friend of mine. Ole Olsen. He owns a security company and owes me a favor. His crew will be out this morning."

"I already have a guy who's coming next week."

"Cancel it. Ole'll do a good job for you and it won't cost you any more than what you were gonna pay."

"Must be quite a favor he owes you," she said, bristling a little at the way he thought he needed to take charge of her life.

"Enough of one." He paused before adding, "Look, about last night . . ." His voice trailed off as if he expected her to jump in. No way. She wanted to hear what he had to say.

"What about it?"

He shoved his fists into the pockets of his slacks. His lips compressed. "I think you should know that I make it a personal rule not to get involved with anyone I work with, either at the department or on the case."

"I think you just broke it."

"Yep."

"But you won't again?"

"No. It was a mistake."

"Oh, *riiiight.* Boy, Bentz, you're a real charmer."

Refusing to be baited, he went on, "I just wanted you to know. In case . . . well . . ."

"In case I'd developed some twisted romantic notion about what happened between us?" she offered.

His jaw clenched. "What happened between us won't be repeated."

"That sounds suspiciously like a challenge."

Bentz shook his head. "I can't let my emotions cloud my judgment."

"Is that possible?" she asked, moving toward him, closing the distance. "Do you have emotions?"

He sliced her a hard look. "I have to get downtown."

"Duty calls?" It sounded harsher than she meant it. She did know what he meant, but she couldn't shake off the sting of his rejection with just a dismissive shrug of her shoulder.

"That's right. It does." His skin grew taunt over his cheekbones. "Thanks for—"

"Don't!" she cut in, lifting a hand as if to ward off a blow. "Just leave it, okay? I'm a big girl. An adult. This isn't an adolescent crush or some fascination I have with you being with a cop, okay? I just want you to understand that. Last night just happened." He lifted a bushy eyebrow as if he didn't believe a word of the garbage she was peddling.

Neither did she. She'd never been into one-night stands and had practiced a rather short and broken chain of serial monogamy since her first real boyfriend her senior year in high school. But she wasn't going to let him know that. Not right now. "Okay, you've got that off your chest. I get it." With a toss of her head, she plunged her fists into the pockets of her robe.

"You're pissed."

"Yeah, a little. It's just that . . . well, I'm not into casual sex."

"Neither am I."

"But I'm not willing to throw last night in the trash just because it doesn't fit in with my book of professional etiquette." She angled her face up at him and his eyes held hers a second too long.

"I just need to keep everything in perspective. Last night, I lost control. It's not like me."

"Maybe it is like you and you just won't admit it."

He looked at her so sharply, she knew she'd hit a nerve.

"Someone really did a number on you, didn't she?"

"It's irrelevant."

"Bull. In case you didn't notice, I was there last night," she said, advancing on him, holding up her bandaged hand and jabbing a finger at his chest. "And I was paying attention. You've got walls built up around you, Bentz. Huge stone walls piled way high, and I'm willing to bet that when anyone starts pulling those stones away, breaking down the walls, you either build 'em up again real fast or you run."

"As I said, it doesn't matter."

"That's where you're wrong." She was angry and couldn't rein it in. "Maybe last night just happened, or maybe it was supposed to happen. Who knows? It all depends upon your cosmic view or lack thereof. But I don't remember asking you for any declarations of love or commitment or anything of the kind, so don't act like I'm some poor, wretched little woman whose heart has been broken. Okay? I'm just saying that we shared something. If it was one time, fine, I can handle that, but don't pretend you're taking the higher ground because of some professional purpose because I'm not buying it."

He hesitated. A muscle worked in his jaw. "What is it you want from me?"

"Honesty."

"Women never want honesty."

"What archaic planet are you coming from?" she demanded, burned. "Most women want honesty, Bentz, and I just happen to be one."

"Then here it is. Short and simple. I can't get involved. With anyone. Last night was a mistake. Not yours. Mine. While I'm on this case, I can't let you . . ."

She arched an angry eyebrow. "Do what?"

"Get too close."

"What about after the case is closed?"

"I don't know," he said and deep furrows etched his brow.

"Nothing will change," she said, starting to understand him and what all this denial was about. "You still won't let me or any female 'get too close.' "

"Maybe you listen to too much Dr. Sam."

"And I'm sticking with my theory that someone really did a number on you. Let me guess . . . your ex-wife." Bingo. His eyes narrowed just a fraction.

"I think we'd better leave her out of this," he said, the corners of his lips tight. He picked up the book on saints and tucked it under his arm.

She wasn't finished. "Let's get something straight. I'm not the kind of woman to sit around and wait. Believe it or not, I, too, have a life."

"That's good."

"You bet it is."

He hesitated, muttered something under his breath, and started for the door. "I'll call you . . . I mean, if anything else comes up, and I expect the same from you." The dog was at his heels.

"Absolutely." Silently counting to ten, Olivia walked Bentz to the front of the house and, while she was at it, pushed aside most of her anger. Rejection wasn't the end of the world and she'd suffered enough of it in the past. Why should Rick Bentz prove to be different than the other men who had left her?

You called him. You invited him upstairs. You wanted last night to happen. You knew the chances. Don't be a child. Clearing her throat, she said, "Look, I didn't mean to come off as the bitch of the century. Thanks for telling me how you felt and . . . thanks for coming over last night. I, um, I was kind of a wreck." She managed a thin smile.

"No one blames you for that. What you saw would have shaken anyone up. I'll talk to the Sheriff's Department; there will be extra patrols and you"—he pointed an accusing finger at Hairy S—"be a guard dog, okay? Not a yapping idiot but a real, bonafide guard dog."

Hairy's tail slid between his legs and his head lowered as he cowered behind Olivia. "He'd rather be a thief. He likes to steal things and hide 'em."

"Wonderful. He'll be a lot of help, that one will," Bentz muttered under his breath as he opened the door, then paused as the moment stretched out awkwardly between them.

"Take care, okay?" Bentz brushed his knuckles under her chin and her stupid heart lurched. "I'll be in touch." He stepped onto the porch, jangling the wind chimes with his shoulder as he took off at a jog to his Jeep.

Standing in the doorway, Olivia watched him swing into his rig, sketch another wave to her, then throw the SUV into gear and tear out of the drive. Leaves and mud scattered in the Jeep's wake. She should've thought *good riddance,* but didn't.

With the tips of her fingers, she touched her chin where Bentz's knuckles had scraped the underside of her jaw. The gesture had been his way of being tender and yet not getting close.

Which was a crock.

The kind of mixed signals she didn't need.

She watched as the Jeep disappeared through the trees. The guy was a cop who'd seen way too much. He'd lost whatever ability he'd had to reach out and connect with another person years ago. He was *not* the kind of man she needed in her life!

So what if he was good-looking? Handsome men were a dime a dozen. Big deal that he was incredible in bed. One had to wonder where he'd picked up that particular skill. It didn't matter that he'd come rushing over here the minute she was upset. After all, it was his job, wasn't it?

So she'd slept with him and made love to him with wild abandon. People did it every night of the week.

But not you, Olivia. This is new ground for you. Virgin territory. You are an idiot. You take so many risks with him. Physical risks, emotional risks. You have no idea if he's involved with some other woman. Just because he's not married doesn't ensure that he doesn't have a girlfriend tucked away—or maybe two or three.

No, that part she didn't believe. Bentz didn't have time for a woman. Not just her, but any woman.

His Jeep was long out of sight as she shut the door and the house seemed suddenly lonely. Cold. As if it had lost some vitality. "Stop it," she growled at herself as she started up the stairs to change. She was halfway up when the phone rang. Down she went. Robe billowing, she flew into the kitchen and nearly yanked the receiver out of the base. "Hello?" she said, half-expecting to hear Bentz's voice on his cell phone. Maybe he forgot something . . .

"Oh, I actually caught you. I thought if I called early I might," Sarah said breathlessly.

"What's up?" Olivia asked, though she knew that, of course, the call would be about Leo. She reached into a cupboard and found a package of sunflower seeds, which she used to fill one of Chia's dishes.

"Leo's in New Orleans."

"What?"

"That's right, he called me last night, wouldn't say where he was, but I had caller ID installed last week and saw the area code."

"What's he doing here?"

"I have no idea . . . well, I have one, but I don't like it. He was at a convention in Nashville last year and ever since then he's been distracted. Spends a lot of time on his e-mail. When I went to log on to check it, I couldn't get in. He's changed his friggin' password. I've been trying to break into it, but so far no luck."

"Why'd he call?"

"I don't know. At first I thought he just wanted me to know that he was okay, to put my mind at ease, but now . . . well, I found his strong box and broke the lock."

"What did you find?" Olivia asked, not really wanting to know.

"Bank statements for an account I didn't know he had and . . . a first draft of some legal papers. Divorce papers," she said and her voice wobbled. "I can't believe it, Olivia, after all these years and all his cheating now *he* thinks he can divorce *me?* No way . . . no . . . freakin' way."

"Oh, Sarah, I'm sorry," Olivia said and she was. She hated to hear the pain and despair in her friend's normally upbeat voice. But she hated Leo Restin for what he was doing to his wife. Olivia wanted to say that divorce might be the best thing, but held her tongue; Sarah was too raw, would argue it to the death.

"Yeah, me too." Sarah's voice cracked with emotion. "I was wondering, how would you feel about a houseguest? Oh, me . . . not Leo." She laughed a little through her tears. Sarah knew how Olivia felt about her husband; Olivia made her position clear often enough. "We could have Thanksgiving together."

"While you track down Leo?"

"I'd take a break for dinner," Sarah kidded, with a hoarse chuckle. "Unless you have other plans. I mean, oh, God, I didn't think that you might be going somewhere or be with someone else."

"Don't worry about that part of it. I don't have anything going." Leaning her head against an upper cupboard, Olivia twisted the phone cord in her fingers and thought of Rick Bentz. She wondered, foolishly, how he would celebrate the holiday. Not that it mattered one little iota. Then she remembered the man in the cathedral. "You know, I think I may have seen Leo—oh, God, was it just yesterday?"

"Where?" Sarah's voice grew tight.

"St. Louis Cathedral."

"Are you kidding? Leo hasn't been to mass in years."

"Maybe I'm mistaken."

Sarah explained, "Leo was so pissed when they threw him out of parochial school, he's never been back to church."

"He went to Catholic school?" Olivia asked, surprised as she glanced at the window to watch sunlight filter through the trees.

"For a couple of years. He played football and they loved that, but . . . well, he got caught getting high on the school grounds and was expelled. Even then he was getting into trouble, not playing by the rules. But I thought he was the greatest." She laughed but the sound was hollow. "Stupid, huh?"

"We all do stupid things when we're in love." She thought fleetingly of Rick Bentz again and reminded herself she wasn't in love with him, would never be in love with him, and to forget any idea of the kind. "So he gave up on the Church?" Olivia asked, her mind beginning to wrap around an idea that was absolutely appalling. Leo, the ex-Catholic. Maybe he'd gotten all screwed up along the way. He was an athlete—a football player and a bow hunter, about six foot three with blue eyes and, from what she'd seen in his dealings with his wife, a cruel streak. But a sadistic murderer? No, she couldn't imagine it.

"Almost completely. Had a real fit when I insisted we get married by a priest. I thought he was gonna call the whole thing off. It was a big scene, but eventually, he agreed. I think there was something else that happened, something bad, but he never talked about it and I didn't pry."

"He's your husband," Olivia pointed out and thought about seeing Leo in the cathedral. He was in New Orleans. Could have been for a while. Had a grudge with the Catholic Church . . . and he had a temper. But that was a long way from murder. A long way, she reminded herself as she found a mug in the cupboard and, cradling the receiver between her shoulder and ear, poured coffee.

"I know he's my husband. Even so, we all have secrets, don't we?" Sarah observed darkly, then added, "So how about it. Want company?"

"Are you kidding? Of course I do. You're welcome to stay here but I just don't know if I'd try to track down Leo if I were you."

"We're still married," Sarah reminded her. "Remember the vow about 'till death do us part'?"

"Yeah."

"Well, I'm working real hard on it."

Olivia braced herself for another session about Sarah's marriage, the kind of conversation where Sarah complained about Leo yet swore she loved him. But instead of launching into that tired old song and dance, Sarah rattled off the time she'd fly in and told Olivia she'd rent a car and drive to the cottage on the bayou, didn't want directions, and promised to call Olivia from her cell when she touched down. "I'll be there tomorrow."

"You got a ticket?"

"That I do. And it only cost me two arms and one leg. I still can hop," she joked.

"I guess I'd better see if I can find a turkey and some cranberries."

"And sweet potatoes. I make a killer sweet-potato pie," Sarah said before hanging up. Olivia's spirits lifted a bit. She hadn't looked forward to spending Thanksgiving alone, and though she thought Sarah's hunt for her husband was a fool's mission, at least she'd be with her friend for a few days. Taking a sip from her mug, Olivia felt the coffee warm a path to her stomach. Maybe Sarah and her problems would make her forget about Rick Bentz.

Maybe.

Then again, maybe not.

Bentz wasn't a man easily forgotten.

And one thing was certain—nothing would put her completely at ease and let her forget that there was a sadistic killer on the loose; a murderer who knew her name. She looked at the picture of her and her grandmother. *Oh, Grannie, if only you were here now,* she thought as she stared at the old photo where Grannie Gin was swinging her off her feet. The hot day. And the shadow. Dark, a somber reminder of the man who had taken the snapshot. *Your father.*

Her hand was beginning to throb and something niggled at the back of her mind, something that had been bothering her ever since Reggie had called . . . what was it? What had he said that didn't ring true. *What?*

They had been talking about the fact that he wanted to see her. He'd been adamant. Determined. What had he said?

"You're the only child I've got left, you know. I've lost the others . . ."

That was it! *Others.* Plural. He wasn't just talking about Chandra. He'd fathered more kids, some she obviously had never heard of. When? With whom? Had he married again or were they the results of affairs? Who were they? Or had he just slipped up?

Maybe it didn't matter. He'd said they, too, were gone. She shivered when she remembered his words.

I've lost the others.

How? Because they were estranged from him?

Cradling her cup, she walked closer to the picture, stared at the shadow looming in the foreground. Was it possible his other children, too, were dead?

Imbeciles!
Ignoramuses!
Absolute morons!

The Chosen One added the new lock of hair to his braid as he listened to the news on the radio, a smarmy air-wave personality who thought he had all the answers and even had the gall to make some inane jokes.

The Chosen One didn't know who was more pathetically stupid—the police or the press. To compare him to the Rosary Killer. How insulting. Father John had been nothing but an apprentice . . . and a foolish one at that. He'd gotten caught.

Deftly The Chosen One went about his task, sitting on a stool near the window, winding the strands, mixing a new lock of shiny black hair with the others. His fingers tangled and stroked in the hair. He closed his eyes, willed his temper to subside. A thrill swept through him as he thought of the last sacrifice and his blood heated. She'd been so willing and then, when she'd awakened to find herself strapped to the wheel, her terror had been complete. "Saint Catherine . . ." But her blood hadn't flowed white as he'd expected; as had been preordained.

He'd wanted her. So badly. His lust had been excruciating as he'd watched her scream and rotate slowly on the wheel, spinning closer to him and then away, her eyes bulging with terror, her face white from the pain . . . he'd longed to lie down with her, to feel the spikes, to somehow thrust into her as the wheel turned and creaked. Yes . . . that was what he'd wanted, the pain and the lust combined. To enter her body as she screamed and he felt the pressure of those sharp spikes.

He was drained. His head pounded. The aching was with him more each day, it seemed, a dull thud that increased as the hours passed. A sacrifice always hyped him up before, during, and immediately after the rite, but later, after reliving it for hours, he was exhausted.

The WSLJ announcer was still blither-blathering on about a serial killer stalking the city. Two victims had been identified as coeds from Loyola and Tulane. So the police were beginning to discover that there had been earlier sacrifices ... good, good ... it had frustrated him that they hadn't connected his earlier work.

Identification of the venerated dead had been bound to happen. The police knowing his method and the dates he would kill might make hunting more difficult ... but he'd prepared for this. He'd already chosen his next victims ... women who needed to be released from their earthly bonds. Twining his fingers in his braid, he walked to the altar, genuflected, and then gazed at the wall where he'd made his offering. It was a beautiful collage of pictures of those saints he'd chosen to be a part of his work. Each image of the saints, a picture of an old portrait of a beautiful young woman with a shimmering halo, would be covered with a newer picture, a photograph he'd taken ... Several were already covered with a new image. St. Joan of Arc, beautiful little Philomena, St. Mary Magdalene, St. Cecilia, and now St. Catherine of Alexandria.

But there were so many more. Kristi Bentz would be a perfect St. Lucy, but what of St. Olivia? The feast day was too far away ... certainly he could redeem Olivia Benchet by renaming her ... that was it. He glanced at his large book, sitting upon a table with the pair of pinking shears he used to clip the pictures from the pages. Yes, that was it, he'd find another worthy daughter of God ...

"Detective Rick Bentz of the New Orleans Police Department ..."

The Chosen One's head snapped up at the mention of

Bentz's name. He glared at his tiny radio and his lips curled. Bentz had robbed him of his pupil; the only person The Chosen One had trusted with his secret. Father John. Now presumed dead. At Bentz's hand.

But Bentz would suffer and suffer well.

The Chosen One stood and let his robe slip to the floor. Slowly and delicately he slid the braid over his nakedness. Staring at his collage, he saw the faces of his victims as the plait slithered silently over his muscles.

They were all beautiful, all bright, all worthy of sainthood.

His breath was coming in uneven gasps. He was rock-hard, his cock throbbing. He tied the braid around it, imagined a dozen sets of hands and luscious lips upon his skin, teasing, taunting . . . promising sinful delights.

He grew light-headed, swallowing hard as he remembered their terror, how they'd begged. He conjured up Kristi Bentz's face . . . oh, yes . . . she would be heaven, but no longer would she be enough. No . . . he had others to redeem. With a grim smile, he thought of Olivia Benchet.

She should thank him for her redemption.

Because she was a daughter of the whore.

Chapter
Twenty-five

"Okay, so what have we got?" Melinda Jaskiel demanded of Bentz and Motoya. "The press is clamoring for more information, the chief is all over me, wondering what the hell we've got going with another serial killer, and I'm speaking with the head of the task force and the FBI in"— she checked her watch—"twenty-three minutes."

"I've talked to the head of the task force and Tortorici with the FBI," Bentz said. It was about two in the afternoon, he and Montoya were sitting in Jaskiel's office, and he'd spent all morning working on the case, shutting his mind down whenever his thoughts strayed to last night with Olivia Benchet.

"Do we think there's any chance this is the Rosary Killer?" Melinda asked. She stood in her crisp navy blue suit, hips and hands resting against the edge of her neat-as-a-pin goverment-issue desk. Bentz and Montoya were seated in front of her in the two visitors' chairs. There were a couple of photos of her parents and two daughters displayed upon her credenza and a crystal vase of ever-changing fresh flowers sat on one corner of the desk. Aside from those little touches, her nameplate, and a few awards displayed on the wall behind her chair, the office could have belonged to anyone. Well, anyone who was a neat freak.

"I've talked to the FBI and Norm Stowell . . . who's an ex-profiler."

"Outside the department?" Behind her lenses, her eyes narrowed.

"Yeah, and—"

"Hold on, Rambo. We're playing this one by the book."

"Of course we are," Bentz said, giving her the acknowledgment she needed should there be a problem. "It doesn't look like this is the Rosary Killer. His signature, the way he displays the bodies, is too different. He's more brutal. Violent. Not the same guy."

"But you think this has to do with saints being killed?"

"Martyred female saints," Bentz said and shifted in his chair. The more he considered the fact that women were being butchered in the manner in which saints had been killed, the more nervous he felt. Some of the women had gone to college and his own daughter attended All Saints— with a name like that it was bound to attract the attention of the killer, even if it was in Baton Rouge.

"All martyrs?"

"Yeah. That narrows the list a little. There are hundreds of Catholic saints and we don't know which ones he'll choose, but they seem to be the ones with bizarre, violent deaths."

"I assume there were a lot of those."

"Amen," Montoya muttered and fanned a list of pages he'd taken off the Internet. "We know about St. Cecilia; Stephanie Jane Keller was killed the same way—beheading with three strokes of a sword, after torture, and we know about St. Joan of Arc and the Jane Doe found at her statue around May thirtieth, the feast day for St. Joan, though we don't know where the victim was burned at the stake; Cathy Adams was different, we think she was portrayed as Mary

Magdalene as she was killed on the feast day of July twenty-second.'' Montoya handed a few of the pages to Jaskiel.

As she skimmed the material, her expression tightened with each page. ''This is worse than the last one.''

Bentz had to agree. ''We think there might be other deaths, two for certain.''

''Because?'' Jaskiel asked, and when Bentz hesitated, she nodded. ''Oh, I get it ... because Olivia Benchet has 'seen' ''—Jaskiel made air quotes with her fingers—''the deaths.''

''She's been right on so far.'' Montoya was still scanning the pages in his hand.

''We're checking missing persons all across the state, especially at the campuses here in town. Stephanie Jane Keller and Cathy Adams went to school part time, one at Tulane, the other at Loyola.'' Bentz hated the connection. He reminded himself that the killer was stalking coeds here in New Orleans, not in Baton Rouge where Kristi was attending school. But didn't most serial killers move? Find new hunting grounds? ''Olivia Benchet is in the master's program at Tulane. We've contacted the local schools, not just the college campuses but the local school districts and private schools, parochial schools, boarding schools, just to put the administrators on alert. They're advising the students to be aware, be extra careful, stay in groups, double-lock doors, stay in at night, the whole nine yards.''

''Do you think that Olivia Benchet, our star witness if you can call her that, is connected to the victims because she's going to grad school?'' Jaskiel's eyebrows drew into a thin continuous line.

''Maybe, but she didn't know either of the victims,'' Bentz said.

Montoya nodded. ''And we're checking out Oscar Cantrell, he was a stepfather, one in a long line, to Benchet. His company, Benchmark Realty, is the management company for the duplex that burned down ... he had access.''

''Did he know the victim?''

''Not that we can establish.''

"We still need to interview him," Bentz said and glanced at the clock. "He was out of town for the holiday, tried to pull a disappearing act, but we got hold of him through his secretary, and rather than deal with the police in Dade County, he's elected to return for an interview."

"Any chance he'll skip out?"

"We've got a man making sure he's on the plane. I'll meet him at the airport," Bentz said.

"What about witnesses? Anyone see anything? I mean, witnesses other than the psychic."

"Nothing that makes any sense." Bentz shook his head. "And the last person to see Stephanie Jane Keller alive was the mechanic where she dropped off the car. He's clean, as is her boyfriend. Townsend's got an alibi we can't break, willingly took a lie detector test, and passed with flying colors. He's not our guy. As for her car—so far no clues."

Montoya added, "I've had a picture of the one guy we can't identify who was caught on video at the scene, but even with computer enhancement, we can't place him. At least not yet. We've already checked out the whereabouts of the owners of the house that burned, the brother and sister who inherited the place. Looks like they're clean, alibis are strong. The brother is probably doing cartwheels for the insurance money. He was working late that night; got the company records and surveillance cameras to prove it. The other owner, his sister, is devastated—loved the place where she grew up. She was home with the husband and kids the night of the murder."

"Somehow the killer had access," Melinda said.

"We're still trying to track down Reggie Benchet." Bentz's thoughts were dark when it came to Olivia's father. "He's connected to Olivia Benchet, who somehow sees the crimes; he's done time for murder, he's on the streets again, and he found religion while he was doing time."

"And probably a few more tricks of the trade. You know those guys," Montoya said. "Send 'em to prison and they learn all the latest scams from the population." He snorted. "Rehabilitation, my ass."

"Have you spoken to his parole officer?" Melinda asked.

Bentz nodded. "So far Reggie's been minding his Ps and Qs."

"My ass," Montoya muttered again.

"The Lafayette Police have interviewed him. I thought I'd stop by today as I'm heading up to Baton Rouge and it's not too far out of the way. Reggie Benchet has recently tried to get into contact with his daughter . . ." Bentz hesitated, thought about what Olivia had confided and figured what the hell. Jaskiel deserved to know all the information. "Olivia called me last night." He explained in detail about what she'd seen, how overwrought she'd been. "It upset her so badly she broke the mirror and cut her hand. She was certain that the killer she saw in the vision knew her name. She somehow knew he was thinking of her and he called her St. Olivia."

"Damn it," Jaskiel muttered.

"You sure she's not making some of this up?" Montoya wasn't buying this new wrinkle in the case.

"She was terrified. Believe me."

Frustrated, Jaskiel slapped the papers she'd been holding on the edge of the desk. "Okay, check out the father. And see that Olivia Benchet has someone watching her and her house round the clock."

"Already done. The FBI authorized it," Bentz said, expecting her to give him a tongue-lashing for not going through the proper channels. Instead she nodded.

"What about the other two killings that you think might have happened?" Melinda asked. "The ones that Olivia Benchet has seen."

"Last night was the feast day of St. Catherine of Alexandria. She was put on a spiked wheel, it broke, and she was beheaded."

Jaskiel's jaw hardened. "Like the last one."

"Yeah."

"The same killer?"

"We assume."

"So now you're a believer?" Melinda asked, a thin eyebrow rising over the tops of her rimless glasses.

"Yeah," he admitted. "I guess I am. She claims she saw another murder. A woman entombed and tortured, left to starve to death. Take a look at this." He handed her a page on St. Philomena, complete with the notes Olivia Benchet had taken. "Now, either she's a scholar of the martyred saints and is jerking our chains, adding extra cases to mess us up, or she's the real thing." An image of Olivia's terrorized expression as she'd flung herself into his arms last night flashed through Bentz's mind. "I'm betting that she's for real."

"All right." Creases furrowed Jaskiel's brow as she checked her watch again. "So you're working with the task force and the FBI."

"Yeah. It's tough with the differing juristictions, but we've got to think that maybe our guy did the same thing in another state. A guy on the force is attempting to cross-reference violent, unsolved cases, committed around the time of some of the saints' feasts days, but even with the FBI and their computers, it'll take time."

"Which we don't have."

"And luck," Bentz added. "So far that's been in short supply, too."

Montoya snorted. "I'm checking with the sword manufacturers. We've got the weapon from the fire at Bayou St. John, no prints, of course, but it's not that common of a sword. My guess is that it was bought secondhand at one of those gun/ammo/weapon shows. Probably not traceable. But we're checking with the local dealers."

"What about the priest connection?"

"So far nothing, just Olivia Benchet's word on that. We're sifting through all the evidence left at the scene, but since everything was burned, it'll take time. We don't have fiber samples. Nor anything under the victim's fingernails. I'm afraid our guy got away clean," Bentz admitted.

Lines of frustration tugged at the corners of Jaskiel's mouth. Her fingernails drummed against the lip of her desk.

"He'll slip up. He's got to. When he does, we'll nail his hide. In the meantime, how do I explain that to the press?" Jaskiel asked, then answered her own question. "I don't . . . Not yet, not about the connections to the saints, otherwise we'll have a copycat and every religious nut in the surrounding parishes coming up with new and innovative ways to torture women making his mark. We'll just keep the same profile. We've got a serial killer, be careful . . . nothing specific."

"Maybe he'll tip his hand if we play it cool," Bentz suggested. "Sometimes when a serial killer doesn't get enough attention, he becomes bolder. Contacts the police. Is frustrated by the lack of attention."

Melinda straightened. "Just as long as the lack of attention doesn't push him into killing again. That would be damned hard to explain to the public."

"So what're you going to do for Thanksgiving?" Kristi asked as she sat in the commons, sipping a Coke while trying to decide if she wanted to "do it" with Brian Thomas. God, he was hot. Dark hair, intense blue eyes, and that secretive air that she found dangerously exciting.

"You mean besides giving thanks?" He shoved his tray aside and leaned his elbows on the scarred table. His class ring glinted under the overhead lights.

"Yeah, besides that."

He was teasing, she saw it in his eyes.

"I think I'll really celebrate by grading papers."

Kristi groaned. "Doesn't sound like much fun."

"No? You wouldn't get turned on by essays discussing the philosophical and political implications of the Catholic Church in Rome during the—"

"Oh, save me," she said, rolling her eyes. "No, *that* wouldn't turn me on."

"Then what would?" He reached across the table and grabbed her wrist, his fingertips grazing the inside of her arm. He rubbed gently and Kristi's heart jolted. "Why don't we find out?"

"Now?"

"No." He shook his head. "I've got class in half an hour, but later . . . I've got a bottle of wine. It's cheap, but effective. Or we could head over to The Dive."

Kristi sighed. "I think I'll have to take a rain check. I've got to meet my dad later. He's picking me up after my last class."

His smile was wicked. "Can't you call and tell him to postpone it a day? Make up some excuse, like you have to study."

"He knows me better than that," she said as he slowly let go of her wrist and the warmth that had invaded her blood and tingled deep between her legs subsided a bit. She chewed on the red and white straw. "He lived with me for eighteen years, remember."

"Maybe you've turned over a new leaf."

"He wouldn't believe it. He's a cop. A detective," she admitted, something she was loath to do. Most boys who heard her dad was on the force, split. Without a second glance. They didn't want to get involved with the daughter of a cop and risk that kind of trouble. It didn't matter if they were into booze, dope, or shoplifting, any little thing and they found a way to leave Kristi behind.

Brian, however, didn't so much as flinch. "Your dad doesn't trust you."

"He doesn't trust *anyone,* and it's only going to get worse now. I read in the papers that they think there's another serial killer in New Orleans. Dad's gonna freak. Just watch. He'll want me to move home, or install a security system in my room, or carry a gallon drum of mace around."

Brian laughed, though his smile didn't quite touch his eyes. "He's paranoid."

"Yeah, he is. He sees all the bad stuff on the streets and it makes him crazy." She mashed the straw between her teeth. "Lucky me, huh? What about your mom and dad? You never talk about them."

His smile seeped away. "Not much to say."

"You're not going home for Thanksgiving."

"No home to go to."

"Oh, come on," she said, thinking he was teasing before she noticed the tightening in the cords at the back of his neck. "Are your folks divorced?"

A muscle worked in his jaw. "Just from me."

"What do you mean?"

"They cut me off when I was eighteen. I got into some . . . trouble and they couldn't deal with it."

"What kind of trouble?" she asked warily. The noise from the kitchen, the rattling of trays and flatwear, and the hum of conversation from nearby tables seemed to be suddenly muffled and distant. Brian glanced down at the table, his fingers, anywhere but her eyes.

"Come on, give. I told you about Dad."

"This is different."

"All I have to do is call my dad and he can do a research number on you like you wouldn't believe."

He tensed. Blue eyes flashed and narrowed on her. "You'd do that?"

"Nah . . . but I could. Come on," she said and reached across the table to link her fingers with him. "What happened?"

"It was a long time ago," he admitted. "Ancient history."

"I won't hold it against you."

One of his eyebrows lifted in disbelief. "You don't know that."

"Is it *that* bad?" she asked and the look in his eyes made her catch her breath.

"You tell me. A girl . . . a girl I dated for six months accused me of rape."

"What?" She wished she'd never asked. Her heart sank. *Rape? Jesus!* She drew back her hand and his lips twisted as if he'd expected her to recoil.

"*Statutory* rape," he clarified. "But still rape. I was eighteen, she wasn't quite sixteen. It was bullshit and the charges were dropped. I was completely exonerated, *completely,* but my parents never believed in me or trusted me again. We had one too many fights about it and they threw me out of the house.''

''Just like that?''

''Why bother with me? They had five more to deal with. I was the proverbial black sheep. My old man and I never got along. Not even when I was a kid.'' He rattled his glass and threw back what little drink was left.

Stunned, Kristi folded her arms around her middle. She'd suspected he had a wild side, a dangerous edge, but this was wilder and more dangerous than she'd expected, and for the first time since meeting Brian, she wondered if she was getting into something that was way over her head. ''So, after they kicked you out, what did you do?''

''The Army for a couple of years, since I was never charged with a crime. But I couldn't see myself as a lifer, so I got out and thought I'd go to the seminary.''

''As in becoming a priest?'' she whispered, thinking of the times they'd made out, how passionate he was, the feeling of urgency she'd sensed in him as he'd touched her and kissed her and stroked her. A priest? ''Aren't they supposed to be celibate?''

''Yeah.'' He nodded, lightening up a bit. ''That was a problem. It was a short-lived ambition, believe me. So I went to college, spent a couple of years working at a job I hated, and ended up here in grad school.''

''How old are you? Forty?''

He laughed. ''Nah. I work fast. I'm thirty-one.''

She gulped. Thirty-one? That was ancient. But that wasn't the worst of it. She was stuck on the rape and his time in the seminary. ''You don't seem like someone who could buy into the whole married-to-God thing.''

''We all go through different phases, especially we *old* guys.'' There was a bite to his words. A sting. As if she'd wounded him.

''I didn't say you were old.''

''Except that you thought I was forty. Anyway, when I went to the seminary, I was just trying to sort things out. I think I was looking for a family. A place to belong . . . oh, who the hell knows? Or cares." He wadded up his napkin and threw it on the table, but his black mood was returning. Storm clouds gathered in his icy eyes.

"I do," she said suddenly. "I care."

"And that's what makes you special, Kristi." He offered a tentative smile. "Are you sure you can't get out of leaving today? I'm sure you and I could have a lot of fun."

"No doubt about it," she said and was tempted to call her dad and make some excuse about having to stay in Baton Rouge for the holiday, pretend she had to write a term paper or something. "But I really have to go home."

"Isn't there any way you could stay?" His hand was so warm.

"*Welllll* . . . I do have a test in Dr. Northrup's class and a paper due for Dr. Sutter."

"Pych?"

"101."

"I had Sutter as an undergrad." Brian frowned. "He didn't like me much."

"Really? Why wouldn't he like you?"

Brian pulled his hand away. "He thought I stole some of my theories off the Internet. It was bullshit and I told him so."

"What happened?"

"Nothing. He couldn't prove it. But he looked like an ass. I can still see him in front of the class, his face red, a tic near his eye. I think it bothers the shit out of him that I'm back."

"And you like that?"

"He deserves to be knocked down a peg or two. Pompous ass!"

She hesitated, but saw the hint of pride in the set of his jaw. "Soooo . . . did you?"

"What? Steal? Plagiarize? No way." He snorted as if the idea were absurd. "If I would have, it would have screwed up everything. My plans, my life, my chance of ever teaching."

"But only if you got caught," she said, unable to stop

playing devil's advocate as she shook her cup, rattling the ice before taking a big swallow. All the while she watched him.

"You think I'd cheat?"

"I don't know. Would you?" she asked and noticed that her heart had started drumming and she was actually sweating a little, as if she were afraid of his answer. Why in the world did he affect her like this?

"No. If you ask me, Sutter was out to get me." As soon as the words were out, he seemed to want to call them back. "I guess I sound paranoid, huh? First my parents, then Dr. Sutter. Watch out, the world has it out for Brian Thomas."

"Is that what you really think?"

"Nah." He lowered his voice as a busboy cleared a nearby table. "What I really think is that I wish you'd stay here for the weekend so we could get to know each other a little better."

"We'll have time later."

"If you say so." He leaned back in his chair and she felt all the intimacy they'd shared evaporate. He suddenly seemed so alone and aloof. The fact that he had no family, that he'd been rejected by his own folks, really got to her, but she couldn't ditch out on her dad.

Or could she?

Maybe there was a way after all.

"I gotta go," he said with a glance at the clock over the register, where a couple of kids were paying for sandwiches. "Damn. I've got five minutes to get across campus." Kicking back his chair, he was on his feet.

She didn't want him to leave, not when she felt that he was angry with her. Not that she'd done anything wrong. She knew he was trying to manipulate her by laying the blame for his misery, his aloneness, at her feet and she didn't want to buy into it, but she really liked him. "So, I'll see ya when I get back."

"Yeah, sure," he said, distracted as he grabbed his backpack and started for the door. Then, as if realizing how he harsh he sounded, he backtracked the few steps, leaned down, and whispered in her ear, "And when you do get back, you'd better be ready."

A tingle slid down her spine. "For what?" she asked.

His grin was slow and decidedly sexy. "You tell me."

Chapter
Twenty-six

"Do I need an attorney?" Oscar Cantrell demanded. Face florid, unlit cigar clamped in his jaw, he strode out of the airport. He was mad as hell and belligerent as all get-out.

"You tell me," Bentz suggested.

"You chargin' me with something?" Cantrell, a short man with an oversized belly, straw hat, and narrow sideburns, sent Bentz a look guaranteed to wither a lesser man. Bentz didn't give a damn. Let him stew. He'd met Cantrell at the gate, flashed his badge, and escorted the shorter man to his Jeep. "Nope. Just have some questions for you."

"Hey, I've got my own car here." Cantrell shifted his carry-on bag from one hand to the other. "I don't need a ride."

"Humor me. I'll bring you back."

"Son of a bitch," Cantrell muttered, shifting his carry-on bag from one hand to the other. But he didn't argue. The road map of veins discoloring Cantrell's cheeks and nose turned a brighter red as he reluctantly climbed into the back-seat of the rig.

Bentz fired the engine and glanced into the rearview mirror. "Tell me about your ex-wife."

"Which one?"

"Bernadette Dubois."

Cantrell snorted and moved his cigar to the corner of his mouth. "Saint Bernadette," he said and Bentz stiffened.

Saint Bernadette? "Is that a special name you have for her?"

"Yeah, right. You ever meet her?" Cantrell asked, and when Bentz shook his head, added, "Well, she's bad news. Big time. A beautiful woman. Downright gorgeous and a manipulator. Always wants more than a man can give. The kind of woman that is nothing but trouble." He threw himself back against the seat. "Sheeeeit, is she in some kind of trouble with the law?" he asked. "Is that what this is all about?"

"I just want to ask you some questions."

"About what?"

"The fire at the rental property you manage over at Bayou St. John."

"I figured." Cantrell was looking out the window, chewing on his cigar, watching the scenery as Bentz headed into the city. "I didn't know nothin' about that. Nothin'. Ask my secretary. I've been out of town. With . . . with a friend. You can call her."

"I will," Bentz said, but figured Cantrell was leveling with him. Probably another dead end. "You know her kid?"

"The girl? Olivia? Yeah, I met her a time or two." He took off his hat and swabbed his forehead with a handkerchief. "Her other daughter died, y'know. I don't think she ever got over it. Felt some kind of guilt. She was nappin' when the kid fell into the pool. Drowned. Bernadette, she blamed the older kid, Olivia, for the baby's death, but deep down I think she felt guilty. Hell, with that woman there was lots of guilt goin' on."

"Is that right?" Bentz hadn't expected Cantrell to be so candid. Cantrell stuffed his hanky into his pocket. "How so? Why all the guilt?"

"Hell if I know. Her dad was dead, her mother half-crazy with all that talk about voodoo and crap. No wonder she was messed up. It probably started with the baby."

"Olivia?"

"No."

"Then the girl who drowned? Chandra?"

"For Christ's sake, no," Cantrell was irritated. "I'm talkin' about the first baby."

Bentz felt something snap in his brain. He glanced in the rearview mirror again.

"The first one?"

"Yeah, her son . . . I think it was supposed to be some big secret, but one night we were drinkin' and she got drunk—more wasted than I've ever seen her. All of a sudden she starts yammerin' about her son. She wouldn't stop belly-achin' about how she got herself in a family way and had to give up her baby. The old lady, Virginia, Bernadette's mother, she wouldn't have it no other way. She insisted upon it."

"Who was the father?"

"Benchet, of course. That's what all the fuss was about. The old lady had Reggie Benchet pegged. Knew he was no-account." Cantrell's lazy gaze met Bentz's in the mirror. "Helluva thing. After that one night, she never brought it up again. Neither did I. Didn't figure it was any of my business, but the thing is, I don't think she ever told Reggie."

"But she confided in you?" Bentz wasn't buying it.

"The demon rum loosened her tongue. Man, that woman was on a supersonic guilt trip. If you ask me, that's when it all started. Giving up that baby."

"When what started?"

"The craziness . . . it runs in the family, y'know." He yanked his cigar from his mouth and punctuated the air with it. "The old woman had it and passed it right down the line. Virginia to Bernadette to Olivia . . . all beautiful women, all not quite right, a little off, sexy as hell, lookers, I tell you, and charming, in a way, but . . . Not your normal woman, if you know what I mean."

Unfortunately Bentz did. He only had to think of last night to remind himself.

Olivia worked a few hours at the Third Eye in the morning, then met Ole Olsen and his crew back at her cabin.

Holed up in the second bedroom, she tried to study while the workmen traipsed through her house, running wire, barking orders, turning off the electricity for a while, and then testing alarm bells. She sat on the daybed flipping the pages of research books, occasionally being interrupted by someone tapping on the closed door, then sticking his head inside to ask a question or two. Her concentration was shot. Not that it wouldn't have been anyway. The night with Bentz seemed now surreal, their fight this morning just another disjointed piece in the jigsaw puzzle that was her life.

Once the electricity was flowing again, she forgot her thesis for a while and logged on to the Internet, where she spent two or three hours researching the lives and deaths of some of the saints. She'd wanted to tell Bentz he was barking up the wrong tree, but as she read about the saints he'd mentioned and remembered the women who had been killed, she was certain there was a link.

But what? Why these saints and why was she involved?

By the time most of the work crew had left, it was nearly dark and she was equipped with a basic security system that would activate whenever it was engaged and a door or window was opened. "So you're saying that I'll never be able to sleep with the windows ajar?" she asked Olsen, a tall, Nordic-looking man with a broad face and a shock of short white hair.

"Oh, yeah, you can turn off certain areas of the house, but I wouldn't recommend it. See here—" He showed her the control panel, and explained about motion detectors and alarms and lag time between setting the thing and activation starting.

"So . . . when the motion detector is on, the dog's got to be locked in another room."

"Unless you want this to happen." With a press of the button, he activated the alarm and a series of ear-splitting shrieks began blasting through the house. Hairy S whined. Olivia learned very quickly how to shut it off.

"Sometimes I hate high-tech," she grumbled.

"Me, too." Olsen grinned and showed off one gold-capped tooth. "But then I remember it's my bread and butter. I shouldn't complain too much." He left her with his business card, a thick instruction and warranty booklet, and a surprisingly small invoice, which he explained was compliments of Detective Bentz. "We go back a few years," he explained. "Helped my kid when she was messed up with drugs. Now, you call me if anything goes wrong, y'hear?" he'd said as he'd ambled out to his truck. "Anything *A*-tall. Bentz said to take care of you and I aim to please."

"I'm sure I'll be able to handle it," she assured him and waved before walking into her newly protected house. She wondered what Grannie Gin would have thought.

Probably that she was foolish. She could almost feel Grannie Gin rolling over in her grave and muttering, "Lawsy-Moley, what's got into you payin' for all those fancy bells and whistles. Trust in the Lord, Livvie, and learn how to use a shotgun. That's all the protection anyone needs."

"Not true, Grannie," Olivia whispered as she sat at the kitchen table and thumbed through the instruction booklet. "Not true *A*-tall." The dog whined and she scratched his ears, then, unable to get past page seven of the booklet, she left it on the table and started for the living room. From the corner of her eye she saw Hairy leap into the chair she'd recently vacated, steal the pamphlet, and hightail it into the laundry room.

"Oh, no, you don't," she warned, chasing after the dog and wrestling the booklet away before he could bury it in his blankets with his other treasures. "I might need this." She tucked the pamphlet into a kitchen cupboard and started through the archway to the living room.

As she did, she felt it—a shifting in atmosphere.

Inside the house.

Like a cold, brittle wind.

"No," she said, her heart drumming. He couldn't be at it again. Not after last night. A cold needle of fear pierced her brain. Glancing in the mirror mounted over the bookcase, she half-expected to see the priest's masked face again, to stare into his cruel blue eyes, but only her own reflection stared back at her, a pale, wild-haired woman who appeared as world-weary as she felt. It was a haunted look. Tortured.

Hairy S whined, but he didn't run to the door or the window as he usually did if he heard something outside. Instead he cowered near her, shivering, as if he sensed some evil presence here, within the core of the house.

"*Sssh.* You're all right," she said, picking him up and holding him close. "We're safe." But he trembled in her arms and scrambled to get down. She set him on the floor and he ran, toenails clicking on the hardwood, to stand in the archway to the kitchen, turn around, and stare back at her. "Hairy, you're fine."

He whined plaintively.

"Oh, you can be such a goose sometimes," she said, but couldn't shake off the feeling that something was horribly, horribly wrong. And not just in her visions, but here in her home. She thought of Grannie Gin's words, her faith in God. Grannie's religion had been skewed a bit, a blend of healthy Roman Catholicism flavored with a sprinkling of voodoo. But harmless. Grannie had found solace in the Bible. This Bible that sat on the top shelf of the short bookcase. The thick, leather-bound volume that had been in the family for ages and rested beneath the antique oval mirror.

Hairy barked and backed up.

"Stop it."

But he wouldn't quit and was barking madly as she opened the Bible. It fell open to the Twenty-third Psalm. Grannie's favorite. Olivia read the familiar passage, and remembered Grannie whispering it to her at night when she tucked her into bed:

"Yea, though I walk through the valley of the shadow of death, I will fear no evil."

Olivia blinked back tears as she thought of her grandmother and how the old woman had pushed Olivia's hair out of her face as she'd whispered the words. Funny, she'd never read this Bible herself; it had been solely Grannie's domain.

Hairy growled. Obviously the passage wasn't calming him down. "Heretic," Olivia teased and set the Bible down, but the front flap sprung open to a page where generations of Duboises had taken the time to record every birth, marriage, and death in the family for the past hundred and twenty years. Grannie Gin had been as careful as her mother-in-law and the woman before her.

Olivia traced her finger down the page, saw where her mother had been born and the mention of three other children Grannie had birthed only to bury as none of the others had lived over a week.

Bernadette had been the exception—strong where all of Grannie's other children had been born weak.

Beneath her mother's name were the listing of her marriages and the children Bernadette had brought into the world.

Olivia stopped short.

Her index finger was poised over the page. There she was, listed by her birth date. Chandra's short life had been recorded as well. But the entry above her name was the one that stopped her cold.

Baby boy. No name. Listed as Bernadette's son, the father being Reggie Benchet. If it was correct, this nameless brother was barely a year older than Olivia.

A brother? She'd had a brother? What had happened to him?

Her head pounded. She searched the notes, thinking she missed something important, but there wasn't a record of the child's death. It couldn't be. She'd never heard his name; he was never mentioned.

As if he had never existed.

Was it a mistake, a nameless baby written in the wrong spot? But no . . . the listing was in her grandmother's hand. Grannie wouldn't have made that kind of error.

So if he hadn't died, where was he?

She felt that chill run through her blood again, and when she glanced into the mirror, she saw the hint of something beneath her own reflection, a shifting shape with no real form.

She dropped the Bible. Backed up. Nearly tripped over her own feet.

Her heart was a terrified tattoo, her hands sweating.

Deep in the reflection she caught a glimpse of something rare. Something deadly. Something evil.

She backed up and told herself that she was letting her imagination run wild, that she was allowing the dog's weird behavior to put her on edge. But the hairs on the back of her arms had lifted and her heart was jack-hammering. *Get a grip, Olivia! You saw nothing,* NOTHING. *You're letting your imagination run away with you.*

Taking several deep breaths, she hurried to the phone, found her address book in the top drawer, and ran her finger down a page where numbers had been erased and crossed out. Finally, she located Bernadette's number.

She dialed quickly, tried to fight the rising tide of panic that was overtaking her. Bentz had said there had to be a connection between her and the killer. Something in her genes . . . could it be? Oh, God, oh, God, oh, God.

The phone rang. Once, twice, three times.

"Answer, damn it!"

After the fourth ring, voice mail picked up and she was instructed to leave a message.

What could she say? "Bernadette . . . this is Olivia. Would you please call me when you—"

"Livvie?" her mother's voice cut in and Olivia's knees threatened to give way. She braced herself against the counter. "What a surprise."

"I need to talk to you."

"As long as it's not a lecture about my husband. I was

considering leaving him, but Jeb and I we're trying to work things out.''

''Are you cra—'' Olivia bit her tongue and slowly counted to ten. ''You know how I feel about that,'' she said, ''but it's not why I called.''

There was a long, strained pause and Olivia wondered how she could ask the next question, how she could accuse her mother of harboring a lie for over thirty years.

''I was going through the Bible,'' she said, ''you know the one. It belonged to Grannie.''

''Yes.''

''Well, it's the weirdest thing. I never knew there was a page dedicated to all the births and marriages and deaths in the family.'' Was it her imagination or had she heard Bernadette's swift intake of breath?

''Is there?''

There was just no way to sugar-coat her question. ''I noticed that Chandra and I were listed as your children, but we weren't the only ones. There was a mention of another child. A boy. Not named and born about a year before I was. My older brother.''

No response.

''Mom?''

A pause and then a long sigh. ''Livvie, this is none of your business.''

''I had a brother and no one told me and it's none of my business?'' she repeated, aghast. ''Of course it's my business.''

''What does it matter now?''

''Bernadette . . . he's my brother. Is he still alive?''
Nothing.

''Is he?'' Olivia demanded again, blood thundering in her head, her fingers clenched over the receiver so tightly they ached.

''I . . . I don't know.''

''Why not?''

''It's complicated.''

"For the love of God, Bernadette! Where is he? What the hell happened? Who is he?"

"I said I don't know," Bernadette snapped, then lowered her voice. "I was young, barely out of high school. Not married . . . back then it was not so accepted to have a child out of wedlock. Not like today. I had to tell my mother and she . . . she arranged a private adoption. I don't know his name, what happened to him. Nothing."

"But—" Olivia leaned against the wall. Her head was spinning with the lie. How many more were there?

"As far as I'm concerned, that baby never existed," Bernadette insisted but her voice shook with emotion. "I don't expect you to understand, Livvie, but I damn well expect you not to judge."

Olivia gasped. "I didn't mean . . . I just want to know the truth."

"The truth's very simple and pretty common. I got pregnant while I was still in high school and your father was . . . Well, he'd shipped out and I wasn't married, so I gave my baby up and I really haven't looked back. I didn't want to. I suppose these days you would call it denial, but there it is."

And it explained so much.

"The only people who knew were your grandmother and me. It was a private adoption. I don't even know the attorney who handled it or the name of the family who adopted him. I didn't want to know then and I don't want to know now. I didn't tell your father."

"He's *not* my father."

"Now who's in denial?" Bernadette threw out. "Leave it be, Olivia. So you have a brother somewhere, what do you care?"

"Aren't you even curious about your son?"

"No, Livvie, I'm not. Now leave it alone."

Olivia couldn't. One way or another, she thought, hanging up, she'd find out who the hell her brother was. Even if he turned out to be a vicious killer.

* * *

Seated at his desk in the station, Bentz glanced at his watch and swore under his breath. He had just enough time to get to Baton Rouge and pick up Kristi. Aside from the suggestion that "Saint Bernadette" had adopted out a son sired by Reggie Benchet, Bentz had learned nothing from Oscar Cantrell. Whatever love the man had once felt for his ex-wife had been killed when Bernadette had started "fucking around" on him. "She was a real slut. Couldn't keep a zipper up to save her life. 'Course that's what had attracted me to her in the first place, but I expect a wife to save it for her husband. *Sheeiiit,* she's a piece of work, Bernadette is," Cantrell had concluded.

Bentz figured there was more to the story, but so far hadn't sorted it out. And now he was late. He threw on his jacket, slid his Glock into its holster, and wended his way through the desks scattered throughout the department.

"Bentz!" Penny, one of the receptionists yelled. "I've got Montoya on the line. He says its important."

"Tell him to call me on the cell." Bentz was already halfway down the stairs. By the time he'd reached his Jeep, his cell was ringing like crazy. "Bentz," he said into the headset as he strapped on his seat belt.

"We found her." Montoya's voice was cold as death.

"Who?"

"St. Catherine of Alexandria."

"What?" Hand over the steering wheel, Bentz froze. "What do you mean? Where?"

"That's just the half of it," Montoya said solemnly. "She isn't alone."

Chapter
Twenty-seven

Talk about a bad day!

This had to be the worst, Kristi thought as she came up with some bullshit answer for the last question on her essay test. This was supposed to be English 101. It was supposed to be a snap. But Dr. Northrup was rumored to be the hardest professor in the English Department, a real perfectionist, and in Kristi's estimation, a prick. He was too precise, too wound-tight. He even dressed the part in his natty suits and perfect hair. She doubted he was more than thirty-five but he seemed older. Harder. Jaded.

Deciding she'd done the best she could, she carried her test paper to the front of the room and dropped it into the half-filled basket on his desk. He was putting on his coat and glanced up at her as she passed. "Going home for Thanksgiving?" he asked.

Kristi was dumbfounded. The entire term he hadn't so much as called on her. Nor had he uttered one word to the kids who had dropped off their exams before she had.

"Yeah." She nodded and hitched her backpack onto her shoulder. "Today."

He flashed a bit of a smile, though it seemed pasted on, as if he did it because it was expected. It wasn't real. But then, the guy was as phony as a three-dollar bill. "Have a nice holiday, Ms. Bentz." He turned to give his T.A. some instructions.

"You, too," she muttered, starting for the door. She didn't even think he knew her name. Wasn't thrilled that he did. The guy was more than a little weird, kind of stuck on himself. It was as if his Ph.D. made him something special, something that should be revered.

It was stupid, in her opinion, and way beyond odd, but then all her professors were a little off. As she pushed the door open and stepped into the cold November day, Kristi wondered if all the teachers at All Saints were weirdos. Or had she just lucked out this term and gotten all the eccentrics?

Rain was pouring from the dark sky. Drops peppered the ground, hitting hard enough to splash and puddle. As she had for three days running, Kristi had forgotten her umbrella. Silently calling herself an idiot, she turned the collar of her jacket up and started cutting across campus, ducking her head against the sheets of cold drops and running through the gloom. Only a few other kids were making their way down the narrow paths that rimmed the tall brick buildings and bisected the lawns of the University. Nightfall was supposed to be several hours off, but the afternoon was dark as twilight.

She jumped over a puddle on the path, began jogging, and thought about her professors. Dr. Zaroster in Philosophy was a nervous, demanding man who barked orders at Brian and looked upon his undergraduate students with an air of superiority—not unlike Northrup.

Perhaps that better-than-thou attitude came with the territory of succeeding in academia.

Kristi's professor in bonehead math, Ms. Wilder, wore tons of makeup and too-tight sweaters, but other than that seemed okay. Dr. Sutter in Psychology tried to appear laid

back, but there was something about him that made her think
he wasn't quite as relaxed as he tried to appear. He seemed
edgy at times. And he'd pulled her aside once to tell her
that her paper hadn't been up to what he knew she could
do. "I'm certain if you spent a little more time doing
research, you would surprise yourself." Oh, yeah, like how
did *he* know? Just because he had a doctorate in psychology
. . . could he psychoanalyze a person on the spot? Then there
was Miss Pratt, the PE teacher. A dyke. No two ways about
it. Pratt kept trying to convince Kristi to try out for the swim
team, but Kristi couldn't shake the feeling that the PE teacher
was hitting on her. Sometimes Kristi even thought Miss
Pratt was a guy. It was just kind of creepy the way she was
always hanging out at the pool or in the locker room, making
herself appear busy but actually watching everyone and
everything that went on around the physical education facili-
ties.

Kristi had never been self-conscious about her body, had
stripped and showered for her gym classes without any hang-
ups, but Miss Roberta Pratt changed all that. The dyke made
her nervous.

Crap. Everyone did these days.

And now Dad was gonna be late. He'd called her on her
cell phone and made some excuse about a major break in
a case, even offered to have someone pick her up.

As if!

The guy her father had in mind was probably a cop friend
and would have rolled up in a department-issued cruiser.
Oh, yeah, *that's* the image she wanted to portray around
campus! Sure, announce to the world that she was a cop's
daughter!

She died a billion deaths just thinking about it. She'd told
Bentz she'd wait. He'd promised he'd be only "a couple
of hours" late. Whatever that meant. She'd lived with him
too long to believe it.

She'd already decided she wasn't going to wait around
forever. If her dad didn't show up in a reasonable time
period, she'd give Brian another call. That thought made

her smile. Taking a sharp left at the statue of St. Mary in the middle of the quad, she thought she heard the sound of footsteps behind her. Someone else was running to get out of the rain. Glancing over her shoulder, she saw no one. The campus was practically deserted.

Kind of creepy in the gloom.

Oh, get over it.

She took a shortcut through the library, taking the steps two at a time and shoving open the old glass doors. Normally packed, the library was now a ghost town with only a handful of students sitting at the old oaken tables or perusing the stacks. The lights were dimmed, it seemed, the entire building desolate.

She hurried outside and crossed the wet lawn to Cramer Hall. Again, she thought she heard someone behind her, another set of footsteps making a mad dash in the rain. Once more, she looked over her shoulder. This time she saw someone in the shadows, a tall man lagging behind. He seemed familiar, someone she should know, but it was too dark to make out his features and he disappeared through the dense curtain of rain—turning his face away as she looked in his direction.

For a heartbeat Kristi wondered if he'd been following her on purpose. But that was ridiculous. Who would be chasing her in this downpour?

You're as paranoid as your old man! For God's sake, the guy behind you was just running like mad to get out of this miserable weather. There's nothing scary about that. Get over yourself!

For a second she thought the guy might have been Brian— his build was about right—but then why wouldn't Brian try to catch up with her? Why would he turn away and head into the shadows? No, that didn't make any sense.

And where was Brian anyway, she wondered, more than a little irritated. Pushing open the door, she tried not to be angry. There was probably a perfectly good reason why he hadn't returned her phone calls.

"Jerk," she muttered under her breath.

Running up two flights of steps, she swabbed the rain from her face, then yanked her cell phone from her pocket. She flipped it open. Nope. No one had called, not since her dad had phoned to tell her he was running late.

Great.

The door to her room was open and Lucretia was lying on her bottom bunk, flipping through a new copy of *Modern Bride.* Kristi recognized the magazine and wanted to puke. All Lucretia ever did was study and dream of graduating so she could get married. Rather than make a nasty comment, Kristi bit her tongue and began peeling off her wet jacket and jeans. "Anyone call?" she asked, squeezing the water from her ponytail as she searched her microcloset for something dry to put on.

"Yeah. Jay." Lucretia was sipping a Diet Coke and munching on Cheetos as she eyed a page displaying several different elaborately decorated cakes.

Kristi cringed.

"He wants to know when you're getting home."

"You talked to him?" Kristi asked, catching sight of her reflection in the mirror. Her skin was red from the cold, her hair starting to frizz. "Why didn't you let him leave a message?

"I didn't think, just picked up the phone without checking caller ID." At Kristi's sour expression, Lucretia rolled her eyes. "Sorry. But he still thinks he's your boyfriend, you know. I didn't think it was that big of a deal." She lifted a dismissive shoulder as she crunched another Cheeto. "He wants you to call him back."

"I think I'll wait until I get home."

"Whatever." Disinterested, Lucretia licked the cheese from her lips.

"Anyone else?"

"Nope." Lucretia looked up with that smug expression that really got under Kristi's skin. "No one. Not even Brian."

Kristi didn't comment, but she couldn't wait to go home and get away from her holier-than-thou roommate. Lucretia

didn't smoke, drink, do drugs, or even listen to any music
other than some Christian station. Just dreamed of being
a wife and mother. BO-ring. Checking her watch Kristi
wondered when the hell her dad would show up.

Bentz parked on the outside of the gate. As he climbed
out of his Jeep, he flashed his badge at a deputy from the
Sheriff's Department who was standing guard. Beyond the
sagging old fence was an abandoned grist mill.

Montoya had been talking to other officers. He broke
away from the cluster standing in the rain, and waved Bentz
in.

"What've we got?" Bentz asked.

"Two Jane Does. Both dead." Montoya was sucking hard
on a cigarette. His jacket was shiny with rainwater, his
features stretched taut in the gathering darkness. Twilight
had descended rapidly in this farming community an hour
out of the city. The rain didn't let up, just kept pummeling
the ground and running off the bill of Bentz's Saints' cap.
"I got a call from a friend of mine in the Sheriff's Department and drove over," Montoya said, "A couple of kids
found the bodies." He motioned to two boys huddled with
an officer and an older woman.

"What were they doin' here?"

"Huntin', though that was behind their mother's back."
Montoya blew out a stream of smoke. "They got more than
they bargained for."

Bentz glared at the mill. The building looked like something straight out of an old horror flick. The windows were
boarded over, the cement walls blacked with age. Vines and
brambles crawled toward the roof while moss dripped over
what remained of the eaves. Part of an old mill wheel sat
unmoving in a stream that angled into the darkness.

"Who's the owner?" Bentz asked.

"We're still digging, but the sheriff thinks the mill's
owner lives out of state."

"He got a name?"

"We're still checking. Locals refer to this place as 'The Old Kayler Place.' Someone named Kayler with roots in the Civil War owned the land a hundred and fifty years ago. The name stuck. The mill came along later but hasn't been operational for a generation or two, probably closed up around World War II sometime. The nearest neighbors are half a mile away."

"Convenient."

"And not as dangerous as the shotgun house off of Esplanade."

"Or an apartment in the Garden District."

Bentz swept his gaze over the exterior again. The place was already crawling with law enforcement personnel. Klieg lights trained bluish illumination on the crumbling walls. Beams from hand-held flashlights bobbed and cut through the shadows as officers, searching every inch of wet, soggy ground, moved slowly through the tall grass, scrub oaks, and brush.

"Did you question the kids?" Bentz asked, sending a glance at the boys.

"Yeah. They don't know much."

"I'll want to talk to them once I've gone inside." Bentz looked back at the mill. Yellow tape surrounded the building. "The scene's been preserved?"

"Best as they could."

"No ID on the victims." It wasn't a question.

"Never that easy," Montoya said. "At least not with this killer. We'll take prints and pictures, blood, and we've always got dental records."

Bentz hiked his collar against the rain. "Let's see what's inside."

"It ain't pretty." Montoya ground out his smoke, picked up the butt, and stuffed it in his pocket.

Bentz braced himself as he walked past two detectives who were searching the muddy lane for tire tracks. Another was sweeping the area with a harsh, intense light.

"You're pretty sure it's our guy?" Bentz asked.

"No doubt." They walked through a sagging doorway

and the stench of death hit Bentz as hard as a fist to the gut. Fetid and rank, the smell was overlaid by another strong odor, the metallic scent of fresh blood.

Inside, rats scurried out of their path and Bentz clenched his teeth as he got his first view of the scene. His stomach tried to revolt, just as it always did. He fought the urge to vomit and forced himself to study the area.

In the center of a large room the murder had taken place. A woman's nude, decapitated body was still strapped to a grotesque, spiked wheel. Blood covered the dirty floor and atop a long workbench, posed upon an overturned, rusted bucket, was her head. Her eyes were closed, a piece of bloody hair missing. "Jesus," Bentz whispered as he spied a chain encircling the stump that had once been her neck. The thin chain draped over the pail. A medal dangled from the fragile links.

"Let me guess. St. Catherine of Alexandria."

"Yep."

Bentz's back teeth ground. "Hell."

"Our man is one sick, sick bastard," Montoya said over the hum of a vacuum that was being wielded by a member of the crime scene and was used to suck up and trap potential evidence. A photographer snapped still shots of the body and surrounding area from all angles. Another photographer used a video camera. Flashes of light strobed, offering glimpses of musty interior walls veined by black rivulets, stains from years of rainwater and filth seeping through the roof.

"Homey, huh?" Montoya mocked, his own gaze traveling over the scene. "You think he could pick anyplace more macabre?"

"Not if he tried, which, I think he does."

Montoya was squatting now, staring at the plywood wheel. "Someone had to make this gizmo," he said. "It's nothing you can pick up at the local five-and-dime."

"Or on ebay."

"So either our killer has a workshop and a truck to haul this thing, or he built it here, or he bought it from someone who has a talent for creating instruments of torture.'' Montoya leaned farther down and rotated his head, shining the beam of his flashlight on the underside of the wheel.

"I'm betting he built it here. It's isolated. He cut some thick plywood, drilled a few holes, put in the biggest spikes he could find, and mounted the whole damned thing on a revolving turret of some kind.''

"It looks like an old wheel balancer, you know the kind they use in garages when they're putting on tires.''

"So you just give it a push and it starts spinning.'' Bentz joined Montoya as the younger cop illuminated the underpinnings, which included an axle screwed into a concrete block. Metal arms supported the blood-stained plywood. Bentz's jaw tightened. "So he's a handyman.''

"How do *you* know about this kind of thing?''

"Because I built one that was similar. Instead of spikes, mine had pegs and was used for a school carnival when Kristi was about ten. The kids spun the wheel to try and win some kind of cheap prize, you know whistles, balloons, toy trucks, and all that useless crap.''

"Like on *The Price is Right.*''

"Well, yeah, but it was called *The Wheel of Fortune.*''

"Vanna would be proud.''

"If you say so,'' Bentz said, not cracking a smile. "But here we've got the goddamned Wheel of Pain.''

"Built by a handyman priest.''

"Who can get his hands on old garage parts as easily as saints' medals.'' Bentz straightened and noticed a large mirror hung on the far wall. The glass was smooth and unbroken, without much dust on the surface. Unlike every other surface in the room. Everything else was covered in a thick, grainy layer of grime. "What's with this?'' he asked, but as the words left his mouth, he knew. "Our boy likes to watch himself while he's working.''

"Shit.'' Montoya scoped out the scene. "You're right. He's a damned egomaniac.''

"Or *Narcissus.* Has it been dusted for prints?''

"Of course,'' a woman officer said, her feathers ruffling

a bit as if Bentz had indicated she and the rest of the team were lax. Wearing latex gloves, she was carefully going over every surface. "Everything has." She muttered something under her breath about "big-city cops" and went about her business.

Bentz didn't let her get to him. "Let's try to find out who manufactured the mirror," he said to Montoya. "Maybe we can come up with someone who purchased something like this in the last month or so—same with the parts on the wheel over there and with the medals. Some of the saints are pretty common, but where would a guy get a St. Catherine of Alexandria medal?"

"Over the Internet or in one of those stores that sells religious crap, probably." Montoya rubbed his goatee. "And the wheel mount. Maybe a garage is missing one. But it looks old, not like the ones that are hooked to computers that they've got today."

"Not every garage in Louisiana is computer friendly. Unless it's been filed off, that piece of equipment should have some serial numbers we can trace."

Bentz scanned the scene once more and noticed a thick pool of blood beneath the wheel, one where there was more blood splattered than around the rest of the perimeter. Obviously the victim had been at that spot in her rotation, right in front of the mirror, when the killer had sliced off her head. Just so the sick bastard could watch himself as he slashed down with his blade. He probably got off on the image.

Again Bentz felt the urge to toss his dinner, but swallowed hard. "Any sign of a weapon?"

"Not that we've found so far." Montoya was still sweeping the mirror with the beam of his flashlight, its bright glare reflected harshly in the glass.

"You said there was another victim."

"Oh, yeah . . ." Using the bright beam to point to a doorway, Montoya led Bentz through a short, dark hallway to another much smaller silo-like room, originally, Bentz guessed, used for storage.

"Jesus!" he whispered as he spied the victim.

Chained to one chipped wall were the remains of a woman, no doubt the woman who had been sacrificed last summer on the feast day of St. Philomena, though her body was so decomposed no one would be able to visually ID her. What parts of her the rats and other scavengers hadn't eaten or dragged away, the heat and maggots had taken care of. Bentz held a handkerchief to his face. This was the crypt Olivia had seen, the tomb.

Once again the victim's head had been severed and it, like the head in the other room, rested atop a rusted bucket. A tiny chain with a medal dangling from what had been her neck glittered in the beam of the flashlight.

The cornerless room was just as Olivia had described, the writing on the wall in big block letters: LUMENA PAXTE CUM FI. Around the letters were the symbols that his brother had explained, the arrows, palm, lilies, anchor, fire, and a scourge.

"Peace be to you, Philomena," Bentz muttered.

"Hardly," Montoya said, scratching his goatee. "The letters are written in what looks like blood, rather than the red paint that was described in the book on saints that I read. My guess? The victim's blood. If what Olivia Benchet says is true, that our man kept the victim here for a long period, then he had to cut her and get blood from her body in order to write his message and fill that." He pointed to a small pottery vial left on the floor.

Bentz had to agree.

"And get this, the head's been messed with."

"What do you mean?"

"It's been moved. We're working on the theory that it fell or was dragged off the bucket, probably by some animal. There's a disturbance in the dust on the table, some blood and hairs and pieces of dried flesh, but it looks like the head was returned to its original resting spot on the pail. Probably by the killer. He must've come back here to build his wheel or drag the latest victim here and checked on his earlier work. Then put things back the way he wanted them."

"The way he wanted us to find them," Bentz added.

"Exactly. This prick is proud of his work. Thinks he's a damned artist."

Bentz didn't like it. Didn't like it at all. It was as if the killer were mocking them, taunting them. "Hell." He glanced around the room, searching for the mirror. It didn't take long, but in this case he found not one, but five narrow full-length panels mounted on one curved wall. "Someone took his time. Look. The spaces between the mirrors are precise, the alignment perfect."

"The guy wants things just so."

"And to see himself in 3D."

On the wall directly opposing the mirrors the victim's chains had been bolted into a thick wooden post. "This is why Olivia only saw fragments," Bentz said. "I thought it was because she was in and out of Louisiana, because she was so far away, but her images were split."

"Because of the curvature of the wall. He couldn't get a big panel that would fit."

"Son of a bitch." Bentz eyed the thin strips of reflective glass. "Let's check with the manufacturer and distributor, then any outlet in the state or over the Internet. It would be odd for an individual to buy five identical mirrors. We'll go back to summer. Before August eleventh. Maybe we'll get lucky," he thought aloud, for the first time sensing there might be a way to track this guy down. "We'll cross-check anyone who bought mirrors, saints' medals, priest vestments, ski wear, tools, and weapons."

"That'll be easy," Montoya remarked.

"Maybe easier than you think," Bentz said as they made their way through the short hallway and larger room to the outside. The rain was sheeting, glistening in the beams of the klieg lights and headlights from the surrounding vehicles. "The FBI should be able to help." He glanced at Montoya. "Where the hell are they?"

"On their way."

Bentz strode to the cruiser where the kids who'd found the bodies and a woman pushing forty were huddled beneath a couple of umbrellas. In hooded sweatshirts, jeans, and hiking boots, the boys looked scared to death. "Kenny and Donny Sawtell," Montoya introduced, "and their mother, Linda. This is Detective Bentz." Montoya motioned to the older of the two brothers. "Why don't you tell Detective Bentz what happened?"

The boys, around eleven and twelve, were white as sheets. They seemed as worried about talking to the cops as they were scared by the gruesome scenes they'd viewed. The older one, Kenny, did most of the talking, but Donny backed him up, for the most part nodding. The story was simple. The boys, who lived about three miles down the main road, had been out hunting behind their mother's back. Packing twenty-twos and following Roscoe, the family's dog, they'd tracked a deer through the woods to the old mill, where they'd ignored the "No Trespassing" sign and slipped through a hole in the fence. Roscoe had smelled something, so they'd broken into the building, thinking it would make a "cool" fort or hideout. Then they'd been scared out of their wits. They'd run home, told their mom, and Linda had called the local authorities.

"You've been here before?" Bentz asked and both boys shook their heads vigorously. Despite the umbrella and hoods, rain dripped down their noses.

"We never crossed the road before," Kenny asserted and Donny nodded his agreement. "Not up here anyways. . . ."

"Never poked around the old mill?"

"No, sir."

"So you've never seen anyone else around here, cars or trucks, maybe ones you don't recognize, or maybe some you did?" Again, in unison, the boys shook their heads. Bentz lifted his eyebrows. "What about you?" he asked the mother.

"Never. I rarely come down this way. It's not on any of the routes I take to work or to the boys' school." Her hair was beginning to frizz in the rain and she had an arm around each of her son's shoulders. As if she were afraid he was going to haul them both into jail for trespassing. "I'm usually going east or south. Not north. And even if I take the main road, I don't go by here.''

Bentz believed her. The turnoff to the mill had to be a quarter-mile off a country road that angled away from the main highway. The mill was so far off the beaten track, probably no one but the old-timers in the local populace knew about it.

Except the killer. Somehow he'd found the Old Kayler Place and used it twice for his grisly work.

''Is there anything else you need?'' Mrs. Sawtell asked. ''The boys' pa will be home anytime and I've got to get supper on. He'll want to talk to Kenny and Donny about taking the dog and the guns out.'' She sent each of her sons a stern look and her fingers tightened over their shoulders.

''No, thanks, that'll do.'' He dug into his wallet and withdrew a card. ''If you think of anything else''—he swept a finger from one kid to the other—''call me.''

''We will,'' Linda promised and hustled her boys through the mud to a pickup truck parked just outside the gate.

''So what do you think?'' Montoya asked.

''The kids are telling the truth. They were scared to death.''

''I'll check on the owner of the place, and the Sheriff's Department is already contacting the neighbors. If anyone's seen anything, we'll know about it.''

''But when?'' Bentz wondered aloud.

''You think he's escalating.''

''Yeah,'' Bentz said, glaring at the fortress-like mill. ''I don't think there's any question about it.''

Chapter
Twenty-eight

"I'm tellin' you I don't know anything' about a baby boy bein' adopted out." Ramsey John Dodd was adamant.

"My grandmother never mentioned it?" Olivia demanded, stretching the cord of the phone so she could fill Hairy S's water dish. She wouldn't put it past the slimeball lawyer to lie through his teeth.

"Not to me."

"I realize you're too young to have been involved," Olivia said as she turned on a faucet, "but I thought she might have said something about the baby or given you the name of a lawyer she used before she hired you."

"I don't know if she had one." Ramsey John's voice was smooth as oil. "But tell you what, I'll go over all my files and see if there's anything in 'em."

"I'd appreciate it," Olivia said and imagined the attorney leaning back in his battered chair, the heels of his shoes resting on the desk in his hole-in-the-wall of an office. "Thanks, R.J." She twisted off the tap.

"Anytime. No problem at all." He hung up and Olivia

set Hairy's dish on the floor. *Just because you have a brother doesn't necessarily mean that he's the killer. Bentz just has a theory that the murderer had to be someone close to you—someone related—but it's only a theory.*

She rubbed the kinks out of her neck.

Then again, it could be true.

She'd gotten nowhere on her quest to find out if her brother was alive

So who would Grannie confide in? If not a lawyer, then who? A sister? They were all dead. Olivia drummed her fingers on the countertop. Bernadette claimed she had no idea what had happened to her son. Reggie supposedly didn't know he existed. Yet . . . that was wrong . . . hadn't he mentioned that she was the only one left, that he'd lost all the others? Did he know what had happened to the baby? Would she have to swallow her pride and talk to the sperm donor again?

From her conversation with her mother, Olivia was certain there were no public records of the birth; no hospital records, but it was the only lead she had.

So you'd better call Bentz. He's a cop. He can get the information faster than you.

She reached for the phone again but pride kept her from lifting the receiver. It had only been hours ago, in this very kitchen, where he'd rejected her. One night of lovemaking . . . a wistful smile tugged at her lips when she thought of lying in his arms, the warmth and security she'd so fleetingly felt as he'd held her close and she'd heard the steady sound of his breathing and the strong beat of his heart.

Well, that was over. He'd made it clear.

She grabbed a broom from the closet and began sweeping the floor. The phone rang and she managed to answer it and balance the receiver between her shoulder and ear as she brushed empty shells from beneath Chia's cage.

"It's Bentz." Cold. Professional. Her heart did a quick little flip before she set the broom aside. From the background noise, the hum of an engine, and the crackle of the police band radio, she guessed he was on his cell phone. "I thought you'd like to know that we found the victims."

Oh, God. "So soon? Wait, victims? Plural?" More than one woman had been killed?

"Jane Does. But just as you described them," he admitted, his voice a little less harsh. "One chained to the wall with the symbols around her, the other strapped to the wheel you described."

"And both . . ."

"Yeah. Beheaded."

Her stomach retched and she shot to the sink, thinking she would throw up. She should have felt a little sense of validation, that she'd been right and proved the skeptics wrong. Instead she just felt horror. Blind, mind-numbing horror.

"Both victims were in the same place," he explained.

Her chest tightened as she remembered the women and their pain. As she kicked out a kitchen chair and dropped into it, Bentz gave her a summarized and, she suspected, sanitized version of what he'd found.

"But it was just as you described. Right on the money. Except that the crypt was really an old storage silo."

Tears threatened. She felt weak. Helpless. All too clearly she remembered her visions, recalled the moments the women were slain. And she could do nothing but watch in horror. Her hands shook as she held the phone. Her right was still bandaged. Her mirror upstairs shattered.

"We'll get him, Liv—Olivia," Bentz said more kindly and her heart twisted.

"When?"

"I don't know."

How many more would she see tortured and killed? The tears began to flow, running down her cheeks and chin to fall to the table. "Listen. I know this is rough—"

She blinked hard. No one could understand. No one.

"—In the meantime, the department's authorized around-the-clock security for you." She swallowed hard, brushed aside her tears with the back of a hand. "Did Ole Olsen's crew come over?"

"Yes." She nodded, glancing around the kitchen, though she knew he couldn't see her. From her perch Chia set out a high-pitched whistle. Olivia forced a smile she didn't feel. "That wasn't part of the system, just Chia's comment, but believe me, I've literally got more bells and whistles than I know what to do with. I think I need a degree in electrical engineering just to lock this place down."

"Just make sure you use it."

"I will . . . if I can ever figure it out." *Buck up, Olivia. Sitting around crying won't help the victims and it certainly won't help you.*

"You're a smart woman. You'll do fine," he said, but she found little warmth in his compliment. Women were dying and she could do nothing. Nothing.

"Olivia? Are you all right?"

She gritted her teeth. "No, I'm not. I feel responsible for this somehow."

"It's not your—"

"I know that, okay! But it's hard." She tried vainly to pull herself together. "Look, I was about to call you. You asked if I had any siblings and I said 'no' but that was before I looked into my family Bible and discovered I have a brother."

"I know."

She froze. "*You* know?"

"I heard that your mother had a son before she was married to your father. She gave him up. Private adoption. So far, no record of it."

"And you didn't tell me?" she asked, her temper instantly igniting. Maybe she didn't know Bentz at all. She'd accepted the fact that they couldn't be lovers. She had come to the painful conclusion that Bentz was breaking off their short-lived relationship not only because he was adhering to his sense of professionalism but also because he was just plain incapable of allowing a woman to get too close. No doubt about it, he'd been burned and burned badly. Nonetheless, he should have had the decency to tell her about her brother. "Didn't you think I'd want to know about this?"

"That's one of the reasons I called. I just found out this afternoon before I got called to the scene. This was my first chance to get hold of you."

Mentally, she counted to ten. Tried to calm down. It didn't work. "How did you find out?"

"From one of your mother's exes. Oscar Cantrell."

"The one who owns Benchmark Realty."

"That's him. Bernadette drank a little too much one night and spilled the beans. I need to talk to her."

"You'll be wasting your time." Olivia leaned a hip against the table and stared outside to the verandah. A crow was hopping along the rail. "I've already spoken to her about my brother. She either doesn't know or won't say who adopted him. I don't know if she went through an attorney or if my grandmother handled it herself."

"The department is already searching the county and state records," Bentz said. "As well as hospitals and clinics."

"I don't think Bernadette went to a hospital," Olivia said. "My grandmother did a lot of things in her life. One of them was priding herself in being a midwife though she wasn't licensed."

"So you don't think your mother ever went to a doctor for prenatal care?"

"That's very, very doubtful."

"I've got to go. Someone's paging me," Bentz said. "But you take care of yourself. If you see anything or feel that you're in any kind of danger, call me."

"I will," she promised, "but just nail this guy, okay?"

"I'm workin' on it."

"Make it soon, Bentz. Make it soon."

Kristi was pissed. She flopped herself into the passenger side of her father's Jeep and folded her arms across her chest. "Three hours," she said as he started the car. "I waited three damned hours!"

"I called," Bentz pointed out. "Told you I got held up."

She glared out the window and wished her dad were anything but a homicide dick. She hated his profession. Being a cop's kid sucked.

He pulled out of the lot next to Cramer Hall. There wasn't much traffic on campus; most of the kids had left earlier. "I offered to have someone pick you up."

"I could have found a ride," she grumbled. "If you were too busy—"

"It was important."

"It's always important," she threw back at him. God, why hadn't she stayed at school? Right now she and Brian could be drinking beer, pretending to study, and kissing in his room . . . instead she was stuck the next five days hanging out in her dad's apartment, dodging calls from Jay and wishing she were back at All Saints. While some kids were pathetically homesick by this time of year, Kristi was already wishing she wasn't going home to that cracker box of an apartment that Rick swore he'd someday move from. Fat chance. He loved it there and now that she was gone . . . she felt a jab of guilt. He was paying for her school. Big bucks. On his salary he couldn't afford anything else while she was in college. But she was still mad. Real mad.

Slumping down in the passenger seat, she scowled out the window. "Mom was never late picking me up," she said and, from the corner of her eye, noticed Bentz's mouth tighten. Just as she knew it would. Rarely did she pull out the "Mom" weapon, only when she was really, really ticked off. Today qualified, so she opened the mental drawer and found the long blade that she knew cut straight to her father's heart. She decided to give it one little twist. "I hate it that you're a cop. Mom did, too."

"She knew I was going to join the force when she married me." He switched on the wipers.

"But *I* didn't have a choice."

"None of us get to choose our parents," he said through lips that barely moved, then slanted a glance at her as he wended his way through the narrow campus streets. "You just got lucky."

Was he kidding? No. There wasn't even a hint of amusement on his face. That was the problem. "Detective" Rick Bentz was always so damned serious. Could barely crack a smile; not that she'd given him any reason to lately. There had been a time when he'd been more easygoing, but that had been long ago. She felt a little bad about the way she'd treated him. Some of her anger had dissipated once she'd gotten her little digs in and she knew he was trying to be a great dad and repair some of the damage between them.

"Jay called. I think he wants you to come to his house for Thanksgiving."

She blew out her breath. "Jay and I are breaking up."

"Oh?" He slowed for a stop sign. "Does he know it yet?"

The ring in her pocket seemed suddenly as big as a tire from one of those monster trucks. "I was waiting to tell him in person."

"Good idea." He frowned, as if he'd been through something similar. Oh, yeah, right. No way. Not the man married to his job. "You might want to let him down slowly."

Now her father was giving her advice on her love life. What a laugh! "Who are you? Dear Abby or Dr. Sam?"

One side of his lip twisted upward. "Jay's an okay guy."

"I thought you didn't like him."

"I don't like anyone you date."

"Don't I know it," she grumbled and considered telling him about Brian but he'd just get on her case about not breaking up with Jay first and he wouldn't like it that she was seeing a guy who was around thirty. No way. Bentz would have a fit. Probably have Brian checked out through the department's computers or, worse yet, meet him and give him the third-degree. No thank you. Time to change the subject. "So you're working on that serial killer case, aren't you?"

"Yeah."

"Is it as bad as the last one?"

"They're all bad," he said and drove past the campus gates, where the traffic increased, the headlights and street-lights chasing away the gloom. "But yes, I think this is worse than the Rosary Killer."

"Why?"

He hesitated.

"God, Dad, you can trust me."

"It's just closer to home. Some of the girls killed have been college coeds."

"Yeah, I figured." She'd known that would freak him out. "I heard some of the kids talking and the school made an announcement. We're supposed to be extra careful."

"You'd better be."

She rolled her eyes, but didn't tell him to butt out of her life. "So are you gonna get this guy?"

"You bet."

"Then you'll be famous again."

"Or infamous." He flashed her a smile as he drove through the city, gunning it as he turned onto the freeway. He didn't even complain when she tuned the radio to "her" station instead of that crappy WSLJ that he listened to. Oldies. Jazz. Obscure music you couldn't find on CDs and, of course, the radio talk show that he found so fascinating, *Midnight Confessions* hosted by Dr. Sam. Ever since last summer when that Rosary Killer was on the loose, her dad had been tuning in. It was weird. Kristi had first introduced him to Dr. Sam and, unbeknownst to Bentz, had even called in a few times and gotten some advice from the radio shrink.

Well, who wouldn't, after what she'd found out about herself, her mother, the man she'd thought was an uncle, and the man who had raised her. They'd all been living a lie. It was probably why her mom had died. Why else would Jennifer have lost control of her car and crashed into the tree? She hadn't been legally drunk—no way. Jennifer Bentz had hated excessive alcohol almost as much as she'd hated her husband being a cop. It had been a clear day. No other car involved. But there had been some traces of Valium in her bloodstream . . . Damn it all.

Kristi was also starting to believe that her mother had hated herself. For all the mistakes she'd made in her life. The more Kristi learned about psychology from weird Dr. Sutter, the more she was convinced her mother had been consumed with self-loathing. Why? Because she'd messed up. Gotten it on with her brother-in-law, a priest no less, ended up pregnant and then lived a lie. Who wouldn't go nuts? Worse yet, years later Jennifer had taken up with Father James again. Like he was some kind of irresistible force or forbidden fruit. No wonder she'd been seeing a shrink and her father had poured himself into a bottle. Then there was the incident when Bentz had killed a kid he thought was going to shoot his partner. That had happened in L.A. Just like everything else.

So they'd moved east. To New Orleans. The only place her dad could get another job as a detective. Yeah, that made a lot of sense. Sometimes Kristi just wished they lived somewhere in the middle of the country—somewhere like Kansas or Oklahoma—and her mom was still alive and really into gardening and her dad sold insurance or real estate, like normal people. They would have a nice two-story house with a picket fence and a dog and a cat, and she would have an older brother to watch over her and a younger sister to confide in and fight with. There would be a patio with a barbecue and maybe one of those old-fashioned swings on the front porch and . . . She snapped herself out of the daydream.

Get real!

She glanced over at the man who called himself her dad. Lines of worry fanned from the corners of his eyes as he squinted against the traffic. His lips were thin and she knew he was thinking about the case. Not that she could blame him.

All in all, he wasn't such a bad guy.

For a paranoid, recovering alcoholic, homicide dick.

* * *

The Chosen One was frantic.

His head thundered, felt as if it was going to explode.

No amount of prayer, nor flogging, could calm him.

Alone in his sanctuary, he stood naked and shaking at the small table, flipping anxiously through the pages of his book. Then, in despair, he rocked back on his heels. His heart was pounding, his head on fire. St. Olivia's feast day was in June . . . no, that would never do. He couldn't wait that long for her sacrifice and Olivia wasn't even canonized . . . no, no . . . He began to sweat. His heart rate accelerated to a fever pitch. Then there was Oliva . . . feast day March fifth, no, no . . . The storm in his head raged and he drew in deep breaths . . .

Calm down.

Think rationally.

The other ones he'd sacrificed had not answered to the names of the saints whom they'd become, had they?

No. He'd had to rename them.

He would have to stick to his original method and baptize Olivia into the proper name. That was all. He was becoming confused. His mission unfocused. Sometimes he doubted himself . . . if only he had someone in whom he could confide. He'd had his apprentice and there had been comfort in sharing . . . but that was over now and he had to resort to confession . . . when the doubts became unbearable, he could confess and not worry about detection.

He closed his eyes and sent up a short prayer for clarity. That's what he needed now. Ever since the last sacrifice, he'd lacked clarity. The rite itself had buoyed him to the God-like state he experienced at each sacrifice but afterward, much too soon this time, he'd tumbled down so far into the black depths of despair, even questioning his mission.

He tried recalling the act, visualizing St. Catherine of Alexandria's face as he'd lifted his sword, but even that did not bring him to euphoria, nor arousal. Because of the woman. Olivia. She was getting nearer. He could feel her. Watching. Wanting to stop him.

This is a test. God is always giving you a challenge and you must not waver on your mission.

"Maintain," he told himself and then, drawing deep breaths, began again, slowly turning the pages of his book, his eyes scanning each thin page. There were many saints to choose from . . . he just had to find the perfect one—yes, that was it, God was speaking to him. It had to be soon. Yes . . . yes . . . Here!

St. Bibiana . . . Vivian . . . not so far from Olivia, many of the same letters in her name, not that it mattered, but . . . oh, yes . . . the way she was martyred. He read hungrily, already thinking of his mission. St. Vivian had been jailed in a madhouse and routinely flogged. Eventually she'd been left for the dogs . . . who surprisingly weren't interested in feasting upon her.

He tapped his fingers on the page.

Obviously, those pathetic curs weren't the right kind of dogs, nor trained properly . . . nor hungry enough.

He would have to do some research. In the library. Rottweiler? Pit bull? Or a hybrid with a wolf . . . oh, that would be a nice touch and there were those lowlifes who bred such animals, all without papers, behind the authorities' backs . . . and the place, well, that was already taken care of . . . He had a whip . . . he glanced to the wall where an ancient cat-o'-nine-tails hung next to a picture of the Madonna. Oh, *yesssss* . . .

The Chosen One finally found peace. His headache abated to a dull, irritating throb. His mission was clear again. He smiled and made the sign of the cross at the altar, then he found his pinking shears and began cutting out the picture of St. Vivian . . . beautiful . . . pious . . . smooth skinned . . . just like Olivia Benchet . . .

Chapter
Twenty-nine

"I can't believe that you actually found this place!" Olivia exclaimed, throwing open the door. It was late Wednesday morning, and Sarah Restin, two bags sitting on the floorboards, was standing on Olivia's front porch. "God, it's so good to see you!" Olivia threw her arms around her friend and said, "Don't pay any attention to the dog." Hairy S was having his usual barking fit, running in crazy circles and setting off a chain reaction of cawing and scolding from the crows and squirrels hiding in the surrounding trees.

"I said I was coming, didn't I?" Sarah said, holding tight and sidestepping Hairy. Olivia remembered that Sarah didn't like animals, had a particular phobia of dogs, the result of having been bitten in the leg while riding her bike as a girl. "I just lucked out and got on an early flight . . . a very early flight," Sarah said, eyeing Hairy S warily.

"But you were going to call first."

"Well, I found directions on the Internet and thought I'd take a chance! This is great," she added. She reached down for the handle of her roll bag. "It's so . . ."

"Un-Tucson?"

"Yeah, maybe that's it," Sarah said, taking in everything. She'd lost weight since Olivia had seen her and her hair was shorter and a deeper shade of red, but her eyes said it all. Worry lines had sprouted near the corners and bluish circles made them appear haunted. "I was going to say it was so remote and isolated . . . in the middle of no-damned where."

"Home sweet home," Olivia teased as Sarah held her at arm's length.

"You look great."

"You, too."

"Don't lie. *I know* what I look like." They each carried a bag inside, and as they passed the bookcase, Sarah glanced into the mirror mounted above. "Ugh. Look at that. I've aged twenty years in the last one." She shook her head. "All this stuff with Leo is killing me. I can't believe he wants a damned divorce."

"Let's not talk about it just yet. We've got plenty of time." She started for the stairs. "Here, follow me, I'll take you to your room."

"Just like the bellman at the Ritz."

"Exactly."

Sarah managed a small laugh as she climbed the stairs and deposited her things in the second bedroom. But a few minutes later, when they were downstairs drinking coffee laced with Baileys, she slipped into her dark mood again. "If I can't get hold of Leo, I'm going to have to get an attorney," she admitted and looked out the window to the bayou. Sunlight battled through a thin mist rising between the skeletal branches of the scrub oak and cypress.

"You should anyway. Just to know your rights. You need someone in your corner."

"I suppose," Sarah said, not sounding convinced as she dropped a hand and scratched Hairy behind his ears. The dog stretched his neck, eager for the attention. "I never, never, never thought I'd be getting a divorce. It's just not something I believe in."

"I know, but Leo's making it damned hard for you to stay married." Olivia finished her coffee as Chia made deep-throated noises from her cage.

"You've got yourself a menagerie here, don't you?"

"Inherited both pets. From Grannie. But you know, now I couldn't live without 'em." As if he understood he was the subject of conversation, Hairy S thumped his tail against the floorboards.

"I'm . . . I'm not really into animals," Sarah admitted.

"I know, but mine are harmless, believe me. Well, unless you get your nose too close to Chia's cage."

"No chance of that. And him?" She motioned with one finger to the dog.

"A pussycat, but don't tell him," Olivia stage-whispered. "It ruins his self-image and I can't afford canine psycho-therapy."

"Very funny."

"I thought so. Oh, crap!" Olivia glanced at her watch. "Look, I hate to leave you, but I've got to work a few hours at the store, then stop by the University and drop off some books at the library. I'll be back later, probably around six."

"I should go into town anyway. I have a receipt for a motel where Leo was staying. I think I'll see if I can find him."

"Are you sure this is what you want to do? I'm getting bad vibes about it."

"He's my husband," Sarah pointed out and drained her cup. She set it firmly on the table, as if she'd finally made a decision she'd been wrestling with. "I'll try to track Leo down, find out if he can look me in the eye, and then attempt to talk to him, see if we can find any way to communicate. I should be back here in a few hours. If not, I'll give you a call."

Short of hog-tying Sarah, locking her in her room, and appointing Hairy S to keep her from leaving, there wasn't much Olivia could do. "Okay," she finally agreed, "but be careful. I mean it. We've got another serial killer on the loose."

"I read that in the headlines as I walked through the airport," Sarah said. "Creepy." But she was obviously more interested in Leo than the killer haunting New Orleans.

"I mean it. Just don't be careless."

"Olivia, has anyone ever told you that you worry too much?"

"No, just the opposite, if you want to know the truth. But there's a reason for it. Somehow I'm in tune with the killer. I actually 'witness' him killing the victims."

"Witness it? Jesus!"

"Not like I'm there."

"Oh, you mean those visions you have . . . come on, Olivia."

"I mean it, I see these things." Something in her expression must have convinced Sarah because she quit arguing. "So you see him kill people in those visions like you got back in Tucson when you had the horrible headaches."

"Just more intense."

Sarah threw her a skeptical glance. "So what have you done about it?' "

"Talked to the police and installed a security system."

"No! Are you serious?"

"Yes, let me show you how it works." She took the time to demonstrate the system and gave Sarah the code to disengage the sensors so she could get in and out of the house without setting off the alarms.

"All right. Got it," Sarah said, though Olivia wasn't certain. Her friend was far more interested in her husband's infidelity than in self-preservation.

"Good. Promise me you'll be careful. I'm dead serious. The police think I may be a target."

"Because of some ESP thing? Oh, come on . . . Really, Olivia, you do worry way too much. And I'm a big girl. I can take care of myself."

"Sarah—"

"Okay, okay, didn't I say I'd be careful? Truly. Now, relax. We're going to have a great Thanksgiving!" Sarah spent the next fifteen minutes "repairing the damage" to her makeup and hair while talking incessantly about how pissed off she was at Leo, then hauled her purse with her and tore off in her rental car.

Olivia was only a few minutes behind.

As she drove into the city, she wondered how much she should confide in her friend. She'd already told her about the visions, tried to warn her, but should she say more? Sarah was going off half-cocked.

And then there were other issues, Olivia thought as she melded into the traffic near the freeway. Sarah's rental was already out of sight. Should Olivia tell her friend about her one-night with Bentz? That she had some weird kind of fascination not only with Bentz but with a parish priest? Or how about the fact that she had a full brother somewhere, one she'd never known existed?

Gripping the steering wheel more tightly and glancing at her own worried eyes in the rearview mirror, she decided to hold her tongue. Sarah wasn't interested anyway. Olivia had warned her friend about the killer. Now all she could offer Sarah was some compassion because Olivia had a feeling that Leo Restin was going to break his wife's heart.

Unless Olivia could stop it.

But how?

No . . . wait . . . Maybe what Sarah needed was some friendly advice, not from Olivia, but from someone she could pour out her heart to, someone she could trust, someone who could help her help herself. For the first time since getting into the car, Olivia felt better. She knew just the person Sarah should talk to. She was Catholic, wasn't she? And there wasn't a more engaging priest than Father James McClaren.

Tonight I have taken a life. The confession had been with James ever since he'd heard it over the phone two nights earlier. He hadn't slept a wink since. Had expected the phone to ring again and that cold whispery voice to seek reconciliation.

Tired to his bones, James walked into the nave. He was troubled, oh, so troubled. He wondered if the Father's sense of humor was so twisted and dark that He would use James's torment, this knowing that a murderer was on the loose and communicating with James, as his own atonement for the sins Father James had committed against his brother, against his vows, and ultimately against God Himself.

James had spent hours in prayer, more hours seeking Monsignor Roy's counsel, and he'd always received the same advice. "Talk to God, James. This is your challenge. You must uphold the faith and trust. You cannot reveal any of the supplicant's sins. This is part of your contract with God." Monsignor Roy had smiled kindly, but beneath his beatific expression there had been something more. Something dark that lurked beneath the surface. An intangible shape that shifted.

James had studied enough human psychology and counseled enough couples and individuals to recognize guilt and fear when he saw them. Brothers they were, walking hand in hand. Had not James himself felt their bristly, uncomfortable presence within his own soul?

He paused at the altar and looked up at the large cross where a sculpted image of Jesus hung, His crown of thorns creating spots of red blood on His forehead, the slash in His side red and oozing blood, the nails in his hands painfully depicted. "Help me," James whispered and genuflected. "Please." He straightened and turned, surprised to find that there was someone near the door. Not just any woman, but the siren of his dreams.

Olivia Benchet.

His heart fluttered for an instant before he reminded himself that he would never allow himself the mistake he'd made once before. She was just another member of his scattered, disjointed flock. Forcing a warm smile that belied the torment in his soul, he walked briskly toward her. "Olivia," he said, holding out a hand. "It's good to see you."

"You, too, Father." She blushed slightly and the stain

of pink accented her wide gold eyes and frivolous curly hair.

"What can I do for you?"

"I need to talk to someone," she said and some of his resolve cracked a bit.

"You've come to the right place. As they say these days, we're open twenty-four seven. The Boss likes it that way."

She smiled, showing off white teeth that overlapped just slightly. "If you're not busy . . ." She glanced toward the nave and noticed the empty pews.

"I think God's reserved this time for you. Follow me." He led her to his office and held the door for her. "Come in. Sit down." As she breezed past him and took a chair, he noticed a provocative hint of jasmine lingering in her wake. His jaw clenched tight and he tried vainly to ignore the scent. He knew he should round the desk and use it as a barrier between them, that he should sit stiffly away from her, but he found it impossible. Instead he slung a leg over the corner of the desk and wrapped his arms around his abdomen. "What's on your mind?"

"First, I was wondering . . . I mean are there any records within the church of private adoptions?"

"What do you mean?"

"I'm talking about a woman, not more than a girl, who gave up a baby around thirty years ago—actually I have the date. I got it out of the family Bible." She rummaged in her purse and handed him a slip of paper on which she'd copied down a birth date and time. "I think it would have been handled through the Church rather than the courts. Maybe even a priest on his own. It might not have been entirely legal."

He felt his eyebrows rise. "Not legal, but with a priest?"

"Yes. Because my grandmother was involved. The baby we're talking about is my brother. It was before . . . before my mother and father were married and I don't think my father even knew the baby existed, at least not at first. Later, I think, he found out."

"And your mother?" James prodded, watching Olivia

shake her head, her blond-streaked curls dancing in the soft light from the desk lamp.

"She doesn't know."

"Or she won't say. It might be that she doesn't want to revisit that particularly painful time." He folded his hands over one knee and tried not to notice the way her eyebrows pulled together or the way she chewed her lower lip.

"I really don't think Bernadette knows, and my grand-mother is dead. The lawyer for my grandmother's estate is too young and didn't act as if he had a clue." She looked into his eyes and he couldn't help but stare back. There was something about her—ethereal, yet oh so earthy. Forbidden stirrings heated his blood. "I don't know where the record would be, what parish, but I think there would be a christen-ing around that time . . . I think the couple who adopted him would have been very religious. Very Catholic. My grandmother was a bit of a free spirit, you might say, but she had strong roots in her faith." He felt himself being mesmerized, thinking thoughts he shouldn't. "I need to find my brother, Father," she whispered, pleading. "It's important."

James thought of his own brother, the pain of his estrange-ment, how he wished he could go back to the days when they trusted each other, fought with each other, wrestled with each other. How the bond that was so strong had been broken. Because of his weakness. Perhaps God was giving him a chance to help someone else. Perhaps *this* was his atonement. "Why don't I look into it?" he offered.

"Would you?" Her face was suddenly alight and his heart buoyed. "Thank you."

"I'm not saying I'll be successful, but I'll give it a try."

A smile teased the corners of her sexy mouth. "Good. Now, there's something else I have to ask."

"Shoot."

"I'd like you to meet a friend of mine," she said suddenly.

"You know priests don't date," he mocked, then decided he shouldn't joke about his vows of celibacy, but Olivia's grin only widened. She knew he was kidding. "Of course I'll meet her. Name the time and place."

"Well, she flew in this morning and she'd kill me if she found out I was discussing this with you, but she's having marital problems. I think she needs someone to talk to."

"Doesn't she have her own priest?" he asked, a bit wary as he realized his main objective had little to do with the friend and a lot to do with Olivia.

"In Tucson, yes. But she's here now and I was hoping that you would spend some time with her. Kind of like a counseling session, I guess. She talks to me but I keep telling her to leave her husband and she doesn't want to hear it. Sarah, that's my friend, and Leo are both Catholic and it might make her feel better to speak to someone in the Church. Someone who could put a positive spin on the situation rather than negative like me."

"Don't you think that's her decision?"

"Yes, but . . ." She shook her head. "I thought you might be able to find a way to help her, or them, you know, make the marriage stronger, help Leo, that's the husband, try and work things out, if that can be accomplished, but I don't think it's possible." She leaned further back in her chair. "Oh, it's a stupid idea, I suppose."

"No, it shows you care." He smiled. "I just don't want this to blow up in your face. She might think you're overstepping your bounds, that she's being bullied or ganged up on, as if this was some kind of intervention."

Sighing, Olivia tapped her fingers on the arm of the chair. "Maybe we could be more subtle." She glanced up at him and he saw the gleam in her tawny eyes, knew the gears in her mind were turning. "Maybe you could just come to the house. For a visit."

"I suppose," he drawled, not certain he liked the way this sounded. It was too much like a pre-teen plot to suit his tastes.

"Then if she wants to talk, fine, and if she doesn't, well, we haven't offended her and I promise I won't push it."

"That would work." He was relieved. "But if Sarah

prefers not to seek counsel, then we would have to accept that.''

"Meaning *I* would have to accept it."

He nodded. "Could you?"

"No problem. I just want to give her the opportunity." Olivia grinned, seeming to like the path her thoughts were taking.

"When?" he asked, checking the open calendar on his desk.

"How about for the holiday? I mean, unless you've got other plans which you probably do, would you . . ." She paused, seemed a bit embarrassed, then said quickly, "Father McClaren, would you like to join Sarah and me for Thanksgiving dinner?"

He hesitated, then looked her squarely in the eye. This was dangerous. He could feel the heat building between them, but he couldn't resist. "I'd love it," he said and, unfortunately, he meant it. Far more than he should have.

". . . so I just don't get it," Jay whined and Kristi, sitting on the edge of the bed cringed as she held the phone to her ear. "Why won't you have dinner with my family?"

"Because my dad's alone."

"I thought you weren't getting along with him," Jay grumbled.

"I wasn't. But I'm trying."

"I guess that's cool. But you still could come over. We need to hook up. It's been a long time."

Tell him. Break up with him now.

"I miss you."

"Jay, I—"

"And I love you, baby."

Oh, God, she felt like a heel, but she couldn't force the words out.

"Look. We do need to talk."

There was silence. She heard the drum of her own heartbeat.

"Jay?"

"I said 'I love you.' "

"I know, but—"

"Hell, Kristi. What's got into you? Ever since you went up to All Saints, you've changed. I think that place is weird, man. It's doin' weird stuff to you."

"Maybe I'm just finding out who I really am."

"Oh, that's such bullshit and you know it. That's what people say when they don't want to talk about what's really bugging 'em." His voice became a high falsetto. "I'm finding myself. I'm getting in touch with my inner woman. I need to have new experiences." His voice lowered again. "I call it bullshit."

"Maybe you're right," she said. No reason to deny it. "It is kinda weird up there, different from high school, but it's supposed to be. It's college."

"Yeah, and so you take a couple of crap psychology and philosophy classes and now you're so into finding yourself that I don't even know you. Listen . . . maybe we should just break up."

"Maybe we should."

There was a sharp intake of breath. "Jesus, Kristi, listen to us. We love each other. Don't we?"

"I don't know, Jay," she admitted, leaning back on the headboard and feeling tears burn at the back of her eyes. She'd thought she'd loved him. But that was high school. Before she'd graduated. Before she'd learned that her dad wasn't really her dad and her uncle . . . oh, God . . . She knew she'd run off to college primarily to get away from the mess. *Avoidance* and *Denial*, stuff weird Dr. Sutter talked about all the time . . . and Jay was right on that score. Some of the people up at All Saints—Dr. Sutter, Dr. Franz and Dr. Northrup included—were definitely beyond "eccentric." Between them, oddball Lucretia, that nerdy Willie Davis who always took a seat behind her in Psychology and stared at her, and the dykie swim coach, All Saints had more than its share of looney tunes.

"You don't know," Jay repeated, disgust tainting his

words. "Well don't you think you'd better figure it out? Oh, shit. I get it. You found someone didn't you? Holy crap, you've only been up there a few months and you're already cheatin' on me. Damn it, Kristi, what is it with you?"

"That's what I'm trying to figure out," she said, matching his anger with her own, then slamming the receiver down, standing, then giving the punching bag a quick kick. So this was the beginning of the end. Big deal. The truth was she'd outgrown Jay. It was better to let him find someone else. Because she had Brian.

The alarm shrieked.

Olivia sat straight up in bed.

Over and over again the sirens bleated. Her dream disappeared. Oh, God, someone was really breaking into her house! She shot out of bed. Hairy S, barking angry, belated warnings, was already at the bedroom door, eager to charge into the hallway.

The gun . . . Shit! The shotgun was down in the closet behind the slickers and boots . . . oh, God, no . . . Her mind cleared, and over the rapid-fire screams of the alarm, she heard her name and a stream of swearing that would make a sailor blush.

Sarah!

Olivia flew out of the bedroom and down the stairs to find Sarah, reeking of gin, at the control panel for the security system. Cursing and red-faced, she was frantically pushing buttons. "How the hell do you turn this damned thing off?" she yelled as the alarm continued to shrill.

"Here . . ."

Someone pounded on the door. "Open up. Police!"

"Holy shit," Sarah said as Olivia punched in the appropriate numbers and the alarm went suddenly quiet.

"It's all right, Officer! I'm coming!" Olivia shouted just as the door splintered open and two plainclothes officers, weapons drawn, burst into the front hallway. Sarah screamed. Hairy was still barking his fool head off.

Olivia and Sarah threw their hands in the air. "It's okay, it's okay, she didn't know how to disengage the security system!" Slowly, the officers lowered their sidearms.

"You're sure everything's all right?" the heavyset one with the crewcut asked.

"Yes! Didn't you see Sarah drive in?" Olivia demanded, her arms coming down to her sides.

Sarah, holding one hand splayed over her heart, braced her back against the wall. "Jesus," she whispered. "Jesus."

"We did see her drive in. But the alarm went off. We couldn't take a chance," the younger one with the square jaw insisted.

"What the hell are you doing here?" Sarah demanded.

"They're watching the house," Olivia said, not knowing whether to be angry or relieved. On the one hand, she was furious that her privacy had been breached; on the other, she was grateful that the police were nearby in case there had been an intruder. "I told you that I could be a target for the serial killer."

"You were serious? God," Sarah whispered, the color draining from her face.

"We're fine," Olivia told the officers. "The system's new, my friend is here visiting, and she isn't used to dealing with this . . ." Olivia gestured to the control panel.

"If you're sure."

"I said we're okay." The officers helped secure the door again, though the door frame would have to be repaired, the lock replaced. Once the officers had left, Sarah followed Olivia upstairs. A few minutes later Sarah had changed into faux leopard pajamas and was brushing her teeth in the bathroom. Olivia flipped down the lid of the toilet and sat with her knees pulled to her chin.

"I nearly peed in my pants," Sarah admitted around a mouth full of foam. "Jesus, it's like we're part of a stakeout."

"It's part of Bentz's plan."

"Who's Bentz?"

Olivia hesitated. "The detective in charge of locating the killer."

"Tell me about him," Sarah said, her eyes narrowing as she gave her teeth a final swipe, then spit into the sink.

Olivia summed up the last week or so, giving her a quick rundown of what had been happening and how Bentz had been involved, though she sidestepped the part about sleeping with the cop. But Sarah glanced at her friend in the mirror before leaning under the tap and rinsing her mouth. "You like that guy, don't you?" she asked, straightening.

"He's okay."

"No, I mean you *really like* him, like in a boy-meets-girl, well, more like a woman-man sort of way."

"As I said, 'He's okay.' "

"Don't bullshit me." She turned, folded her arms over her chest. "You're falling for the cop. My God, Olivia, are you out of your ever-lovin' mind?"

"I'm *not* falling for him."

"Bull*shit!* I don't sell tons of Dr. Miranda's Love Beads to lovesick teenagers and don't recognize the symptoms. You've got the hots for Detective Bentz! Oh, no, don't tell me you're into handcuffs and some of that weird kind of stuff that I sell."

"No, not that it's any of your business. And since when are you the expert on love?"

"Well . . ." She sighed and shook her head. "Maybe not, considering the situation." Ducking her head under the sink, she rinsed her mouth a final time, then wiped her lips with the sleeve of her pajamas. "So don't try to dodge the issue, you'd like to be involved with the cop."

"It's not going to happen," Olivia said, drawing her knees up to her chest and balancing her bare feet on the edge of the toilet lid. She felt like a kid at a slumber party discussing the new boy in school. "So tell me, what happened to you tonight?"

"Nothin' good."

"You find Leo?"

Sarah shook her head. "I think he was with *her,* the bitch he met at that convention in Nashville."

"You're sure?"

"No, but I called her."

"What?" Olivia shrieked. Oh, no, this wasn't good.

"Yeah, I had a couple of martinis and got up my nerve. Phoned her at her place." She turned to the mirror and plucked an errant hair from the corner of one eyebrows.

"You didn't."

"Sure did. He's *my* husband." Sarah seemed proud of herself.

Olivia groaned. "I don't think I want to know what happened."

"I told her to back off."

"And?"

"She hung up. I called back and the phone just rang and rang. She must've unplugged it."

"You really think Leo was there?"

"Probably. The chicken shit!" Some of the starch left her spine. With a sad, humiliated sigh, she closed her eyes. "Oh, Olivia," she said, resting her forehead on the mirror. "What am I going to do?"

"For now, you're going to bed. It's late. We'll talk in the morning. Maybe things will be clearer."

"I doubt it, but," she said, her shoulders sagging, "I'm beginning to think you're right. Somehow I've got to get over Leo. This . . . this emotional tornado we're in is killin' me."

"Then we'll cook up a storm for Thanksgiving."

Sarah managed a smile. "Turkey, stuffing, sweet-potato pie . . . comfort food."

"And maybe I'll whip up a surprise," Olivia said with a wink as she snapped off the bathroom light. It was a long shot, considering Sarah's current state of mind, but maybe Father James McClaren could help.

* * *

"You're going to work on Thanksgiving?" Kristi groaned from beneath the covers.

"Someone has to keep the streets of this city safe for law-abiding citizens, ma'am." Bentz was standing in the doorway of her room, staring at the lump in the middle of the bed that was his daughter.

"Save me," she said.

"It's just for a couple of hours."

"Oh, yeah, right. I've heard that one before."

"I'll be back in time to get the turkey into the oven."

"You're actually cooking?" She lowered one edge of the coverlet and opened a bleary eye. Bentz drew in a swift breath. Sometimes, in the right light, Kristi looked enough like her mother to stop him short. "I thought we'd go out to a restaurant and a movie or somethin'," she said around a yawn.

"Didn't you see the turkey in the refrigerator?" he asked.

"I figured it was just for show. Like the false face of a building. That you were trying to impress me."

"It's the real thing, kiddo. But did I?"

"Impress me? No!" Then she giggled the way she had when she was a little girl, and the sound brought back memories of a happier time. "Well, yeah, you did, okay. I'm superimpressed. Now go, leave me alone. What time is it anyway?" She lifted her head off the pillow. "Eight-fifteen? On Thanksgiving? Are you crazy, Dad?"

"Some people think so."

"Well, they're right!" She pulled the blankets over her head and rolled over. "You can wake me up around noon. Maybe."

"Count on it. You're on to mash the potatoes."

She groaned again as he slid out of the room and closed the door behind him. It was nice to have her back, even if she was a little grumpy. He'd missed her. When she'd lived at home, they'd fought all the time, about her curfew, her grades, her boyfriend, her attitude. She'd been quick to point out that he was far from being fault-free. His being a cop "sucked," her having to clean up the place was part of his "medieval thinking," her lack of a car was "the worst," and the fact that he suspected her of having sex was a violation of a basic trust issue. When he'd left some condoms on her dresser, she'd been "grossed out" and accused him of being jealous because he "wasn't getting any."

Living with her the last three months had been hell.

And he missed it. He drove to the station and joined the crew that had elected to work the holiday. The first thing he saw was a report that Olivia's new security system had gone off the night before last. The officers indicated it had been a mistake, a friend had tripped the alarm and not been able to reset it at one-thirty in the morning.

Bentz dialed her number. She answered groggily. "Hello?"

His heart twisted a little. "It's Rick. I heard you had trouble the other night."

"Oh . . . no, Sarah's visiting . . . my friend from Tucson. She was out late and the alarm system got the better of her." Her voice sounded thick, still full of sleep, and he remembered how it had been to hold her and smell her scent all night long, to hear her soft breath as she cuddled up next to him.

"I just wanted to make sure you were all right."

"Fine . . . fine . . ." she said and explained what had happened. Her story gelled with the report and she promised that she'd get the door fixed permanently after the holidays, then later, as she sounded a little clearer, she thanked him for calling and wished him a "Happy Thanksgiving," but he heard the change in her tone, the wariness. Somehow she'd found a way to deal with the fact that whatever they'd shared the other night couldn't be repeated. And it bothered him. Not that he wanted her clinging to some belief that they actually could have something together, but the fact that he knew it would never work. The world seemed a little colder when he hung up and severed the connection.

Refusing to dwell on stupid romantic visions, he checked his e-mail and in-basket and made some calls, hoping to come up with an ID of either of the newly found victims.

So far, he didn't have IDs or an autopsy report on either, but the cause of death was pretty evident and he was fairly certain that the times of death would coincide with the timing of Olivia's visions. If they were lucky, the killer had slipped up and the crime scene team had found some evidence linking someone to the murder scene—a hair, a piece of fabric, skin under one of the victim's fingernails, a fingerprint left carelessly, a tire track, a witness who'd seen a car or truck . . . anything.

They just needed a break—one tiny break. Something more concrete than Olivia's revelations

Olivia. Even though he'd called her earlier he'd tried not to think too much about her and had attempted to close his mind to all thoughts of the night he'd shared with her. Nonetheless he was worried about her and had checked to make sure that her place was being kept under police watch. He only prayed the killer wouldn't strike again soon.

Oh, yeah, and why not?

Sipping bitter coffee, he glanced down the list he'd put together on a legal pad, a list of martyred women saints whose feast days were coming up. It wasn't good news. In the next few weeks the calendar was ass-deep in feast days and Bentz had written down the ones that he expected would appeal to the killer.

December second, St. Vivian or Bibiana, flogged and left for the dogs; December ninth, St. Gorgonia, trampled by a team of mules, her bones crushed, her internal organs mashed to a pulp. She supposedly survived not only the trampling— oh, yeah, right—but some other form of paralysis, to end up dying of "natural causes." Then there was December thirteenth, the feast day of St. Lucy. Lucy had been hitched to a team of oxen who couldn't budge her. When the oxen failed to drag her to death or pull her apart, she was tortured by having her eyes ripped out before she was set afire. Apparently she survived the blaze because she ended up being stabbed to death.

Brutal. Ugly. Twisted.

A priest?

He didn't think so.

He shoved his notes aside. The feast days he'd pulled were only a few, those celebrating the deaths of martyrs before the middle of the December. There were more . . . lots more. With each day that passed.

Rubbing the back of his neck, Bentz stood and looked out the window to the gray, wet day. Pigeons fluttered and cooed, perching beneath the eaves.

In New York there was the traditional parade, while all around the country, people were hosting their families, gorging themselves, and sitting around the television to watch football.

But here, in New Orleans, there was a killer. And he was waiting, ready to strike again.

Chapter Thirty

"I told you I know nothin' about any of these murders and I don't 'preciate my ass being dragged down here on Thanksgivin'." Reggie Benchet's eyes glittered angrily as he sat under the harsh fluorescent glare in the interrogation room. His scrawny butt was balanced on the edge of a battered chair, his elbows propped on the table. Thin to the point of being gaunt, appearing older than his sixty-eight years, he spat a stream of tobacco juice into a tin can on the floor. "Now, do I need a lawyer? You gonna charge me with somethin' or you gonna let me walk out of here?" Pointing a gnarled finger at Bentz, he added, "I know my rights. You cain't hold me without chargin' me, so unless you boys come up with somethin', I got me a Thanksgivin' dinner to go to."

"Where?"

"It don't matter none, but at my girlfriend's place."

Bentz checked his notes. "Claudette DuFresne?"

"Yeah, but don't you be botherin' her now, not on the

holiday. She's got herself a bad heart and she don't need any trouble.''

"She was arrested for selling crack," Bentz said, flipping through a two-page rap sheet that included everything from soliciting to dealing. "Yeah, she's a real sweetheart.''

"That was a few years back. She's cleaned herself up and taken Jesus into her heart. She's a good Christian woman, takes care of her sick ma and works down ta the senior center in Lafayette.'' He scrabbled in a pocket of his shirt and pulled out a pack of Camel straights. "Mind if I smoke?'' He didn't wait for an answer and lit up, chewing and smoking all at once. A tobacco company exec's dream consumer.

"You found God yourself, didn't ya?''

"That I did and you all can rest easy that I'll be sendin' up prayers for your souls.''

"You're not a priest," Montoya interjected from his spot near the door. His arms were folded over his chest, his usually neat goatee a little ratty, and he was wearing an I'm-not-buying-it expression.

"Nah. 'Course not. I'm born again. Found Christ in stir ... hell, that sounds like a great country song, now, don't it?'' he asked, coughing as he laughed at his own joke.

"But you were Catholic?''

"Me? Hell, no. That was my wife. 'Scuse me, my *ex-*wife. Bernadette.'' He shook his head violently, as if he were trying to dislodge water from inside his ear. "Now there's a woman I should never have gotten myself hitched to.''

"Let's talk about that.''

"Ancient history.''

"You had three children with her.''

His smile faded. He spat again.

"We know that one daughter survived and another drowned as a toddler, but you had a son as well.''

"For all the good it did me. No one ever told me 'bout the boy, y'know. I suspected, though, found some old doctor bills when I was married to Bernadette, but she always got real quiet and claimed she had a miscarriage. Years later, when I was locked up, she came clean. I guess her conscience got the better of her and she wrote me a letter, told me the boy was out there, she just didn't know where. I did what I could from prison, which wasn't much. Once I tried to get more information from her, then from her mother, and even from the doc. But he was dead. I didn't get squat.''

"And that's where you left it?''

He paused, took a long drag, then blew a smoke ring to the ceiling. "Not me. That there's my only boy and he was took from me. Thirty damned years ago. I ain't done lookin' for him.''

"Maybe we can help,'' Bentz offered.

"And why would you do that?''

"We're looking for him, too.''

Reggie was instantly wary. "Why?''

"We just need to talk to him, like we're talking to you,'' Montoya explained.

Reggie's eyebrows drew togther. "I don't see how. If you don't know who he is, why do you need to talk to him?''

"We think he can help us.''

Reggie wasn't buying it. "No way—''

"I thought you wanted to see your boy. Tell us what you know.''

Hesitating, stalling for time, Reggie mashed out his Camel, leaving a piece of it to smolder. "You'll quit hasslin' me then?''

"If you've kept your nose clean.''

"Shit, yes, I have. You talk to my parole officer. He'll tell ya so hisself.''

"So what've you got?''

He snorted and finally lifted a thin shoulder. "Not much. I told you that already. All I know is that Virginia told me it was a private adoption, and by that I'm sure she meant illegal, and no one would ever find out. A priest had handled the whole damned thing and he was sworn to secrecy. But while I was doin' time, I remembered another inmate who told me about a Father Harris or Henry, who got himself in a passel of trouble. Not only was he sellin' babies and pocketin' the money, but he got caught with his pants down. With a fifteen-year-old boy.''

''He was charged?'' Bentz asked. Now they were getting somewhere.

Montoya's eyes glittered in interest.

''I don't think so. According to the inmate—Victor Spitz—the boy was paid off, the charges dropped, and the priest was moved out of state.''

''You say his name was Henry or Harris?''

''That's what I was told.''

''First name? Or last?''

''That I don't know.'' Reggie shook his head. ''That's all I can tell ya,'' he said and checked his watch again. ''Now... I expect a ride back ta Lafayette before my damned dinner gets cold and I find myself in the doghouse.''

''You didn't! You didn't invite a priest to dinner,'' Sarah said, horrified. She was folding bread cubes into sautéed vegetables, turkey giblets, and oysters, all of which she claimed were part of her mother's ''famous'' stuffing. ''Why?''

Peeling parboiled sweet potatoes, Olivia said, ''I could lie to you and say that he seemed lonely and that I like him and that I wanted him to feel included in some kind of Thanksgiving tradition and it wouldn't really be a lie, but the real reason is that I did it because of you, because you seem depressed and I thought—''

''That what? I needed to confess something? Jesus H. Christ, Livvie, that's nervy of you!''

''You don't have to say a word to him, okay?''

''Good, 'cuz I won't.'' Sarah was livid. She stirred the giblets with a vengeance.

''I was just trying to help.''

Sarah set her mixing spoon aside and let out a long,

calming breath. "Yeah, I know and I appreciate it, really, but . . . I just need to talk to Leo."

Olivia wasn't about to argue.

Two hours later when the doorbell rang and Hairy S ran howling to the front door, she wondered if she'd made a mistake. "Great, the priest's here," Sarah said, still keeping her distance from the dog. "Just what we need."

"You'll like him."

"Oh, come on . . ."

"Just . . . relax. Have a good time." Olivia threw open the door and found Father James dressed in slacks, casual sweater, and a bomber jacket. Bent on one knee, he eyed the damage to her lock. Beside him on the porch mat was a bottle of wine.

"Have a little trouble?" he asked, looking up at her, and she was reminded that he was too good-looking to be a priest. Square jaw, thick hair, wide shoulders, and a killer smile that didn't quite touch his eyes.

"A little. Alarm system malfunction."

"And the door blew up?"

"Was kicked in by the police," she said and realized he probably thought the security company had sent the cops. No reason to explain. "Come in," she invited as, while still crouched, he extended his hand, allowing the dog to sniff it cautiously. "That's Hairy S, he came with the house."

"No doubt a selling feature." Blue eyes flashed humor.

"Depends upon your point of view."

He straightened and dusted off his hands. "I can fix that for you," he said, motioning toward the doorjamb.

"That's right, you're the handyman priest. That would be great. But maybe later. Right now, come on in. There's someone I'd like you to meet."

Sarah stood by the bookcase inside the front door.

Olivia motioned to her friend. "Sarah Restin, Father James McClaren."

"You're a priest?" Sarah was obviously skeptical as she eyed his casual attire.

"That's right, but I left my alb in the car," he joked and took her hand in his. "Nice to meet you."

"You . . . you, too." Stunned, she looked him up and down as Olivia ushered them into the kitchen.

Father James offered the bottle of wine. "My contribution to dinner."

"Thanks. We'll eat in about half an hour. In the meantime, you can do the honors." Olivia handed him a corkscrew. He poured wine and they each had a glass. Any reservations Sarah had seemed to melt away as they talked and got to know each other. Father James carved the turkey as Olivia placed dishes on the table and Sarah lit candles. Hairy S settled into his spot near the back door, Chia chortled, and once he'd held chairs out for each of the women, Father James sat at the table, bowed his head, and said a short grace. They talked about everything and nothing and Olivia thought again what a waste it was that he'd accepted a calling with the Church. He would have made someone a great husband and, she assumed, would have been a fabulous father.

He joked, was effusive about the meal, and helped clear the table. After the dishes were stacked near the sink, he insisted that Olivia bring out her grandfather's tool box, then went to work on the door.

"He's not like any priest I've ever met," Sarah said as she whipped cream for the pie while Olivia wrapped the leftovers in plastic wrap. "I mean . . . he looks like he should be on a soap opera, for God's sake. He brings wine and then fixes things . . . and, if I didn't know better, I think he's got the hots for you."

"The 'hots'? Come on. He's married to the Church." Olivia felt heat crawl up her neck.

"Church-smurch, he's still a man." Sarah sneaked a peak past the archway and bit her lip. Over the whir of the mixer she said, "I know he was trying to hide it, but I'll bet you the deed to the store that he would be great in bed!"

"Don't even say it! Sarah!"

"Come on, admit it. Haven't you ever wondered what it would be like to do it with a priest?"

"No!"

"Why? Because you're in love with the cop?" She pulled a face.

"I'm not in love with anyone," Olivia insisted as Chia whistled and the mixer whined. She wiped her hands on a dish towel and started to pour coffee. "So hush."

But Sarah's smile was positively naughty. "I'm just telling you if I was single and that man looked at me the way he looked at you over dinner, I don't know if I could contain myself."

"Enough!" She glared at her guest, and Sarah, rolling her eyes, turned her attention to the cream again.

"I think we're about there . . . See, it's the stiff peak stage."

"The stiff peak stage . . . ?"

Sarah burst out laughing as she switched off the mixer and disconnected one of the beaters.

"You're bad, Sarah Restin."

"Don't I know it?" Licking whipped cream off the beater and winking, she proved her point.

"Save me!" But Olivia laughed.

"What's so funny?" Father James asked as he appeared in the doorway. He was wiping his hands on a handkerchief.

Both women laughed even harder.

"I think I missed the joke," Father James said.

"It's nothing. We were just being silly." Olivia shot Sarah a warning glare. "My houseguest has a vivid imagination." To change the subject, she walked through the archway and looked toward the front of the house. "So, is my door fixed?"

"Good as new." He showed her his handiwork and explained how he'd managed to fix the lock. "A little paint and no one will be the wiser."

"How can I repay you?" she asked and from the corner of her eye saw Sarah lift a suggestive eyebrow.

"Dinner was a start," he said, and one side of his mouth

curved upward. "Maybe I could convince you to attend
mass once in a while."

"You drive a hard bargain," she teased, "but sure.
Maybe. Now, come on, we can have dessert in the living
room. Why don't you see if you can find something decent
to listen to on the radio and I'll light a fire?"

"Leave that to me," he said. "Just point me in the direction of the woodshed. I was an Eagle Scout, you know."

"Why doesn't that surprise me?"

For the next hour, while a fire crackled in the old grate and
smooth jazz compliments of WSLJ played through Grannie
Gin's ancient radio, they made small talk. Father James was
as charming as ever but Olivia noticed that beneath his
veneer of affability and calm, there was a hint of tension,
a disturbance that was visible only upon occasion, something
dark in his blue eyes.

Sarah was right. He was handsome. Even drop-dead gorgeous. Though Olivia tried to ignore the feeling, she noticed
a little spark, a connection whenever he looked at her. It
was almost as if there were an unspoken message in his
gaze—an unasked question, one, she was certain, would
scare her to death if she knew what it was.

And it bothered her. He was a priest, for God's sake.
Any bond she felt for him was unthinkable, perhaps her
imagination working double time. She couldn't think of
Father James McClaren as anything but a man of God. She
wouldn't.

First the cop; now the priest.

No way. She sat on one end of Grannie Gin's lumpy
couch, he on the other. Sarah, more relaxed than she'd been
since she'd shown up on Olivia's front porch, kicked off
her shoes and tucked her stocking feet beneath her as she
slowly rocked in Grannie's old swivel chair.

Olivia thought about Sarah's observation—what it would
be like to make love to a priest.

*For God's sake, it's only been a few days since you were
with Bentz.*

She felt the heat wash up her face but managed to keep

up with the conversation, which was turning toward Sarah and her life in Tucson. Sarah, gesturing as she spoke, explained that she and Olivia had owned a store together and it had "never been the same" since Olivia had returned to Louisiana.

This was a good time to make a quick exit and leave Sarah to talk to the priest. Olivia excused herself and started on the dishes, refusing all help in the kitchen, claiming the room was too small for more than one person and she could probably work faster by herself.

Sarah didn't put up much of a fight, and when Olivia hazarded a glance through the open doorway, she noticed that Sarah had moved to the couch, was deep in conversation with Father James, and was dabbing at her eyes with a tissue. Good. Now, if she could make herself scarce without being obvious about it.

She washed, dried, and put away the dishes, wiped down the counters and table, even swept the floor. Over the soft hum of music, she heard Sarah talking rapidly, her words punctuated with sobs, then Father James's deeper, calmer voice. Maybe he was helping her; getting through to her. Olivia crossed her fingers and sent up a prayer that Sarah would somehow find a way to come to terms with her marriage and Leo, the jerk of a husband.

Olivia was about to offer an after-dinner drink when the phone rang, and for a heartbeat, she thought Bentz might be calling again. "Hello?"

"Hello, darlin'." She froze. Recognized the voice. Her heart turned to stone. What did she have to say to her father? "Just wanted to wish you a Happy Thanksgivin'."

"The—the same to you," she managed, though she wasn't sure she meant it.

"I don't have time to stop by today and like as not you've got other things goin' on, but someday, Livvie, we need to see each other and catch up on old times. I'm a man of God now. A minister. You can talk to me."

"There were no old times, Reggie." She had to nip this father-daughter thing in the bud.

"See, here? That's 'xactly what I'm talkin' 'bout. We
need to bridge some rifts, darlin'."

"Please, don't call me that. Not ever again. You can call
me Olivia."

"Hell, that ain't no fun."

She was bristling now, angry that he'd disturbed her holiday. "You know, Reggie, for a minister, you swear a lot."

"Maybe I'm from the Church of Tellin' It Like It Is. I
just called to wish you a good day." She could tell he was
about to hang up and thought twice about her harsh words.
After all, it was Thanksgiving.

"Wait," she said. "Look, I, uh, hope you have a good
day, okay?" That was the best she could do.

"I will, *Olivia.*"

"Reggie? There's something I want to ask you," she
said, barreling on. Since he'd called, she may as well take
advantage of it. "I was digging through some things of
Grannie Gin's and I found a note that I have an older brother.
Bernadette confirmed it, but she couldn't tell me where he
is or even if he's alive. I was thinking you might know
something."

"Well, don't that beat all? Not a word about the kid in
thirty years and now twice in one day. I don't know nothin'
more than I told that detective who had the nerve to haul
me down ta New Orleans on Thanksgivin'. I told him everything I know, which isn't a helluva lot. The boy was kept
a secret from me. Your damned mother, she never gave me
a chance to know my own son!" He was agitated, his raspy
voice strained. "Why all the interest now?"

"Because I never knew about him before."

"What about the cop?"

"That's between you and him," she said. "I assume it's
about a case."

"Hell, yes, a case. He had the nerve to ask me where I
was when those women were kilt. Like I'd know! You fuck
up once and the system gets ya, Livvie. I'll never be free
even though I did my time. Anytime there's trouble, the
cops, they'll be knockin' on my door.

"Listen, if you track that brother of yours down, you tell him he's got a pa—a real one—who'd like to meet him. Seems the whole fam-damn-ily is a helluva lot more interested in him than they are in his father. Goodbye, Olivia," he said angrily and hung up so loudly Olivia jumped. Well, fine.

After replacing the receiver, she decided to pour herself an after-dinner drink. That was the way Reggie Benchet affected her. He drove her straight to the bottle. Scrounging through the cupboards, she found half a pint of Black Velvet and added a healthy shot to her coffee. "Cheers," she muttered to herself and heard Sarah's voice droning on over the faint sounds of jazz. Good. With a smile, she took a sip. Not bad. She hummed as she finished putting the last pot away.

The phone jangled again.

Now who? Admonishing herself for a fool, she couldn't help but hope Bentz was calling again.

"Olivia, let me talk to Sarah," Leo Restin said without so much as a "hi," or "hello." Great. "I know she's there. She called a friend of mine last night, so get her on the line."

"Leo—"

"Now!" he ordered. Olivia didn't like his tone of voice. She looked at the receiver, then promptly hung up.

"Bastard," she whispered before taking another swallow from her cup. "How do you like those apples?"

The phone rang sharply. She considered unplugging the damned thing and let Leo stew in his own juices. She drained her cup.

On the fourth ring, she answered sweetly, "Hello?"

"Olivia, don't you hang up on me," Leo commanded.

"Uh-oh? Not nice, Leo. You can't boss people around." She dangled the receiver over its cradle.

"Olivia!"

Sighing, she held the phone to her ear.

Leo was nearly choking with rage. "I want to talk to my wife, and if you don't put her on the goddamned line, I'll come over there and—'' She dropped the receiver again and considered another drink, but the phone rang immediately. She picked it up. Before she could say a word, Leo said, ''Please put my wife on the phone.'' His voice was strained. He was forcing the words between clenched teeth.

''Then behave, Leo. It's Thanksgiving,'' she said.

''You have no right to—''

''Ah, ah, aahhh.''

''Okay, okay. Just let me talk to her.''

Olivia was considering hanging up again when she looked up and found Father James standing in the archway, his blue eyes trained on her. ''Trouble?'' he asked.

''Nothing serious. Leo Restin is on the phone. Does Sarah want to talk to him?''

As if she'd been lurking around the corner, Sarah shot into the kitchen. ''I thought I heard you say his name,'' she charged. Her eyes were still wet, tears clinging to her lashes, but she threw Olivia a *how-dare-you-screen-my-calls* look and snatched the phone from her hands. ''Hello?'' she said brokenly, then the tears began to roll rapidly down her cheeks again. ''Oh, God, Leo, where are you? I've been so worried . . .'' She turned an ostracizing shoulder toward Olivia, who, shaking her head, poured herself and James each another cup of coffee. She reached into the cupboard again and silently she held up the near-empty bottle of Black Velvet. To her surprise, the priest nodded. Olivia poured them each a healthy shot then, as Sarah whispered, sniffed, and sobbed into the phone, carried their drinks into the living room.

Hairy S, snoring softly, was curled beneath the window.

''Did you get through to her?'' Olivia asked as they settled onto the couch.

Father James took a sip of his drink. ''Privileged information,'' he said. ''Confidential.''

''I just want to help.''

''You've done all you can. Now it's up to Sarah and Leo.''

''Jerk,'' Olivia muttered. She wanted to confide in Father

James, to tell him what a no-good, two-timing, mean-as-the-devil creep Leo Restin was, but she kept her comments to the one word. Before she had a chance to second-guess herself, Sarah swept out of the kitchen.

"I've got to go. Leo wants to meet." Her eyes were bright with hope, a tremulous smile upon her lips.

Olivia was certain her friend's heart was going to be ripped out and stomped on all over again. "Are you sure—?"

"Yes! And I don't have any time for a lecture. I'll tell you all about it when I get back—" She started for the staircase then thought better of it. Hurrying back to the living room, she extended her hand to the priest. "Thank you, Father," she said. "You . . . you really helped." And then she was gone, racing up the stairs, rattling around in the bathroom and flying back down again. "I'll see you later," she said to Olivia and then winked wickedly. "Unless I get lucky."

She was out the door before Olivia could clap a hand to her forehead. "This is never gonna work."

"That's her decision."

"I know, I know, but she did come here, to my house, broken into a million pieces."

"Maybe not so many," James said and sipped from his coffee cup as the strains of an old Frank Sinatra tune filled the room. Red embers glowed as the fire hissed and sparked. The whiskey was taking effect. Olivia's bones melted a bit and she nudged off her shoes with her toes. Looking at James seated at the far end of the couch, his long legs stretched in front of him, she felt lucky that he was there. Without his clerical collar, he seemed so real. So approachable. So downright male.

He stared at the fire, his brow knit in concentration, his jaw hard. A scholar's mind, an athlete's body, usually hidden beneath a priest's vestments.

"Something's bothering you."

"Me?" He glanced up at her and flashed a quick smile. "Nah."

"Yes, there is . . . and don't try to deny it. I'm a little bit of a psychic, you know.'' When he didn't respond, she added, ''It's true. My grandmother used to read tarot cards and tea leaves, and even though she was a devout Catholic, she dabbled in voodoo.''

''How does one 'dabble' in something like that?'' he asked.

''Well, voodoo isn't all about killing chickens and pushing pins in dolls to curse people, you know.''

''I do know.'' He slid her a glance. ''I've studied all kinds of religion and theology and not just through the seminary. It's one of my passions.''

''Any other ones?''

He chuckled. ''Oh, yeah . . .'' he said and his voice softened but he didn't elaborate. ''What about you?''

''Uh-uh. We weren't talking about me. I said that something's troubling you and you tried to change the subject.''

''Even priests have problems,'' he admitted and she watched as firelight played upon the sharp angles of his face. Yes, there was something bothering him, a sadness he tried to hide.

''Maybe I can help.''

''You have. Already.'' Edging a little closer, he took her hand in his and she was surprised to feel calluses upon his skin. ''Just inviting me here, letting me be a part of your little family of friends, that helped. It reminded me of what it feels like to be a part of a family.'' He held her hand a second longer than necessary, then dropped it.

Olivia's breath caught. ''I had ulterior motives because of Sarah. Besides, you have a family.''

His eyes darkened even more. ''That I do.''

''Where are they?''

''Around. But . . . my folks are gone, one a year after the other, and I've got a half-brother but we don't see each other that often.'' He stared at her for a few seconds, his concentration intense, and she suspected he was waging some kind of inner battle. ''I think I'd better go.'' Placing his hands on his knees, he stood quickly, as if he were afraid he might change his mind. ''I'm on duty later.''

"A priest's work is never done?" she quipped.

"Amen, sister."

They laughed and the tension between them broke; she was able to breathe again as she walked him to the door. "Thanks for coming and talking with Sarah."

"Anytime." His voice was soft and she knew he meant it. Maybe Sarah was right, she thought, retrieving his jacket and watching as he slid his arms through the sleeves. He looked down at her, his dark hair falling over his forehead and the intensity of his gaze damn near heart-stopping. She had the unlikely urge to kiss him goodbye, just a brush of her lips over one cheek, but she didn't dare.

He reached into his pocket. "Oh. I nearly forgot," he said, retrieving a folded piece of paper. "These are all matters of public record, so I'm not breaking any Church laws here, but it's a list of the christenings during the time you mentioned. Because of the birth date, I've narrowed it down quite a bit. I hope it helps."

"It will," she promised him as he handed her the computer printout. "Thanks."

"The least I could do." This time she thought he might lean down and graze his lips over her temple, but he didn't, and if he'd even considered it, he held back. "Goodbye, Olivia." He squeezed her hand. "Don't be a stranger. The door to God's house is always open." She watched as he turned his collar to the wind and jogged to his car.

James felt Olivia's gaze. It seemed to burn right through his jacket. Gritting his teeth against the heat flooding his veins, he didn't stop running until he reached his Chevy. Gazing into her eyes had been his undoing, and the hard-on stretching the crotch of his slacks was evidence enough of that. What the devil was wrong with him? He climbed into his four-door, started the engine and waved. As if he wasn't thinking about jetting out of the car, running back to the porch, swooping her off of her feet and carrying her up the stairs so that he could bed her. That's what he wanted.

To strip her of her clothes, climb atop her body and bury himself in her as deep as he could. He hazarded a last glance in her direction. She'd picked up the dog and was holding the scruffy little beast to her chest as she leaned against the siding on the porch.

It wasn't just sex he craved. It was all of it. His heart ached. A beautiful woman, a cozy little cabin in the woods, and a mutt of a dog. All the things he'd given up in life. For his calling. For God. Because he believed. He'd always believed and he knew in his heart that he could help others with their faith, that it was his purpose on life, God's plan for him.

Gritting his teeth, he stepped hard on the accelerator and the car sped over a little bridge to land in the rutted, leaf-strewn lane. He couldn't allow himself to have these doubts. Not now. Not ever. Because it wouldn't take much to propel him into taking a step over the threshold of sin. He cranked the wheel at the main road and skidded onto the highway. Rain splattered the windshield and he began to pray.

He was losing his battle with lust.

Chapter
Thirty-one

Kristi spun and kicked hard, then punched the boxing bag hanging from the ceiling of her bedroom. *Thud.* The bag took the hit. It swayed and came back for more. "Can't get enough, eh? Ah, so!" She was covered in sweat, her hair ringing wet, but all the old tae kwon do moves she'd learned as a kid came back to her. *Just like riding a bike,* she thought.

The punching bag swung crazily; it wasn't what Master Kim, her once-upon-a-time instructor, would have called a worthy sparring opponent, but the bag did the trick as far as giving her the workout she needed, both mentally and physically. One more spinning hook kick, then a side kick, and finally a one-step punch. "Die," she growled at the bag.

She was almost over being mad at her dad.

Almost.

So he'd come back late from the office? So it was Thanksgiving? So what else was new? He used to drive her mother crazy—C-R-A-Z-Y—with all his cop shit. At the time, Kristi hadn't understood it; she'd been a little kid. But she had recognized the tension that escalated between her parents whenever her dad was eyeball deep in a case. He'd never change. His work came first.

No, that wasn't really true. She did believe that she was his first priority. If nothing else, Rick Bentz loved her whether he was her "real" dad or not. It was so weird to think that her uncle, the priest, was her biological father and Rick, the man who raised her and whom she still considered "Daddy," was really her uncle. Sick, sick, sick. She gave the bag a couple more quick kicks then ended with a chop to the throat—well, if it had had a throat, it would have been dead!

Bentz stuck his head through the door. "Come on, Cassius, time to mash the potatoes."

"Who?"

"Cassius Clay, you know—"

"Oh, right, Ali. The Great One."

"No, that's Gretsky."

"The hockey guy."

"Muhammad Ali was The Greatest."

"You know too much about this shi—garbage," she said. "Just let me run through the shower and I'll be out." When he looked about to protest, she pointed a long finger at his nose. "Don't even think about touching *my* 'taters, got it? I'll be out of the shower in ten minutes. They can wait."

Before he could put up any kind of argument, she dashed into the bathroom, locked the door and twisted on the faucet. She didn't quite make her ten minute time frame but before a half hour was out, she'd cleaned up, thrown on her favorite sweats, snapped her hair into a ponytail and mashed the damned potatoes.

Bentz had sliced the hell out of the over-cooked turkey and though his stuffing was on the mushy side and the gravy looked like it had a serious case of acne, the canned cranberry sauce and pumpkin pie and chocolate eclairs he'd bought at the local bakery made up for it. And he'd tried. Kristi would give him that. He'd left fresh flowers in a vase on her bedside table, her favorite stuffed animal, a gray raccoon with a button eye missing had been positioned on the pillows of her bed, and he'd even managed to find two candles that he'd lit and placed on the tiny kitchen table for "just the right ambiance." They sat with the table pushed against the wall, the three counters and sink filled with messy dishes. But it didn't matter.

The best part was that he hadn't touched a drop of Wild Turkey or whatever it was that he used to pour down his throat every holiday. Those were the bad times. And now she understood why. He'd drunk a lot for as long as she could remember, probably ever since finding out that she wasn't really his kid, but then, after the accident when he'd shot the kid, he'd poured himself into a bottle . . . She remembered her parents' fights, how each holiday had been a battle. Other kids had looked forward to Christmas, but she'd felt the tension building and in her pre-teen years, wanted to skip the whole thing. And then Jennifer had died. Rick had given up drinking for good. Kristi figured he deserved an "A" for effort.

They were nearly done with the main course when he brought up all the bad subjects at once. "You talked to Jay yet?"

Kristi poked her mashed potatoes with her fork. "Yeah. On the phone. We had a fight."

"Did you explain what's going on?"

"Not really." She didn't want to think about Jay. Not now.

"Don't you think you should?"

"I will when I'm ready, okay?" she said defensively. Noticing how his eyebrows had climbed halfway up his forehead, she sighed and set down her fork. "I'll see him tomorrow or Saturday. I didn't want a big scene on Thanksgiving. Why ruin the holiday?"

The lines on her dad's forehead deepened, but he nodded, obviously trying to give her some space. "You're right. And I should butt out."

"Now there's an idea." She aimed her fork at him, pointing across the table. "But I'll talk to him before I leave." She took a couple more bites, and decided she had to bring up Brian. Her dad was bound to find out anyway. "I guess you should know that I'm seeing someone else."

"Some*one*. I figured you'd date a lot of different guys." He cut a bite of turkey and pronged it with his fork.

"Wellll . . . I *was* supposed to be pre-engaged to Jay."

"Whatever that means."

"So I wasn't really looking, but this one guy, he's a T.A. and don't freak out, okay, just because he's a little bit older."

"How much is a 'little bit?' " Bentz had stopped eating and was looking at her intently.

Maybe she should have kept her mouth shut. "A few years and it's not serious, okay."

"I hope not. I didn't know T.A.s were allowed to date students."

"It's frowned upon if the T.A. is assigned to your class, and yes, I can guess your next question, Dad. Brian is assigned to my class, but believe me, it hasn't affected my grade in Philosophy. In fact, you'd probably think just the opposite."

Bentz's frown deepened. Geez, she was blowing this!

"Omigod, don't even go there, Dad, my grades are fine, just not stellar, okay. And Zaroster's class is tough. Philosophy of Religion. God, why did I sign up for that one? But, really, none of my classes are a snap. It's not like high school. Zaroster, Sutter and Northrup are three of the hardest professors on campus and I've got them all."

"That's not so bad," he said, digging into the soggy stuffing again. "Tough is good."

"Then how about weird? I swear I ended up with the strangest teachers at All Saints. Even Mrs. Wilder, the bonehead math teacher is kinda freaky. I bet she lives with twelve cats and knits little sweaters for them." Kristi laughed at her own joke, hoping to derail her father, but, of course, it hadn't worked. He hadn't so much as cracked a smile.

"Why do you think your teachers are strange?" he asked and this time he put his fork down.

"I don't know. They just are. Come on, think about what kind of people spend their whole lives wrapped up in one subject and being a part of academia. They're bound to be a little off-center." She lifted a shoulder. "Enough with the interrogation, okay. My grades will be fine. Let's not think about it now. It's Thanksgiving."

He was about to say something else, but thought better of it. "Yeah, I guess it is." One side of his mouth lifted. "I'm glad you're home."

"Well, I'm glad to be here, although, I gotta admit it was touch-and-go for a while. When you were late picking me up, I thought, 'screw this, I'll just stay here.' "

"Because of the T.A.? Brian?"

"He had something to do with it."

"He got a last name?"

"Yeah, he does . . . ." she hesitated but decided her father with all of his police connections would find a way to dig up the information. "It's Thomas, okay? Now, make me a promise. Swear to me that you won't go looking him up on the computers at work. He doesn't need his privacy invaded. It's bad enough that mine is."

"It's not—"

"Yeah, Dad, it is and not just because you're my father, but because you're paranoid and a cop and a single parent."

"Paranoid?" The phone rang and Kristi jumped.

Brian was on her mind and she'd given him the number. Then again it could be Jay. She answered with a quick "Hello?"

There was a pause. "Kristi?"

"Yeah?"

"This is Uncle . . . this is James."

She felt sick inside. Her biological father. The priest. Her dad's brother. She looked over at her dad. Bentz was staring at her. "Hi," she forced out. "How are you?"

"I just wanted to wish you a Happy Thanksgiving."

"Oh. Right. You, too," she said, her mind racing. How would she get him off the phone? She didn't want to talk to him. Ever. What a creep! And to think . . . She didn't even want to go there. She'd trusted him once. When she'd thought he was "Uncle James" and didn't understand

Bentz's stand-offish attitude toward his brother, the gleam of jealousy in his eye. Now she did and she didn't want to talk to him. Not ever. As far as she was concerned Bentz was and always had been her father. Period. He'd always been there for her. Always. Even during the bad times with his drinking, she'd never doubted that he loved her. Oh, he drove her nuts, no doubt about it, but didn't every dad? This guy—James—he was slime spit, a real dick-head. She never wanted to set eyes on him again. But here he was on the phone, his voice so damned calm and serene, it was enough to make her want to puke.

"I'd like to see you," he was saying. "I did talk to your dad—my brother—the other day and he suggested I not push the relationship, but I did want to say that I'm thinking of you and of him. My prayers are with you."

"Fine. Thanks." She hung up quickly and noticed her palms were sweaty, her heart racing and when she caught a glimpse of herself in the mirror, she saw that her skin had turned the color of chalk.

"Jay?" Bentz asked and she shook her head as she slumped into her chair.

"Father McClaren."

"Shit! I told him not to—" Bentz caught himself.

"He just wanted to wish us both a nice Thanksgiving. You know, Dad, that shouldn't be threatening."

"It isn't."

"But it is strange. I mean, really wacked out. Swear to God, we must be the most dysfunctional family on the planet."

He laughed and tossed his napkin onto his plate. "We're not even in the top ten in this city. Just when I think I've seen it all, something else comes along. Believe it or not, our family still hovers in the normal range."

"Oh, yeah, right."

That was hard to believe. "That's because all you deal with are scum bags."

"My point exactly."

Kristi wasn't buying it. She helped him clear the table,

then slice thick slabs of the pie, but she knew that their family wasn't anywhere near normal. Not when her biological father was her uncle and the guy who raised her was an alcoholic cop who'd accidentally killed a kid in the line of duty, and her mother probably got loaded on downers and committed suicide by driving a minivan into a tree. No matter what Bentz said, no way did they brush normal.

He was deluding himself.

James clutched the phone for several seconds after Kristi had hung up. He replayed their short conversation in his mind. Yes, it had been brief, but then he'd expected as much. *Time* he told himself, *it will take time.*

He lived in a small house one block from St. Luke's and he considered going over to the church early and speaking with Monsignor O'Hara. He hung up the phone.

Father James, who so many turned to for counseling, needed someone in whom to confide. He had so many issues to deal with.

First and foremost there was Kristi. His child. How he'd once wanted to give up the priesthood, marry Jennifer, claim Kristi as his own. Failing that, at least he'd hoped for interaction with her. He could never be recognized as her father, he knew that much now, but he could still have the role of uncle . . . if she'd let him.

He didn't want to take away anything from Rick. Bentz had done a fine job with Kristi. Better than fine. And raising a daughter alone was never easy.

Then there was the issue of Olivia. Dear Father, help him.

James walked to his desk and found his Bible. It had been his mother's and he found solace in the thin pages. Where was the passage he wanted? He flipped to the Book of Proverbs just as the phone rang loud enough to startle him.

He picked up the receiver but his eyes were skimming the pages, searching for the passage that would give him peace.

"Forgive me, Father . . ."

James didn't move a muscle. The midnight confessor was calling again. The clock ticked on the wall, counting off the seconds. He was sweating, his hand around the phone in a death grip. "What can I do for you, my child?" he forced out.

"I . . . I . . . must complete my mission . . . but sometimes I have doubts."

"We all have doubts. What is your mission?"

"It is from God. To find the saints. To see that they make their way to heaven."

No. This can't be right. James sank back in his chair. Was he actually talking to the serial murderer? The killer Bentz was trying to stop? "It is not for you to decide who is to be venerated or canonized," he said carefully.

"But God has chosen me to find them, to offer them to Him."

The hairs on the back of Father James's neck rose one by one. "You must've misinterpreted what He's saying. It's a sin to take a life. Remember that 'Thou shalt not kill' is one of the Ten Commandments. God would not ask you to sin."

"He speaks to me, Father. He tells me who to choose. It's His divine will. And this, my confession, is between you and me, Father. What shall be my penance?"

James's heart was beating a fast tattoo, his mind spinning rapidly. He'd considered the question. "Your penance, my son, will be to pray the rosary and to turn yourself in to the authorities."

There was a long pause. James would have thought that the penitent had hung up except he heard music in the background—soft choral chords. No . . . it was a Christmas carol, an instrumental version of "Silent Night." His stomach turned over at the thought.

"The rosary," the penitent finally repeated. "Pray the rosary?"

"Yes, and never kill again. Go to the police."

"So that they can jail me for doing God's will? So that

you would not carry the burden of my confession?'' There was a hint of anger in the voice.

''So that you would not sin again. This is your penitence. You must go to—''

Click. The line went dead. James closed his eyes and dropped his head into his hands. He'd failed. The killer was certain to murder again. In the name of God.

And James could do nothing about it.

Montoya was waiting for him when Bentz arrived at his office Friday morning. His expression said it all. And it wasn't good news. Montoya looked like hell. Though he was dressed in his standard leather jacket and black jeans, his hair was uncombed, his goatee untrimmed and ragged, and his usually cocky smile was nowhere to be found.

''You okay?''

''Fine,'' he clipped out.

''But—''

''I said I'm fine.'' His dark eyes flashed, the set of his jaw was rock-hard, and every muscle in his body was flexed, as if he were spoiling for a fight. As Bentz hung up his coat, Montoya leaned against the file cabinet. ''Three women were called in missing Monday night. One came home— she'd just had it with her husband and teenaged sons and took herself a little unscheduled break. The second one's still unaccounted for, but the third one, Leslie Franz, is probably the victim we found on the wheel. She's married, no kids, teaches in a preschool, but get this, her husband is a professor at Loyola.''

''Let me guess—she was a part-time student.''

''Bingo.''

Bentz's back teeth gnashed. He thought of Kristi at home in bed. ''No positive ID yet?''

''Just a matter of time.'' Montoya motioned to Bentz's computer. ''I scanned the photos over from missing persons. And she has two tattoos. One on her right ankle, the other on her left shoulder.''

"Does she?"

"Yep. A dolphin and a cross."

As Bentz settled into his chair and clicked on the icons on the computer screen, Montoya walked to the window, his hands in the front pockets of his jeans, his eyes fixed on the dismal day outside. Gray clouds hung over the tops of the buildings and rain spat against the window.

Bentz found the file and opened the picture. Sure enough, St. Catherine of Alexandria smiled up at him. She was clinging to the jib of a sailing ship, her blond hair pulled into a ponytail, her smile as bright as the sunlight spangling the blue water. Bentz's gut clenched. She was either the victim posed as St. Catherine of Alexandria or she was her twin.

"Once again everyone who knows her is locked tight in alibis, at least that's the way it seems. The husband, Bertrand, is older, pushing fifty. Leslie is his second wife. The trophy, I guess. His first one is another professor, up at All Saints."

Bentz stiffened. Damn!

"That's where he met wife number two. Leslie Jones was an undergraduate. Big scandal. Bertrand divorced the first wife, married the second, and took a position in the Psych Department at Tulane."

"With Dr. Leeds." Bentz didn't like it. Because Kristi attended classes there, because the Rosary Killer had attended school there, and because of the name "All Saints." Coincidence? Not hardly. He reached into the top drawer and found a half-used package of Tums.

"When he married Leslie, Old Bert was forty-eight and she was half his age. Nasty. Nasty."

Bentz popped two antacids and washed them down with a swallow of yesterday's coffee. "We'll have to check out the ex-wife, though I don't know how she could be involved."

"I've already started. Her name's Nancoise and she's got credentials up the ass. All kinds of awards for scholarship and philanthropic shit. She's a long shot."

"Remember the guy who wrote *The Scarsdale Diet?* He

was shot by a scorned lover who was headmistress of some
hoity-toity school. It's happened before. What's the old saying, something like 'Hell hath no fury like a woman
scorned'?''

"Close enough." Montoya scratched at his goatee and
continued to stare through the glass as noises from the outer
office filtered in through the door, which was slightly ajar.
Phones rang and conversation buzzed. Once in a while,
someone shouted.

"What's eating you?" Bentz asked, leaning back in his
chair. "Bad turkey? Holiday depression? What?"

Montoya's jaw clenched. "Woman trouble."

"What? That I can't believe, *Diego*."

"Believe it," Montoya said grimly. A muscle worked near
his temple, and his eyes narrowed. "That second woman, I
mentioned, the one still missing?"

"Yeah." Bentz got a bad feeling.

"She's my girlfriend. Marta Vasquez. I filed the report.
We had a fight Monday night at my place. She never made
it home. Took off in her car like a bat out of hell. No one's
seen her or her Camaro since." He glanced over his shoulder
and his dark eyes had lost their spark. "I was the last one
to see her and I've got no idea where she is, man, not one
fuckin' idea. The worst part of it is she was taking a couple
of night classes at Loyola."

Looking up from his desk chair, Bentz waved Olivia
inside. But he didn't so much as crack a smile, and what
little spark of hope Olivia had experienced that he would
be glad to see her was quickly extinguished.

"Hi," she said just as the phone rang. He nodded at her
as he grabbed the receiver. "Bentz." His expression grew
darker and he held up a finger indicating that he'd be a
minute or two. Then he rotated the chair so that his back
was to her, the phone cord stretched, and his end of the
conversation was just quick answers. "No . . . not yet . . .
waiting for the autopsy . . . Yeah, you'd hope, but so far we

haven't gotten lucky . . . ass-deep in this shit . . . I'll see what I can do . . ."

His office looked about the same as it had the first time she'd visited him—had it been only a week ago? So much had happened. The clutter—files, mail, legal pads on which notes had been scribbled, still remained as did the pictures of his daughter on the desk. His window was cracked a bit, allowing in the noise of traffic below floating in on a cool November breeze.

". . . I'll call as soon as I hear anything. Yeah . . . you got it . . . You, too." He spun around and hung up.

"How are you?" he asked without much inflection. She looked for warmth in his steely eyes. Saw not a drop.

"Fine."

"Nice Thanksgiving?"

"Yeah, it was. A couple of friends came over. You?"

"Just Kristi and me. It was good. Now, what can I do for you?"

So much for pleasantries. "I thought I'd share something." Reaching into her purse, she pulled out the sheet of paper James had given her. "I asked a priest I know for a favor."

One of Bentz's eyebrows lifted. "Didn't know you were close to any priests. The last I heard, you were having nightmares about them."

"About one," she corrected as she handed him the list of names. "Anyway, Father McClaren was good enough to—"

"Father McClaren?" Bentz said and his eyes narrowed harshly. "Father James McClaren at St. Luke's?"

"Yes. Do you know him?" She was surprised.

"Kristi and I attend mass there once in a while."

"You never mentioned that—"

"It's not very often. How do you know him?"

"I was looking for information after the fire. St. Luke's is the closest church . . ."

"Go on, what did Father McClaren come up with?" Bentz asked and the skin over his face seemed to draw tighter. It ticked her off. So they'd slept together and he decided he couldn't handle it. The least he could do is act decently.

"It's a list of christenings," she explained, "all of which happened within the three months after my brother was born. You seemed so convinced that a blood relative might be involved that I thought it was worth checking out."

"It is." He scanned the notes. There were sixty-three names. Olivia had counted them. "Any of these turn out to be priests?"

"I don't know. I didn't ask that."

"Does he know you're looking for a priest who might be a killer?"

"He doesn't know anything about the murders. I only asked him about my brother," she said. "And we talked a little. He gave me some advice."

Bentz lifted an eyebrow.

"About how to deal with a hard-ass cop who shuts off emotionally anytime someone gets close."

A ghost of a smile flickered over Bentz's mouth. "And what was Father McClaren's advice?"

"To tell the jerk to 'go to hell.' "

"That was a direct quote?"

"No. That's how I interpreted it," she snapped and noticed the set of his jaw shift a bit.

"Maybe he knows what he's talking about." Bentz's chair groaned as he leaned over the desk. Resting his elbows on an open file, he held her gaze. "Look, Olivia. I'm sorry."

"Bull."

"No, I am." For a second the facade came down and she caught a glimpse of the man beneath the tough-as-nails, emotionally detached cop. "But it would be best if we—"

"Yeah, I know. I got it the last time," she said, standing. "I'll let you know if I have any more visions, okay?"

"That would be good."

"No, Bentz, it would be hell," she said, shifting the strap of her purse to her shoulder. "Find this guy and do it fast. Then you won't have to keep explaining to me why you can't see me anymore."

She reached for the door, but he was out of his chair and around the desk in one swift motion. She was pulling on the knob, but he slammed the door shut hard enough to rattle panels. The flat of his hand held the door tight in its frame. His was so close she caught a whiff of his aftershave. "Don't," he warned, his eyes flashing. "Don't play any woman-games with me. We made a mistake the other night, and that's all there is to it. I didn't mean to let it go so far and you didn't mean to get involved, either. It just happens sometimes."

"Not to me."

"Well, it did the other night."

She didn't argue. Couldn't.

"For that, I'm sorry. But you and I can't let anything get started, at least not for a while. We have to be able to work together professionally. I thought I made that clear."

"As glass," she said.

"You'll be able to handle it?"

"With no problem." They both knew she was lying, but as he removed his hand and she opened the door, she added, "Call me if you ever need a psychic, okay? Because I can see into your future and it looks like it's going to be lonely as hell."

The dogs were howling again. Chained, muzzled, and hungry, they put up a clamor that would wake the dead. The Chosen One told himself to remain calm; no one other than himself could hear the beasts. The feast day of St. Vivian was fast approaching and then the dogs would be satisfied.

He'd bought the curs from a backwoods redneck who lived in a rusted shell of a trailer, spat tobacco juice between his front teeth, and bragged about outsmarting the law while he poached "gators," distilled his own brand of moonshine, and sold half-breed dogs and "fightin' cocks" to anyone who paid cash.

The deal had transpired in near darkness, the only illumination the smoky glow of the parking lights of a battered pickup and an SUV. Neither vehicle had plates. The Chosen One had unscrewed the license plates of his stolen Ford before he'd made the journey to this part of bayou country. The owner of the dogs probably just didn't bother with legalities or the DMV. Both parties felt better not having a clear view of the face of the other, and after the cash was exchanged for "one quality male and the meanest bitch this side of Arkansas," The Chosen One had driven the dogs here, then driven back to the college, parked the stolen car in a lot not far from where he'd found it, replaced the plates, and jogged to the spot where he'd tucked his own car. Then he'd driven back to his sanctuary.

He was proud of himself. Of his resourcefulness. He'd found the dogs through an ad in a local paper that was chock-full of cheap items for sale—everything from used mattress and springs to farm equipment and exotic pets. The animals had been described as "guard dogs—Doberman/Rottweiler mix." They were perfect.

Except for their incessant howling from the basement. This, of course, was not where he lived; just where he spent most of his time. He lived in a cramped space only a few blocks from the college. His furnishings, books, and clothing were there. He'd left a few things strewn about to make it seem as if he entertained women in those quarters, and he found this the most exciting part for they were earrings, or necklaces, or even scarves of some of the women he'd immortalized.

Now, he untied his cincture and let his alb slide to the floor. He stood naked before the altar, but he couldn't concentrate, the dogs were too loud. Music didn't help and even the caress of the jeweled whip striking his flesh wasn't enough to satisfy him. His prayers seemed empty and unanswered, and when he fondled his braid, rubbing the plait slowly between his fingers or upon his cock, he had only the hint of an erection. Closing his eyes, he conjured up the image of St. Catherine of Alexandria rotating on the wheel, her white body spinning and dripping blood, the horror upon her face as he withdrew his blade ... but, no ... he didn't get hard, didn't feel the presence of God ... began to doubt.

The barking continued. If one of the beasts quieted, it seemed the other took up the call. He strode to the landing and screamed down, "Shut up!" Spawn of the devil, that's what the curs were. His head began to pound harder and harder with each yowl.

Perhaps he should beat them again. Take the leather straps and whip them until they turned and snarled at him. They had water and a couple of bones with tattered pieces of meat but he'd offered them no solid food. He wanted them ravenous for St. Vivian.

As his head ached, he sensed, from somewhere in the back of his brain, that he should repent. It was so confusing at times. God meant him to do His will. Yes, of course, but ... the priest had insisted that he stop; that his sacrifices were a sin ... but then the priest didn't understand. Couldn't.

Pray the rosary and go to the police.

What kind of a priest was Father James?

At the altar The Chosen One slid to his knees and bowed his head. He prayed until his knees ached, until his neck hurt, but it was no good. He needed to confess and the phone wasn't good enough. No ... he needed to visit the confessional and hear Father McClaren's breath, feel the heat from his body through the thin partition ... yes ... it would be dangerous, but necessary.

God would expect no less.

Chapter Thirty-two

". . . a bar in Lafayette, one in Baton Rouge, two in New Orleans, and one in Cambrai," the owner of Nick's Neon Lighting said from his office in Montgomery. Seated at his desk with the phone receiver wedged between his ear and shoulder, Bentz was scribbling notes. "Those are the only places I've sold a neon sign like the one you described, with the pink martini glass. I'd be glad to fax you over the information."

"Do that," Bentz said and gave him the fax number. Irritated, he plowed stiff fingers through his hair. The case was getting to him. He'd viewed every shred of evidence and was working with the damned task force but he still felt as if his wheels were spinning, they were getting nowhere.

Fast.

And now a neon sign of a pink martini glass could be linked to Baton Rouge, only a few blocks from the campus where Kristi was attending school. At All *Saints*. Even though there were other bars who had the same signs displayed, Bentz focused on the one in the window of The Dive. He didn't like it. Not one bit.

As soon as he got the fax, he'd give a copy to the task force, just as he'd taken them a copy of the list of names Olivia had provided him with. The team was sorting through it, locating those infants, comparing the list to recorded births, Social Security numbers, DMV records, and arrests. They were sifting through class lists, faculty lists, alumni lists, and employee records for the colleges the victims had attended, scouring the information for a link. The FBI was comparing the murders to others in the data base in the hope of finding similarities with other crimes that had been committed across the country, just in case New Orleans wasn't the killer's first or only hunting ground.

The task force had established a hot line and had given more facts to the press in case anyone knew of anything suspicious.

In the matter of a week, evidence was being collected, sifted, and classified, but so far the task force hadn't come up with dick and Bentz felt as if they were running out of time. More feast days loomed, each day bringing them closer to another murder. Loosening his collar, he read through the list of names on his copy of Olivia's list for the dozenth time ... He felt as if he were missing something, as if somewhere in those sixty-odd names, was the killer. "Who are you, you bastard?" he wondered aloud.

Had any of these newborns grown up to be priests? Had any attended the colleges in the area? How many now lived around New Orleans? The computers would sort this out. If there were any matches ...

A secretary rapped on his door, then dropped off the fax and some mail, all of which had been opened, none of which was valuable. He skimmed the fax from Nick's Neon Lighting, then shot a copy to the coordinator of the task force. None of the addresses for the bars was near the victims' homes, or their places of employ, or from where they were assumed to have been abducted.

Except for The Dive in Baton Rouge. Only three blocks

off the campus of All Saints College. Hell, why couldn't he shake his bad feeling about this one? He glanced at the bifold pictures of Kristi, then remembered seeing her buried beneath the covers of her bed on Thanksgiving morning. Later he'd caught her kicking the hell out of his punching bag. At dinner she'd tried heroically to pretend that his miserable attempt at Thanksgiving dinner was fabulous.

He grinned. Kristi was right. He was paranoid. He didn't know what he'd do if he lost her. His daughter—and he'd beat the living tar out of anyone who even suggested she wasn't rightfully his—was the one constant in his life, the reason he'd quit booze and women.

He knew he had to let her go, and hell, he was trying. Half the time she was pushing him away, telling him to "get a life." He glanced around the small, cluttered office where he spent more hours than he wanted to count. Case files and empty cups cluttered his desk. Pictures of grizzly murder scenes had been tacked to his bulletin board. Dust collected on the few pictures he had mounted on the walls. This wasn't a life. When he went home, it was more of the same. Aside from watching sports or sometimes taking a few swings at the punching bag.

He threw down his pencil and closed his eyes as he leaned back in his chair. She was right. He did need something more in his life.

*Some*thing *or some*one *like Olivia Benchet?*

"Shit." He didn't have time for a woman. Especially not one who had somehow befriended Father James.

Why not? Hell, Bentz, she came here offering a damned olive branch and you treated her like dirt.

His jaw clenched so hard it ached. He didn't want to think about a relationship with anyone right now, not even Olivia. When this was all over, when the madman was either dead or behind bars, maybe then there would be time for a woman in his life.

Like Montoya's life? Bentz scowled darkly. Montoya's girlfriend still hadn't shown up. Disappeared without a trace.

An APB hadn't come up with the girl or her car. And she was a part-time student.

That was the connection . . . but he was missing something . . . something important. He reached into his drawer, found a pack of nicotine gum, and shoved the tasteless stick into his mouth. The schools, it all had to do with the schools.

He picked up the information sheet he'd put together on Brian Thomas. In less than twenty-four hours, Bentz had figured out that Thomas was thirty-one, estranged from his parents, had gotten into trouble when he was younger when an underage girl had cried rape, and gone to the army as well as been enrolled for a while in a seminary.

There were too many damned red flags waving around the guy. Olivia thought she'd seen a priest behead Stephanie Jane Keller in her vision and the guy was about the same weight and height as Thomas, athletic and blue-eyed. Thomas had been trained with all sorts of weapons while he was in the military and at one time had a deluded vision of becoming a priest. His days at the seminary had been numbered and somehow Thomas ended up at All Damned *Saints* while victims were being slaughtered in accordance with saints' feast days.

And what if he was the killer? Why would he be dating Kristi? Is that how the killer got to know his victims—by cozying up to them, dating them? That MO seemed unlikely and dangerous; the killer would take a big chance of being seen with the women he eventually killed. So far no one had connected the murderer with the women who had been slaughtered.

That you know of. Maybe he was clever. Maybe Thomas had dated them in the past.

There were too many damned coincidences for Bentz's way of thinking.

Time to have a chat with Kristi's boyfriend. Behind his daughter's back.

If she found out and was pissed as hell, that was too bad. At least she would be alive.

* * *

"So that's it, I have to face it. Leo wants a divorce and there's not a whole lot I can do about it except get the best damned lawyer in Tucson . . . no, make that Phoenix," Sarah decided.

She'd returned around five that morning, had slept until two, then rattled around in the bathroom for ten minutes before appearing with her two bags in the kitchen. Her eyes were puffy and she looked as if she hadn't slept a wink, but she wasn't crying now. She appeared calm and determined. "He wants to marry the bitch. Can you believe it? He's"— she made air quotes with two sets of fingers—" 'in love.' He didn't want this to happen, you know, it just did."

She took the cup of coffee Olivia handed to her. "It's such bullshit. When I think of all the years I looked the other way, put up with his nonsense, figured that someday he'd grow up . . . Jesus, I was a fool."

"You were married to him. Quit beating yourself up."

"Oh, and that's the best part. He and the bitch are already planning their wedding. As soon as the divorce is final. He's quitting his job in Tucson, well, they've probably fired him by now anyway, and moving in with her. They're . . ." Sarah's chin wobbled. She buried her nose in her cup and took a big gulp. ". . . they're even talking about having a baby together. Her kids are six and eight. Girls. They want a son."

"Oh, for crying out loud. Sarah—"

A solitary tear tracked from one of her eyes and she held up a hand, palm outward. "Here's the kicker. She's married, too. Her husband just found out last weekend and he's shell-shocked. Had no idea his wife was foolin' around on him."

"They deserve each other."

"I know . . ." She set her half-full cup on the counter. "Look, I've got to get home. I have a lawyer to see, a store to run, a cat to adopt, and I think I'll sign up for one of those dating services on-line."

"Are you sure? Cats? Dating services?"

"I'm not sure about anything except that I'm through sitting around and bawling my eyes out over that loser. The cat will be better company and I'm going to meet some men, damn it. Somewhere there's got to be a better guy out there." Again her chin trembled and her eyes filled. "Damn it, why do I even care? Leo's a bastard. Always was."

"And you're the winner. Keep reminding yourself of that . . . call me anytime and . . . are you sure you have to leave?" Olivia asked, touching her friend on the arm. "I've got the extra room."

"Thanks, you're a love, but I have to put my life back together. And you . . . figure it out with the cop and Father James."

"What? I'm not—"

"*Shh.*" Sarah shook her head and held up a hand. "Don't lie to me. I know you've got some kind of thing for the detective but I saw the way Father James looked at you."

"If you remember, he's a priest."

"He's a man who just happens to be a priest. And he's a hunk."

"You really have flipped."

A sad smile twisted her friend's lips. "Maybe I have," she admitted. "Maybe I should amend my earlier goals. Make it that I have a lawyer to see, a store to run, a cat to adopt, a dating service to join, and a shrink to visit. Is that better?"

"Much," Olivia said, sad that Sarah was leaving. It had been nice to have someone in the house again. They hugged and sighed, then Olivia helped Sarah stash her things in the trunk of her rented compact. A squirrel scolded them both as she drove away. Hairy S whined as the little car disappeared over the bridge and through the trees. "She'll be back," Olivia predicted, glancing down at the dog. "And you be good. She's not all that crazy about you. Come on." She whistled to the dog, who took off after a squirrel. "Hairy!"

The phone rang.

"Hairy, you get in here!"

The dog ignored her. Again the phone rang.

"Fine!" She left the door open and ran to the kitchen in time to hear her own voice on the recorder. "This is Olivia. I'm either out or—" She grabbed the receiver. "Hello?"

"Oh, hi . . . It's James," Father McClaren said and she smiled as she conjured up his handsome, if worried face. "I'm glad I caught you . . . I feel like a fool to admit this but I think I may have left my wallet at your house. Maybe I dropped it while looking in the toolbox or while I was sitting on the couch . . . I don't remember."

"Let me check. Hold on a minute." Olivia did a quick search. The toolbox didn't hold anything other than her grandfather's assortment of screwdrivers, pliers, hammers, and wrenches, and the couch only gave up a few quarters, lint, and kernels of popcorn, but then she looked beneath the blankets in Hairy S's bed in the part of the porch that had been converted to the laundry room and sure enough she found a slim, black leather wallet. Father James McClaren's picture stared up at her from his driver's license.

"Got it," she said as she returned to the kitchen and picked up the phone again. "My dog's a thief. I found it in his bed. I could bring it to you tomorrow. I've got to drive into the city anyway."

"I'm afraid I'll need it before then, so unless it's inconvenient, I'd like to stop by and pick it up later. Right after mass tonight?"

"That would be fine, " Olivia said, leaning a hip against the counter and seeing Hairy appear at the back door, where he began to pound against the glass. "I was just trying to save you a trip." She unlocked the door and cracked it open. Hairy galloped inside.

"I'll see you later then," Father James was saying. "How about around eight-thirty?"

"Great."

"How's Sarah?"

"She just left." Olivia sighed. "It's a long story. I'll tell you all about it when you get here."

"See you later."

Olivia hung up and set the wallet on the counter, where the dog couldn't get to it. "Shame on you," she said to Hairy S as she walked to the front of the house and shut the door. "Stealing from a priest." *That's worse than lusting after one.* She *"tsked, tsked,"* then fed both animals and, telling herself that she was *not* paying any attention to Sarah's assessment of Father James's feelings for her, changed into black slacks and a sweater, touched up her makeup, tried and failed to tame her hair, and spritzed on a couple of shots of perfume.

Reminding herself she wasn't getting ready for a date, she switched on the television. The screen flickered to show an African-American newswoman standing in front of an old, dilapidated building surrounded by trees and brush. Police cars, lights flashing, were parked haphazardly around what looked to be a warehouse until she realized that she was viewing the grist mill where the most recent victims had been found.

She swallowed hard. So this was where they had died— in a desolate, crumbling building.

". . . as you can see, the police are still here, searching for clues. Last night the bodies of two women were discovered by . . ."

Olivia, mesmerized by the report, dropped onto the couch. She'd avoided watching the news for the last few days, hadn't wanted to dwell on the murders, but now, viewing the crumbling mill and knowing what had happened inside, she listened, transfixed, as the reporter warned the citizens about a brutal serial murderer on the loose. ". . . though not many details have been released, the police have issued a warning to all citizens . . ." Other images flashed before the scene. Photographs of the victims interspersed with footage from the archives which displayed the apartment house in the Garden District where Cathy Adams's nude body had been found, the statue of St. Joan of Arc, and the burned-out shell of a house in Bayou St. John where Stephanie Jane Keller had been slain. ". . . and now, here, two women found in what an anonymous source has called macabre, brutal, and ritualistic slayings reminiscent of the Rosary Killer, who prowled the streets of New Orleans just last summer.'' The screen changed to footage of Bentz talking to the press. It was a hot summer day and Bentz was sweating as he answered the reporter's questions, assuring the viewers that the Rosary Killer had been killed.

"But, Detective, isn't it true that the killer's body was never recovered?'' a sharp-featured reporter asked.

The screen cut to the anchor desk, where a man and woman were seated. The anchorman stared solemnly into the camera. "And now the streets of New Orleans are being prowled by a serial killer again, barely six months later. Has the Rosary Killer returned? Or is this a new menace? For continuing coverage of this, and other area news, tune in at—''

Olivia snapped off the set. Seeing Bentz's image only made her angry all over again. Yes, she understood his feelings about getting involved with her, but come on, it wasn't as if she'd been expecting a marriage proposal. Not that she would have accepted one anyway. She had this thing about avoiding relationships that could ultimately result in marriage. Ever since finding out that her fiancé had cheated on her with her best friend, she'd decided marriage wasn't for her—at least in the foreseeable future—and her biological clock could just quit ticking for a while.

Is that why you pick men who are off-limits?

"No,'' she said so loudly that Hairy S growled. She pushed all images of Bentz out of her mind and spent the next two hours in the second bedroom, catching up on some assignments for her classes the following week, then, seeing headlights splash illumination on the lane, hurried downstairs. She threw open the door before Father McClaren had a chance to knock.

"I was expecting you,'' she explained, noting that, tonight, he was wearing his clerical collar along with a black shirt, black slacks, and his leather bomber jacket.

"And you're clairvoyant. Like your grandmother. You mentioned it.''

"Did I also mention that it's a royal pain? Come in."
She walked him into the kitchen and handed him his wallet.
With a glance at the dog, she said, "I don't think he had
enough time to do any real damage with your credit cards.
But he could've gotten on the Internet. Let me know if you
see charges for flea collars and dog biscuits and I'll see that
he pays you back."

James actually grinned. "I'll go over my statements with
a fine-tooth comb."

She slapped his wallet into his hand. "Is there anything
else I can do for you?"

He hesitated and for a second she expected him to say
something clever . . . even suggestive. Instead, he said, "No,
thanks."

"How about a glass of wine?" she asked. She liked his
company. Wanted him to hang around.

Again the hesitation in his blue eyes, the indecision.
"Fine. *A* glass." He glanced around the small cottage. "You
said that Sarah left. As in for the night?"

"As in she flew back to Tucson." Olivia opened the
refrigerator door. "Leo wants a divorce. He's already got
wife number two all lined up." She handed Father James
the bottle and a corkscrew then found a wedge of brie and,
in the cupboard, a box of crackers that were well past their
pull date.

"How did she seem?" he asked as he found a couple of
glasses and poured the wine.

"Better than I expected. Maybe that's because she talked
to you."

"I doubt it." He handed her a goblet and touched the rim
of his to hers. "Cheers," he said.

"To new friends."

"And happiness."

"Don't suppose I can twist your arm and ask you to build
me another fire?" she suggested. "You did such a great job
last night."

"Flattery will get you everywhere," he said. "Let's see what we can do." Together they hauled chunks of dry oak and kindling into the living room. Olivia wadded up newspaper and Father James fussed over a "back log," then arranged the paper and kindling before striking a match.

"Perfect," she said as hungry flames devoured the dry tinder.

"Let's see . . . give it time . . . sometimes it starts out fast and then dies out. You have to be careful. And patient."

"Do you?"

"Mmm." He slid her a look and she wondered if they were still talking about the fire.

"That's the way it is with everything, isn't it?"

"The good things."

They sipped the Chardonnay, made small talk, and Father James loosened up a bit, even accepting a second glass. "You know, you could do something else for me," she suggested and one of his eyebrows rose.

Her heart nearly stopped.

Dear Lord, what was wrong with her? Why the devil was she flirting with him?

"What's that?" he asked and the irreverent smile that teased his lips was at odds with his profession.

"Nothing that will get you into trouble."

"Oh, darn."

"How about helping me string some Christmas lights over the mantel?"

"And here I thought you were offering me food and drink because you enjoyed my company."

"No such luck," she kidded. "Now, come on, handyman, mush!" She set down her glass, rummaged in the closet under the stairs, and gently set her grandmother's shotgun to one side so that she could pull out a box of ancient decorations.

"Isn't it a little early?" he asked, helping her carry two cartons of lights to the living room.

"Once it's after Thanksgiving, 'tis the season," she

quipped and, to prove it, turned on the radio. WSLJ made a point of playing one holiday song an hour the week after Thanksgiving. Within ten minutes, before they were finished stringing the lights, a jazzy instrumental version of "Let It Snow" filled the room.

"Didn't I tell you?" she asked as she switched off the table lamps, and other than the glow from the fire and the pinpoints of colored light draped over the mantel, the room was dim. Cozy.

"That's not really a Christmas carol."

"But it's seasonal. Come on, you *never* hear that played in July."

He laughed. "When I hear 'White Christmas,' it's officially Christmastime."

"But—"

"I'm not kidding." He sat beside her on the couch and stared at the fire. " 'Frosty the Snowman,' or 'Winter Wonderland' don't cut it either."

"Purist," she muttered, sipping from her glass.

"Comes with the territory." His eyes danced, reflecting the green and red pinpricks of light. "And this"—he hoisted his stemmed glass into the air—"doesn't."

"No?"

"Uh-uh. Definitely off-limits." But as he shook his head, he poured them each another glass. "However, we can't let it go to waste," he said. "After all, it's imported."

"It is?"

"All the way from California. If you haven't noticed, it's another country out there."

"How would you know?"

"I lived there."

"Really."

"Yes, ma'am. And I've got a secret about that time in my life." His smile was positively seductive. She leaned back on the couch. "What?"

"It was before I was a priest."

"Oh-oh, something dark and evil."

"You might say." He laughed. "Before I found my calling, I was a surfer."

"No way!"

"Oh, yeah . . . you should have seen me hang ten."

"Give me a break." She grinned, the wine and intimate room going to her head.

"Maybe someday I'll give you a demonstration."

She was taking a gulp of wine but laughed so hard she choked. The thought of Father James, clerical collar in place, priestly robes flying as he crouched upon a surf board and rode the crest of a wave off of Malibu, gave her a fit of giggles. She coughed so hard she had to set her glass down. "I . . . don't . . . believe . . ."

Suddenly he was holding her, patting her on the back. "Are you all right?"

"Yes . . . no . . ." she gasped.

"Olivia . . ." His pats were harder on her back, helping her cough. "Breathe."

"Does . . . does the Pope know about the surfing?" she asked, still trying to catch her breath.

He laughed loudly, a deep rumbling sound as he pulled her close to him. "Do I detect a note of irreverence?"

"From me?" Pinning a look of shock on her face, she shook her head in mock innocence and noticed that his arms still surrounded her. "Never."

"You are incredible," he said, his voice a whisper as the smile slowly slid from his face and she realized how close they were, that their noses were nearly touching, that the smell of him was overpowering, that her breasts were flattened to his chest. It was crazy. And so emotionally dangerous. *Stop this, Olivia. Before you do something you can't stop. Before you make the biggest mistake of your life!* But she didn't move. Couldn't.

She swallowed hard and his eyes flicked to her throat.

Though he didn't open his mouth, she swore she heard him groan. "I don't think I should be here," he said, but didn't let go. "In fact, I know I shouldn't." His words slurred a bit.

"Probably." She sighed. "But . . . ?"

"Olivia, I can't . . ." He stopped. As if he'd witnessed the sadness in her eyes. As if he knew exactly what she was thinking. "Oh, hell," he ground out, then added, "Forgive me," before he glanced down at her lips and kissed her. Hard. Without a tremor of reluctance.

Warning bells screamed through Olivia's mind. This was wrong. So wrong. They both knew it. Hadn't he just tried to say as much? But she kissed him back. Between the wine and the darkened room and the sense that they both needed to reach out to someone, she pushed aside all the doubts that plagued her, doubts that continued to echo through her mind.

He's a priest, for God's sake. And probably half drunk.

How will you feel tomorrow?

How will he?

Don't throw away the friendship he's offering . . . This is a sin, Olivia. A sin!

Think!

Her heart pounded, her skin tingled and deep inside she began to heat.

She couldn't stop. Didn't want to.

He was eager once he'd crossed that invisible barrier between them. His hands searched beneath her sweater, scaling her ribs, delving into her bra, kneading her breasts. She melted like butter inside, knowing she was making the biggest mistake of her life. *Don't do this, Olivia. For God's sake, don't!*

Anxiously he pulled her sweater over her head and kissed her all over, her cheeks, her neck, the tops of her breasts. His mouth burned a scorching path, touching and caressing, his tongue was rough and wet. Her mind spun crazily with erotic images she couldn't control.

His lips found her nipple and she dug her fingers into his thick hair, holding him closer.

He groaned as if from his very soul.

God help me, she thought, closing her eyes as the wicked sensations swept through her blood. She wanted him, ached for him, longed for more of his fevered touch. And she wasn't disappointed. Sweat slid down his body as he unbuttoned the waistband of her slacks. The zipper slid down with a soft, slithering hiss. His hands scraped her clothes from her, caressing her buttocks and legs, creating a whirlpool of heat that kept building as he kissed her.

Perspiration dotted her skin and her mind was spinning.

"You're so damned beautiful," he whispered as he flung her panties onto the floor. She was stark naked in the half light while he was still in all of his clothes, including the white collar that announced to the world he was a priest, a celibate man dedicated to God. He must've noticed her gaze drop to his neck because in one swift, angry motion he ripped the collar from his throat. His lips crashed down on hers.

Closing her eyes and her mind to the thought that she was seducing him into sin, she kissed him back. Their tongues touched and collided. She yanked at the buttons of his shirt and pushed the fabric over lean, hard, sinuous shoulders. The muscles of his back were strong and she felt his erection hard through his pants. Her mind clouded and spun, she wanted him and yet . . . it felt wrong . . . and not only because of his station in life. For a blinding instant she thought of Rick Bentz and how she still felt about him. This lovemaking wasn't the same. It wasn't about love; it was about sex— forbidden sex, angry sex, get-back-because-she-was-hurt sex.

James kissed her hard and she tried to blot out Rick's image—for God's sake he'd rejected her—but when she found the zipper of his slacks, and James, breathing hard, started to guide her hand inside, she stopped.

"I . . . we can't," she said in a rush. This was so wrong in so many ways.

His eyes flared angrily and she felt like an idiot, a tease. She pulled the quilt around her as he leaned backward. "Olivia—"

"Shh . . . I know . . . I'm sorry. I didn't mean things to go this far," she said and fought tears. Regret tore through her as she saw the pain etched in his features. "I think, no I *know* I was using you. I was hurting and . . ." Her chin trembled. ". . . you know you're just too damned good-looking to be a priest. I think the term today is 'hottie.' "

He groaned, but cracked a weak smile. "Is that some kind of consolation?" he asked thickly.

"No." She shook her head and took in a deep breath as she pulled the afghan more tightly around her naked body. "It's a compliment. I care too much about you for this to happen."

"Forgive me, but that sounds like a cliché, part of a rehearsed speech. I'm not buying it."

Wrapping her arms around her knees, she sighed. "Okay, so I feel like the ultimate tease here. But it wasn't intentional. Really. I care for you. A lot. But if we took this one step further, I think—no, I'm sure, that we'll both regret it. Maybe even before morning."

"You're in love with someone else."

She gritted her teeth. "I was. Yes. No more."

He snorted as he scooped up her bra and panties and handed them to her. "You're kidding yourself, Olivia." His blue eyes held hers. "You and I both know it. Now, I think we should both get dressed and I'd better leave before I change my mind."

Grabbing his wrist, she said, "Please. I don't think you should drive. You can stay. In the spare room. It seems kind of empty now that Sarah's gone."

"I don't know . . ." But he hesitated. "I am a little dizzy."

"I promise to make you the most fabulous breakfast you've ever eaten in the morning," she said, wanting him to stay, to cement their friendship, so that she would know that they could get over what had just happened between them. "Boiled crawfish, shrimp omelette, biscuits with gravy . . . my grandmother's favorite recipes."

He hesitated, then glanced around the cozy room with its sparkling colored lights and the crackle of the fire. "Okay, you've tempted me and I can't resist." His eyes grew serious. "I guess I've already proved that."

Wiggling into her clothes, she said, "We're putting that behind us, right?"

"Right."

"Good." She pressed a chaste kiss to his forehead. "Thanks, James. For understanding."

"No problem," he said, though she guessed it was a lie. "It's all part of the job."

Chapter
Thirty-three

"Are you nuts?" Kristi said as she shoved her extra pair of running shoes into her backpack. "Me, not go back to school? Come on, Dad, I thought you were into me getting a higher education." She glanced at her father standing in the doorway, his chin all rock-hard, his lips compressed. Jesus, did he always have to play the heavy? She was *not* in the mood for it. Her period had started this morning and she'd already had to deal with Jay. For God's sake, he'd actually gotten red-faced and cried when she'd handed him back his ring in the parking lot of the Dairy Queen. On top of all that, Brian hadn't called this entire four days and she had two papers due. One for Zaroster and another for Sutter. Now her dad was pulling this overprotective stuff again.

She didn't have time for any of this crap.

"I just don't see what it would hurt if you waited a few days to go back," Bentz said, walking into the room and looking all tough. As if *that* would change her mind.

"It's college, Dad, and no, they don't take roll, but I've got some assignments that are due pronto and I can't afford to miss class. It's not like I'm this brainiac stellar student, you know.'' She zipped up the bag and glanced around her room one more time. The bed was still unmade. Just the way she'd kept it when she lived here and she knew it bugged the hell out of her father. She flipped the covers over the pillows in a halfhearted stab at straightening up, then noticed the bouquet of carnations and rosebuds, still fresh, that her father had placed in the vase on her nightstand before she'd arrived. ''Look, I know you're worried. There's a serious bad guy on the loose, but I still have to live my life, you know.''

''I don't think you get how dangerous this is. The creep is lurking around college campuses. There's a connection to All Saints.''

''Is it serious? Or just a theory? I thought some of the victims went to Tulane or Loyola.''

''That's true, but I think his hunting ground is wider.''

'' 'Hunting ground?' Yuk, you *try* to make it sound creepy.''

''It is,'' he said soberly. ''I don't have to try. These women weren't just killed, Kristi. They were sacrificed. Butchered. The public information officer is letting out some more info on the son of a bitch, to warn the public and to ask for their help in tracking him down.''

''Good. You'll catch him faster.'' She hauled her backpack onto her shoulder.

''Let's go.''

''I want you to have a bodyguard,'' he said, trying a new tack.

''What? No friggin' way.'' But she could tell he was serious. ''Think about it. I can't have some guys following me all over campus like I'm the daughter of the president or anything. No, Bentz. It's not going to happen. And don't start messing with my friends, either. Doing background checks and all that shit. It's not going to work. Come on, Dad, I've really got to get back to campus.'' Then she saw it, a tightening in the cords at the base of his neck. ''You already have, haven't you? You've checked into someone—

oh, no, don't tell me it's Brian. You wouldn't." She saw it in his eyes. "You can be such a bastard!"

"Did you know that he was in trouble with the law?"

"Yeah, he told me all about it. Statutory rape. And he doesn't get along with his folks. Okay. Yeah, I know. Now, let's go." She stormed out of the room. "It's time to rock 'n' roll."

The dogs were driving him out of his mind. They howled from dawn to dusk and then some.

The Chosen One reminded himself that he didn't have long to wait. December second was barely a week away . . . and he needed to spend that time flogging Bibiana while the dogs watched and grew hungrier.

He crossed himself at the altar and changed into street clothes, surveying himself in the mirror, smiling as he thought of his next mission. This one was more personal than the others . . . Bibiana . . . Sister . . . it was time to meet . . . How had it happened that his mother, named for St. Bernadette of Lourdes, had been such a whore? A woman capable of giving up her child, her only son, then marrying the very man who had sired that boy and having more children—girls—which she kept. Never once had she tried to contact him. Never once had she attempted to explain. It was as if he'd never existed.

It was an outrage; a sin.

Who had the son been given to? Hayseeds! Hicks! A barren farming couple who wanted him only to put him to work, sunup to sundown, a couple whose strict interpretation of Catholic dogma had been corrupted by their need to survive. He, the son they'd wanted so desperately, had been flogged and cursed, forced into servitude, told incessantly how much he cost his parents with his parochial education which, of course, they'd insisted upon. And a strict school it had been, an institution where there had been no girls, no distractions, a school which concentrated on learning and higher education, a school where he'd excelled and managed to receive scholarships and where he'd learned that he'd had a different calling, that God had chosen him to suffer, the Father in all His wisdom, had picked him to rid the earth of sinners . . . first his parents, but slowly . . . so that it would appear natural.

First the "accident" with the tractor that had left his father a cripple. Then, over time, the slow effects of the fertilizer supplements added to his medications, swirled carefully into tall glasses of sweet-tasting, over-the-counter concoctions for everything from cough syrup to constipation remedies. His "mother" had been just as easy with her belief in "natural" herbs, pills that could be easily doctored, capsules that could be swapped all too easily. She'd been half-blind, so dependent. No one had suspected. They'd been in their late forties when they'd adopted him, and then, when he'd found his calling, when God had first spoken to him, they had already started to decline.

Freda had died in her La-Z-Boy watching *Jeopardy!*, Tom from a heart attack not a year later.

Simple.

Neat.

Tidy.

And just the beginning, he thought now as he heard the dogs' howls over the soft strains of classical music. Bach. Usually calming. But not tonight.

Tonight he was restless. He needed to find Bibiana, to convince her to meet with him. She would be wary, so he would have to be careful. But then . . . he had just the bait.

Adjusting his jacket, he walked down the stairs to the basement where a single red bulb glowed, giving the old cement walls a faint crimson glow.

The woman laying naked in the straw was still unconscious. Her hands were bound behind her, a shackle chaining one ankle to the wall. He'd left her a bucket to use should she need to defecate and he gave her enough water to keep her alive. She was groggy still, the discoloration on her face unfortunate. He hadn't expected her to struggle. Stupid bitch of a woman. Whore. Out drinking and flirting . . . a married woman. He would keep her. Alive. For a while. Until she'd lured St. Bibiana here. His hands clenched as he thought of his sister. Olivia Benchet, the privileged one.

Soon to be sacrificed.

God was waiting for her.

The dogs bayed and growled from their kennels and he noticed that their ribs were beginning to show. Drool dripped from their muzzles. He tossed them each a bone from the meat market . . . and they, snapping and snarling, dark eyes glittering, pounced on their morsels.

The woman moaned. He'd have to tend to her. Take off her gag so that she could lap water . . . stupid whoring bitch . . .

One eye opened, blinked, and focused for a second. She jerked away, scrambling as best she could toward the wall. Fear widened her eyes over the gag. One cur growled and the woman snapped her head, caught sight of the dogs and scrambled closer to the wall.

His cock twitched when he saw her terror. He thought of what he could make her do . . . the sexual acts he'd imagined . . . he was suddenly hard. It would be so simple to rut with her. To debase her. To show her what a filthy whore she was . . . but he couldn't. It would be unclean. Unworthy.

Carnal pleasure is not part of the mission. His headache grew. The tic beneath his eye began again. His mission seemed cloudy.

Confess. You need to confess.

The prisoner's gaze was fastened on the spasm on his face, then when he caught her looking, her eyes moved and saw the bulge in his pants. Her terror was complete . . . or was it . . . there was something else in her eyes—a cool calculation. She was planning her escape. Even in her foggy mind. He clucked his tongue. He thought of putting her under again, then decided to let her consider her fate. One dog sent up a wild yip and she glanced over at it, new horror showing in her eyes. She hated them. And rightly so.

The Chosen One turned to the stairs and he heard her mewling behind him. Soon she would beg for her life, do anything he wanted, and he'd have absolute power over her. He turned on the third step and gazed down at the windowless cavern with its reddish light. She scooted closer, supplicating.

Yes, she was beginning to understand. He was her master. He alone decided her fate. He felt a spot of tenderness for her shackled and naked. But he had work to do. Time was passing. He felt a twinge of regret, of conscience. Sometimes his mission seemed wrong . . . other times he knew he was right. His head thundered. *Remember, you are the cleanser, one whom the Father has told to go forth and purge the earth from the depravity of sinning women. This is about purity. And retribution.*

The Chosen One fought the pain and doubts knifing through his brain. He needed counsel, direction. To reaffirm that which he knew to be true. He sucked in his breath against the agony roaring through his head. Unlike the sweet bite of the whip, the pleasure that the kiss of the leather straps invoked, this was sheer agony. This pain was far different. Debilitating. Blinding. He needed to talk to someone. Father James . . . yes . . .

The woman made another strangled cry and The Chosen One turned from her. Before he clicked off the light, he glanced back. She knew only fear. She had no concept that he was going to make her immortal, that she would become a saint.

His was a heavy burden. He snapped off the light and said, "Good night, Sarah."

". . . it'll all be in my report," Officer Calvin Smith, one of the deputies assigned to watch Olivia, was saying, "but I thought you'd want to know that besides her friend, Sarah Restin, who left and drove to the airport, Ms. Benchet has had another regular visitor. He visited her for Thanksgiving and then stayed over the next night. I wasn't too worried about it because I saw her greet him and they obviously knew each other, but now I'm thinkin' it was kinda odd."

Every muscle in Bentz's body tensed. "He stayed over?" Bentz repeated, jealousy spurting through his blood.

"Yeah, and that's what's odd. I ran the plates of his vehicle a little while ago and the car belongs to the Church."

"What?" Bentz whispered, dread chasing away the jealousy. "The Church?" *No!*

"Yeah. The guy's a damned priest."

Bentz shot to his feet. He wanted to reach through the phone lines and strangle the man. Fear gelled in the darkest reaches of his soul. "Who?" he demanded, envisioning Olivia tied up somewhere. Tortured. Images of Leslie Franz strapped to the wheel of death and Stephanie Jane Keller chained to a pedestal sink zipped through his mind in horrid, vibrant technicolor.

"Father James McClaren." The officer laughed. "I guess even priests have to get their rocks off sometimes."

Bentz's teeth ground together. "Why didn't you call me immediately?"

"What do you mean?"

"Don't you know we're looking for a priest? That the serial killer—"

"Jesus, no! I've been on vacation. Just got into town and pulled this duty. My partner never said anything about the suspect being a priest."

"Where is she now?"

"I don't know. I'm off duty."

"Dammit. Find out and call me back. On my cell phone. Pronto." He gave the idiot his number. "You got that?"

"Yes, sir."

"Repeat it back to me."

Smith did. "What do you want me to do?" he asked.

"Pray, Smith," he said. "Then sit tight. I think you've done enough." Swearing, Bentz slammed down the phone. He strode out of his office and flew down the steps. He was in his Jeep within minutes. Throwing the rig into gear, he closed his mind to the grotesque images that chased after him. Olivia and James . . . lovers . . . like Jennifer and James

... no way. No way! He pounded a fist against the steering wheel and snapped on his lights. Blowing through a stop sign, he considered the evidence. James? James was the killer? He was the right size, athletic, about the right age if Norm Stowell, the profiler, was to be believed and hell ... he had blue eyes ... didn't he? But why would Olivia get herself entangled with a priest after experiencing the horror of her own visions? It didn't make any sense. What had she said? That she'd gone to St. Luke's because it was the closest church to the fire that had taken Stephanie Jane Keller's life? That she'd asked Father James, the parish priest, to get the list of babies who'd been christened about the time of her brother's birth?

Bentz whipped around a double-parked van. Had he been wrong? He'd assumed the killer was related to Olivia somehow, but he could have made a mistake ... and now Olivia might be paying with her life! He blasted his horn when a middle-aged BMW driver cut him off.

His cell phone beeped and he picked it up, bracing himself for the worst. That there was another victim, that the son of a bitch had somehow gotten Olivia ... "This is Bentz," he snapped.

"Rick? It's Olivia." She sounded frightened. Scared out of her mind. Oh, God. No ...

"Where are you?"

"At work ... but something's wrong ... I can feel it," she said. "He's ... he's conflicted. Confused. The killer wants to talk to someone ..."

"Who?" Relief washed over him. At least she was safe. Unharmed.

"I don't know ... but I have the feeling that he needs to unburden himself, that he will do something worse ... he's desperate."

"Stay put. I'll be there in five minutes." He cranked on the wheel at the next light and nosed his Jeep toward the French Quarter.

*　*　*

The Chosen One slunk through the shadows of St. Luke's. He'd walked these halls before and knew the hidden closets and doorways, the places to hide or flee if he needed to. He was familiar with the cloister and the gardens and had used the tiny clear panel in one stained glass window to view inside.

On silent footsteps, he made his way through the chancel, then, as his eyes became accustomed to the dim light, stopped short.

He wasn't alone.

An altar boy, still dressed in cassock and surplice, had rummaged through the sacristy and was drinking the priests' wine from a gold chalice. The hooligan had a nearly shaved head and an earring that winked in the dim light.

The Chosen One slid into a dark niche. His head was beginning to ache again. *Ignore the boy. He is not part of the plan.*

Or was he? Perhaps . . .

Blatantly abusing his privilege, the thief of about fourteen was pouring more wine into the chalice—*the chalice*—and then as if he had every right, took the blessed cup to his lips and guzzled wine as if he were a street wino.

Sacrilegious!

Making a mockery of all that was holy.

From his position in the shadows, The Chosen One realized that he had been drawn here not for confession, but because he had work to do. God had sent him here to punish the heretic in altar boy vestments. And . . . for another reason, one more intimately entwined with his higher calling. Yes . . . the boy would provide a distraction for the police . . . Perfect.

Withdrawing the small knife from his pocket, The Chosen One moved noiselessly and swiftly. The heretic, caught up in his sinful deeds, didn't notice. Nor did he hear the click of the blade switching into place. His lips were stained from the wine, his wicked smile surrounding the cup as he thought, no doubt, of how he'd brag to his peers at school.

He wouldn't have the chance.

The Chosen One yanked back the pagan's head, exposing his white throat. The boy cried out. But it was too late. The Chosen One clamped one gloved hand over the boy's mouth and used the other to slash his throat. Blood spilled. The chalice fell to the floor, rolling and shimmering in the dim lights. The boy struggled as The Chosen One dragged him through the darkened ambulatory to the altar and left him there, not only as a sacrifice but as a warning.

Wiping his blade on the black skirt of the boy's cassock, he smiled. This was his purpose. To rid the world of sinners. Adrenalin sang through his blood as he snapped his deadly weapon shut and slipped into the night again. Outside, breathing the heavy air scented by the Mississippi River, he realized that his headache had vanished.

"Nooo!"

Olivia's knees buckled. She was polishing small pyramids in the Third Eye when she caught her reflection in the windowpane. But beneath her own image she noticed something darker, a distorted face, wide and evil. In her mind's eye she saw a small, finely honed blade. It slashed down. Blood sprayed. She fell into the display, knocking over candlesticks and incense holders and picture frames.

"What the hell's goin' on?" Tawilda said, pushing aside the beaded curtain to find Olivia slinking to the floor, her head in her hands. "Olivia? Jesus Christ, are you okay? Do I need to call nine-one-one?" She'd already whipped her cell phone from her purse and was kneeling beside Olivia. "Honey—"

"No, I'll be all right," Olivia whispered, her head pounding, tears blurring her eyes. But she wouldn't. Not as long as the monster was free.

"Well, you don't look all right to me. You look like you've just seen a damned ghost. I'm callin'—"

The front door burst open, chimes tinkling. Rick Bentz took one look around, vaulted over a wagon displaying unique Christmas ornaments, and landed next to Olivia. "What happened?" he demanded.

"She collapsed!" Tawilda said. "And what the hell are you doin' here? I thought she gave you the heave-ho."

"Are you all right?" he asked, ignoring Olivia's coworker.

"Yes, but he's at it again," she said, shaking and cold.

Bentz's arms surrounded her and she clung to him, barely hearing Tawilda's *"Tsk, tsk,* if that don't beat all."

"Tell me," Rick insisted. "What did you see?"

"He killed someone. Quickly, with a knife, I don't think it was planned." She was breathing in gasps. "It wasn't expected . . . and he . . . he wasn't wearing a mask, I saw his face." She shuddered and leaned into Bentz.

"He killed someone? What the devil are you talkin' about?" Tawilda cut in.

Olivia hardly heard her. "But the image was distorted this time. As if he were looking into one of those fun-house mirrors . . . He . . . he had blue eyes and had dark hair and . . . I think." She squeezed her eyes shut. "I caught an image of a ring of some kind."

"A wedding ring?"

"No . . . I mean, I don't know . . . but it had a stone in it." She was shaking. "Oh, God, I think . . . I think the victim was a child . . ." Tears ran down her face as she clung to him. "A girl in a long black dress with an apron . . . or . . ." Her eyebrows knit and she shook her head. "I . . . I'm not sure . . ."

"We'll check it out," he promised, wanting to reassure her. But he couldn't. They were out of time. "Can you describe the scene?"

She nodded. "I have the feeling that it was in a church . . . He killed the child in a closet of some kind and then dragged her to an altar." No, that wasn't right, the victim didn't have any hair. Swallowing hard, she looked over Bentz's shoulder toward a rack of Mardi Gras beads, but he knew she wasn't focusing on the display, that she was seeing inward, viewing the scene in her mind's eye. "I don't know why, but it seemed somehow familiar . . . but I only caught glimpses . . . It was violent. Brutal and the killer . . . the killer was enraged." She shuddered in his arms, then, as if realizing how close they were, she seemed to gather herself and push gently away. She bit her lip. "I think this might have happened at St. Luke's," she said, her eyes darkened. "I caught a glimpse of bright colors, panels of color from a stained glass window I'd seen before at St. Luke's. It was distorted, but . . . I'm nearly positive."

His gut clenched. "Then I'd better go check it out." He reached for his cell phone to call the station, but her fingers clamped around his wrist.

"I'm coming with you."

"I don't think so."

"You heard the lady," Tawilda interjected. "Seein' what she's goin' through here, I think you'd best take her along."

"If you don't, I'll just follow. No!" She said as if she finally understood. "It wasn't a dress. But a robe. Like a choir person would wear . . . or an altar boy." Her eyes met his and he read the fear in her gaze, the concern. Whether she admitted it or not, she, too, thought somehow James could be involved in all of this.

And it was tearing her up inside.

So are you going to give up the priesthood? Renounce your vows? Change the course of your life forever because of one woman?

Father James reached the church and found the back door ajar. Again. Monsignor O'Hara was oftentimes careless about locking up and when James pointed out the need for security, he'd snorted the same tired litany, "The doors to God's house are always open." *The very same quote you said to Olivia when you tried to lure her back to mass.*

Olivia. His heart twisted at the thought of her. Their one night together when they'd nearly made love had been heart-wrenching, and in the morning, she'd met him in the kitchen with a cup of coffee, then, her fists plunged into the pockets of her robe, she'd apologized for making a horrid mistake, the guilt in her large gold eyes reflecting his own misery. He'd drunk the coffee, eaten the breakfast she'd made, cracked a couple of lame jokes that now caused him to wince and had walked out of the house into the wintry morning. Throughout the drive to the church he'd thought of her, never noticing the traffic nor the threat of rain.

Now, as he strode through the back door of St. Luke's he noticed the lock hadn't been forced. He'd have to speak to the monsignor. The "open door to God's house" theory was a nice idea but impractical. There was always a chance for trouble, either thievery or vandalism or worse. Father James didn't believe in inviting trouble.

Except when it involves women.

Cringing at the turn of his thoughts he walked through a back corridor and felt something amiss . . . a coolness to the air. He discovered that the chalice was on the floor of the sacristy, having rolled there and wine had spilled . . . *What in the world?* The hairs at the back of his nape lifted. He picked up the cup and then squatted down by the stains on the floor . . . wine, yes . . . but . . . the walls were splattered with purple-red drops . . . his heart began to pound. Not wine. Blood. Someone's blood.

Leaping to his feet he sensed the evil still lurking in the house of God and, heart hammering, throat dry, he followed the trail of blood, red stains leading to the altar where . . .

"Dear Father!"

James stopped dead in his tracks. His eyes couldn't believe the horrible sight of an altar boy lying upon the altar. Blood streaked from a crevice in the boy's neck. James bounded down the ambulatory but as he reached the boy and saw his bloodless face, the stains over his white surplice he knew he was dead.

"Please, God, no," he cried. The boy was Mickey Gains . . . a tough kid who never had much of a break in life.

James listened for the boy's heartbeat and heard nothing. No breath came from his nostrils.

James had witnessed death before, had comforted the dying but never had he seen something so brutal or savage. Stumbling backward he ran to the church office and frantically punched out 9-1-1. Blood was on his hands, on his shirt, on the receiver as an operator answered.

"Help me," he cried. "There's a boy . . . he's dead. Mickey Gains was murdered, here at St. Luke's," he yelled into the receiver. "Oh, God, send someone. Call Rick Bentz! Get Detective Bentz over here now!"

Chapter
Thirty-four

Bentz's cell phone rang when they were only five blocks from St. Luke's.

"Detective Bentz," he answered . . . then cursed vividly into the phone as he swerved in and out of traffic. ". . .Yeah, I'm almost there. Two minutes, tops. Call Montoya!" He hung up and swore again, his skin turning a lighter shade. With a flip of a switch, he snapped on his lights and siren. "Looks like you were right," he admitted to Olivia though his eyes never strayed from the traffic as he barely braked for a corner. The Jeep shimmied, its tires squealing in protest when he slid around a double-parked delivery van.

"No . . ." She didn't want to believe it even though she knew the truth.

"An altar boy."

"At St. Luke's?" Olivia slumped against the passenger door. She was numb inside. Empty. The image of the child being slaughtered burned through her mind and she felt some great responsibility, as if she could have prevented the tragedy. Tears filled her eyes. *A child.* The monster had killed a child!

"So what's your connection to St. Luke's?" he asked, hazarding a glance from the corner of his eye.

Her heart stopped. Guilt filled that hollow place in her soul. "I already told you that I know the priest. He's the one who gave me the names of those boys who were christened about the time my brother was born." She looked out the window where the streets shimmered under the glare of street lamps. St. Luke's Church with its white-washed walls, spire, and bell tower loomed above the surrounding buildings.

Olivia had always looked to the Church for faith and comfort, a place of solace, but tonight it represented everything dark and evil in the world. Shuddering, she wrapped her arms around her middle as Bentz twisted the wheel into the parking lot, then stood on the brakes.

In the distance another siren wailed plaintively.

Bentz threw open the door, but looked back at her. "You'd better stay here."

"Like hell." She was already opening her door and stepping into the pockmarked lot. In three quick steps she'd caught Bentz and was jogging up the steps to the front doors.

Lights flashing, a police car roared into the lot and an ambulance was right on its tail. It screeched to a halt in front of the church. EMTs exploded out of the vehicle, joining officers as they ran inside.

A uniformed cop tried to stop her.

"It's all right." Bentz flipped open his badge.

"But—"

"She's with me!" he insisted and the other cop backed down. From the side of his mouth, he ordered, "Just stay inside the door and don't touch anything." His hands clamped over her elbow as he shouldered open the door. Inside every light was on, flooding the nave. Bentz planted her near the rack of brochures. "Don't move," he ordered, both his hands gripping her upper arms. His hard expression allowed no argument. He was in charge.

"But—" Her gaze drifted over her shoulder to the altar, where the EMTs were already working over the victim. A boy. In a blood-soaked cassock. Father James, his own shirt smeared with blood, was staring at the victim, his expression dark as the night outside. Her heart twisted. What was this all about?

"Don't argue." Bentz's fingers tightened and she was aware of the metallic scent of fresh blood. "If we're gonna catch this son of a bitch, you have to help me. Okay? Don't move. Otherwise you're outside or in the Jeep."

"He's gone," one of the EMTs said, shaking his bald head as he checked vital signs of the victim. Olivia swallowed back tears while Father James whispered something then made the sign of the cross. When he looked up, his eyes found hers. Shock registered across his handsome features, then there was a hint of an emotion akin to relief. He extricated himself from the altar and started down the aisle past the empty pews.

"What are you doing here?" James's gaze, which had been focused on Olivia, shifted slightly to take in Bentz. He stopped dead in his tracks. As if he'd come upon an invisible barrier. Bentz's hands released her. "You know each other?" James asked, bewildered.

Outside, more sirens tore through the night.

"I think that's the question I should be asking you," Bentz said.

James's jaw turned to stone and Olivia sensed that something more, something deeper than priest and parishioner, bound them. "Wait a minute."

"Jesus Christ, James, you have one helluva time with your vows, don't you?" Bentz said, pushing his nose into the priest's face.

Olivia saw it then, the faint resemblance, the same dark hair, strong jaw, and high cheekbones, but it wasn't just the physical, no it was more. How they interacted. As if they were related . . . cousins, maybe, not brothers, oh, God, no . . . She felt sick inside. No way. They had different last names.

"I don't have time for any of this shit. Who's the victim?" Bentz asked, then sent Olivia another warning glance to stay put.

"Mickey . . . Mickey Gains. Please don't use the Lord's name in—"

"And you were the one who discovered him?"

"Yes." James shoved his hair from his eyes and pulled his gaze from Olivia. "I found him here on the altar about ten . . . maybe fifteen minutes ago. He's fourteen, lives a few blocks away, his family has been with the parish for years . . ." Again James's eyes strayed to her. Olivia looked quickly away, afraid her guilt would be evident. "I came in to do some paperwork and talk with God. I've been . . . I've been having some issues I need to deal with. I wanted to seek His counsel," Father James explained. "And then . . . then . . . I walked through the back door and found blood and spilled wine in the sacristy. I followed the trail and found Mickey . . . just as he is."

"Let's have a look," Bentz said, but held a hand, palm outward, toward Olivia. "If you want, Officer Clarke would be glad to see that you get home." He motioned to a red-haired female cop who'd just walked in. Officer Clarke, obviously used to taking orders from Bentz, nodded, her hand on a cell phone.

"I'll think about it." Olivia was left standing in the shadows of the upper balcony, watching the two men who had become close to her—the homicide detective and the priest—as they approached the altar, then made way for the crime scene team as policemen and women arrived to seal off the area and start collecting evidence.

This was a nightmare of the highest order. The dead boy. Bentz. Father James. Rather than fight the officers, Olivia walked outside to the night and rubbed her arms as the winter cold seeped through her jacket and sweater. News crews arrived, reporters and curious onlookers collected, kept at bay by the police. Olivia stood near Bentz's Jeep and looked down the darkened streets. Somewhere out there in the darkness a killer lurked, one who was connected to her and to the two new men in her life, two men she'd let into her heart.

"I thought we could get together tonight," Brian said and Kristi, lying on the lower bunk, her legs stretched toward the bottom of the upper bunk, grinned. She'd been bothered that he hadn't called for the few days she'd been back at school, distant in class, and she couldn't help wondering if she'd done something wrong, if, over the holiday, he'd become disinterested.

Obviously she'd been wrong.

"Sure. What time?" She couldn't wait to see him again, and all her talk to her dad about reports and papers that were due immediately was quickly forgotten.

"How about ten-thirty?"

She glanced at the clock. Nine-fifteen. "That could work." It was kinda late and she had an early class in the morning, but so what?

"Why don't we meet at The Dive?"

"I'll be there," she promised and was already wondering what to wear. Something sexy. And just in case, she'd take a shower and put on a black bra and panties . . . She hung up and started to hum as she rolled off her bed. Wondering vaguely if this was what it was like to fall in love, she rummaged in her closet for her favorite black miniskirt and boots. She had the perfect maroon sweater—turtlenecked and sleeveless—which would look great with a short black jacket.

She planned to knock Brian Thomas's socks off . . . well, his socks and maybe a few other articles of clothing as well.

"So that's it. All you know." Bentz wanted to twist his brother's clerical collar until it choked the life out of him. What the devil was wrong with James? A priest who couldn't keep his hands off women—Bentz's women.

Not true, Bentz, you cut Olivia loose, his conscience reminded him.

The crime scene team was still collecting evidence while Montoya was outside dealing with the press and interviewing the neighbors, hoping to find someone who had seen something, *anything.*

James had repeated his story to half a dozen officers. It hadn't changed. Bentz almost believed him. *Almost.* Seated here in the church office, seeing the lines of strain on his brother's face, the torture in his gaze, the way he nervously rubbed his hands together, James seemed genuinely distraught. Not a killer.

He's a priest, his hair is dark, his eyes are blue, and he wears a ring with a dark stone . . . He knows Olivia, intimately it seems, so he doesn't keep his vows; he discovered the body and he had blood, most likely the victim's, all over him.

"So what about your parishioners? Any one of them seem as if they're not dealing with a full deck?"

"Several. Some, the older ones, are suffering from dementia and we have a few who are mentally challenged, but do we have anyone who I might think is deranged and sadistic, someone who could slaughter someone? No . . . some are odd, of course and others I don't really know, but no, I don't think any of them . . ." His voice trailed off. "I wouldn't know."

"Sure you would. If they were good Catholics, wouldn't they confess to you?"

James didn't move for a second. His lips rolled over his teeth and he twisted his ring. Bentz had hit a nerve. He waited. James finally said, "Good Catholics wouldn't commit murder."

"What about bad ones?"

James's throat worked. "All of God's children are—"

Bentz threw himself across the desk and his fingers curled into his brother's clean shirt. The bloody one had been already taken for evidence. "Don't give me any of that premixed, parochial pablum, okay? Not all of God's children are good people who've wandered astray. Some are bad. Sick. Demented. Their wires misfunction and short-circuit. They're bad, James. Evil. So don't give me any of this shit! Do you know of anyone who might have killed Mickey Gains or any of the other victims?''

''I—I have no proof of anything.''

''So what about insight? A gut feeling? Anything, James. We're talking lives here; do you want to see what happened to that kid''—he used his free arm to flail it toward the door, taking in the church and the altar—''happen to someone else? You know what I think? You were the one who explained about the way the saints were martyred. I'm willing to bet my pension that it's the same guy who was here tonight. So help me out, will ya?''

''I'm trying, but I don't know who did this,'' he said, his eyes tortured, his face suddenly a dozen years older than it had been.

''You know something!'' Bentz charged, so angry spit sprayed from his mouth.

James, weighted down by some inner beast, shook his head. ''I can tell you nothing.''

''You pious, hypocritical son of a bitch. People are being slaughtered! Hideously. Micky Gains out there is just the tip of the iceberg.'' His fingers tightened in the smooth fabric of his brother's shirt. ''If you can, you've got to help me stop this!''

''I'll do anything I can.''

''Like hell!'' Bentz dropped his hand, but stayed close enough that his nose was nearly touching James's. ''You said you had some issues with God.''

''Yes.'' James licked his lips.

''What issues?''

A muscle worked in James's jaw.

''What issues?'' Bentz repeated, his eyes narrowing.

''Celibacy,'' he said in a low whisper.

Bingo. Bentz felt as if he'd taken a sucker punch to the gut. ''Anything else?''

''Isn't that enough?'' James's blue eyes fastened on his.

"You're involved with Olivia Benchet." It wasn't a question. The room was silent for a moment. So still that the sounds of the night seemed to seep in through the closed windows.

"How do you know her?" James finally asked.

"She didn't tell you?" Bentz's eyes narrowed.

James shook his head, then leaned back in his chair and rotated so that he could study the window, so that he wouldn't have to face his half-brother. "No."

"And you didn't mention that we were half-brothers?" Bentz had backed off, away from the desk, put some distance between them so he wouldn't lunge at his brother again and knock him senseless. He was running on raw energy tonight—adrenalin fired by rage.

"Why would I? All she knows is that I have a half-brother who's estranged." His lips twisted into a dark, self-deprecating grin. "Why didn't you tell her?"

"It never came up."

James made a dismissive noise as the door to the office sprang open and banged against the wall with a thud.

Bentz nearly jumped out of his skin as a stately older priest marched in. "What's going on?" he asked. His eyes were an imperious blue, his voice low, angry, and laced with derision. Self-righteousness oozed from beneath his alb. "Why are the police and the press crawling all over God's house? I got a call from Mrs. Flanders down the street saying that there was some trouble here . . ." His gaze landed on Bentz, who had already opened the wallet holding his badge.

"There's been a murder, Monsignor. Here in the church," James explained. "Mickey Gains."

The monsignor's legs gave way. His face turned white as death. "No . . . but I just saw him . . . he was to lock up . . ." His voice faded as he leaned against the wall, slammed his eyes shut, and made the sign of the cross over his chest. All of the life seemed to have been squeezed out of him. "I can't believe it."

"You left the doors open?" James charged.

"You know how I feel about it . . . Mickey? Dear God." Blinking as if to clear his head, he sketched another quick sign of the cross over his heart as he shook his head in disbelief.

"Tell me what you know," Bentz said and flipped open his notebook again.

"Nothing . . . he's just one of the boys who helps with the services . . ." His voice cracked and he buried his face in his hands. "I can't believe . . . not Mickey . . . not Mickey." A tap on the door and Montoya poked in his head. His gaze flicked from one priest to the other. "Are you Roy O'Hara?" he asked and the monsignor nodded, then found the strength to pull himself to his full height.

"Yes, why?"

Montoya's dark eyes met Bentz's. "There was a case a few years back. A boy in Jackson, Mississippi."

More blood drained from Father O'Hara's face and Bentz made the connection. What had Reggie Benchet told him, that there was a pedophile but the charges had been dropped on a Father Harris or Henry or . . . could he have meant *O'Hara?*

"That was all a mistake," the monsignor said but spittle seemed to collect at the corners of his mouth and his hands were shaking. "A solitary case of one boy's malicious lies. The charges were dropped for lack of evidence. I was reassigned. To St. Luke's."

"Were the charges dropped because of lack of evidence or because of a payoff?" Montoya asked.

"No—the family decided the boy was lying. I'd caught him in the closet doing unthinkable things . . . it was all a mistake."

"Then you wouldn't mind coming downtown with me to make a formal statement." Montoya's dark gaze slid to Father James. "You, too."

"Gladly," James said.

Montoya escorted both of the priests outside. Bentz took in the scene one more time. He felt in his gut that this was the work of the same twisted brain who had slaughtered the

women on the saints' feast days. It had to be. Unless there
was a copycat around, unless whoever had killed Mickey
Gains had put together enough information from the press
releases and the media information to come up with his own
kind of sick, brutal crime, one similar enough to confuse
the issue.

It had happened before.

Two killers involved with the Catholic Church?

Or one?

His eyes swept the nave, empty now, except for a few
remaining police officers.

Bentz wasn't religious; wasn't really sure where he stood
on God. But he'd been raised by the Church and this was
his parish. As irreverent as he was, he'd come to St. Luke's
on Christmas and an Easter or two, had even attended mass
once in a while in between, usually with Kristi. He'd seen
two fellow officers married at the very altar where Mickey
Gains had been slain. Bentz had been here once for a funeral
and even been invited to a christening.

Two killers?

Bentz didn't buy it.

Then who?

Father Roy O'Hara, apparent pedophile.

Father James McClaren, a priest who couldn't come to
terms with his vows and Bentz's half-brother.

Brian Thomas, the boy interested in Kristi who had once
been in the seminary and had a beef with the Church and
his parents?

Olivia's brother, whoever the hell he was? The genetic
link that could maybe explain why she saw visions of the
killings and through the killer's eyes.

A student at one of the universities who knew the victims?

A faculty member?

Nancois Franz?

The clue was here at St. Luke's . . . The killer had been
here for a reason. But what?

If the murderer wasn't the priest, then why would he be

in the church? To pray? To confess? To feel the presence of God in some way? Or to search out his next victim?

Bentz craved a smoke and a drink. He needed time to sit and think, a Camel straight burning in an ashtray, a shot of Jack Daniels cooling over ice in a short glass. Nicotine and alcohol—just enough to relax him and help him concentrate ... Now, as he stood in the back of the nave, his eyes narrowed at the altar and the huge sculpture of the Crucifixion rising to the cathedral ceiling. Stained glass glittered under the lights and blood stained the altar.

There had been murder.

In God's house.

In Bentz's city.

Why *here?* Why not St. Louis Cathedral? Why not some other church? There had to be a connection.

He wondered what he'd find if he tapped the priests' phones. Rubbing his beard shadow, Bentz considered his options. He could go to the DA and a judge, but knew he didn't have enough evidence. However, he knew how to bug a phone himself and had some equipment stashed in a back closet. It would take only a few hours. And there was his connection down at the phone company's investigative department. Larry would help him out; had in the past. For a six-pack.

We're going to play this one by the book, Melinda Jaskiel's words echoed through his brain, but Bentz decided the book wasn't helping out a whole helluva lot right now. He owed Jaskiel a lot. She'd stretched her neck pretty damned thin all so that he could land this miserable job a few years back. And he was going to pay her back by hooking up an illegal wiretap and surveillance camera, then removing the equipment, and with the information gained, force the killer's hand. No one, except for Larry Dillis, would be the wiser. Not even Montoya. Bentz figured if he was going down, he was going down alone.

Maybe the bug wouldn't turn up anything.

But maybe it would. As he started for the doors to look for Olivia, Bentz told himself that the wiretap wasn't because he wanted to know what was going on between her and James. It wasn't any of his damned business anyway. This was only about nailing the killer.

Jesus, he could use a smoke.

He walked into the night. And a madhouse. Police cars, press vans, curious neighbors, reporters with microphones, and dozens of questions were swarming in the night. Olivia wasn't visible.

"Detective Bentz, can you tell us more about the murder?"

"The department will issue a statement later."

"Is this the latest victim of the same killer?"

"I don't know."

"Is the victim another coed?"

"No comment."

"This murder took place in a church. Could it possibly be the work of the Rosary Killer?"

Bentz paused and looked at the group of eager reporters and cameramen, none of them much over thirty, all hoping for a scoop, interested in the facts, not the victim.

"As I said, the department will issue a statement," he said, practicing the same old litany. "I can't comment until it does. Thank you." Then he strode to his Jeep and found a piece of gum in his pocket. As he did, he spotted her.

Huddled in the passenger seat, Olivia watched him through the windshield. She looked exhausted. Drained. He didn't blame her. He opened the door, climbed behind the wheel, and jammed his key into the ignition. "Sorry it took so long. I thought Officer Clarke was going to escort you home."

"She tried. I refused." Her eyes snapped gold fire in the night. "Why the hell didn't you tell me that Father James was your brother?" she demanded, and before he could answer, added, "And don't make any lame excuse that it just didn't come up, okay? I told you all about him when I gave you that list of names of babys who'd been christened thirty years ago."

"I didn't think it was important," he said, twisting the ignition. The engine caught.

"Not important?" she repeated with a snort. "Oh, give me a break, Bentz. He's your brother, isn't he?"

"Half brother." He twisted in his seat, backed up, then jammed the rig into drive. The Jeep bounced through the puddles and potholes as he wended it through the other vehicles parked haphazardly in the lot.

"Oh. *Half* brother. Is that why you didn't bother to mention it?"

His frayed temper snapped. "I think that makes us even. You didn't figure I needed to know that you were sleeping with him."

She stiffened, muttered something under her breath, then poked a finger at Bentz's shoulder. "It's not your business, Bentz. You made it perfectly clear that nothing could happen between us. What I do with my personal business is just that—my business."

"Even if you're sleeping with a priest, a primary suspect in the case?"

"What?" she demanded, outraged. "Father James? He's not—"

"You sleep with him and you still call him *Father* James?"

"I'm *not* sleeping with him."

"But you did," he said flatly.

She opened her mouth, then snapped it shut. From the corner of his eye he saw her try to rein in her anger. "I *nearly* did, okay? Not that I need to explain myself. The whole thing was a mistake." She folded her arms over her chest. "I seem to be making a lot of them lately."

"That son of a bitch." Bentz slowed for a stop sign, then took the corner.

"It wasn't his fault."

"No?" Bentz snorted.

"No! And nothing happened . . . God, Bentz, get over it! And quit trying to blame someone."

"If it makes you feel any better, Livvie, this isn't the first time James has had trouble keeping his vows."

"I don't think I want to hear this," she said sharply, but he saw the pain in her expression and he immediately felt like a heel. "It's none of my business."

He had no claim on her. She was right. What happened between James and Olivia had nothing to do with him.

"Well, it was mine," he said as he accelerated through a light just turning yellow. "I caught him in bed with my wife about nineteen years ago."

Chapter
Thirty-five

The headlines were magnificent. The Chosen One had bought copies of all the local papers and now, in his sanctuary, as he clipped them with his pinking shears, he softly sang a Christmas carol and read the bold print.

"Hark the herald angels sing . . ."

POLICE STYMIED IN CHURCH MURDER

"Glory to the newborn King."

ROSARY KILLER RESURRECTED?

"Peace on earth and mercy mild."

COLLEGE COED SERIAL KILLER BAFFLES NOPD

"God and sinner, reconciled . . ."

ALTAR BOY SLAIN.

"Again . . ." he paused, then sang to a crescendo, "God and sinner reconciled." He liked that line in particular.

The Chosen One smiled at his work as he tacked the banners of his newly found fame to the calendar where his saints had been displayed. St. Joan of Arc, St. Catherine of Alexandria, beautiful little St. Philomena, St. Mary Magdalen . . . such lovelies.

But the press didn't understand him, nor did the public know of his work.

The police, of course, were idiots even if the press was giving him his due respect. Finally. Yet there had been not one mention of God's work, of the mission. Of course they didn't know. The police were keeping the members of the Fourth Estate sheltered from the real truth with words like "ritualistic slayings," or "brutal murder," so as not to bring out the copycats or those who would claim to have done the deeds for a few minutes of fame. So the press hadn't been allowed to understand what was his mission . . . unless he corrected them. A letter to a newspaper or a call to a radio station . . . all risky, but . . . . perhaps . . . He paused as he considered the disc jockey he would call.

Dr. Sam on her show *Midnight Confessions.*

Perfect.

Yes . . . but first things first.

He had to capture his next two victims. First St. Bibiana, then St. Lucy. Time was running short and while the police were busy trying to figure out how that miserable altar boy was connected to the other murders, it was time to make his move. He just needed a little help.

Humming to himself, he walked down the stairs to the basement. Opening the door his nostrils were immediately burned with the foul stench of the dogs and fecal matter. The animals were quiet now, but as he opened the door and snapped on the red light they sent up a cacophony of howls. Worse yet, the bitch was in heat . . . and the male dog was more interested in breaking into her kennel than snarling at the terrified woman backed against the wall.

She looked up at him as he approached and then to the weapon swinging from his cincture, the stun gun at odds with the gold-colored cord holding his alb in place. "Would you like to get out of here, my child?" he asked in soft, dulcet tones.

She nodded wildly, her round eyes darting from him to the dogs and back to the gun.

"Well, I think it's time. I've made my point. You will be obedient, now, won't you?"

Again she nodded and he bent down to release her bonds, but as he did, he clipped a collar around her throat, the same collar that surrounded each mutt's neck. The collars were the kind used in training dogs, each neck band equipped with metal prongs that pressed into the soft skin of the throat. Activated electronically by a remote control device he kept in his deep pockets the collars would sizzle with electricity, shocking the wearer. Should they be wet, from holy water or sweat, the shock was even more severe. With the press of a button The Chosen One could zap her or the dogs into submission.

To prove his point, he withdrew a control and aimed it at her. She withered away, shrinking into the wall, shaking her head violently and making anxious cries beneath her gag. He smiled, a faint erection beginning beneath his robes. "Trust me," he said and pushed the button. She squeezed her eyes shut and the bitch in heat squealed and yipped as a shock went through her mangy body.

He released the button and the woman opened her eyes in terror. Tears rained from her face and she looked beyond him to the kennels where the female dog, tail between her legs looked confused and whimpered.

"Now, will you do as I say?" he asked her and there was no hesitation. He saw complete compliance in her eyes. "Good. Come along then, I have a job for you." He released the shackles on her feet, but kept her hands restrained and helping her to her feet, urged her up the stairs. "If you do anything I don't like, anything at all, I'll be forced to activate the collar, and . . . yes, the stun gun. Remember that? You didn't like that, did you?

She shook her head vigorously as if she remembered all too vividly how he'd approached her just after she'd returned her rental car and before she could make her way to the airport terminal.

Dressed in jeans, sweatshirt and jacket, he'd blended in, then taken out the gun and zapped her, catching her before she hit the ground and half dragging her into the car he'd stolen at the campus . . . just like before. It had been raining furiously and he'd used an umbrella to shield them not only from the weather but prying eyes as well. She'd only made one cry—the stun gun and his knife had convinced her to remain quiet as she'd roused. Then he'd gagged and cuffed her and brought her here.

She was a fine specimen, could probably be offered as a sacrifice. He watched the muscles of her rump—tight and rounded, as she walked up the steps. Again the pleasantly painful erection . . . yes, spilling her blood would be a pleasure. He stopped her in the upper hallway before she reached the entrance. No one was allowed into his sanctuary. Just God.

"Here we go." He stood her against a curtained wall and took several pictures with his Polaroid. "Now, if you're good . . . very, very good, next time I'll let you out; I'll have a more difficult task for you," he said, thinking of her cell phone. "For now, though, you must go back downstairs."

She shook her head.

"It's only for a little while," he assured her as the tears ran again. "And then, I'll get you out of the basement for good. But you have to promise that you'll help me." She didn't hesitate, but nodded violently. Her hands were on his sleeves, clutching at his alb, reaching for his chasuble, trying to wind her fingers into its satiny folds. "I understand," he said. "I know this is difficult, but nothing worthwhile comes easily. There must be pain and suffering and sacrifice involved. Now . . . off with you." When she started to shake her head he reached into his pocket and brought out his remote control. "Be a good girl," he warned and she turned quickly and on dirty bare feet scrambled down the stairs. He wanted to give her one little shock, to hustle her along, but resisted.

Sarah needed to fully comprehend the difference between reward and punishment.

* * *

". . . Forgive me, Father, for I have sinned . . ."

James felt his knees turn to water. It had been over a week since the last time he'd heard this raspy confession. "What is it, my son?" he said, forgetting all the rules, sitting on the edge of the desk in his apartment. His spine was stiff, his heart pounding with dread.

"It has been a week since my last confession and these are my sins."

James braced himself.

"I have taken the Lord's name in vain and I have lusted in my heart."

So far, so good.

"For your penance say ten Hail Marys and five Our Fathers." James's throat was dry and his lungs so tight he couldn't breathe. Surely the penitent had not killed again . . . and then he knew.

"And I broke the commandment again. I took a life."

James's blood was thundering in his ears. "Another one?" Father O'Hara had been interrogated, but set free as he could prove his whereabouts. The scandal had been horrible of course and he was being scrutinized by the press and the parishioners and the clergy . . . O'Hara's name would forever be associated with the killing though he was innocent of the murder. However, there were other charges that Mickey's parents' attorney was making, claims of improper touching, sodomy and rape . . . and now this . . .

"Oh, yes . . . I found the sinner in the house of God."

"The sinner?" James felt sick inside.

"The altar boy who desecrated the church," the voice thundered. "The hooligan who stole wine and had the audacity to drink from the chalice, all in the guise of piety. Yes, I spilled his blood, gladly. Let it be a lesson to all those who defy God, who do not revere His house, who commit sins."

The man was mad. He had it all twisted around.

"Listen, my son," James begged, though he wanted to

somehow strangle the man. *Give me strength, Lord, please, let me find a way to stop him.* "I, too, have sought God's counsel. He has told me that the killings must stop, that it is not His will. No more lives be taken."

"You?" A haughty sneer was evident in the voice. "You have talked to God?"

"Yes, many times."

"And you heard Him speak?"

"I know what He wants and this violence is not His will."

There was a snort. "The world is a violent place, Father. Haven't you noticed? And the atrocities committed in the name of religion have been around since the beginning of time."

"Then commit no more. Sin no more."

"But I, *I* have actually spoken to God and heard His voice and my mission is clear. I am to make a sacrifice to Him. For the martyred saints. To reaffirm their martyrdom."

"What?" James said, his gut clenching. Bentz had been right.

"You don't understand, do you? I knew you had not spoken to the Father." And then he went on and on about his mission, about how he would find the perfect person to sacrifice on the feast days, just as Rick Bentz had surmised. He hardly paused for a breath, as if he were glad for a chance to explain himself. His speech pattern was that of a lecturer . . . as if he were used to people listening to him, an orator. A priest? A politician? A CEO? A teacher . . . the coeds taken from the local campuses . . . a scholar?

"Have I a penance?" he finally asked.

"Of course . . . of course . . . it is the same as before. You are to say the rosary and confess to the police—"

"I'll not be judged by mortals! My confession is only to the Father through you."

He clicked off and James was left with the receiver to his ear. He dropped it, didn't realize that the connection wasn't severed, that the receiver dangled over the edge of the desk.

James sank to his knees and prayed harder than he ever had in his life.

Bentz taped the entire conversation. He felt some measure of relief that James wasn't the killer. But hearing the bastard's raspy voice, feeling his presence had made Bentz's skin crawl. He didn't waste any time, just popped a couple of Rolaids he found in the desk drawer at home, then dialed up his friend with the phone company. Maybe Larry would have some information for him. Maybe he was about to catch the killer. Maybe he'd get lucky.

"What the fuck is this?" Brian Thomas asked as he threw open the door to his studio apartment and found two cops on his doorstep. One had a swarthy complexion and had a don't-fuck-with-me attitude stamped across his face, the other guy was older, tough-looking but . . . oh, shit, he recognized Kristi Bentz's father from a picture he'd seen in her wallet.

"We'd just like to talk to you," Bentz explained.

"I haven't done anything to your daughter."

"So you know who I am?" His smile was cold as death.

"She said you'd be calling." He stepped back and let them into his one room. It was sparsely furnished and messy, but he didn't really give a rat's ass. The cops couldn't bust him on anything. The weed he'd smoked last night was all gone, he didn't do anything stronger, so he was home free. But he was sweating and no doubt both cops, their gazes scraping over his bookcase and . . . oh, shit . . . the bong. He'd left the bong and a six pack of empties by the bed and sure enough Bentz spied it.

His lips compressed. "We need to ask you some questions," he said and pointed to a secondhand recliner near the window. "Why don't you sit down?"

Brian was sweating bullets. What did the cops have on him? He'd been through this before, a long time ago, and memories of being arrested, of having his hands yanked hard behind his back as he was cuffed, of the charges and arrest, the hours of interrogation, being fingerprinted and stripped, thrown in a locked cage with the lowlifes of the world . . . Now, he gritted his teeth and tried to think. He'd done nothing wrong. They couldn't prove anything.

"Kristi said you'd eventually come by, that anyone who dated her was subjected to some kind of interrogation."

"Just a few questions," Montoya said. "No big deal, man. You just stay cool and this'll be over in a few minutes."

"Maybe I should call my lawyer."

"You need one?" Bentz asked, thick eyebrows lifting over suspicious gray eyes. What a piece of work.

"I don't know, do I?"

"Not if you haven't done anything wrong," Montoya said and kicked out a kitchen chair. "Sit down. Relax. It's just a couple of questions."

Bullshit, Brian thought, but settled into the recliner and wondered if they smelled the wafts of burnt weed still lingering in the air. Bentz didn't sit down. He also didn't hide the fact that he didn't trust Brian. Not one little bit. Obviously he didn't like the fact that Brian was dating his daughter and for a second Brian thought about all those movies he'd seen, the bad cops who planted evidence, then threatened charges unless they could squeeze a confession from the guy. He swallowed hard. Even if he beat the charges, his career here at the University would be ruined.

It would be smarter to cooperate.

They asked him a million questions. Some of them had to do with faculty and students, but a lot of the questions surrounded Dr. Franz and his two wives. Brian had been at All Saints as an undergrad at the time and had done some work for the first wife, Dr. Nancoise Franz. They also asked him about women he'd read about in the papers, Leslie Franz, Cathy Anderson and Stephanie Jane Keller—victims of the serial killer. And they'd stared at the two swords he had mounted over his bed, then asked him about weaponry and what he'd done while in the military. He should call a lawyer; it was obvious they thought he might be connected to the killer stalking the college campuses.

Or more likely, Bentz had a hard-on for him because he was dating his precious daughter. Didn't the cops have more important things to do than intimidate innocent people, for Christ's sake?

They couldn't think he was really involved? That was crazy. He didn't know those girls.

Bentz asked him about the rape charges and about him spending time in the seminary. They even brought up the names of some of the patron saints—now what the fuck was that all about? Bentz had done enough homework to bring up the fact that before Brian had transferred to All Saints he'd spent his freshman and sophomore years at Tulane and studied psych under Dr. Leeds.

"That guy, he's a real prick," Brian said, wiping the sweat from his palms on his jeans. "Stuck on himself. Between him and Dr. Sutter, here, I gave up on psychology, decided to do my doctorate work in philosophy. I came up with a theory that everyone gets interested in psych because they need it themselves. They have problems, go to a shrink, get off on talking about themselves and decide they could make some money at it . . ." Brian shut up. Why rattle on? Years ago, when there had been all that trouble with the rape charges his lawyer had told him to answer precisely, give no more information than what was asked.

The cops left about an hour and a half after they'd arrived, thank God. Brian walked to the window and looked through the grimy panes and checked out the parking lot. Within minutes they climbed into a Jeep with Bentz at the wheel. What the hell were they doing all the way up here? How serious were they to be talking to him? An uneasy feeling crawled across his skin.

He thought about calling Kristi and reading her the riot act, but decided against it. But seeing her tonight would be out. Bentz would probably drop by and visit his daughter and he was the last person Brian wanted to run into again.

No, he needed time to think. What the hell was he doing with a cop's daughter anyway?

Brian walked to the refrigerator and pulled out a beer. He was just twisting off the top when the doorbell rang again. Shit. Not the cops again. Please! He took a long swallow and walked to the window. The Jeep was gone. Good.

So who was ringing his door? Grinning, he thought he knew the answer.

The edge from the detectives' visit had worn off. He'd cooled it a little with Kristi since she'd returned from visiting her dick of an old man at Thanksgiving. Not because Brian didn't want to see her, but because he thought playing a little hard to get wouldn't be such a bad idea. He sensed she liked a challenge, so he was going to give her one. Maybe then he'd be able to score. How would the old man like that? Huh?

The bell rang again and he yelled, "Coming!" then under his breath, "Keep your panties on." Running fingers through his hair, he walked to the door and pulled it open. The smile plastered onto his face slid away when he recognized the guy standing in the hallway. "What the hell are you doing here?" he demanded a second before he saw the stun gun. "Hey—wait!"

But it was too late. He felt the blast, fell backward and watched his beer fall to the floor.

"Is he a suspect, Dad? Are you gonna arrest him?" Kristi demanded, ignoring the hot dog and Coke her dad had bought her. He and Montoya had taken her to a hasty dinner in a little hamburger shack just off campus and he'd dropped the bomb—admitted that he'd been talking to Brian. A few other students were hanging out at the counter and she hid her head, didn't want to be seen with her dad when he was on duty.

"Let's just say he's a 'person of interest.' " Her father was seated across the table with its fake wood top. Bentz was all business.

" 'Person of interest.' What the hell does that mean?''

"That I'm going to be watching him.''

"No.'' She wanted to shake some sense into her old man. "Are you trying to ruin my life? Because you are!'' She shot a glance at Montoya. "He's just hassling Brian because I've been seeing him, right?''

"No. The dude could be bad.'' Montoya wasn't his usual self. Seemed harder, angry. Like the case was getting to him, too.

"What happened to 'innocent until proven guilty?' Huh? Isn't that what this country is all about. Jesus, Dad, give me some breathing room, okay?''

"This guy is dangerous.''

"The killer is dangerous, Dad. Not Brian. I *know* him. He's not a killer.''

"Bull. I want you to come home with me. Now.'' Bentz rose to his full height. "It's not safe here.''

"For who? Everyone? Or just me? Are you going to send everyone on campus home just because you think one of the T.A.s might know something about the murderers?''

Bentz's jaw grew tight. "No, I guess I can't do that, but I can arrest him. There's enough circumstantial evidence to hold him for a while,'' he said, knowing that he was stretching the truth. He didn't have anything concrete. Just a gut feeling. And the prick was seeing his daughter. But he had seen the bong and the empties in his apartment. He could bust the guy for drugs, and if he had any underage students in his apartment, for serving alcohol. "Either you come home with me, or I arrest him. What's it gonna be?''

"You're serious.''

"Damned straight.''

"This is so outrageous. You'd embarrass me?''

"In a heartbeat if I thought it would keep you alive,'' he said.

Her chin shivered, then she clamped her jaw tight. "If you do this, I will never, *never* forgive you.''

He checked his watch. "You're got one hour to turn in

your papers and pack. You can drive up here every day to attend your classes. A bodyguard will come with you.''

"Like hell. I''m eighteen. You can't force me—''The look in his eyes made her clamp her mouth shut. She was supposed to meet Brian at the library in half an hour.

Then she could explain everything, but if she capitulated all of a sudden her dad would be suspicious. ''So my choice is to leave school or be humiliated to death. Either way Brian will hate me.''

"You'll get over it.''

"You can really be a bastard, you know that, don't you?''

He checked his watch. ''You've got fifty-eight minutes.''

Olivia rang up the sale, quickly wrapped tissue paper around the cranberry-scented candles and handed the bag to a hefty woman with tight gray curls who smiled and wished her a ''Merry Christmas.'' She winked as she tucked her bag under her arm. ''Less than a month away, you know. Tomorrow's the first of December.''

"That it is, Merry Christmas to you, too.'' The woman bustled out of the store, jangling the jingle bells that hung from a bright red bow that Tawilda had tacked over the door.

Olivia checked her watch . . . only an hour until the shop closed. She planned to spend a couple hours in the library on campus and then go home and soak in a long bath. She didn't relish the thought of Christmas; this year would be the first without Grannie Gin and she was here in Louisiana, alone, instead of in Tucson where she'd made friends.

Speaking of which, she was getting irritated with Sarah. It wasn't unusual not to hear from her friend for a week or two, but it wasn't Sarah's style not to call and tell her she'd made it home safely, that she'd really enjoyed staying with Olivia, or that she really loved Leo and couldn't go through with the divorce. Olivia had called her friend twice, leaving messages each time.

Maybe Sarah was overwhelmed. It could be that the

thought of the impending divorce coupled with the Christmas season was too much for her.

And what about you? What are you going to do for Christmas? Who are you going to spend it with?

Rick Bentz? Not hardly. Their conversations had been all business and she was still angry with him for not telling her about Father James McClaren.

What about Father James? Oh, God, she didn't want to think about that. She'd nearly made love to him, barely a week after she'd done the same thing with his half brother. No, she was better off without a man in her life. She could make it on her own. In fact, she'd probably need years of therapy after the last two men in her life. Bentz had been bad enough, but then to nearly sleep with a priest. How desperate had she been? James McClaren was a good, kind man and she'd almost led him astray . . . no, she wouldn't even go there.

Thank God they'd stopped when they had, that they'd realized before it was too late that they'd come close to making a mistake that would have ruined their lives.

The phone rang just as another customer walked through the door, jangling the jingle bells. "The Third Eye," Olivia said, picking up the phone.

"Hi, Livvie, did you have a nice Thanksgiving?" Bernadette asked.

"Yeah, I did," Olivia said automatically and tried to keep her cool. He mother was reaching out to her. That was good. *Just don't let her get to you.* "My friend Sarah, from Tucson, was with me."

"Good."

"And you?"

"It was all right . . . well, no, it wasn't. Jeb and I are splitting up. I decided you were right. I don't need this. I went to San Antonio, spent a weekend alone, and sorted it all out. I'd already filed papers a while ago, but the divorce was on hold, now . . . I don't think I'll ever marry again."

Olivia almost laughed. "I think you're the marrying

kind." *As opposed to me,* she added silently. "So, you're okay with the divorce?"

"Yes," Bernadette said firmly. "And I'm hoping that you and me, we can patch things up. I haven't been a great mother, I know that, but maybe now that you're grown we could be friends or something." Olivia was stunned. This was her mother talking? Self-centered Bernadette?

"That would be nice . . ." Olivia said then saw one of the women who had entered the store, a short, slim woman in a navy jacket, pocket a glass paperweight. "Uh . . . I've got to run, Mom."

"Before you go—"

The shoplifter looked over her shoulder as she reached for another item, a crystal reindeer ornament, then, spying Olivia watching her, casually looked over the item and replaced it. Olivia was only half-listening to her mother. "The real reason I called is that I remembered a name associated with the adoption of my son."

"What?" Olivia asked. Now her attention was dragged from the shoplifter.

"It was Thomas."

"Thomas?"

"Yes, I'm sure of it. My son was adopted by a couple named Thomas."

"Thomas who?"

"I think it was their last name . . . but maybe I'm mistaken . . ." Bernadette faltered. "I overheard your grandmother talking once and she said something about the Thomases, I think. I hope this helps."

"It does, Mom, thanks," Olivia said, her heart racing as the shoplifter edged toward the door. "Just a minute," she called to the woman and dropped the receiver. "I think you may have taken some merchandise—" The woman was out of the door in a heartbeat. Olivia gave chase, but as soon as she stepped out of the store, she lost the thief in the crowd. It was dark and raining and in her navy jacket she blended into the jostling crowd. Christmas lights illuminated Jackson Square but Olivia didn't feel the spirit. "Great," Olivia muttered, unable to leave the shop alone. Tawilda wasn't due back from her dinner for another fifteen minutes.

Olivia started into the store but caught her reflection in the window panes. Her hair was windblown and her face was pale. Taking a step toward the doorway, for the first time in a week, she sensed him . . . saw a quicksilver image behind her own.

No.

The people on the street walking by shrank, the noise of the street seemed to fade and her head began to ache. He was there, staring back at her—blue eyes and dark hair, angular features, not unlike her own, but not Father James no . . . . and . . . then he turned his vision to another spot . . . as if someone had called his name. He focused on his quarry and Olivia saw the woman's face. The dull ache behind Olivia's eyes banged painfully. A young girl with long auburn hair and an attitude of confidence . . . a face Olivia had seen before, not in person, but framed as it was tonight, in a bifold picture sitting squarely in the middle of Detective Rick Bentz's desk.

Chapter Thirty-six

Where the hell was Brian? He was supposed to have met her fifteen minutes ago. Kristi stood on the porch of the library looking through the sheeting rain. It shimmered against the streets, and poured from the sky. Though barely five in the afternoon the day was gloomy and dark.

And she only had seventeen minutes before she had to hook up with her dad in front of the dorm. She'd made the date with Brian five minutes before her dad had shown up. On the phone Brian had sounded weird, like he was high, or scared, or *pissed*. And who could blame him? Come *on*. To have your girlfriend's dad, the cop, show up and start an interrogation. Her cheeks burned at the thought of it. Sometimes she hated her dad.

He's not really your dad, is he?

Maybe that was the problem. Anyway around it, Bentz had only messed things up with Brian even more than they were to begin with.

Ever since she'd gotten back from Thanksgiving, things had been strained with Brian. He'd been moody and uptight.

Something was eating at him. He blamed the stress of the end of the term, that Zaroster had been giving him a hard time, but Kristi sensed there was more going on.

They'd made out a couple of times, but she'd always broken it off because it hadn't felt right. There was something missing, something she couldn't define. She thought of Jay. He loved her. Brian didn't. She knew it and it almost seemed as if she was . . . well, it seemed archaic, but it was almost as if he was using her, that she was just another conquest.

That was backward thinking. She could turn it around, consider it the other way, that he was just another notch in her garter belt. Oh, yeah, right. *Face it, Bentz, that's not the way you're made.* She glanced up the street and saw his car slowly approaching. He hadn't stood her up! He was just late again. Waving, she pulled her hood over her hair and blinked against the rain as she jogged down the puddle-strewn path to the spot where he'd slowed.

"Hi!" She climbed into the passenger seat, yanked the door shut and leaned over to kiss him, but he didn't respond, just stared straight ahead and pressed on the accelerator. Only then did she notice that there was someone in the back seat, a guy in a ski mask. Her breath stopped short. Oh, shit. There was a collar around Brian's neck, some kind of weird-looking choker. "What's going on?" she asked, reaching for the door as the man behind her drew his arm around to the front and pointed a gun at her chest.

"No!" she screamed, reaching for the handle of the door. Her last thought was that her dad had been right. Oh, she'd been a fool. "Don't—"

A jolt of electricity hissed through her body.

Bentz glanced at his watch as his cell phone rang. He and Montoya were double parked in front of Cramer Hall waiting for Kristi. So far she was ten minutes late. He snapped on his cell. "Detective Bentz."

"It's Olivia. He's hunting again," she said, her words pouring out in a rush. "He's looking for Kristi, Bentz; I saw through his eyes." Rick went cold to the bottom of his heart.

"What the hell are you talking about?" No! It couldn't be. Not when he was here and Kristi was in her dorm. He started running. Fast. The cell phone was pressed to his ear and Montoya was on his heels. He pushed through a startled group of girls coming down the stairs.

"I'm saying he's after her, I think he's gotten her."

"No. He can't have." Bentz wouldn't believe it.

"Wait a minute—" a woman behind the front desk called.

"I'm here at the dorm," he said into the phone.

"Find her!"

"I will."

"Bentz, there's something else. My mother called. She said the couple who adopted my brother were named Thomas."

"Shit!"

"And I can identify him." she added. "I saw his face."

"Go to the station, have someone draw the composite and look at pictures of Brian Thomas. He's the guy Kristi's been dating." He clicked off as they took the stairs two at a time, then flipped the phone at Montoya. "Call for a back-up. Send someone over to Brian Thomas's apartment. Olivia just identified him." He reached for his weapon, found Kristi's room and pushed open the door.

"What're you doing here?" Kristi's roommate asked. She twisted in her desk chair.

"Looking for my daughter. Where is she?" Panic squeezed his chest.

Lucretia rolled her eyes. "Did she know you were coming? She left about half an hour ago."

"To go where?" he demanded, his heart drumming with dread.

"I don't know. I think she said something about the library. I think she might've had a date with Brian Thomas, the T.A. You might want to warn her about that. She could get in big trouble, him being the T.A. for one of her classes . . ."

He didn't hear the rest. He was already halfway down the hall.

"No, that's not him . . ." Olivia insisted, shaking her head as she stared at a picture of Brian Thomas.

"It has to be." Bentz, seated on the other side of his desk, glared at her. The desk was strewn with files, the bulletin board covered with pictures of the crime scenes Olivia had seen in her mind's eye—the victims posed as saints—Cecilia, Mary Magdalen, Joan of Arc . . . and the others. All brutal grisly scenes. And now Kristi was with the killer. Olivia's knees went weak. She sank into a desk chair.

Bentz thumped a finger onto the grainy photo and leaned over the desk. "Look again," he ordered. "This has got to be our guy!"

She studied the picture again. It was no use.

"I'm sorry, Rick. It's not him. I'm sure," she insisted, enduring Bentz's furious glare. She recognized the fear congealing in his expression, knew that he was dying inside, desperate to save his daughter. Olivia ached for him. For Kristi. Even now the girl could be dead . . . or suffering some horrible torture. Olivia's blood was cold as ice water. "I wish I could help, but—"

"Then, try, damn it. Give me a name. You said your mother thought a couple named Thomas adopted the bastard, so this is the guy!" He pounded a fist on his desk and forgotten coffee jumped out of a cup on the desk. "Shit!" He mopped up the spreading dark stain with his handkerchief.

"Get a grip, man," Montoya said, slipping through the doorway.

"Go to hell!" Bentz pointed a damning finger at his partner, then something snapped in his face. He crammed the handkerchief into his pocket.

"You go first."

"I'm already there."

Montoya snapped back, "That makes two of us."

"Damn." Sleeves rolled up, Bentz plowed his fingers through hair that hadn't seen a comb in hours. "Take her downstairs," he said, motioning toward Olivia. Their gazes touched and she saw more than fear, a deeper distrust in his eyes. "Work with the damned artist. Get me a sketch, a computer composite, anything, and get it fast!" He glance down at the photo of Kristi on his desk. His throat worked and his shoulders slumped, but only for a second. In the next breath he was angry all over again, the cords of his neck standing out, his lips flat against his teeth. "One way or another, if we have to tear that school apart, we've got to find that son of a bitch!" He motioned to Montoya. "Get pictures of every male over twenty who has stepped foot on All Saints in the last year or two." Bentz trapped Olivia in his determined stare. "Maybe you'll recognize one of them," he said coldly, as if he didn't trust her again. Just like before when she'd first entered this very office a few weeks earlier. As he if he couldn't stand gazing at her, he turned to Montoya. "Take her to the artist!"

The phone shrilled and Bentz rotated a muscular shoulder, effectively ostracizing Olivia as he snatched up the receiver. She got the message: he couldn't stand to be in the same room with her.

"Come on, let's check with the artist," Montoya said and she stood on wooden legs, managing to put some starch in her shoulders as she followed him downstairs.

Three hours later after the artist and computer had come up with a reasonable sketch, she walked into the bright New Orleans night. Christmas lights glittered throughout the city, businesses were festooned with greenery, and even the police department was decorated for the holidays, but she couldn't conjure up a bit of Christmas spirit. Not a solitary drop. She climbed into her truck, thought about going back inside and facing Bentz again, but knew she'd only get in the way. She had no more information to give him.

Hopefully he could save his daughter and locate the monster. *The monster who could be your brother.*

Damn it all.

Her cell phone beeped as she started the engine. She picked up and said, "Hello?" as she checked traffic.

"Olivia?" Sarah said, her voice tremulous.

"Sarah!" Olivia felt a second's relief. "Where are you? I've been calling and calling. I keep getting your machine."

"I didn't go back to Tucson."

"What?" Sarah sounded strange. Maybe tired? Or so Olivia thought as she strained to hear her friend's voice over the rumble of the engine, the buzz of traffic and the crackle of a bad connection. "You didn't go back? But it's been over a week."

"I know. I . . . I thought I could work things out with Leo."

"Wait a minute." Olivia switched off the fan for the defrost, hoping she could hear more clearly. "You said you were going through with the divorce."

"I was . . . I am . . . I . . . uh, I'm confused . . ." That explained the weird tone to her voice. "I hoped that you would meet me at St. Luke's that we could talk to Father James."

Olivia bit her lip as she thought of the priest. "Father James might not be available," she said, cringing at the thought of the slain altar boy. "There was trouble at the church last week."

"I know, I heard about it, but . . . but I've already spoken with Father James. He wants you to be there."

"Does he?" Olivia was surprised. Since the night of Mickey Gains's death they hadn't seen each other, hadn't so much as spoken. And wouldn't James rather speak to Sarah alone—to counsel her one-on-one? Or was there a chance he wanted to see Olivia again?

"Please," Sarah said, sounding desperate.

That did it. Her friend needed her. "When do you want me to meet you?" she asked.

"Soon. As . . . as soon as possible." Sarah's voice wavered, as if she were on the verge of tears. "Father James is going to the church now."

Olivia glanced at the clock in the car. It was nearly nine

and she was dead tired. But Sarah needed her; Olivia assumed the strain in her friend's voice was because she felt foolish, that she'd hated to make the call and admit that she'd lied. "I can meet you in fifteen minutes."

"Thanks, Livvie."

"I'm on my way." Olivia hung up and put her car in gear. What the devil had gotten into Sarah? Olivia had known her friend hadn't wanted the divorce but when she'd left after Thanksgiving, Sarah had sounded so confident and sure of her decision. Maybe something else was going on. Olivia had the eerie sensation that something deeper was bothering Sarah. Or was Olivia just getting paranoid? All the murders were making her overly suspicious. Nonetheless as she turned on the fan and the window cleared well enough that she could pull into traffic, Olivia, picked up her cell phone again and punched a button. The last caller was displayed. Olivia recognized Sarah's cell number. *So now you're second guessing your best friend—bad karma, Olivia.*

She nosed her truck through traffic and tried to shake the bad feeling that clung to her as surely as if it had claws. What was it? Why did she keep thinking something wasn't on the up and up. The trouble was Olivia had a bad feeling about everything these days. Her head still ached from the vision and she was worried sick about Kristi. She was just on edge. Jittery. That was it.

"Thanks, Livvie," Sarah had said. Which was odd. Sarah always called her Olivia except when she was teasing her . . . but then Sarah obviously hadn't been herself tonight.

She stopped at a red light and tapped her fingers impatiently on the steering wheel. Where had Sarah been staying this past week? With Leo? Were they back together? Then why the hesitation and . . . fear, that was it, fear, in her voice. Jesus, surely Leo hadn't beaten her . . . That son of a bitch!

The light turned green and Olivia tromped on the accelerator, spraying water from the puddles that shimmered on the street. Her teeth gritted at the thought of her friend's loser of a husband. She ran the next yellow light and rounded the corner to spy St. Luke's three blocks down. Security lamps splashed against the whitewashed bell tower and a small creche was illuminated beneath the spreading magnolia tree. Wise men, angels, shepherds, Mary, Joseph and a manger with Baby Jesus lying swaddled in the straw. The church itself was dark except for a few exterior lights and a warm glow from the stained glass windows near the altar.

Despite the nativity scene, the block was desolate, the street empty, most of the surrounding houses dark. Olivia turned into the rutted parking lot and scanned the area for Sarah's rental. No luck. Maybe she hadn't arrived yet.

Odd. Sarah had sounded as if she was near the church or in the church . . . maybe she'd already turned in the car.

Climbing out of her pickup, feeling the night close in on her, Olivia pocketed her keys and avoided the puddles that collected on the uneven asphalt. She tried not to think of the last time she'd been here, of poor little Mickey Gains being ruthlessly slaughtered within the sacred walls of the church.

Cinching her jacket more tightly, she headed for the main doors. A wind, dank with the scent of the river, moaned as it cut through the surrounding trees and the iridescence from the street lamps cast the street an eerie, watery blue. The hairs on the back of her neck raised as she strode along the sidewalk, but she dismissed any sense of premonition, blaming her case of nerves on her intricate knowledge of the murders and the fact that Kristi Bentz was missing. Still, the night felt creepy and out of sync.

She was near the church doors when she heard a car on the next block. It's engine was racing, tires humming. Sarah!

Turning, she spied a black European car fishtail around the corner, then scream to a stop in front of St. Luke's. Goose bumps rose on Olivia's flesh. This was wrong. All wrong. She reached for the handle of the church door when she spied Sarah seated on the passenger side, through the window facing Olivia.

"Thank God!" Olivia whispered and started for the car . . . but something was still wrong with Sarah. She wasn't getting out of the Mercedes. She was leaning against the window, barely moving. Pale and thin, she looked at Olivia with haunted, dark eyes. Slowly she shook her head.

"Sarah? What's wrong?" Olivia took two steps toward the sedan before she slid her gaze toward the driver. He had to be Father James, didn't he? But the car—the driver shoved open the door and swung onto the street. His alb shined pure white in the dark night.

Instantly, Olivia recognized her mistake. This wasn't James, he wouldn't be wearing vestments. Damn.

Her blood turned to ice. She stared straight into the cruel blue eyes of the killer.

"Oh, God . . . no . . ." What was Sarah doing with him? What the hell was happening? "Drive away!" Olivia screamed, suddenly propelled into motion. She broke into a dead run. He rounded the Mercedes.

"Sarah! Drive!" Damn it, why wasn't Sarah moving?

Olivia sprinted hard. Toward the parking lot. "Help me! Please! Someone, help us!" she screamed and heard him behind her. Lightning fast footsteps, closing in, slapping the pavement. Terror spurred her forward. *Faster! Faster! Run faster!* She reached into her purse, her fingers scrabbling for her cell phone. Her pickup was only ten yards away. Five. Shit, he was closing in! She heard the sound of his breathing! Hard. Fast.

Run! "Help! Someone! HELP!" Not one porch light snapped on.

Her truck was so close! If she could just get inside! She glanced down at the phone in her hand. Managed to punch out 9-1-1.

"Ahhh!" Pain rocketed through her body. Gasping, she bounced against the fender, then fell to the ground. Her chin bounced on the asphalt, her purse and cell phone skated away. Lipstick, pens and wallet flew into the shadows.

She'd been shot, she thought dully, aching everywhere, unable to move. The killer had shot her . . . at least her death would be quick . . . no wheel of torture or burning at the stake or beheading. . . . Through blurry eyes, she saw him approaching and noticed his weapon, then went weak inside as she recognized the stun gun. No bullets. Just shock. She wasn't going to die quickly after all. She tried to scream. Couldn't muster a sound.

"Come along," he said in a calm, steady voice. "We have work to do, Bibiana."

"No . . ." she whispered, shaking her head weakly as he snapped a collar around her neck and dragged her back to his car. "No, no . . . no . . ." Her fingers scraped along the uneven pavement; blood dripped from her chin and the world was spinning crazily as she tried vainly to focus on a face that was similar to her own. Her brother . . . So evil and vile in his white vestments. "Bastard," she muttered. He cuffed her with the back of his hand, then yanked open the back door of his car.

In the front seat, Sarah didn't so much as flinch.

"Help—" Olivia tried to cry out. If Sarah would help, there was a chance they could overpower him, but her friend was propped listlessly against the glass of the passenger window.

She tried to kick. Missed. He clucked his tongue and shoved her into the backseat. "Bitch." Olivia fought and was rewarded with a jolt that singed her neck and caused her body to arch. She screamed.

"Be calm!" he insisted, roughly pushing her into the backseat. As she fell inside, she thought she saw something in the shadows, a movement.

Help me, she tried to yell, but no words came and pain screamed down her body.

The door slammed shut.

Her murdering bastard of a brother climbed behind the wheel and accelerated away from the church. Lying on her back on a smooth leather seat, Olivia looked through the back window of the Mercedes and through the glass to the Stygian black heavens. She knew that if she didn't do something and soon, the monster would kill her, kill Sarah and kill Kristi.

Give me strength, she silently prayed to the dark sky. She hoped to hell that God was listening.

"I'm telling you he's got Olivia!" James screamed to the dispatch officer. Adrenalin shot through his veins and fear clutched his heart as he drove crazily through the thick traffic on the freeway. "Patch me in or get me Rick Bentz. The killer's got Olivia Benchet. I'm following them now . . . but I'm afraid he's losing me. I'm on the freeway heading north, toward Baton Rouge!" The taillights of the Mercedes were visible in the darkness, three cars up and James lagged back though he knew nothing about tailing a vehicle . . . only what he'd watched on some of those police shows on television. Who knew how accurate they were?

"Sir, if you would—"

"Call Rick Bentz!" James repeated into his cell phone. "Do it *now*. Tell him his brother, James McClaren called and the killer's got Olivia! He grabbed her at St. Luke's. Her truck is still there. I'm on the 10 heading North. For God's sake, woman, send help!"

"Sir—"

"He's in a black Mercedes . . . an older model, Louisiana plates but I don't have the number. I can't get close enough to see." James had walked out the side door of the church only to witness a priest dressed in a white alb stuffing a groggy woman into the car. In a split second James had recognized Olivia, then spotted her pickup in the empty lot. His own car had been parked around the corner. James had sprinted to his Chevy as he'd heard the Mercedes roar away. Muttering every prayer he could think of, James had climbed inside his car and ignored the speed limit as he'd taken off in the direction the black car had taken. By luck he'd seen the sleek car stuck at a traffic light. From there, he'd followed, his head pounding with fear, his hands sweaty over the steering wheel. "You've got to send someone," he screamed at the dispatcher. "I could lose them, and whatever else you do, call Detective Rick Bentz," he ordered as his cell phone began to bleep and sputter as the battery died. "Damn it all . . . Father, if you're listening, please, help me save them. I beg of you." He ended his prayer and slammed the phone down, then concentrated on the traffic, ribbons of red taillights in front of him, the Mercedes moving easily up the freeway.

His fingers clenched around the steering wheel in a death grip. Not Olivia, he thought frantically. Oh, God, not Olivia. Could this be his punishment? For all his sins? No . . . oh, God no. He made a quick sign of the cross and fought tears that burned hard against the back of his eyes. "Please, Father, take me . . . spare her, I beg of you . . . take my life first."

She should recognize him, Olivia thought as the car turned off the smooth road to bounce through the darkness. Dried weeds brushed the sides of the Mercedes and the tires spun against gravel. Sarah hadn't moved. The driver had been quiet and when she'd tried to open the back door several times, she'd found it locked. So who was he and where were they? She'd seen enough to know that they'd headed north toward Baton Rouge, but when he'd taken an unfamiliar exit off the freeway, she'd become disoriented in the darkness. They'd left the city lights long behind them to this desolate stretch of land . . . He glanced at her in the rearview mirror. She froze. Every time he caught her moving, he did something and stinging, burning pain shot through her body, an electrical shock that made her cry out and brought tears to her eyes. She tugged at the collar, but it was locked and he was watching her in the rearview mirror, somehow able to discern any movement and shoot a jolt of electricity through her. Or perhaps he was playing with her, trying to scare her or beat her into a near-catatonic state. Like Sarah.

That was it! Mind games . . . learned behavior . . . psychology . . . She closed her eyes for a minute but her mind was racing in circles. She called up the names of the newly christened babies from the sheet that Father James had given her. She'd gone over them dozens of times . . . Thomas . . .

Brian Thomas was the only baby listed with the last name of Thomas.

"Who are you?" she cried, her toe inching toward the door again.

Zap! Pain sizzled through her throat. She squealed.

"Ask nothing," he commanded. "Don't speak."

As the car turned sharply and bounced upon a rutted road, Sarah began to mewl.

"You, too, shut up!" he growled

Thomas . . . she went through the list again, remembering the names. Bill and Monica Trent, Seth and Rosemary Bailey, Ralph and Primrose Stafford . . . but . . . but wasn't there a . . . then it hit her . . . *Tom* and Frieda Sutter had christened a baby boy. Tom as in Thomas and the baby's name had been . . . William, no, Warren . . . Warren Sutter . . . the name rang a distant bell. She'd heard it somewhere. Hadn't she? Or was she imagining it? Her head pounded, her muscles were weak and she was vaguely aware that the car was slowing. Warren Sutter . . . Oh, God . . . She'd heard the name at Tulane! Hadn't Dr. Leeds mentioned him by name when Leeds had been late for his appointment with Olivia? He'd said something about getting caught in a conversation with Dr. Sutter . . . her brother . . . a sadistic murderer. Not a priest but a professor.

Brittle grass scraped the underbelly of the car as it twisted and turned along a long, dark lane. Olivia's heart pounded crazily. He was taking them to some remote, isolated spot— just like he did with the women found butchered in the mill. Dear God . . . how could she save herself? Sarah? Kristi . . . where was Bentz's daughter? A dozen horrifying scenarios scorched her mind. Was she alive?

The Mercedes's tires crunched on gravel as the car slowed, rolling to a stop. He cut the engine. It cooled and ticked, but there were other sounds as well . . . the low, mournful rush of the wind, Sarah's whimpering and more . . . the muffled howl of dogs.

Sarah was shaking in the front seat, staring through the windshield. Obviously she'd been here for days, possibly a week, and whatever she'd seen in this building . . . Olivia trained her eyes on the tall structure. Dark and looming with a peaked gables, it rose from the ground, a barn with a sharply pitched roof. The baying was coming from inside and it was scaring the hell out of Sarah.

And why wouldn't it? Think of what this man's capable of.

Olivia's throat went dry with fear.

Whatever was inside the dark structure, it meant certain death.

He'd climbed out of the car, rounded it and opened one back door. "Come along, Bibiana . . . or do you prefer Vivian?" he asked, then answered, "No, I prefer Bibiana. You're home now and Lucy is waiting."

"I don't know any Lucy," she rasped out, but her heart chilled. She knew what was coming.

"Surely you do, Bibiana. You're a clever one, aren't you? With your visions and all. You know who Lucy is, there's no reason for denial."

"Kristi," she whispered, sick inside. Though she'd expected it. Bentz's daughter. But at least she was alive.

And probably tortured. Maybe disfigured . . .

"I knew you'd figure it out." Remote control aimed at her throat, he yanked first Sarah, then Olivia from the car. "Make one false step and I'll zap you. And your friend as well. If you try to escape, the other women will suffer. Horribly."

Olivia bit her lip. She withered inside. She knew he meant every word. But it was all too horrible. To think that Bentz's daughter was to be sacrificed as St. Lucy . . . but the feast day was over a week away, nearly two. Maybe Kristi could escape before she met her horrid end. Somehow Olivia would help her get free.

Olivia's own death was imminent, within days, she remembered, but still there was time for Kristi.

"Hurry up, Bibiana, your fate awaits. You know what that is, don't you?"

It came to Olivia in a horrid rush. She remembered studying the martyred saints for the coming months. St. Bibiana had died monstrously, flogged until she was bleeding and then . . . then fed to the dogs.

She heard the howling again, a deep, insidious rumbling that echoed through the night. Terror sliced through her. She didn't have to be told that the dogs were hungry, probably half starved.

Sarah mewled and cowered as he herded them both toward the horrid, monstrous edifice.

There was no escape. The forest closed around them, the smell of the river musty and thick. A drizzle as dense as fog collected in patches. Each time Olivia took a misstep, he blasted her and she went weak. "Move it!" he snapped, his patience worn thin. She had to get the stun gun from him and turn the weapon on him. Somehow . . . when the time was right. He prodded them through the door, forcing them inside a long hallway without windows. At a door at the end of a hall, the dogs were scratching and snarling.

Olivia nearly threw up.

Take him—try and overpower him. Don't let him lock you in here or you're dead for sure!

Her heart pounded. Her chin throbbed. She was so weak, but if she could grab his weapon.

Ignoring the stairs leading upward, Sutter pushed them forward. "Hurry up."

Try to take him, Olivia! You have no choice. Otherwise you, Sarah and Krisiti are as good as dead!

Sarah's cries were louder. Tears ran down her face. "No . . . no . . . no . . ." She hung back and he shoved her hard as he opened the door and snapped on the lights.

Now!

Olivia lunged. Scratching and clawing, fighting for the control.

Sarah screamed and fell into the horrid room. "For God's sake, Sarah, help me!" Olivia yelled.

With a yowl, Warren pushed on the remote and agony shrieked through Olivia's body. She scratched at his eyes, her fingernails scraping skin from his cheek.

He backhanded her into the room. "You stupid, stupid cunt!"

She fell to the floor, scraping her knee. Though she didn't move, he jolted her again. Pain ripped through her muscles. She screamed.

Again he pressed the horrid button. Her body flailed. Pain sizzled down her spine. She shrieked in agony.

Again!

"No—oooohhhhh!" She couldn't breathe.

Again!

He didn't stop until she was gasping and crying, her throat raw from screaming, every nerve in her body jangled as she flopped on the filth-encrusted floor. Lying on patches of straw she saw the dogs . . . chained but pacing near their kennels.

"Now, Bibiana, obey, or I'll set the dogs on you," he snarled and Olivia didn't have any strength left to fight him. She could barely lift her head to study the cavernous room. Red illumination offered a dim view of a filthy lair, where the two dogs paced near their metal cages and a girl, naked, was chained to the opposing wall.

Kristi.

Olivia retched.

How could she possibly save them? *How?*

This windowless room was a grotesque torture chamber. And a horrid shrine. Mounted between hideous whips and chains and swords, in stark, blasphemous contrast, were intricate crosses, crucifixes and religious symbols, including a picture of St. Mary. As if that wasn't enough, the room had dozens of mirrors tacked to the wall, glittering in the red light, reflecting every inch of the grotesque den. The mirrors gave her a view of herself and what was happening behind her while she watched the others . . . sick, oh, so twisted . . .

Terror, the like of which she'd never known, turned her insides to jelly. Whatever was to happen here would be horrendous.

"Where is Brian, Sutter?" Kristi demanded, straining at

her shackles, her lean, athletic body tense. She was as furious as Sarah was docile. "You son of a godcamned bitch, what the hell did you do with Brian?"

"Tut, tut, Lucy, such language." Sutter's eyes sparked cruelly. "*Never* take the Lord's name in vain," he warned.

Oh, no—

"I'm not fuckin' Lucy, okay—and oh!" Her body arced as he aimed a remote control at her. She fell onto dirty hay. "You bastard!" Another jolt and she jumped, screaming, "You're an animal! Worse than an animal! Worse that your ugly dogs. You get your jollies torturing women, don't you? Well, listen up! My dad is going to fucking kill you. Whatever you do to me is gonna be nothing compared to what he'll do to you! It'll be a million times worse when he gets ahold of you, you son of a bitch."

He blasted her with the stun gun, then pressed the remote for good measure. Kristi screamed and flailed in wild agony, the dogs howled and snarled and Sarah wailed piteously.

"Shut up," Sutter screamed. He slapped Sarah against the wall. "I've had it with your whining!" He pounced on her, gagged her with a piece of tape hanging on the wall and snapped a chain to her collar. His alb was now dirty and he was sweating, his skin glowing red in the light. Olivia edged toward the stairs and was rewarded with another blast from the stun gun. "Strip," he ordered and then tore off Sarah's clothes, literally ripping them from her body. She was terrified, screaming, and he jolted her into submission as her limbs jerked like a marionette.

Olivia didn't move.

"I said 'strip'," he repeated and his gaze narrowed on her. "Or would you rather me do it for you, sister?" Pure evil twisted his lips. Pinpoints of lust shined red in his eyes.

She had to do his bidding.

For now.

But only for now. She already felt her strength returning a bit . . . she just needed time to recover.

"Now!" he bellowed.

Quivering with fear, her mind racing to find a means of

escape she began to unbutton her shirt. She pretended not to notice his erection, stiff and protruding against his vestment. *Dirty, sick pervert,* she thought, pulling her arms free of her sleeves.

She swallowed back her disgust. *I'll get out of here and I'll take them with me, even if I have to kill you myself,* she silently vowed. She couldn't allow fear to get the better of her. She had to be sane. Think straight. Find a way to get free.

Chapter Thirty-seven

"I'll kill him with my bare hands," Bentz muttered as his Jeep barreled off the freeway to this godforsaken strip of brushy farmland. Flat and dark with thickets of scrub oak and pine. "If he touches so much as one hair on Kristi or Olivia's head, I swear to God, I'll rip his fuckin' head off."

Montoya glowered into the foggy night, smoking a cigarette, listening to the police band. "You won't get the chance. I'll blow him away, man." He patted his sidearm. Was it enough? As smoke drifted from Montoya's nostrils, Bentz silently prayed they could save them.

He'd heard the replay of James's call, and police from several jurisdictions were converging on a piece of property near the river not fifteen miles from Baton Rouge. The Baton Rouge Police had been called and they'd gotten into Sutter's home where they'd searched and come up with an address for another piece of property . . . one that was located on the river, an old farm that had once been owned by Tom and Freda, Sutter's adoptive parents. But they were behind Bentz. Because of the homing device he'd surreptitiously mounted behind the rear bumper of James's car, he was closer to the farm. He heard the other sirens, but they wailed in the distance.

He prayed that he wasn't too late as the miles of old asphalt rolled under the Jeep's tires.

If only Kristi and Olivia were still alive. His daughter meant everything to him . . . *everything*. If he lost her . . . his throat clogged. He'd never forgive himself. Why hadn't he saved her when he'd had the chance? Why had he let her go back in that dormitory alone? Why, why, why? He beat on the steering wheel and Montoya flipped his cigarette through a crack in the window. Bentz told himself not to think the worst. Kristi was alive. She had to be. And Olivia. He ached when he thought that she, too, was in the monster's clutches, maybe even dead. He'd been so cold to her earlier. Not just detached, but ruthless and mean. He'd seen the pleading in her eyes, the silent need to connect with him and he'd cut her loose. Because he was scared for his daughter. Because he was pissed that she'd been with James.

And now . . . now he might have already lost her. His jaw clenched so hard it ached. His throat burned. Olivia— why hadn't he trusted her? Forgiven her? Told her he loved her before it was too late? Now, the two women he cared about were in horrid peril. Because he'd failed to save them.

And what about James? According to the homing device James had followed the Mercedes to the Stutter farm. His life too was in serious danger. Everyone Bentz held dear was caught up in this vile mess . . . their lives in jeopardy. Bentz tried not to think about the horrors the killer had committed . . . the photographs that he'd mounted on his bulletin board and committed to memory, the bloody crime scenes.

"The bastard's goin' down," Montoya said as they spun around a corner and a skunk, caught in the Jeep's headlights, waddled quickly into a ditch. "And if he's got Marta, he'll wish he'd never set eyes on her. Or me." Montoya glanced at Bentz and for once there wasn't the hint of the younger man's usual cockiness. In the dark car, his face illuminated by the glow of the dash lights, Montoya was sober as death, his face hard with conviction. "He's goin' down," Montoya vowed again. "Even if I have to go with him."

"I'm with ya," Bentz said and eased off the throttle as he glimpsed the turn-off for the lane leading to Sutter's farm. His headlights flashed on a rusted, listing mailbox, its door gaping open in the rising mist. Bentz's heart clenched as he cranked on the steering wheel.

God help him if he was too late.

"Help me, Father," James whispered, sneaking through the wet grass and overgrown bushes that surrounded the building. Mist was his cover, fear his companion. Dogs were baying from within the tall, gloomy building. Despair congealed in James's heart, but he forced himself toward the door, his footsteps muffled by wet leaves and bent grass. This was a test, surely. The Father was challenging his courage.

James would have the element of surprise on his side but he had no real weapon, nothing to use in a battle aside from the useless cell phone in his pocket and a bottle of wiper cleaner that he hoped to squirt in the killer's eyes. Stupid. Another TV cop trick. But all he had.

Remember Daniel and the lion's den.

Maybe he would find something inside to help him . . . a shotgun or a knife or . . . Could he do it? Could he take another life? It was a sin . . . He'd reached the door and he pushed all of his vows out of his mind. He had to save Olivia . . . nothing else mattered. He made a quick sign of the cross, then grabbed the door handle and pushed.

No lock held him back. The door creaked open. His muscles ached from the tension as he crept into a darkened hallway at the end of which he saw a faint red glow . . . a shimmering scarlet line at the level of the floor, reddish light seeping beneath another door. Noises, the dogs and voices came from within. He scanned the dark walls with the hint of visibility. He saw nothing to use as a weapon here, but there was a stairway leading upward into quiet murky darkness . . . Did he have time to search? Did he dare risk a few precious moments to race up the stairs and try to find something to arm himself? He had to. Otherwise he didn't have a chance.

The dogs were baying crazily from behind the door and he knew he was nearly out of time. "Help me," he whispered and noiselessly took the stairs two at a time.

Olivia quaked with fear as she faced her brother.

"I've been saving this for you," Warren said, and pulled a nasty-looking whip which had been mounted on brackets in the wall. It was small, made of leather and had nearly a dozen wicked tips. "Know what this is?" With a flick of his wrist it cracked abominably. Sarah jumped. Didn't cry out. "It's a cat o' nine tails . . . a perfect little whip." Warren handled the damned weapon almost lovingly, caressing the smooth handle. "Now," he motioned with the whip to Olivia. The tails sizzled around his hand. "Turn around and don't move. Yes, there in front of the dogs. But don't try anything foolish. If you do, I'll not only have to use my stun gun again, but I'll sacrifice your friend here. You see, I have no saint yet picked for her and so she can be eliminated anytime."

Sarah was screaming behind the tape on her mouth now, her eyes round with panic. "Shhh. . . . I'm sure St. Bibiana will be a good penitent." He hit one of the buttons on the remote control and Sarah squealed before sliding down the wall and collapsing into tears.

"You merciless bastard," Olivia charged, unable to hold her tongue. She felt stronger now, couldn't pretend to be meek and weak. "How can you do all this in the name of God? This is blasphemy! Heresy. Sick, twisted tripe!"

"Blasphemy?" He seemed amused.

"You dress like a priest, you spout all kinds of religious quotes, you . . . you hang crosses with whips and you kill innocent women and boys, butcher them. These aren't acts for God, they're acts against *Him*."

"I save the sinners," he said, a tic beginning near his eye.

"You save them from nothing. *Nothing.* You're so sick you've twisted it all around in your scrambled brain," she said, wheeling to face him. "It's an excuse. You like to kill. That's it. You're so sick you enjoy the pain and the power." The tic was working overtime now and his lip twitched. "You're a pathetic murdering coward, hiding in vestments you didn't earn and somehow you try to justify your sickness."

"I speak with God."

"Bull."

The tic was pounding now. "I'm The Chosen One."

"You're a lunatic."

"The Father speaks to me." A twitch was moving his eyebrow and eyelid.

"You're a freak, that's what you are!" Kristi cried.

"Shh! Don't!" Olivia warned. It was one thing for her to bait this monster, but she didn't dare risk Kristi's life.

"Protective, are you?" he asked her and she didn't speak, afraid for Kristi's life. Warren's smile returned, the tic slowed. "I expected some fight in you, *sister*, but obviously you are smarter than I thought. Now, turn around and look at the dogs. . . ."

She hesitated.

The Chosen One—Warren—moved a step closer to Kristi.

Quickly, Olivia did as she was told, but her mind was racing. No way would she allow herself to be filleted for some starving mutt's meal. In the mirror, she saw him raise his whip. She braced herself.

Crack!

Pain ricocheted through her. Nine bites to her flesh. She flinched. Bit down so she wouldn't cry out.

"Don't move!" he ordered.

She caught his glare in one of the mirrors.

His eyes thinned in anticipation. Again he snapped his wrist.

The whip stung again. Scorching pain erupted on her back. She didn't so much as wince and held his glare. In the mirror she saw the pink tip of his tongue as it ran over his lips. His gaze was fastened on her bare rump and red flesh. He was a sicko. A crazy. But maybe she could use that. . . .

Snap!

Fire ripped through her. She sucked in air through her teeth. Tears sprang to her eyes. She had to stop this. She heard something. Footsteps? Her heart leapt at the thought, but it was crazy. The dogs were barking and turning toward the door. Warren looked over his shoulder but there was silence again. She couldn't hope for outside help.

It was up to her.

She thought quickly. How? She couldn't just turn and run at him. But . . . if she could endure the pain until the right moment, if, before she was exhausted from the flailing, she could summon the courage and energy to roll into a ball and somersault backward toward him while he had his weapon raised; she could knock him off his feet, grab the stun gun and aim it at him.

Or he'd kill her.

Well, he was going to do that one way or another.

This was the only way. Their only chance. She had to try it. He would either kill her slowly by flailing her to death, try and feed her to the dogs or chain her up and leave her for another session. Either way she and Kristi and Sarah were doomed.

Smack!

The whip blistered her back like a million little knives. She jolted. Managed to stay on her feet.

"Tough one, aren't you? A true daughter of Reggie Benchet," he snarled and in one mirror, Olivia caught Kristi's eye.

Look at me. Kristi! Look at me. We have to do this together.

Kristi glanced to the mirror. The male dog whined and looked at the door. Olivia thought she heard something—

Snap! The whip snaked. Pain exploded on Olivia's back. Bright lights flashed behind her eyes. Her knees threatened to buckle. *Don't lose it, not now.* But she didn't have much time.

Sutter was sweating, his erection protruding, his concentration on Olivia's rump.

Kristi nodded ever so slowly and Olivia gave a tiny nod back as he flipped his wrist again. *Now! It has to be now!* The whip sizzled through the air. It sliced into her back— burning. Olivia tucked, rolled backward and jerked upward in one swift motion. She grabbed hold of the whip.

"You bitch!" Warren, startled, took a step backward, close enough to Kristi that the girl, ready, kicked hard and upward, landing a blow to his chest.

Craaack, his ribs split.

"You pathetic cunt!" he cried, whirling.

The dogs bayed and footsteps pounded. Someone had found them!

"Down here!" Olivia bellowed. "Help!" She pounced on Sutter, but he'd managed to aim the remote. Furious, he jabbed a button.

Sheer agony sizzled down her spine. Her body arced crazily. Pain ripped through her body. Lights flashed, spangling her vision. Blindly she dug at him with her fingernails. He stumbled back another step. Kristi twisted, rounding to kick him hard in the groin.

The Chosen One buckled, dropped his remote.

The door flew open. James tumbled into the room. In one hand he held a fine whip edged in glass. His other arm was extended, fingers splayed in supplication. "Stop! Please." His face was pale and chalk-white as if he'd seen a horrific specter.

"What the hell?" The Chosen One was on his feet.

"You must stop! Kristi! In the name of God, this has to come to an end!"

"Help us!" Olivia screamed, then bucked as she was shocked again.

Sutter had the stun gun! She fell to the floor, twisting her ankle as she looked into the gold eyes of the female dog. "Stay," she ordered.

The dog growled low in her throat and the male moved behind her. In a mirror she saw Warren, one arm wrapped around his broken ribs, the other holding the stun gun. "Father McClaren, put down my whip," he ordered, but he was weakening. Spittle clung to his lip. "You made a grave mistake in coming here."

"Help us, Uncle James," Kristi cried.

"I will, honey." He was walking forward slowly, his gaze steady on Warren though the dogs circled and snapped on their leashes. "I will. Please, you must stop this. I don't know why you're doing this, but it's not God's will. Release these women and repent. I will help you with the police and with the Church, but please, I beg of you, by all that is holy—"

Warren aimed the stun gun at James and pressed a finger. "What would you know of holiness, you sanctimonious bastard?" he snarled. He pressed a button. James yelped and fell to the floor.

No! He had to be stopped! Pushing herself, Olivia sprang. Her twisted ankle throbbing, she flung herself at her brother and felt the electricity before she'd landed a blow to his face. The Chosen One staggered, stumbling backward. Kristi leaped onto his back. She wrapped her chain around his neck and pulled, screaming and crying, volts of electricity streaking down her body as he pressed the gun against her thigh. Flailing, Warren slammed Kristi into a wall, his hands scrabbling for another weapon. He came up with a crucifix— a black wrought iron cross with a pointed end. James climbed to his feet, swayed and rushed Warren.

"Watch out!" Olivia screamed in horror. No—she staggered to her feet, threw herself toward the two men.

But it was too late. James wobbled forward.

"Noooooo!" Krisiti cried.

The Chosen One's hand slashed downward.

Thud! The crucifix plunged deep into James's chest.

James jerked backward. Blood seeped around the weapon.

"No, no, no!" Olivia cried, tears falling from her eyes as she struggled to crawl to reach James . . . not dear James . . . "Oh, God, oh, God . . ." She inched toward him, but it was too late. Blood appeared around his lips.

"Forgive me, Father," he whispered, then sank to his knees.

Bentz heard the screams as he threw himself out of the Jeep before it stopped rolling. He was too late! Whatever horror the monster had planned it was happening. To Olivia. To Kristi. To everyone he loved.

With Montoya on his heels and sirens screaming through the night around them, he rushed the building, his weapon drawn. He couldn't lose them. Not now. Dear God, not now. His heart was pounding, his pulse thundering. *Let them be alive,* he silently prayed. *And give me a clear shot. That's all I need. Just one.*

Other officers were surrounding the building but he pushed open the door and found himself in a long hallway by a staircase, and ahead, through a door that was ajar, in the blood-red glow of the lights he looked into his own personal hell.

"No!" Kristi screamed, yanking hard on the chain surrounding the prick's neck. He'd killed Uncle James . . . . Oh, God . . . Sobbing, kicking, grief tearing her from the inside out, she wanted to kill the bastard. She would!

All the years of hatred and confusion muddled in her mind as she saw the man who had sired her collapse on the floor. He couldn't be dead. No! No! No! Not James! From the corner of her eye Kristi glimpsed Olivia pulling a sword off the wall. She was half-dead, too. Bleeding and raw, limping. As the creep aimed the stun gun at her again, Olivia rushed forward, swung and sliced his hand, sending the gun into the deep dirty straw.

She drew back to swing at his head, but he twisted, rolling around so that Kristi, upon his back, was his shield. "Jump off!" Olivia ordered, the bloody sword still pointed at him. He backed up, using the mirror to try and skewer Kristi on the weapon. Kristi kicked all the harder. Olivia dropped the sword.

Footsteps thundered. The door banged open. Bentz stood in the doorway. "Drop your weapons! Police!" Bentz, his Glock drawn, strode into the room. His eyes locked with hers. "Kristi, let go," he yelled.

"Daddy," she said weakly and willingly gave up her grip to crumple into a heap and start to cry. He was here to save her—to save them!

The Chosen One retrieved his stun gun and aimed it at Bentz.

"Rick, watch out!" Olivia cried.

Bentz fired.

With a horrible yelp, The Chosen One fell just as the stun gun fired. Bentz jolted, then sprang forward, blasting more shots into the crumpling man.

"Daddy . . . oh, Daddy . . ." In a heartbeat Bentz crossed the room, sweeping her off the dirty floor and holding onto her as if his life depended upon it. She buried her face in his neck and sobbed brokenly. "Uncle James . . . he's dead," she said and grief tore at her. The man she'd rejected. The uncle who had adored her. The man who had given her life and she'd been petty and mean to him. When all he'd tried to do was love her. She thought of the gifts he'd showered upon her, the kindness and patience and . . . and how, in the end, she'd rejected him, slamming down the phone the last time he'd called. And now . . . and now . . . she squeezed her eyes shut but that horrible moment when The Chosen One had slammed the cross into James's chest burned through her brain. Shaking violently, Kristi clung to Bentz as if she'd never let go.

And Bentz wouldn't let her. He held onto her and

screamed orders, felt the wash of warm tears run down the back of his neck as other officers poured into the room. Olivia—she looked like she'd survive, but James . . . Bentz stared in horror at his brother and the horrid cross imbedded in his chest. He crawled to James while still holding Kristi. "James! Can you hear me?" he demanded, instantly on his knees.

Flashlights bobbed. The dogs growled. Policemen barked orders. Some rounded up the dogs, others searched the premises while still others checked the wounded.

"Get the keys off him," Bentz ordered, pointing his sidearm at the killer. "And get an EMT in here. Now!"

A policewoman dropped to James's side. "Hold on, Father," she said softly.

Montoya, after checking for Sutter's pulse, slid his fingers into the monster's pockets. He found a set of keys and threw them at Bentz. "I'll get you out of here," Bentz promised as he unlocked Kristi's chains and felt a rage as hot as all of hell's fires burn deep within him as he glanced at this fetid, brutal room.

Then his eyes locked with Olivia's as she sat crumpled in a corner. She was propped against one wall, breathing hard, naked but for some kind of dog collar and shivering. Scrapes and bruises covered her face and arms. Damn the bastard.

Kristi whimpered as her chains fell away.

"Shh . . . honey . . . it'll be okay. I promise . . ." he said, knowing he lied as he made his way to Olivia. Still holding his child, he knelt and found a key that unlocked the collar surrounding her throat. "Are you all right?"

"No . . . yes . . ." She was crying too, tears glistening red from the weird light as they streaked down her face. Juggling Kristi, Bentz took off his jacket and draped it over Olivia's shoulders. She flinched before he saw the red welts . . . deep cuts slicing across her back.

"That son of a bitch."

"It's all right," she said, her chin quivering. "I'll be okay."

"I'd like to kill him all over again." He slid a finger along her jaw and swallowed hard. "I'm so sorry—"

She grabbed his fingers. "Later . . . now . . . James . . ." she said brokenly as an officer approached and offered a blanket which Bentz swaddled around his daughter.

Kristi sobbed as Bentz looked back at his brother where the policewoman was still working over him. But James was quivering and shaking, his face white as death.

"Shit . . ." Carrying Kristi, Bentz dived to the other side of the room. "James . . . no . . ." He fell to one knee. "Hang in there," he said to his brother and yelled, "Where the hell are the EMTs?" He placed a hand on James's shoulder. "You're gonna be all right, James, you got that? You're gonna be fine."

Barely conscious, James rolled glazed eyes at Bentz. A crucifix was buried deep in his chest, blood stained his pale lips. Bentz wanted to throw up.

"No . . . It's too late . . ." James's breathing was ragged and slow, blood spreading across his shirt. With an odd, peaceful smile, he rasped, "No doctor, Rick. I need a priest."

"No, don't talk that way!" Bentz swivelled his head in Montoya's direction. "Where's the damned ambulance?"

"It's here."

"Forgive me, Rick. I wronged you," James forced out, his voice a wheeze, a horrid rattle deep in his lungs. Then his gaze moved to Kristi. "And you, too . . . I . . . I . . . love you. So much."

His eyes seemed to glaze and Bentz felt as if a thousand fingernails were scraping the inside of his soul. Images of James as a young adoring pup, the kid who always tagged after him flashed through Bentz's mind. They'd spent so many hours while growing up talking of baseball and hunting and girls. His throat clogged. "There's nothing to forgive, James, and you're going to be fine."

"But Jennifer—"

"Ancient history. And I've got . . . we've got Kristi." Without James's betrayal, Bentz wouldn't have a daughter.

"Please . . . please don't die, Uncle James," Kristi said and a tiny, faltering smile curved James's lips. "Daddy!"

"God is calling me."

"Not yet! Fight, James!" Rick ordered, cradling his brother's head, feeling James's silky hair against his palms. "Fight, damn it! We need you. I need you. Kristi needs you! Don't give up, do you hear me!"

Kristi was sobbing and James's eyes closed slowly.

"I—can't!" he rasped, his chest rattling.

"Don't you give up! James! James! Damn it, don't you give up!" Bentz swung his head toward the rest of the room. "Get an EMT over here! Now!" Bentz bellowed, his eyes moist as one of the dogs snapped and yipped while an officer forced it into a cage.

He couldn't lose James. Not this way. Not at the hands of a serial murderer whom Bentz should have put away. There was so much to say, to do, so many fences to mend . . .

Half a dozen emergency workers lugging equipment, jogged into the room. Shouting orders, they split up to attend the fallen.

"Holy shit," one whispered as he reached James.

"Over here, this one's traumatized, maybe worse!" Another EMT was already with the woman chained to the wall.

"Sarah!" Olivia cried, but her friend didn't respond.

"I'll take care of her!" a young policeman threw over his shoulder as he unlatched Sarah's bonds and pulled the tape from her mouth.

"This one's dead." A third was leaning over Warren Sutter where bullet holes riddled his alb and the pure white cloth was now stained a dark, oozing red. Bentz glanced at the man as an EMT ordered him aside and started working over James. "Out of the way. Christ, I need some help here . . . we're losing this guy!"

"No," Olivia cried. She'd managed to get to her feet and stumble across the room. Her fingers clasped a department-issued blanket around her body. "No—James!" she whis-

pered and fell to the floor. "Please . . . please . . ." Tears
rained from her eyes as she touched James's limp hand.

Bentz's guts twisted as James's eyes fluttered open, just
barely. "Be good to Rick. He's a good man . . . you deserve
someone who . . . who can love you . . . totally." Olivia was
crying openly now. "And Bentz . . . he . . . he needs . . . a
strong woman . . . you." James's voice cracked, then faded.
Kristi sent up a wail that echoed hollowly through the dank,
dark chamber.

Tears streamed from Bentz's eyes. It was too late. "Oh,
Daddy, he can't be—"

But the EMT shook his head and Bentz ached inside,
guilt and anger roiling deep within. "It's over, honey," he
whispered, fighting a losing battle with tears as he held his
daughter. James's daughter. Their daughter.

"But Uncle James . . ."

"Shh. He's with God now."

"You don't even believe in God," she charged. "You
said so."

"I lied."

"Another ambulance is on its way." Montoya clicked off
his cell phone and took the time to look around the room
as if for the first time. The dogs were finally penned, but
the mirrors and weapons glittered in the red light, glittering
more harshly by the flashlights the officers were using.
"Jesus H. Christ."

Bentz, holding Kristi, moved closer to Olivia. She looked
down at his brother and shook her head. Tears streamed
from her eyes and her chin wobbled in her vain attempt to
rein in her emotions. Bentz wrapped his free arm around
her. "We'll get through this. Together."

"I don't know how."

"Have faith," he said and the words struck an old forgotten chord, one he'd denied for so many years. "It was James
who followed you here and called it in," he explained. "He
saved you." His other arm tightened over his daughter.
"And Kristi."

"But how did you know where to come?"

"I bugged his house, his phone, and his car." His admission reminded him of how he'd doubted his own brother, the anger and jealousy he'd felt toward a good, if sometimes weak man. "I'm a great brother, aren't I?" he asked, hating his black suspicions. "I guess I don't trust anyone." His gaze fastened on Olivia. "But I'm working on changing that. I promise."

In the distance, the bleat of additional sirens cut through the night. "Come on," Bentz said to his daughter and Olivia as body bags were carried in. "It's time for us to go home."

"No, Dad," Kristi said. "We have to find Brian. The . . . the creep's got Brian somewhere!"

"Too late." Montoya's face was grim, as if he'd aged twenty years. "We already found him in the trunk of the Mercedes."

"Is he okay—?"

"I'm sorry, Kris," Montoya said with a shake of his head.

Kristi convulsed, screaming and kicking. "No, no, no!" Tiny fists flailed, but Bentz held on, wouldn't let her go. "He can't be dead. Not because of me. Noooooo!" Kristi let out a painful screech louder than either the dogs or the approaching ambulances. Guilt chasing through him, Bentz wondered if she'd ever be all right. And Olivia, what of her? She looked into Bentz's eyes.

"Shh . . ." he said to his daughter. "It's over."

"It'll never be over," Kristi argued, sobbing hysterically.

"You're right." He held Olivia's eyes with his as somehow his daughter seemed to get a grip on herself. Her sobs quieted though her face was wrenched in agony. "But it'll be better," Bentz promised, though he wasn't sure he believed his own words. "Much better. For all of us. I swear to God we'll all get past this. Somehow. Now, come on. It's time to go home."

Epilogue

"I know pronounce you man and wife. Ladies and gentle-men, I'd like to introduce Mr. and Mrs. Tyler Wheeler." The minister held up his hands as the couple turned and faced a small gathering of friends and family. In a long cream-colored gown, Samantha looked radiant as she walked through the guests sitting in the huge open courtyard of the St. Suzanne Hotel nestled deep in the French Quarter. Her new husband, in black tuxedo, was tall and handsome, a man whose book on the Rosary Killer would be in the stores within the next year.

The setting was perfect, Olivia thought.

It was the Saturday after Christmas and the centuries old brothel-turned hotel was still dressed in garlands and wreaths. Millions of lights spiraled through the foliage while outdoor heaters hummed as they warmed the courtyard and the friends and family of Dr. Sam and her new husband.

Olivia glanced through the jeweled fronts of palm trees and ferns to a dark sky where stars twinkled and a crescent moon hovered. Next to her, tugging at his tie, Rick Bentz watched the ceremony. It had been nearly a month since the horrid night at The Chosen One's lair, but Bentz, true to his vow that night, was trying to make things better and giving their relationship another shot. Olivia had been a hard sell. They'd spent hours talking and she wasn't sure she was ready to trust him again, but she did care about him; probably loved him, fool that she was. At that thought she smiled.

Things were far from perfect. Sarah Restin was in serious counseling and on anti-anxiety drugs, Kristi, too, was traumatized, but, it seemed would be able to go back to school after the winter break. Olivia had mended fences with her mother, but the specter of The Chosen One hadn't quite died. The press kept him alive long after he should have been buried.

Slowly the case had unwound. The Jane Doe laid at the foot of St. Joan of Arc had been identified as a transient woman from El Paso. No family had come forward to claim her remains. St. Philomena had been a runaway teen from Detroit. Their IDs had been found in The Chosen One's lair, an indecent, deranged shrine in the upper floor that had once been living quarters in the loft of the old barn. Eventually there had been a connection made to the universities as both women had at one time or another been seen by other students on the campus of All Saints. The transient had worked one week as a maid, the runaway had shown up uninvited to a party.

The only person missing was a woman named Marta Vasquez. She'd been Montoya's girlfriend and she'd vanished. Apparently into thin air.

Bentz worried that she'd been taken by The Chosen One and killed elsewhere, her remains not yet located, but so far, thank God, no one had been able to make that link. Everything Dr. Warren Sutter had ever owned or touched had been gone over with a fine-tooth comb. Including his personal lair, the small farm in the middle of nowhere that Sutter's family had bought years ago. He'd turned it into his sanctuary, complete with an altar. And a torture chamber.

Olivia shuddered as she thought of it. Not only had the

police found a horrific calendar with Polaroid pictures of The Chosen One's victims in the upper room, but also they discovered a closet of vestments and trophies, including an obscene braid he'd plaited from the hanks of hair he'd scalped from his victims.

Bentz speculated that the killer had found his other killing grounds by snooping around and discovering vacant buildings—even ones in the middle of the city like the shotgun house at Bayou St. John.

But Olivia didn't want to dwell on the past. Her visions had died with her brother and she was now taking tentative steps in this new relationship with a very wary man. He seemed to have believed her that she and James, though close, had never actually made love, though she was certain, at this point, Bentz wouldn't have held it against her if she had slept with his brother. For her part, Olivia had forgiven Bentz for pushing her away during the course of the investigation.

It was all water under the bridge.

They were starting over. Or at least trying to. She watched the dance floor and recognized the people that Bentz had pointed out. Everyone from Samantha's workplace, WSLJ, had attended and had blended into the sprinkling of Ty and Sam's family, friends and neighbors. One woman had even had the audacity to bring her tiny dog—a pug named Hannibal—though he'd been kept in a kennel at the desk. Samantha's father had given his daughter away, but, Bentz had explained after talking to the bride, Sam's brother, Peter, hadn't shown up, nor had her best friend, Corky Griffith, dealing with her own mother's recent heart attack, been able to fly to New Orleans.

Nonetheless Sam was radiant; her red hair gleamed under the tiny lights, her dress sparkled and as she danced, she whispered something to her groom. Ty tipped back his head and laughed, then swung Samantha off her feet.

"We should dance," Olivia suggested.

"I don't dance."

"Never?"

"Never."

"Don't tell me, another one of your rules." She rolled her eyes.

"That's right," he said, pulling at his tie as he winked at her. "But for you, I'm willing to bend a few." With that, he took her into his arms and warned her, "Just don't you dare complain if I step on your toes."

"Have I so far?" She laughed. "I have a feeling that for as long as I know you, you'll be stepping on a lot of toes."

"I guess you've figured me out."

"Oh, Bentz, that'll take a lifetime. Maybe two. But I'm trying. I think you just may be worth it. *May* be."

"Has anyone told you you're a sick woman?" he asked as he spun her with surprising agility.

"Just you, Bentz," she said with a smile and winked at him. "Just . . . you."

Dear Reader,

As you may have noticed, there are some questions left unanswered in COLD BLOODED. Rest assured they will be answered in THE NIGHT BEFORE, my next romantic suspense novel for Zebra Books.

THE NIGHT BEFORE is a change of pace. Once again we're in the old South—Savannah, Georgia, but this time the heroine of the book, Caitlyn Montgomery Bandeaux, a woman who's not known for her stability literally wakes up with blood on her hands. In fact there's blood everywhere, in the bed, on the walls, in the bathroom . . .

She has only tiny shards of a memory from THE NIGHT BEFORE. Is the blood her own? Or someone else's? Most of the people in her large, eccentric family will be no help so she's forced to turn to her twin sister, Kelly, a woman with secrets and desires all her own. Kelly assures her twin that everything will be all right. But Caitlyn has the feeling Kelly knows more than she's saying—more secrets she's keeping locked away. Afraid to confide in rugged Detective Pierce Reed or the new psychologist in town, Dr. Adam Hunt, a handsome but mysterious man who has taken over her counselor's practice, Caitlyn has to solve the mystery alone. Is she a cold-blooded killer, or the victim of a morbid psychopath?

THE NIGHT BEFORE will be on the shelves in March 2003, so look for it. In the meantime, visit me on the web. I've revamped my website and there are interactive contests and tidbits about current releases and future projects. Sign my guest book and let me know what you thought of COLD BLOODED. There's tons of information and fun on the website—contests and puzzles that only those of you who have read COLD BLOODED—can figure out! So grab your mouse and click onto: www.lisajackson.com.

You'll also get a peek at my next medieval romance novel, IMPOSTRESS for Signet Books. IMPOSTRESS is the story of Kiera of Lawenydd, who, because of a bargain made long ago, must pay back her sister, Elyn, by disguising herself as Elyn, and marrying Kelan of Penbrooke. Kiera knows she's making a vast mistake, but goes through with the dare, not knowing that the man she expects to be ancient, balding and boring, is the most handsome, intriguing baron in all of Wales. For his part, Kelan has no idea his marriage is a sham until after the wedding night and that's when the fun really begins!

Look for IMPOSTRESS in April 2003, after the release of THE NIGHT BEFORE.

The best to all of you!

Lisa Jackson